LIBERTY BELL

AND

THE LAST AMERICAN

LIBERTY BELL

AND

THE LAST AMERICAN

JAMES STODDARD

Ransom Books

Visit www.james-stoddard.com to learn more about the author.

For a list of the quotations used in this book, please
go to www.james-stoddard.com/quotes

To contact James Stoddard email: evenmere@gmail.com

Cover illustration and design by Mimer E.
Additional cover consultation by Scott Faris www.fariswheel.com

Edited by Betsy Mitchell www.betsymitchelleditorial.com

Heyoka Coyoté's tribal history includes quotations from John
G. Neihardt's *Black Elk Speaks*, and is used by permission of
the John G. Neihardt Trust.

A Ransom Book
Printed in the United States of America.

First Printing: April 2021

10 9 8 7 6 5 4 3 2 1

Antonio's Map
With the Yooessay
Superimposed

TO THE REPUBLIC

For Which It Stands

AUTHOR'S NOTES

The characters in this book speak the language of a people a thousand years in our future. Having changed over time, its resemblance to modern English is comparable to the relationship between our English and the language of Chaucer. Despite that, a number of names and words from our culture remain, especially in old expressions.

In my translation of this future language, when certain words have become distorted from their original spelling or meaning, I have used an alternate spelling, such as the word *fizzicist* for *physicist*. Likewise, many words we would normally capitalize, such as names of cities, linger only as figures of speech and are not capitalized herein.

This book was written in 2015 and was not influenced by the 2016 election and the following four years. Nothing herein is intended as a statement for or against any political party.

The purpose of all government, as best promoted by the practice of virtuous policies, ought to be the aggregate happiness of society.
–George Washington

In this business, by the time you realize you're in trouble, it's too late to save yourself. *–Bill Gates*

CHAPTER ONE

We still do not understand the cause of the Great Blackout of the late 21st century: an electromagnetic pulse, a series of iron-core comet strikes in the upper atmosphere, a weapon deployed by an alien civilization — many theories have been suggested. Whatever the cause, the devastation was worldwide and nearly total. Electricity ceased to function for centuries; earthquakes and volcanic activity shook the planet. The oceans flooded the coastlines of every continent for two hundred miles, leaving major cities forever inundated. Continents split, sundered by unbelievable forces. The destruction and resulting plagues depopulated whole nations, with mortality rates in many regions reaching one hundred percent. In the Americas, perhaps less than one-eighth of one percent of the human population survived.

Long before the cataclysm, all books and documents had been converted to electronic storage and the original paper versions either shredded or left to rot. The end of electricity did more than herald a Dark Age — it erased the history and literature of the Earth, even as the accompanying geological catastrophes obliterated cities and landmarks.

Fortunately, three hundred years after the Great Blackout, a scholar and poet named Benjamin Aguilar discovered a surviving book printed before the disaster, a volume consisting of the quotations of famous Americans. Reading the words of these great men and women inspired Aguilar to travel the American continent, collecting the stories and legends of early history passed down through the generations. These, he adapted — along with the book of quotations — into a single written narrative he called The Americana. Over the next several centuries, it would become the cultural cornerstone for the newly emerging nation-states of the American continent. Though we can expect little accuracy from a people dependent on electronic data storage rather than oral tradition, I believe, like Aguilar, that there is always a grain of truth concealed within the tales. But to quote one of the figures in the The Americana itself: "When the Legend becomes fact, print the Legend."

—The Day the World Ended by Madison Humphrey

* * *

In his people's language, Washington's first name, "General," meant "pertaining in common to all," and that was what he became, a leader to the American colonists in Virginia. As a youth, an enchantment had been laid upon him by the Star Weaver, Betsee Ross, that he could never tell a lie. Because of this, some called him "Honest Gen." —The Americana

* * *

800 Years After the Great Blackout

The day was glorious, the sky cloudless, and Liberty tried not to let her apprehension show as she wheeled her suitcase along the concrete sidewalk, past coaches, wagons, and horses tied to hitching rails. Men in levite jeans or goochegoo suits hurried by, and she forced herself to appear serene, knowing the best way to keep evildoers and roughnecks at bay was with a display of confidence. The women she passed wore short, dark skirts over long, cotton pants with matching blouses, making her feel overdressed in her ankle-length yellow dress, long tunic, yellow jacket, and orange beret. She had only been to Mayberry once before, when she was a little girl. Her mother had been with her then; and she struggled not to gawk at the sights and sounds of a big city of nearly two thousand souls.

Still, she felt pretty as a picasso in a pawnshop, as Gramps liked to say, with her face and eyelashes done, and her hair put up and curled, though her stockings were hot and her pumps pinched. Her mother had sewn the dress just for the trip, a two-week visit to her aunt in Bedford Falls; and as she had left, Gramps said she looked real kodaky.

She crossed the petrol-resin street, so much smoother and elegant than the dusty roads of her village, resisting the urge, in her excitement, to skip along the way. She had to remember to act the lady, or she'd look like a rookie to the sophisticated townies. But it was hard. Everyone appeared so stern and busy. Unlike at home, they didn't even greet each other as they passed; and she couldn't help but gape as a circuit judge strode by, regal in his black and white striped shirt, his yellow cape billowing from his shoulders, his silver whistle dangling from his neck. Nor could she resist wistfully pressing her face against the window of the first bookstore she had ever seen. Not only were there three periodicals and a newspaper on display, but she counted twelve books, surely worth a Bezos' ransom.

Three men already stood in line at the window of the ticket office, and momentary timidity held her back. When people started getting in front of her, however, she clucked her tongue, murmured *Charge for the guns*, and strode forward.

When her turn came, she looked the teller full in the face, trying to appear cool as she asked for a ticket to Bedford Falls, but to her chagrin her voice faltered into a stammer. Mentally berating herself, she missed hearing the fare price and eyed the teller stupidly until he repeated it. She counted the debit coins from her handbag, struggling to remain unruffled.

"Thank you, sir," she said, turning away.

"Don't forget your ticket, miss," the man standing in line behind her said.

Avoiding his eyes, face burning, she murmured her thanks and scooped up the ticket.

She moved quickly along the sidewalk, then halted in confusion, uncertain what to do next. There were so many people, all going different directions. Not far away, an old man set a wooden box on the sidewalk, stood on it, and began declaiming in a loud voice against the corrupt policies of the government. Forgetting herself, she gaped in wonder. To her dismay, before the orator had uttered enough words for her to follow his argument, two uniformed men rushed up and dragged him away.

She stood aghast. Were people in Mayberry forbidden to speak freely? She had heard stories of repression but hadn't believed them true.

Through her confusion, she realized someone was addressing her.

"You look like you could use some help." She focused her thoughts, recognizing the pleasant voice of the man who had reminded her of her ticket.

Taking a deep breath, she turned and glanced up at a dark-haired stranger with a thin moustache and iron-gray eyes, wearing a gray suit and matching cowboy hat. His good looks startled her, and it took her a moment too long to answer. "If you could show me where to go . . ." Her voice trailed away into sudden shyness.

"Right this direction." He gave her a boyish grin. "May I?" Before she could answer, he picked up her suitcase, not bothering to roll it.

Less than twenty yards away stood a door with a wooden sign above it marked *Terminal*; she would have seen it herself if she hadn't been so fuddled. They entered a large room with a wooden floor and a long counter to their right. The stranger passed her suitcase through a cutout in the counter to a man in a blue uniform.

"Tickets, please," the man said.

Liberty held out her ticket and the stranger took it, added it to his own, and handed it to the official. "We'd like to board early enough to get a good seat. The young lady is a bit nervous about traveling."

Liberty was about to protest when she saw the corner of a twenty-debit bill protruding from beneath the tickets.

"I think that can be arranged, sir." Tickets and money vanished behind the counter, only to reappear with their boarding numbers scratched out and replaced in pencil.

As they walked away, Liberty exclaimed under her breath, "You bribed that man!"

"More like a generous tip." He smiled at her, his eyes mischievous. "I was only thinking of you. It'll be less hectic if you board early."

The room had three seating areas, arranged in rows of four. A desk and double doors stood at the end of each. Speechless, she let him lead her to one of these, where they found their seat numbers in the second row closest to the front. Several people were already waiting.

"What do we tell the ones who are legally entitled to these seats?" she asked.

"We don't have to tell them anything. The porters always keep back some extras."

"For the bribes."

"Oiled palms make the wheels turn. It's the way things are done here."

"We cannot afford to differ on the question of honesty if we expect our Republic permanently to endure," she said without thinking.

He looked at her in surprise. "Mighty pretty words. They yours?"

"Teddy Roosevelt."

He chuckled. "I see."

"So, we are riding the same train," she said. He was clearly a man of questionable character. She had read of conners and nixons preying on the unsuspecting in large towns. Despite his good looks and seeming kindness, she determined to find an excuse to desert his company. To avoid further conversation, she withdrew a large book from her handbag.

"I'm going to Fort Annie Oakley," he said. "I noticed your ticket was for Bedford Falls. Nice little town. My uncle owns the grocery store. Revere is his last name, same as mine."

Liberty couldn't help but smile. "Like Paul the Watchman. 'One if by land, two if by sea; if from the sky, there shall be three.'"

"He's a distant ancestor."

"Really?" Seeing his expression, she reddened. "Oh, you're teasing."

"Well, I could be related, I suppose. I've never put much stock in a name. Mine's Brett, by the way."

"Revere is a good and honorable name," she said, weighing its worth against the bribing of the official. Despite his open, smiling face, she kept her tone aloof. "I'm pleased to meet you. My name is Liberty Bell."

They shook hands. He had a strong grip.

"That's a pretty handle. A tad unusual."

"Gramps says we're Southern Bells and should be proud as Henry Ford on a freeway." She tapped her book for emphasis.

He glanced down at the brown leather volume, splotched and stained from use. "What you got there?"

She showed him the title page.

Brett's eyes narrowed. "What kind of writing is that?"

"Old American," Liberty said, surprised at his lack of recognition. "The language of Washington himself."

"You can read that stuff? What does it say?"

"It's *The Americana*. My gramps' copy. I was afraid to bring it, but my Aunt Rosalynn wanted to see it; it has our family tree in the back."

"What does that line under the title mean?"

"*Incorporating the Quotations of the Founders*. It's on every copy."

"So that's where you get all the grand sayings. I haven't read *The Americana* since school."

"Actually, the modern school editions are abridged and para-phrased, useful as a way to expose children to the stories, but not entirely constitutional."

"I don't follow you."

"Constitutional. You know." Seeing his confusion, she added, "That it's good and honorable, and the truth. Like what's written here." She stroked the page. "For years, my gramps read it to us every morning at breakfast. I've always been able to memorize almost anything once I've heard it."

"We had a copy growing up, a modern Inglish version, of course; but I can't say I ever read it."

She frowned, furrowing her brow. "You've never . . . I thought everyone had. I love the histories of General Washington and his Knights and Representatives of the Pentagonal Table. The Boston Redsocks' Tea Party, the Dee Day Invasion, the—why are you looking at me like that?"

"I guess I never met a lady who liked the old yarns so much. They always seemed long-ago and far away to me."

A man carrying a megaphone walked up to the desk. "Ladies and Gentlemen, welcome to the Short Line Railroad. We will begin pre-boarding at this time. Please have your tickets ready."

A pair of tall Yooessay marshals approached the desk, tanned men with handlebar moustaches, their eyes wary beneath the ovals of their black and white futball helmets. Each wore a silver star pinned to his black-leather uniform and black boots shining with polish; their pistols, unconcealed, sat firmly in their shoulder holsters. Two men in dark leather jackets followed, one bearing a briefcase handcuffed to his wrist, and another pair of marshals brought up the rear. Liberty watched them with frank curiosity.

As soon as the marshals had passed through the double doors, the man at the desk called rows one through ten for boarding, and Liberty and Brett Revere followed the line into the train yard. Skycaps loaded luggage into baggage cars; the smell of the engines and the rumble of the locomotives filled the air. Liberty had expected to see dozens of trains, but there were only two, sleek and silver, rounded in front, with spiraling smokestacks, their cars wide as barns. It was loud and not a little frightening, and she was suddenly glad to have an escort.

Brett studied the train a moment, his iron-gray eyes sharp beneath the brim of his cowboy hat, before leading her past two cars and toward a third. Liberty wondered how he knew which to choose when they all looked alike. The marshals were standing outside the car talking to a steward.

The interior proved even more spacious than she had expected, with rows of seats on either side, turned to face one another, and a row of single seats in the center, also facing in pairs. The width of the compartment left plenty of walking room. Petrol lamps, installed along the walls, burned brightly but without odor, their fumes siphoned away through tubes. Mr. Revere led her toward the front of the car to two of the center seats.

"You wait right here, little miss. I need to speak to the steward. Won't be a minute."

"All right." But the instant he left she felt abandoned. Drawing a compact from her purse, she checked her hair. She really should find a way to gently part from Brett. Her gramps had said a hundred times a Southern Bell should never be seen in the company of a man who wasn't a husband, a relative, or a friend of the family, and here she was being escorted by an absolute stranger, one lots older than her seventeen years—probably almost thirty. She blushed at the thought of her mother seeing her in such a situation. Yet, she couldn't help but welcome a bit of protection. And she'd be leaving the train before him.

She glanced around, her insides quivering with excitement. She wanted to see everything! The car was filling up. A group of four ladies boarded, as dressed-up as Liberty, followed by three boys garbed in gray dusters like their father, a half-dozen little girls wearing sky-blue dresses and embossed berets, and four men with roughneck looks. One of this last group came her way.

"This seat taken?" He wore a slouch hat that hid most of his unshaven face; he reeked of beer.

"There's someone coming," she said. "A friend."

He looked her over, gave a lecherous grin, and swaggered away. She glanced at the door, suddenly wishing for Brett's return.

The marshals entered the compartment. The younger of the two dark-suited men, the one without the briefcase, came directly to Liberty. Opening his wallet, he flashed a badge. "I am a person of authority requiring your seat. You must move to another."

He wore a flat-brimmed, black hat fringed with dangling black beads. The handle of a pistol protruded from beneath his leather jacket. His eyes were brown and haughty. Liberty stared at him, shocked by his effrontery.

"Are you unable to hear me?" he demanded. "We are on official Yooessay business and require your seat."

She rose, her temper rising with her. "You, sir, are a disreputable servant of the public. My rights are assailed and my liberty usurped."

She turned and made her way to a window seat. She had barely settled in, cutting her eyes to the side to watch the young man and his associate occupy her former place, when Brett Revere reappeared.

"Why'd you move?" He sounded irritated.

"I was forced to abandon my position by a hooligan in the guise of authority." She told him the story.

Brett eyed the man. "Best not make too much of it. He's pretty young; his hat hasn't shrunk down to his brain size yet. This is a better seat, anyway."

The doors were closed with a piercing rattle. A stewardess in a blue lace dress and matching conductor's hat spoke into a megaphone, while another woman, similarly clad, stood at the front of the compartment.

"Welcome, ladies and gentlemen, to the Short Line, traveling to Adamsville, Bedford Falls, and Fort Annie Oakley. Please pay close attention as we inform you of our safety regulations."

Most of the passengers ignored her, but Liberty watched, wide-eyed, as she explained about the sicky sacks and the wooden flotation devices beneath the seats, while the other woman held the items up and gestured broadly with her hands to point out the two emergency exits. Liberty thought it quite grand, their following so closely the customs set out in *The Americana*, back when life had been luxurious and lectricity had existed to power a train's engines and lights.

When they were done, one of the stewardesses addressed Liberty. "In case of an emergency, are you comfortable opening the door?"

Liberty glanced at the red letters painted on the exit beside her. "What kind of emergency?"

The stewardess looked annoyed.

"We'll change places," Brett said. "I can handle the door."

As they switched seats, Liberty said, "People sure don't like you to sit where you want around here."

Brett grinned. "You'll get used to it."

An elderly gentleman and his wife took the seats across from them, and Liberty saw the compartment was nearly full. A bell rang; the train's air-horn gave a long blast and gently moved forward. Liberty stared in fascination as they pulled away from the station, past the petrol-resin streets and stone buildings.

"Oh my stars and stripes!" she exclaimed, clapping her hands together in delight.

"Is this your first train ride?" the old gentleman asked. He had silver hair and kind eyes.

"Since I was a little girl, but I don't remember much about it. It's absolutely yankee dandy, the blue sky above and the town running by, pretty as floats in a rosy bowl. Will it go faster than this?"

The old man chuckled. "Much faster, my dear. She'll soon be doing nearly forty miles per hour."

"It's a wonder we can breathe," she said, breathless herself.

They left the town behind, hurtling down the tracks past rolling, grassy hills, stands of larch and elmoak, and scattered farmhouses surrounded by long fields of bread-corn and petrol-barrel bushes, plants created by jenetic wizardry before the Great Blackout. The world, she reflected, was certainly a big place.

For the first half hour, she did nothing but watch the country blast past. "It's so fast my eyes are turning crooked."

"Best not overdo it, dear," the gentleman's wife said. "You'll get a migraine."

Her husband, a farmacist from Jefferson Corners, was a good conversationalist, and the four of them fell into an easy discussion. The couple was traveling to Fort Annie Oakley to see their new grandson, and Liberty learned that Mr. Revere was a grain buyer for Southern Mills. But when it came out that she and he weren't traveling together, the woman gave him a sharp glance. "You're awfully young and pretty to be traveling alone, my dear. A woman should always be careful. Couldn't your parents accompany you?"

"My daddy died when I was eight, kicked in the stomach by a

horse, and mama and I moved in with my gramps. She had to stay home with my brothers and sisters, but I'm really independent. I've taken care of my siblings most of my life, though Tink—that's my sister Tinker—is only a couple years younger, and she helps."

"The three of us can watch over her as long as we're on the train," Brett said, giving the woman a disarming smile.

Liberty frowned, not certain she liked being 'watched over.'

The miles rolled on. The stewardesses handed out cups of grapple juice. The travelers played cards awhile. The old gentleman wanted to place nickel-debit bets, but Liberty declined. "General Washington called games of chance 'the child of avarice, the brother of iniquity, and father of mischief.' So I really couldn't."

"That's a bit provincial, isn't it?" the woman asked.

"No, ma'am. Gramps says we're going to hades in a walmart cart— the government out west all corrupt; even the governor himself appointing cronies and taking bribes." She gave Revere a rebuking look. "That's why it's so important to have standards. Course, where I come from, around Farwell, people are honest. And I like to think most folks in the Yooessay are, even if there are some rotten chips in the ram. Like Dolley Madison said when she made those little cakes to appease the Reds who came to burn down the White House: 'Be a good neighbor to everybody, and just like a good neighbor they'll be there for you; and there won't be any thugs or ruffians in the hood.'"

"I wish I had your rose-colored shades, Sunshine," Brett said.

"A cynic, Mr. Revere," Liberty returned, "is a man who knows the price of everything, but the value of nothing."

Brett burst into a pleasant rumble of laughter. "Well, I'll be! You're a regular nuke-fire! I didn't think there were any like you left in the world."

"I admire your directness, young lady," the old gentleman said. His wife, shooting Revere another suspicious glance, smiled and nodded her approval.

"You're right about our government, too," the gentleman continued. "Everybody talks about it wherever I go: the governor and his Committees stripping authority from our judges, ignoring legitimate protests from the town councils—why, only last month, the Outlook Press in Fort Annie Oakley, an opponent of the governor's policies, burned to the ground under suspicious circumstances. These are dangerous times."

After the cards, Liberty dozed for a while. Then there was a stop at Adamsville so everyone could stretch their legs and eat lunch. Once back aboard, the country began to change, becoming more wooded with fewer farmhouses.

"We're at the edge of No Man's Land," Brett said. "As close as we'll come to it this trip."

Liberty peered out the window, half-expecting to see roughnecks and fizzicists lurking beneath the shadows of the elmoaks, but there were only a herd of mule-deer and scattered turtledoves. A light breeze stirred the leaves, peaceful as the Potomac.

The afternoon passed. They ascended a ridgeline, the train slowing to a crawl as it made its way up the long slope. Brett had been quiet, almost sullen, for the last hour, and Liberty studied his handsome face. His eyes darted back and forth across the compartment, as if searching for something; she followed his gaze but saw nothing unusual. Most of the passengers slept or read. The marshals had removed their helmets. One of them studied a map while his comrade across from him nodded in his seat. The rude official, as Liberty thought of him, sat upright and alert, watching the courier with the briefcase handcuffed to his wrist. Liberty noticed that the four roughnecks who had entered the car together each sat in different parts of the compartment and were awake and vigilant.

Brett retrieved his hat from where he had placed it beneath his seat. As he put it on, Liberty noticed a drop of sweat drifting down his forehead.

Suddenly, he reached into his jacket and pulled out his pistol. Holding it directly above Liberty's head, he aimed it at the rude official.

Without thinking, Liberty grabbed the weapon, pulling it down just as he squeezed the trigger. So close to her ear, the shot sounded like a cannon in the closed compartment.

Everything happened all at once but seemed to occur in slow motion. A woman screamed, followed by others. The four roughnecks had their revolvers drawn; Liberty realized they had intentionally positioned themselves to surround their targets. The rude official and the marshals fumbled for their weapons. One burly marshal rose from his seat but was cut down by shots from the four corners of the car. Still, he had drawn the outlaws' fire, and another marshal got one of them before he too was felled. A brave passenger grabbed a roughneck's pistol and fought to tear it from his grasp.

The rude official drew his revolver in one smooth motion, only to lose his grip on it, flinging it half-way across the aisle. The courier with the briefcase threw himself to the floor, his revolver out and blazing before he landed. He hit his target multiple times, sending the outlaw sprawling.

Liberty witnessed all this in a moment. Revere cursed in her ear and tried to raise his gun back into line. She gripped it with all her strength to keep it down. Drawing his other arm back, he cuffed her across the face, throwing her out of her seat onto the floor. Somehow, she wound up with his pistol.

She knew how to shoot, though she usually used a rifle. She pointed the gun at Brett's stomach. *If anybody comes at you, don't aim for the head,* Gramps always told her. *Go for the chest.*

For an instant their eyes locked; she saw scorn for this schoolgirl threatening him with a gun. A line from *The Americana* ran through her mind, about firing when you see the whites of their eyes. She pulled the trigger.

And missed—much to her surprise—from less than three feet away. She had always known pistols could be tricky. Before she could fire again, he ripped the weapon from her grasp, turned it expertly, and shot the man with the briefcase. Without pausing, he jerked Liberty to her feet, whirled her around, wrapped one hand around her neck, and put the gun to her head.

Liberty's eyes swept the compartment. A hush had fallen. The air hung thick with gun-smoke. All the marshals were down, either wounded or killed. The courier lay on his back, staring lifeless at the ceiling. Three of the outlaws were dead; the passenger who had struggled with one of them lay groaning and clutching his stomach. The other outlaw stood holding his gun, his shoulder bloody. The rude official reached for the courier's revolver lying on the floor.

"Hold it!" Revere commanded. "Go for that gun and I kill the girl!"

He froze.

"That's the way, junior," Revere said. "Now give me the map from that briefcase."

"It is the property of the Yooessay government," the official said. "If you take it, the full weight of justice will fall upon you."

"If you don't give it to me, I'm going to blow this girl's head off. Get the key and hand me the briefcase. No tricks."

"We never had the key with us."

Revere aimed his gun and fired, putting a hole dead-center in the briefcase lock. "Give me the map."

As the man obeyed, Revere opened the emergency exit behind him. The air rushed in. The train had topped the ridge line and begun its descent, its speed increasing. The other outlaw came up behind the official, took the scrolled document out of his hand, and brought it to his boss.

"Unroll it," Revere ordered. "Make sure we have what we want."

The man complied, showing it to him. Revere nodded. "That's it.

Now we and this little lady are leaving. Don't try to do anything stupid, junior. That goes for all of you."

A wave of panic swept through Liberty. So far she had only had time to react. But to be in the hands of these evildoers, at the edge of No Man's Land, filled her with terror. Her copy of *The Americana* lay on the seat; she stretched her arms to reach it.

"Not the girl," the elderly farmacist spoke up, rising to his feet. "Take me instead."

Revere struck him a savage blow to the side of the head with the butt of his pistol; the gentleman crumpled back into his seat. His wife shrieked. But Revere's grip on Liberty momentarily loosened. With a snarl of rage, she snatched up *The Americana*. Swiveling her hips to increase her momentum, she brought the corner of the book into Brett's stomach with all the force of her body.

The air rushed from his lungs, doubling him over. He dropped to his knees. The other outlaw stepped forward, his pistol aimed right at her.

The official, apparently waiting his chance, leapt forward, tearing the map from Revere's hands. With another bound, he sprang for the exit just as Liberty stepped backward to avoid the outlaw's gun. Liberty and the official collided and she fell backward, instinctively clutching him as they toppled through the doorway toward the rushing earth.

CHAPTER TWO

Cortez Coronado and his conquistadors crossed the deep Atlantic from the shadowy realms of the Old World, where the tyrants and despots reign, seeking to plunder the Seven Cities of Gold. Only the Alamo, a tiny fortress, barred their path.

Five days Davy Crockett and his men held the fort, three hundred against Coronado's fifty thousand, but one by one the defenders fell: Roy Rogers, Samhooston, Wild Bill Hickok, and others. At last, only Davy remained. They pierced his body with many arrows, even as he slew Coronado with a throw of his great tomahawk, Old Betsy.

But the valor of the defenders gave Eisenhower Iron-Hewer time to rally the Continental Army and defeat the conquistadors. And the gold from the Seven Cities was taken to Fort Knocks. — *The Americana*

* * *

Liberty and the official tumbled out of the compartment together. She felt the sudden tug of the wind and saw a whirl of blue sky, green trees, and the brown earth rising to meet them. They separated in the air, and she tried to get her hands in front of her but couldn't do it in time. She hit the ground on her side and went rolling. It seemed to go on and on, an endless tumble.

She finally came to rest on her stomach, her head turned, her eyes level with blades of grass, scattered rocks, and a black beetle who scuttled away as she tried to focus her vision.

Am I hurt? she thought. Am I dead?

She lifted her head and moved her legs, relieved to discover she could. "No paralysis from the neck down," she murmured. She raised herself on her arms. Her dress was nearly pulled up to her waist, showing her petticoat. She glanced around. The rude official was already on his feet. He picked up a rock and drew his arm back, apparently prepared to hurl it if Brett Revere followed from the departing train. When the outlaw did not appear and the last car passed, he dropped the stone and turned in her direction.

With a flood of embarrassment, Liberty clambered up, smoothing her dress. Her handbag was still on the train; her copy of *The Americana* lay open a few feet away. Still dazed, she staggered to the book and picked it up. One section of the binding had come loose, and several pages were being carried away by the breeze. She rushed to collect them, tears springing to her eyes, while the man retrieved his beaded cowboy hat, brushed the dirt off his black jacket and pants, and swaggered over to her.

"Don't be afraid," he said. "All is well. You are under the protection of Antonio Ice, Secret Service Agent for the Yooessay government." He raised his arms and gave a half-bow. "I am only too pleased to have rescued you."

"I should've let him shoot you and saved the trouble. You've ruined my book! Help me gather the pages."

"You speak of a book after such a narrow escape?"

"It's been in our family for generations!" She struggled not to cry in front of him. "Who were those men? What did they want?"

Antonio looked down at his hand, which still held the scroll. He grinned in triumph and held it aloft. "I saved the map!"

She clutched at a page of the book, but it blew out of her grasp, forcing her to hop to catch it. She glanced back at him. "Looks like you only saved half the map. Would you please help me?"

"Half the . . . ?" He looked at the scroll again. It was clearly torn and less than its original size. He unrolled it, studied it, and sat on the ground, one hand on his forehead.

The breeze stiffened, sending the pages whirling away. Liberty chased them, running awkwardly in her pumps. Most of them got caught in a bramble-bush, and she gathered them quickly, seizing the last with a cry of success.

She trudged back toward Antonio, who was muttering something she couldn't understand. The shock of the battle began to sink in, and her relief at retrieving the pages gave way to shame. Brett Revere had used her from the moment they met, both to appear an innocent traveler and to board the train early. She groaned.

"This is a disaster," Antonio said, both hands over his eyes. "My partner is dead; half the map is gone. What will I tell the Bureau Chief?"

His words brought home all she had witnessed. Suddenly trembling, she sat down beside him to keep her knees from giving way.

"I'm sorry about your partner," she said.

"I've been with him ever since I finished school. I was like a son to him."

Liberty patted his shoulder. He had black hair and a strong chin. "I know what it's like to lose someone close. How long had you worked together?"

"Since the end of April."

Liberty paused. "Of what year?"

"This one."

She gave him a sideways glance. "This is the middle of May."

His brown eyes turned sadly toward the ground. "Yes. It's nearly spring." He reached down and plucked an orange wildflower.

She took her hand off his shoulder. "You only knew him two weeks."

"We grew close in a short time."

Before she could answer, his eyes abruptly widened and he leapt to his feet. "Wait! We have to get out of here! We have half the map and they have the other. They'll be coming back for us. Come on!"

He grabbed her wrist and pulled her to her feet.

"Wait, yourself!" Liberty said. "I am not going into the wilderness with some stranger. I'll wait for the next train if you please."

"You'll be waiting for a bullet. Whoever those men are, they mean business. Believe me, I know the profile of their kind—I have extensive training. After the way you treated their leader, they'll show no mercy."

"There were only two of them left alive, and one was wounded."

Antonio frantically cut his eyes toward the top of the ridge. "Clearly, they intended to leave the train as it slowed at the crest of the hill, but our vigorous resistance threw off their timetable. They must have confederates waiting out here with horses. We have to get away, get some transportation, and send a message to my Bureau."

The thought of more outlaws alarmed her, but so did the idea of traveling with this stranger. Still, if he was right, they couldn't stay there. "Very well. Maybe we can find a farmhouse and get help."

She clutched her damaged copy of *The Americana* as they marched away from the railroad tracks, passing around elmoak groves. Antonio Ice took long strides and Liberty struggled to keep up.

"Can't you walk any faster?" he asked. "This is an emergency situation requiring Bold Moves."

Liberty narrowed her eyes at him. "You may have failed to notice that my legs are short, and these shoes are not made for hiking. Next time you throw a woman off a train, pick one wearing boots."

"You shouldn't have stepped in my way. Now on top of everything else, I have to be responsible for a girl."

Liberty halted and stamped her foot. "I am perfectly capable of taking care of myself. If you don't want my company, I'll find my own way."

His eyes flashed. "That's fine with me."

They stood glaring at one another. After a moment, his face softened. "As much as I would like it, I can't leave you. It would be dishonorable."

Liberty raised her eyebrows.

Antonio lifted his hand. "You don't understand. In ancient times, my ancestors crossed the waters from the Islands of Mexico. Despite being aristocrats and gentry of the Royal Brotherhood of Builders, they abandoned their wealth and glory to join with the poor, underprivileged Americans, who had neither roofs over their heads nor roads to travel on, to help them build a great nation. With such distinguished lineage, I cannot desert a woman in need."

"*The Americana* mentions that," Liberty said, grudgingly impressed. "General Washington met them on the shoreline and—"

Antonio waved a dismissive hand. "The story of my heritage was passed down to my family through the generations. General Washington is a myth told to children."

"What?"

"Those stories—all moon rocks, fanciful as chocolate."

Liberty clenched her fists against her sides, mouth gaping in indignation. She sputtered a moment before regaining her voice. "You, sir, are a villain and a cab, so just taxi yourself out of here! *The Americana* is the best and truest book in the world. When I think how the Founders bled and died for our freedom—"

He held his hand in front of her face. "Stop! We have no time for fantasies. Real criminals will soon be nipping at our heels. Come along."

He turned and strode away, leaving her quivering in exasperation. "I am among anarchists and commies!" she shouted at his back.

She looked behind her. The railroad tracks were still visible between the tree branches. She could go back, but the outlaws might be waiting. She turned toward Antonio, who had nearly vanished behind the vegetation. The sun was westering; it would be dark in two hours, leaving her alone at the edge of No Man's Land. She licked her lips, feeling her courage slip away.

"Wait!" She ran after him as fast as her pumps allowed.

* * *

The sun slid toward the horizon and they had yet to see a farm-house. Antonio led them east, traveling parallel to the tracks but far enough away to be hidden by the trees. He occasionally muttered to himself, as if in inner debate.

"What are you mumbling?" she finally asked.

He gave her the perplexed expression of a lost calf. "I'm not allowed to say." He sighed. "It's top secret, for my superiors' ears only. I'm under oath."

"Well, a man is only as good as his word, so that's that."

"I'd tell you if I could."

"I understand completely."

"It's just that we were taking the map to Fort Annie Oakley, then south to New Washington; but with half of it lost I must determine my course of action. Only specialists at the capitol can read the map, which is written in Old American. But if the men who stole the other half have someone who can understand that language—I know it's unlikely— but if they do, and if there's enough there for them to decipher it, they might get . . . it could be bad for our country, that's all. I wish we could find a farmhouse."

"Can I see it?"

"I couldn't let you since you're a civilian. It's classified. Besides, you could never understand it."

"So why not let me try?"

He gave her a suspicious glance. "The Secret Service Guide says trust no one when out in the field."

She looked around. "Well, we're definitely out in a field."

"That's not what it means."

"I was joking. I'm only trying to help. But if the spy guy manual says you shouldn't let me—"

"I am an agent of the Secret Service of the Yooessay. Spy guy is a vulgar term used by the masses. Why are you doing that?"

"Doing what?"

"Putting your hand over your heart any time anyone says Yooessay. See, you're doing it now."

"It's a sign of respect. I've done it since I was a little girl."

He tilted his head back and studied her carefully, rubbing his chin, which was beginning to show stubble. The beads on his hat quivered with the breeze. "A field agent must be prepared to improvise at all times." He handed her the scroll. "Be careful; it's very old."

She halted, glad to stop because her feet were killing her. If they didn't find a farmhouse soon, she was going to have blisters. She sat down with her back against a tree, took off her shoes, and curled her legs beneath her so her dress covered them. The scroll was soft, made of an unfamiliar material the texture of leather but smooth and supple; she decided it must be ancient indeed. The map was a real work of art, with a compass rose and drawings of mountains and forests.

"As you can see," Antonio said, "the writing is beyond your understanding. It's—"

"Oh my stars and stripes! You're trying to find the gold of Fort Knocks!"

He rushed to her side, reaching for the map. "What makes you think—"

She gripped it, refusing to let go. He sat down beside her.

"This says The Rocky Mountains, I'd guess, though it's partially torn away." She pointed at the writing, her excitement growing. "And there's the Grand Canyon. And look! Yoosemitee, the Old Forest. I'll bet the other half shows the Everglades and the Falls of Niagara. And here!" She tapped the map. "It says: Golden Treasure, except the last letter is missing."

She leapt to her feet. "This is genuine!"

"How do you know Old American?"

"My gramps taught me so I could read *The Americana* in the original." She opened her copy of the book and pointed to a page. "See? It's the same writing. Where did you get this?"

He stared up at the book and the map. "It was found in the ruins of one of the old cities. Do you have any idea how few there are who comprehend this language?"

"I thought lots of people could. I mean, Gramps and I are the only ones in Farwell, but I assumed in the larger cities—"

"So you understand all this?"

"It makes sense if you think about the story."

"Perhaps you could refresh my memory. I haven't heard it since I was a child."

Liberty rolled her eyes. "Did you even know the map's contents before I told you?"

He shrugged. "With my honed agent skills, I've surmised much."

Taking the tone she used when telling a story to the younger children at school, she related the tale of Davy Crockett and the 300 Americans. When she was done, he said, "I remember parts of it because the Royal Brotherhood of Builders fought against the conquistadors. But what makes you think this map shows the way to the gold?"

"Because it's the only Great Treasure mentioned in *The Americana*, which further states that Fort Knocks was moved to the Rocky Mountains just before the Great Blackout."

Antonio looked at the map. "Can the old legends really be true?"

"Your skepticism reflects our watered-down and dissipated educational system. There is one other detail: The Fountain of Youth was said to be at Fort Knocks. Anyone who drinks from it becomes immortal. And the map says right here, 'The Valley of the Fountain,' so, clearly—"

Antonio raised his hand for silence, then stood up and paced back and forth in front of her, gesticulating as he went. "If you, a mere girl from the unsophisticated suburbs of the countryside, can read this map, couldn't there be others?"

"I'm not a girl. I'm seventeen and—"

Antonio shook his finger at her as he strode past. "Can we then assume our adversaries might be able to do the same? Don't say a word! Old A.I. is thinking."

Liberty watched in annoyance as he paced, his hand on his chin, his hat pushed back, bold as a banty rooster in a motel-six.

"Can you tell where the gold is located?" he finally asked.

Liberty studied the map. "There were so many changes after the Great Blackout: floods, volcanic eruptions, earthquakes. If this map was made before that—and that's an assumption . . . It's hard to know. It was hundreds of years ago."

"But could you use it to find Fort Knocks?"

"Maybe. But with half of it missing—"

"I must consider. Wait! I have done so. When in the field a spy guy must be willing to make Bold Moves."

"I thought spy guy was a vulgar term."

"Not if spoken in the correct spirit." He put his hand to his chin. "Even with a horse, it would take three days to reach Adamsville, and another three for a Fedecks messenger to arrive at New Washington. By that time, our enemies could decipher the map and be far ahead of us. You and I must beat the bandits to the gold."

"You and me? I have to be at my aunt's in Bedford Falls."

"Your aunt can wait. You must do this for the sake of your country. Your knowledge of Old American will prove invaluable."

Liberty felt herself growing flustered. "This map would take us straight through the middle of No Man's Land, home of roughnecks, rednecks, and fizzicists, and if it's as old as you think, it might not be accurate. Besides, even if we found the gold, how could we get it out?"

"These are mere details. My superiors at the Bureau believe the map to be legitimate, so that's enough for me. The rest can be dealt with once the treasure is found."

"Why don't I just translate the map for you, so you'd know what it says?"

"Unacceptable. In the course of our journey, we may discover other clues written in Old American."

"I'll tell you what's unacceptable: you telling me what to do. James Madison tells us that wherever the real power lies in a government, there is a danger of oppression."

He looked directly into her eyes. "It's funny. Since you know so much about the Founders, I assumed you were a patriot. Apparently, you aren't."

Liberty put her hands to her hips, eyes wide in astonishment. "How dare you call me unpatriotic? I love the Yooessay!" Her hand drifted unconsciously to her heart. "I believe in everything the Founders handed down to us."

Antonio shrugged. "It's just that ours is a poor country with few resources and many enemies. The barbarians border us to the east, the Great Desert restricts us to the west, and the Mexican Islands, much to our shame, are no longer our allies. But," he pointed his index finger toward the sky, "with the gold of Fort Knocks, think what our people could accomplish: paving streets and constructing water services, improving our agriculture, hiring more teachers for our schools, perhaps even increasing our trade with outlying communities. And if our enemies get it, consider the harm they can do us, for make no mistake, the outlaws on the train were doubtless agents of some foreign power. You would be performing an inestimable service to your country."

Liberty hesitated. She had no desire to go anywhere with this blusterer, much less into the perils of No Man's Land. Yet, if it was for her country. . .

"You have to ask yourself," Antonio said, "what would General Washington do?"

"Your attempts at manipulation are unnecessary," she snapped. "Besides, General Washington would send his Knights and Representatives. Better to ask what Mac Arthur or Marshal Dillon would do. Let me think!"

A multitask of emotions filled Liberty as she considered the situation: suspicion of Antonio, trepidation for the journey, and concern for the consternation it would cause Gramps, her mother, and her aunt. But beyond that lay a thrill at the thought of undertaking such an adventure. She had lived her entire life less than three miles from home; here was an opportunity to see the world. Wasn't this exactly what happened to Lewison Clark when Representative Thomas Jefferson sent him to explore the wild? Or to Dorothy, a woman younger than Liberty, summoned from Kansas by a whirlwind to free the Emerald City from the tyranny of the Wicked Wizard?

"I'll do it!" she exclaimed. She lowered her voice. "At least, I'll go with you part-way until you can send a message for instructions from your superiors. But only as long as you act in a civil and constitutional manner."

"A descendent of the Royal Brotherhood of Builders always acts honorably. Now let's find somewhere to spend the night."

Liberty put her shoes back on and rose to her feet, regretting her decision the minute she felt her rising blisters.

The sun drifted below the treeline, sending shafts of light shooting between the scattered boughs, throwing long shadows across the travelers' path. They crossed deer trails and stands of wildflowers humming with bees. Struck by how much it resembled the common woods back home, Liberty had to remind herself they were on the edge of No Man's Land, the lair not just of evildoers, but reputedly a haven for goblins, ghosts, and giant spiders. Not that she believed in them, but she shivered at the thought of being caught out after dark.

As twilight descended, the birds ceased their chirping, and the crickets took up the call. The breeze dropped; the air grew still; the world narrowed until Antonio appeared only a shadow by her side.

"Have you been out in the woods much?" she asked.

"I am a master of outdoor survival. Fear nothing with old A.I. by your side."

"I'm not afraid. It's just that we're going to be fluttering around in the dark soon."

"True. But since we have nothing to eat, no bedrolls, and dare not start a fire that could alert our enemies, we might as well keep walking."

"You sure you've done a lot of camping?"

She saw his shoulders shrug in the dimness. "During our survival course in Secret Service school we were left alone in the woods without provisions for three days."

They walked in silence as she digested this. The brambles and wildflowers brushed uncomfortably against her skirt.

"Did you pass?" she finally asked.

It took him a moment to answer. "I got pretty hungry, you know."

"That's what I thought. Well, Captain Cook, I suggest we stop where we are before we lame ourselves."

Even as she spoke, they passed a stand of trees filled with looming shadows.

"It would be a shame to halt now," Antonio said, "when we've reached a farmhouse."

The vague outline of a house and barn stretched before them. Liberty gave a mental sigh of relief until she realized none of the lights were on. "It looks deserted."

"Maybe they go to bed early. Let's see what's in the barn."

"That's private property."

"We won't hurt anything. Come on."

Antonio unlatched the barn door, and the smell of hay and horses filled their nostrils. It was completely dark, but Antonio stepped inside and struck a match, revealing painted red walls, stables, and a lantern hanging from a peg. Liberty snatched up the lamp before the light failed. Working together they soon got it burning. As its flame rose, a horse snorted; two bay mares and a piebald gelding stood in the stalls. Saddles, bridles, and blankets hung on wall pegs. A hand-painted sign, nailed between two studs, depicted a snake labeled with a popular slogan from *The Americana*: *Don't Tread On Me*.

"We can stay here tonight," Antonio said.

"I've slept in barns before when a cow needed help calving, but never by choice. Let's knock on the door and find out if anyone's home."

Seeing his hesitation, she said, "Come on! You can tell by the sign they're patriotic. They'll surely help us."

Holding the lantern, Liberty led out of the barn, following a dirt path toward the house. Before they had gone a dozen steps Antonio grasped her arm and hissed, "Wait! Look there."

From the direction they had come glowed the orange flame of a campfire, its light wavering between the tree branches.

"The bandits have pursued us," Antonio whispered. "Quickly! Back into the barn."

They retreated, his hand guiding her.

"We don't even know it's them," Liberty protested.

"A camp in the middle of No Man's Land—who else could it be? The outlaws must have left the train and met up with their waiting confederates. Believe me, I have experience in these matters."

"Is that from a Secret Service class on interpreting campfires?"

He pulled her into the barn and shut the door. "It isn't a subject for levity. They're less than two miles behind us, undoubtedly on horseback. We have to leave at once."

Taking a bridle from its peg, he entered the gelding's stall. "Easy, boy." The horse blew, making its lips quiver in protest at the lateness of the hour, but it allowed Antonio to put the bit in its mouth.

"What are you doing?" Liberty demanded.

"Under the authority of the government of the Yooessay, as a deputized officer of the Secret Service, I am confiscating two horses." He threw a blanket and saddle onto the gelding's back, tightened the cinch strap, and turned to one of the mares.

"You can't steal those horses! We have to go back to the house. I'm sure the owner will give us transportation."

"Patriotic sign or no, we can't take chances on his loyalty. He might not believe us—or considering where he lives—might be an outlaw himself. Besides, I'm not stealing them, I'm procuring them for official government business, to be reimbursed by my agency at the first opportunity."

"I will not be a party to vigilante search and seizure under the guise of bureaucratic authority," Liberty replied. "Thomas Jefferson tells us that even the best forms of government will eventually be turned to tyranny by those entrusted with power. You can't take the horses."

His back to Liberty, Antonio continued saddling the mare. She walked around to where she could see the side of his face. "Mister Ice, I don't think you understand. I will have no part in this. Eternal vigilance is the price of liberty, and rampant abuses of power must be opposed. You will stop at once."

Without replying, he took a rope from its place on the wall, cut two lengths of it from a long knife hidden in a sheath in his boot, and tied one of them into a loop. Stepping over to Liberty with a suddenness that made her shriek in surprise, he twisted it around her wrists, making her drop her copy of *The Americana*.

"Stop that! What are you doing?"

He drew the rope tight and jerked a bandana from his pocket and tried to put it over her mouth. She pulled her head away.

"Don't you dare!" She tried to hit him with her tied hands, but he was too strong. She got a solid kick to his calf, making him grunt in pain. He came at her with the gag again and she lost her balance. He tripped over her, falling across her legs, but before she could regain her feet, he straddled her, his knees pinning her shoulders. She kicked, vainly trying to reach his head.

"Hold still," he ordered, bringing the gag closer.

"I'll scream from here to the Olympics, I swear I will. I will fight you in the fields! I will fight you in the—"

Her last words were lost as he tied the gag. He jumped up and wrapped another rope around her ankles. Scooping her up, he threw her over the mare's saddle. A few quick lashings bound her hands and feet together around the horse's belly.

"Knot-tying class." He picked up *The Americana* and stuffed it into a saddlebag. "I got excellent grades at that. You have my sincerest apologies, Miss Bell, but there is no time for debate."

Taking the lantern, he led both horses into the night. He climbed onto the gelding and they set out through the darkness along a narrow cow path.

* * *

For the first three minutes, Liberty struggled with all her strength, until the gag left her breathless, the ropes made her wrists ache, and the jouncing of the horse made her stomach churn. For the next five minutes she chided herself for ever being nixoned into accompanying this lunatic. Five minutes more were spent wondering, with mounting horror, whether he really was who he claimed to be, or a homicide who had somehow managed to spin his way into the confidence of the Yooessay marshals. So far, he had lost his gun in the middle of a fight, thrown her off a train, and stolen two horses. She did have to admit he could tie an excellent knot. But had he acted any better than Brett Revere? She blushed. Throughout her journey she had been naïve as a popsicle in a microwave. If she ever got off this horse, she was going to take the initiative.

After she had fretted for twenty minutes more, Antonio strode back to her, carrying the lantern. "We are beyond the hearing of both the farmer and the bandits. If I release you, will you promise not to run away?"

She nodded her head.

"Most cool," he said. "I take you at your word." He untied the gag.

She groaned. "I have become the accomplice to a horse thief. Be aware that an oath given under duress is neither morally nor legally binding."

"Be aware I can leave you tied to the horse."

"I will suspend any intentions of flight."

He released her and helped her down.

With calm resolve, she braced herself and slapped him across the face as hard as she could, throwing all her fury into the blow. "You will *never* do that to me again!"

His mouth opened in surprise. By the light of the lantern, she saw his eyes narrow in anger; she thought he was going to hit her. Instead, he stood his ground, his fists doubled, and after a moment, said, "I suppose I deserved that."

"I want to see your badge more closely, and I want to see it right now!"

He drew his wallet from his hip pocket and held it open, unveiling a silver badge embroidered with gold at its center, embossed with the words *To Protect and Serve*. She took it, studying it carefully. It was made of heavy metal that glistened in the light.

"It appears to be authentic," she admitted. "If so, your disgraceful manhandling of my person only tarnishes its luster."

"I answer to a higher purpose, Miss Bell. We must ride as long as we can, for our very lives."

"Very well. But I expect no more chicanery. As far as I'm concerned, until you prove otherwise you are nothing more than a brigand with credentials. Now, let me see your knife."

He drew his blade from his boot and handed it to her rather carefully, though he stayed his ground. She used it to slit one side of her dress and petticoat.

"It will have to do." She returned it to him. It was immodest to ride with half her leg exposed, but she could hardly travel sidesaddle.

"Let me help you back on."

Ignoring his waiting hands, she swung herself easily onto the horse, the feel of leather cold against her thigh. The air was cool; their path lay among stands of tall trees.

"Giddy up," she ordered the mare, prodding it gently with her heels. She rode forward without glancing back at her companion, keeping her head high, but she was suddenly trembling. She had, after her humiliation, established boundaries between them, but it had been a dreadful gamble; he could have killed her for slapping him. He had shown at least some sliver of decency, this uncertain man.

The full moon soon rose, gigantic as a fabled Florida orange. She gazed wistfully at its mountains and the dark blue rectangle along its left side, the remnants of Armstrong City, the old American moon base. She wondered if anyone lived there still and if so—as they rode ever deeper into No Man's Land—if it too was a country of ghouls and madmen.

CHAPTER THREE

According to the author's own words, the quotations incorporated into the tales of The Americana came from a book written before the Great Blackout. As such, they must be far older and more accurate than the oral histories the author compiled. —A Study of Ancient America by Armstrong Thomas

* * *

Then the immortal Pilgrim, Waynejon, said to Lincoln, beneath the shadowed boughs of Yoosemitee: "From its beginning, the Union was founded as an eternal struggle between the rights of the states and the power of the Federal Government. It survives through compromise."

Abraham Lincoln brooded a moment. "These are indeed perilous times for the Union, and I will do what is necessary to preserve it. I am willing to compromise, yet some things cannot be compromised, no matter the cost."

"Because that is so, your life will be hard," Waynejon drawled, "and for the sake of your country you will die in the end."

"So be it," Lincoln said. —The Americana

* * *

Liberty and Antonio rode until the moon stood high overhead, its ancient city a blue blush on its blanched cheek. They finally climbed from their mounts, weak from hunger, thirst, and fatigue. They dared not light a fire for fear of its being seen, and lacking bedrolls, lay beneath a gnarled elmoak using their saddles for pillows.

"We need to be off at dawn," Antonio said, extinguishing the lantern.

Liberty groaned her reply and fell at once into a sleep troubled by her empty stomach and the chill night air. She dreamed of her long, bizarre day: the train station, the gunfight, Brett Revere and the dying marshals, Antonio losing his gun, his lashing her to the horse, the long ride through darkness.

She woke on her back in the dawn's early light, gazing up at wisps of lightening sky between the branches of the elmoak. A purple butter-dragon sat on a weed beside her, flexing the dew from its wings. She sat up. The riding and the hard ground had left her stiff, and she was ravenously hungry. Antonio lay comatose a few feet away, his boots resting beside him, his hat pulled down over his eyes. She rose and tapped his toes with her foot.

He bolted upright with a shout, fumbling for his missing gun.

"Whoa, there!" Liberty said, startled herself. "It's just me. You said we needed to get up early."

His expression grew less wild. He ran a hand through his thick black hair. "I was just resting my eyes."

They bumbled around, still half-asleep as they saddled their mounts, but were soon on their way. Liberty glanced cautiously behind her, thinking the horses' owners would be looking for them; it was customary in the wild to shoot horse thieves first and hold the trial later.

"Do you think the outlaws are still after us?" she asked.

"Beyond a doubt. They're vicious, clever men, else they never would have succeeded in their ambush." He narrowed his eyes at the surrounding vegetation. "Be careful not to let your clothing get caught on a shrub. Trackers often find their quarry by such torn remnants."

Liberty grimaced. "You didn't grow up in the country, did you?"

"It's in the Secret Service Guide."

"I've lived my whole life around Farwell without leaving a shred of clothing on a thorn bush, but I'll tell you what we should do, constitutional for sure; we should ride down the next stream we find to hide our tracks, the way General Washington saved the Brits at Dunkirk when the Notsies had the Allies pinned."

"You know a lot about *The Americana*, don't you?"

"'Those who don't know history are destined to repeat it,'" Liberty quoted, "'and forfeit all coupons, discounts, and travel miles.'"

"I don't believe it's history at all. All those heroic deeds they're supposed to have done, constructing buildings hundreds of miles high, creating weapons that could destroy thousands, defeating Space Aliens. Why didn't some of the cities survive? Where's the evidence?"

"You sound like Brett Revere," Liberty said. "All the records were lost in the Great Blackout. It was—"

"Because the knowledge was stored in lectricity. I know the story. But lectricity is a myth, too."

Liberty raised her voice in irritation. "Lectricity is not a myth! It made everything work. And the ruins were lost in the earthquakes, volcanoes, and rising oceans. Whole continents were shattered like lego logs in a kindergarten. And then the plagues came, killing millions."

"Millions!" Antonio snorted. "Do you have any idea how many people it takes to make a million? The legends always exaggerate. No, Miss Bell, there was never any great, idyllic civilization where people flew through the air on gigantic birds and lectricity made robots move. Besides, how could General Washington have done all they say: fighting in the French and American Native War, the War of Independence, the Civil War, the World War, and also been President? He would have to live two hundred years."

"Because of lectricity, medicine was better and people lived longer. Everyone knows that. And those weren't separate wars. They were skirmishes in the Great War against Hitler, the Wolf Prince from the rotten vileness of the Old World, a continent of darkness and shadow where kings and despots ruled in totalitarian lands of blackest evil, just like *The Americana* says."

"Useless nonsense," he said, "a bunch of fruit-filling."

"If it's so useless, why do you need me to read the map? Besides, maybe General Washington lived for centuries because he drank from the Fountain of Youth at Fort Knocks."

Antonio threw up his hands and waved them in the air.

They rode in fuming silence until they reached a stream. Cottonwoods and cattails grew along its banks; its waters slipped slowly by, a tired traveler from distant mountains. Lacking a container, Liberty and Antonio knelt, cupping their hands to drink, while the horses guzzled greedily beside them.

"Makes me wish I had a longer neck." Liberty pushed the mare's head up to keep her from drinking too much.

"Makes me wish I had found a canteen in that barn."

Liberty refrained from replying, though she thought they had stolen more than enough. She knew how she'd feel if someone had taken Gramps' horses.

Antonio cleared his throat. "Riding in the stream, that seems like a good idea. Does the direction matter?"

"Upstream or down, makes no druthers."

They rode their mounts through the shallow water, over pebbles round and white as eggs. Hoowaukers spread their red fantails, giving stuttering calls from the upper tree branches. The air was warm but not uncomfortable. Liberty smelled lilac and the musky scent of her horse. Momentarily lost in the joy of riding through green trees on a spring day, her hunger and irritation faded, making her forget they were journeying through No Man's Land pursued by villains.

As if to turn contentment to perfection, the stream soon opened onto a small pool populated by golden trout. Liberty dismounted.

"What are you doing?" Antonio asked.

"I need a long stick. We're having brunch." Seeing his look, she said, "Don't worry. I'll be quick."

Borrowing Antonio's knife to cut off a short length of her bridle, she tied the blade to the end of a broken tree branch. Circling along the banks of the stream, she quickly speared a pair of fish and threw them flopping to the ground.

When she looked up, Antonio was staring at her in frank admiration. "I wish I . . . I mean, let me try that!"

He sprang from his horse and took the spear from her hand, his eyes fixed on the pond.

"It's harder than it looks," Liberty said.

He gave a quick thrust with the spear. When he pulled it out of the water, two fish wiggled on its point.

Liberty laughed. "Talk about a rookie hit! You could never do that again."

He grinned at her. "Watch old A.I."

Tossing the fish to the ground, he searched the pond and struck again, once more catching his prey. He held it up in triumph, arms straight over his head. "Ha! The Master! I'm a quick learner, Miss Bell."

Liberty clapped her hands in delight. "I know how to cook them with hardly any smoke."

Sobering, Antonio looked behind them. "All right, but we have to hurry."

"We need dry wood, nothing green."

Within moments, she had a tiny fire going. She gutted the fish with the knife and cooked them on a sharpened stick, silently thanking Gramps for teaching her so many survival skills. She burned the trout around the edges, but when she and Antonio sat down to eat, she thought nothing had ever tasted so good. Afterward, she wrapped the two remaining fish in Antonio's bandana to save them for dinner. Together, they buried all signs of the trout and the fire, and were soon in the saddle again. It annoyed her a little that Antonio didn't thank her for feeding them, until she reminded herself that a deed done expecting thanks wasn't a good deed at all.

They traveled the river another two miles until its banks began to rise, making it difficult to exit and leaving them open to attack from above. Departing from it, they journeyed north. Throughout the afternoon they saw no sign of pursuit.

With the westering sun, the ground began a gradual ascent, a long slope leading to a series of tall hills. As they reached the crest, Liberty glanced over her shoulder and saw distant movement below them, a line of approaching horses passing between the stands of trees.

"Sure as a subway, that's either a police squad or Revere's men," she said. "I wonder which is most likely to shoot us on sight?"

Even as she spoke, the riders broke into a gallop.

"C'mon!" Antonio ordered, kicking the sides of his horse. "Riding in the river, it didn't work so good."

They hurried down the back side of the hills, not running but keeping to a quick trot. Their pursuers were easily two miles away, riding uphill, and would have to slow down or risk exhausting their mounts. The biggest danger lay in staying out of rifle range.

They made good time and were safely out of sight behind the trees before the riders finally topped the rise. They angled northwest, hoping to avoid being seen.

"The odds are against us," Antonio admitted. "These men are clearly expert trackers. I wish I had my pistol."

"I wish you had a busload of dynamite. We need a moovey moment."

For two hours they traveled, zigzagging their way, staying among the densest groves of trees, alternating the horses between a walk and a trot. When pushed, Liberty's mare proved to be a natural pacer, falling into a gentle rolling jog easy as sunshine in El-lay, but at any moment she expected the riders to break through the vegetation.

The sun dipped below the trees. The horses were beginning to tire, and between her anxiety and the day's journey, Liberty felt almost as weary. The only comfort was that their enemies' mounts would be equally fatigued.

Behind distant clouds, the sun turned to smoking ruins and faded to twilight. They dismounted near another creek, watered themselves and the horses, and led the animals a mile along the riverbed, then beyond it a short distance, where they made camp in a stand of locust trees. After tending to their mounts, they sat on the ground in the dark, their backs against their saddles, and ate the last of the trout, a meager meal; it looked to be another hungry night.

Keeping his voice low so it wouldn't carry, Antonio said, "At least the outlaws won't be able to track us in the dark."

"The spy manual again?" Liberty softly replied.

"You shouldn't mock the Secret Service Guide, especially if you value the old stories as much as you say. In school they told us it was written by Edgar Zimblis Hoover himself. He was—"

"Head spy guy; I know. That's a good story, but no more constitutional than a red light at a Macy's Day Parade. Edgar's brother, Herbert Hoover, who could fly using his vacuum powers, was the real head of the F.I.B., as it was called back then."

They fell into silent disagreement. The crickets sang; the wind lay still. Liberty was miserable. Her whole body ached. She hadn't missed many meals in her life and had to fight the urge to burst into tears. She wanted to tell her disagreeable companion she would head for home at first light, but she didn't like appearing weak. Besides, she had given her word.

The moon, waning from full, rose above the trees, and by its light Liberty noticed something. She stood, excited.

"What's the matter?" Antonio asked, startled by her sudden movement.

"Those bushes." She hurried to the nearest of them—and despite the earliness of the season—found it covered with berries. She picked one, half as big as her palm. "Some kind of blueberries."

"Can we eat them?"

"Their texture is unusual, but they look all right." If Liberty hadn't been too tired to debate, she would have reminded Antonio that the berries' size demonstrated the veracity of *The Americana* story of Johnnie Appleseed jeneticizing the trees and fruits of the nation to their fullest potential. Instead, she handed him a berry and took a bite herself.

"Oh my stars and stripes, this is good!" Juice ran down her chin, which wasn't ladylike at all, but she didn't care. The minute she swallowed, her hunger swelled within her. "I wish we had these back home." She looked at Antonio, who was eating just as fast as she, and they exchanged sudden childish grins, then both looked away.

"It melts in your mouth, not in your hand," he said, making her smile at that common *Americana* phrase, a quote from Auntie Emm.

They sat down. Liberty felt like she could eat forever. Her spirits lifted with every bite.

"Where did you grow up?" she asked, remembering to speak quietly. She might as well get to know him if they were going to travel together.

"Fort Annie Oakley."

"It's really big, isn't it?"

"Bigger even than New Washington, a population of nearly twenty thousand."

"I can't imagine," Liberty said. "How do you ever learn every-body's names?"

He laughed. "You don't. There are too many. That's just the way it is in a great metro. But it was a good place to grow up. Ours is a big family. I have three brothers and two sisters. I'm the youngest."

"I'm the oldest," Liberty said, "which can sometimes be a bit of a dragster, because I have to help take care of everyone else: my brothers, Graham and Blue, and my sisters, Tinker, Jingle, and Barb. It's a lot of responsibility."

"My eldest brother is the most responsible, I guess. Being descended from the Royal Brotherhood of Builders, and my mother a cultured woman, we were always high-class. But my father—Old Hombre we call him—he doesn't care much for culture. He wants to get off work, relax, and drink a few beers. He likes to laugh and tell jokes. We mostly get along. Old Hombre, he's all right. But we haven't always heard ear-to-ear. He wanted me to follow in my brother's tennies and join the police and fire department. He said I could make Fahrenheit Inspector in five years. I refused."

"I don't remember much about my daddy." Liberty spoke with a sudden pang of yearning. If he were still alive, she couldn't imagine ever disobeying him. Or Gramps, for that matter. "Was your father upset?"

"He was angry when I dropped out of thirteenth grade, but I didn't see the sense of it. Old A.I. is made for bigger things." Antonio thumped his chest with one fist. "Anyway, the city mayor surrounds himself with bullyboys, and I won't work for him. I was a carpenter for a while, then went to Secret Service School. I liked it a lot."

He took another bite of berry. It struck her he wasn't such a bad sort. And he was pretty cute, his dark eyes and bronze skin. Perhaps she had judged him too harshly.

"What about you?" he asked. "I know you can start a fire, catch a fish, and read Old American."

She shrugged. "There's nothing glamorous about where I grew up, but my gramps taught me that everyone's special, that we're all here for a purpose. Sometimes I just ache to find out what mine is." She turned her head toward the night sky. "I like to look at the stars and think of them shining through the universe on a million, gazillion planets, maybe some of them like ours. And I think they're shining just for me, but that every other person feels the same way, so they're shining for each individual in a particular way. And from each person's gifts, we can build great things. Out of the Many, One. And we don't have to stand alone. I think the world's a wonderful place and I dream sometimes of doing great things. Maybe not like General Washington. None of us are that great. But maybe like Patrick Henry or Susan Anthony."

"That's poetic," Antonio said.

"You don't think it sounds silly?"

"No. You got to be yourself, you know. That's the important thing."

"I don't think it's the most important. I think it's better to do something for somebody else."

They gabbed on, warming to one another, laughing and eating until Liberty thought she would burst. But when they were satisfied, their mirth abruptly died, slipping away like cats down an escalator. Liberty shook her head, wondering at her giddiness. Why had she suddenly taken a liking to this rude man?

"What just happened?" Antonio asked, shaking his head.

Liberty put her hand over her mouth. "Oh my stars and stripes. It must be the fruit. It's jeneticized to be intoxicating."

"Will it hurt us?" Antonio asked.

"I hope not. I don't feel sick or anything. I guess we're all right."

Embarrassed by their frankness, they fell silent and lay down with their heads against their saddles. Liberty shuddered, reminded that they were traveling through the wilderness and would have to be more careful; the berries might easily have been poisonous. Chiding herself, she fell asleep.

* * *

If it had been up to Liberty, they would have overslept, for she was so weary she spent the night in a smog-dead slumber, waking only when Antonio lightly shook her. It took her a moment to remember where she was, and when she did, she couldn't quite believe it. It seemed wholly incredible that she, a Southern Bell, should find herself alone in the wilderness looking for the gold of Fort Knocks with a complete stranger, riding stolen horses and pursued by outlaws. She fought the urge to cry.

I have to be stout as a Federalist, she thought, rising to her feet. The moon was nearly down; the stars said it must be close to four o'clock. They saddled the horses in silence, fuzzy-headed, shivering in the darkness, the animals blowing in protest and lifting their necks to avoid their bridles. They led the beasts out of the trees and mounted. Gradually, the horses warmed to the work, falling into their accustomed pace. Within the hour, the faint glow of sunrise grayed the eastern sky.

Liberty drew a pair of berries from her saddle-pack and handed one to Antonio.

"You sure it's safe?" he asked.

"Long as we don't start doing somersaults on the horses' backs. They didn't hurt us last night, so we should be fine."

The fruit proved as good as the evening before, but when its elation swept through her, she suppressed the urge to start blabbing again. Antonio must have decided to do the same, and they rode along, wordless and grinning.

By the time the sun rose, their euphoria turned to horror, however, as the pounding of hooves caused them to whirl around. A dozen outlaws, led by Brett Revere, thundered toward them.

"Ride!" Antonio yelled.

"My stars and stripes!" Liberty kicked her horse wildly.

It took a moment to convey the urgency to their animals, but they finally sprang into a gallop. The ground was fairly even, and they could go full-out. Liberty couldn't remember the first time she had been on a horse. She could ride well, but it was one thing to gallop a few yards on a familiar road and another to run triple-crown over alien terrain with pursuit at her back.

We're in the crisco now, she thought, relaxing her arms and pushing her feet against the stirrups to keep her balance.

The mare hit her stride, that moment when a horse's movements grow fluid and easy as riding on a cloud. At the same time, a tree branch to Liberty's left splintered and fell, clipped off by a bullet. She dared a glance behind her. Revere's men were fifty yards away; she couldn't tell if they were gaining.

She turned back to find a fallen tree directly in their path. For a wild instant she thought of leaping it, but a horse must be trained for that. She veered to the right and Antonio dodged to the left, splitting to either side of it, coming back together moments later.

The ride was a blur, the passing stands of trees, the rocks and stones, the staccato hooves, the mare's labored breath, the wind blowing Liberty's hair behind her, the popping pistols, the shade and sunlight through distant hills. Sooner or later, a bullet would hit one of their horses.

There was nowhere to flee, no avenue of escape, no hope of outdistancing the outlaws. They could only succeed in running their animals to death.

She looked back again and saw one of the pursuers' mounts stumble and crash to the earth, sending its rider flying. The wrong piece of ground and it could happen to her as well. Liberty put her head against the mare's neck, urging her on.

A mile passed, then two. Green foam flecked the mare's mouth. Three of the outlaws had fallen behind, unwilling to kill their valuable steeds.

Antonio's gelding screamed, struck by a bullet. It staggered and dropped, unable to carry its own weight. For an instant Antonio held on, until the animal hit the ground rolling, throwing him just far enough ahead to prevent the horse from landing on top of him.

Liberty jerked the reins to halt the mare. It took precious seconds to slow her momentum and even longer to return to her companion. Antonio was already back on his feet. The riders were nearly upon them.

"Get on!" she shouted.

Instead, he pulled the map from his pocket. "Get it to the Bureau! Ride on! For the Yooessay!"

She took it, but hesitated. The mare could never get away carrying two, and it made no sense for her to stay to be caught. But to leave him like this . . .

Feeling a deserter and a coward, she tightened her lips and turned the slavering horse, preparing to leap away. To her shock, another set of riders approached from that direction. There was no way out.

But instead of aiming their guns at her, the newcomers shouted and fired into the air. She turned her horse and saw Brett Revere and his men thunder to a halt, then veer away, fleeing back the way they had come.

Not knowing what else to do, Liberty trotted back to Antonio and dismounted. A score of riders surrounded them. The men halted and waited with guns drawn, studying their captives. Each wore identical garb: a brown shirt and levites, and a brown cowboy hat with twin oval tabs rising three inches on each side of its brim.

While Liberty stood breathless and shaking, one of their number, a big man, dismounted and strode toward them. He touched his hat in Liberty's direction. "Happy trails. My name is Jesse James, and this here's my gang. You are in the hands of the Rough Riders."

CHAPTER FOUR

Some scholars have suggested there were actually two Roosevelts. I do not find the argument compelling. Recent philological evidence suggests that the etymology of the name 'Franklin' derives from 'Free Man,' and may well have been a title such as "mayor" or "mister." Thus, in formal situations Roosevelt would have been addressed as Franklin Teddy Roosevelt. Such a title certainly suits the tone of the Old American culture.
—*A Study of Ancient America* by Armstrong Thomas

* * *

Liberty sat momentarily paralyzed, remembering all *The Americana* said about the great Jesse James. In No Man's Land, at the border of the Old Forest, where haunts and specters were rumored to roam, could the dead return to ride in the sunlight?

She shook her head firmly, saying the first thing that came to mind. "No, you're not."

"Not what?" Jesse drawled.

"Jesse James."

"My daddy said I was, and my mama backed him up."

"Sir." Antonio limped forward, right hand upraised as if swearing an oath. "I am Antonio Ice, representing the Yooessay government on a mission of national importance. You will impede our passage at your own peril."

Laughter ran around the circle of James' men.

"What's funny?" Antonio demanded.

"By all visuals you weren't proceeding so pleasantly before our arrival," Jesse said. "I think we will escort you to our condos."

"If you intend to take us prisoner," Antonio replied, "I ask you to let the girl go free. She is an innocent, undeserving of mistreatment."

"I wasn't at this juncture planning on torturing either one of you.

Let's see about your horse."

Despite its wound, the gelding was struggling to rise. A pair of the Rough Riders dismounted and approached it. One seized its bridle and helped it to stand. It waited pathetically, holding its back leg curled against its stomach, wild-eyed and shivering in shock and pain. Blood ran down its hip where the bullet had entered.

"These animals look familiar," Jesse said. "Farmer Duncan has a pair not unlike them."

"You won't have to put him down?" Liberty asked, hoping to change the subject.

Jesse stared at Antonio with narrowing eyes. "If you mean the horse, I've never shot a good animal except at necessity. I can't say the same for some men." He turned to Liberty. "We have a smattering of skill in veterinary medicine. If I may help the lady back onto her saddle?"

He strode over to her. A bear of a man, broad-shouldered and powerfully built, he was round-faced with round spectacles, a red, neatly trimmed moustache, and pale blue eyes. Despite being the leader, he appeared less than thirty years old. He scrutinized Liberty as he took her arm and guided her into the saddle; the amount of leg revealed by her slit dress embarrassed her, and she pulled the cloth over her knee.

Jesse turned back to Antonio. "You'll have to walk, but our domiciles are nearby."

Antonio nodded and Liberty felt momentary satisfaction at seeing him humbled by having to trudge behind the horses. His plea for her freedom made her regret the thought, however. It wasn't constitutional to be spiteful. She recalled Representatives Jefferson and Adams, lifelong opponents, but friends in the end, dying together on the Fourth of July.

Jesse rode beside Liberty. She could sense him watching her out of the corner of his eye. Each of the Rough Riders carried not only a rifle in his saddle scabbard, but a thick, wooden club four feet in length, its handle carved into the face of a smiling, moustached bear wearing round spectacles. Following her gaze, Jesse lifted his from its scabbard and expertly twirled it. He tossed it spinning into the air and caught it with his other hand. "This is an innovation of our own, useful as a staff, a weapon, and a tool for prodding cattle. We call them roosey-canes."

He returned the weapon to its scabbard. "I don't suppose Farmer Duncan loaned you those horses?"

"I know it was wrong," she said, "but we were desperate."

"That's why we call 'em desperados."

Liberty blushed. "The end doesn't justify, I know. But Antonio really is a government agent. I've seen his badge; it's metal and everything."

"I'd love to see it; and I hope to hear the story of how a pretty woman in a fine dress winds up with a yahoo in No Man's Land. Seems a trifle interesting."

"Would you believe I fell off a train?"

"I'd believe you were pushed."

She grew silent, exasperated by how transparent she was. After a moment, she asked, "Are you outlaws?"

"We're nothing of the sort, and I'm aquiver that our countenances fail to show it. We're the Brotherhood of the Rough Riders." He reached up and tweaked one of the two round, furry tabs rising from his hat. "We farm and raise livestock, and occasionally, when men of ill-repute pass through the territory, such as those evildoers who assaulted you, we take from the advantaged and give to the disadvantaged. We're the law in a lawless country, upholding justice in the spirit of the great American hero, Teddy Roosevelt, whose ideals our brotherhood embodies."

"I assumed your idol would be the man for whom you are named."

"I have immense admiration for him, but he isn't my pop-star. I've naturally spent time studying his life, and find it a shame that he, who did so much for so many, should have his flame cut short by a cowardly shot in the back. Had he lived longer, perhaps he would have achieved as much greatness as Teddy. Up yonder are our condos."

Liberty noticed nothing at first, until she perceived a house nestled among stands of tall elmoaks, painted in such clever camo it could scarcely be seen. Wagons and corrals stood beside it, all equally disguised.

"It's a wonder you don't paint your horses," she said.

Jesse laughed, a pleasant rumble. "In the badlands, it's best to be circumspect. Welcome to the Elkhorn Ranch, home of the Rough Riders."

"Did you grow up here?"

"I and my father before me."

As they drew near the two-story mansion of wood and stone, Liberty could see it had been added onto several times. A pair of powerful black-and-white dogs sprang barking from the porch, tails wagging, circling the riders to give Antonio a careful sniffing-over while he eyed them warily. He apparently met their approval, for they trotted away.

"Have you and your fancy-hat friend eaten lately?" Jesse asked.

"Only some berries this morning."

"Come along, then." He dismounted, carrying his roosey-cane with him. Helping her down, he beckoned Antonio to follow, leaving the horses to the care of his men. They passed onto a wooden porch and through a pair of camo double doors.

"Mama, we got company!" Jesse called as soon as they crossed the threshold. The room was filled with light; the long windows stood open, allowing a cool breeze; a staircase swept to the upper floors, and the entire chamber was filled with bears.

Bears were carved into the legs and arms of the chairs and tables; their features were chiseled into the fireplace mantle; they sat on shelves near the ceiling, peered from the bric-a-brac and doorknobs, looked out from every drawer-pull, from silver trays and stone statues. A bear nutcracker lay beside a bowl of pecans; several bear-shaped umbrella stands stood by the door, half-filled with the gang's roosey-canes. Jesse put his own among them.

A tall, middle-aged woman appeared, with laugh lines and eyes the same blue as Jesse's.

"Mercedes me!" she exclaimed, seeing the newcomers. "If these aren't petunias in a pool hall! Where did you find them, Jesse?"

"Just around the hood, Mom. This fellow is Antonio Icicle."

"Ice," Antonio corrected, doffing his hat. "My pleasure."

"The other one doesn't have a name," Jesse said.

Liberty shook the woman's hand. "I neglected to introduce myself. Liberty Bell, ma'am."

"Happy trails to you both. I'm Maddie James. We don't see too many pretty girls wandering the wilderness, Miss Bell."

"They're both horse thieves," Jesse said. "We shall hang them directly after supper."

Liberty and Antonio exchanged alarmed glances.

"Well," Mrs. James said, "perhaps you would like to bathe before supper and the lynching."

"Yes, ma'am." Liberty struggled to hold down a rising panic.

Mrs. James led them up the curving stairway and down a long hall. Bears glowered at them from every newel post and painting. The floors were pine plank, with handmade rugs before each door, all with bear motifs.

"This is your room, Miss Bell. The next one is yours, Mr. Ice. Each has its own bath."

Liberty struggled to hold back her tears. "But, Mrs. James, is he really going to hang us?"

"Oh, child." She patted Liberty's shoulder. "Jesse has never hanged anyone in his life. He *has* shot a few roughnecks over the years, but only when it was called for."

"I knew he was joking," Antonio said.

"How?" Liberty wiped a corner of her eye.

"People such as myself are trained to read others' expressions. I'll explain later." He stepped into his room and shut the door.

"It's a good thing you told us," Liberty said, "or I'm pretty sure Mister Deduction would be climbing out a window right now."

"He'd break his neck. You'll find everything you need laid out in the bathroom. I'm going to see if I can google up some clothes for both of you."

Her hostess departed and Liberty looked around the room. It contained a dresser, nightstand, and four-poster bed, all made of burl elmoak. A down comforter covered the bed. A large painting hung on the wall, displaying Teddy Roosevelt and his Rough Riders hunting a fox. She wondered how long Elkhorn Ranch had been in existence to accumulate such opulence.

Her image displayed in the full-length mirror proved an unpleasant surprise. Despite her efforts, her hair was a catastrophe, sticking out in oily wisps from under her hairpins; her dress, torn and stained, was completely ruined. Tears filled her eyes when she remembered how many hours her mother had spent sewing it, and she suddenly regretted hooking her fate to Antonio's questionable quest. His theft of the horses without a twinge of remorse had shaken her. And the way he had hollywooded her with his badge and Secret Service talk—she wondered if he knew anything at all. Perhaps it would be best if she took this opportunity to give the whole thing up and return to civilization.

She stepped into the bathroom and brightened. Indoor plumbing and a boiler for hot water were common in the Yooessay, but she had never seen anything this elegant. All the fixtures, including the bathtub, were made of marble. She ran her hands along the smooth counter surface, wondering at the Old American feel of it. Towels, washcloths, and even fragrant soap sat beside the sink. She raised the bar to her nose, her eyes closed to breathe in its lilac scent. Putting it down, she sniffed the sleeve of her dress. She smelled like a coyote in a carwash.

She luxuriated in the bath until her fingers wrinkled. Upon finally leaving it, she found clothes more suitable for travel lying on the bed: brown levites, a tree-bark brown blouse, and a matching cowboy hat and boots. Donning them, she felt comfortably dressed for the first time since leaving the train. She brushed her hair and straightened her bangs in the mirror, leaving it loose on her shoulders, blonde against brown. She didn't look too bad for someone who had spent three days in the wilderness. Having been the Pompom Car Nation Queen back in Farwell, she knew she was pretty, but couldn't help wondering what Jesse, the inhabitant of a world much larger than her small village, would think of her.

She shook her head, clearing such thoughts away. She was on a mission for her government and had no time for such fancies.

Stepping out of her room, she found Antonio pacing the hall, dressed in black levites and a white cotton shirt. He had left his hat in his room, and his thick dark hair, combed back and glistening with gel, made him look handsome. This did nothing to allay her annoyance at him, brought on by her earlier suspicions. He studied her with his dark eyes, his expression odd and unreadable.

"We need to talk," he said, speaking softly. "It's critical that you keep from mentioning the thing we carry."

"The map?"

"Hsst! Don't name it aloud. From now on, call it the *tonic*."

"Why would I call a map a tonic? That's like calling a duck a weathervane."

"Please, Liberty, try to understand. It's a code word. Agents use them all the time."

"Must be confusing, calling everything something else. If a pig is a horse and a gun is a piano, you'd say 'Drop your keyboard and get down from that sow.' Do you have code words for each other?"

"Sometimes. We—"

"So, are you the Creampuff Kid, or what?"

"Liberty!" he hissed. "You . . ." He studied her expression. "You're teasing me."

She giggled. "Maybe."

"You don't see the seriousness of the situation. We're in the hands of desperate men who would murder us without hesitation. James is clearly the ruthless head of a petty kingdom."

"Except he saved our lives. We're the horse thieves."

"Nonetheless, you mustn't mention our mission, not even under torture. Do you understand?"

"I do."

"Good. Let's go down. Act nonchalant."

His earnestness touched her. He might or might not know what he was doing, but he was surely sincere. "Before we join the others," she said, "I wanted to thank you for your gallant attempt to protect me."

"It was the least I could do. Besides, you had the tonic."

She frowned. "You did it for that? I see. It seems I misconstrued your intent." She pulled the map from her pocket, thrust it into his hands, and brushed past him, descending the stairs.

"Liberty! I didn't mean . . ."

She felt his eyes upon her back, then heard him sigh and follow her down.

Mrs. James met them at the bottom. "What a handsome pair you two make."

"We ain't a pair of nothin'," Liberty snapped, then immediately softened. "Begging your pardon, ma'am. Antonio and I have been thrown together by the sheer chance of a quickpick lotto, as my gramps likes to say."

"I see. Well, dinner is ready in the cafe. If you'll follow me."

They passed down a hall with a tall tapestry depicting Teddy Roosevelt grinning at a bear—man and animal both wearing identical spectacles and short moustaches—and entered a room filled with at least two hundred people seated around long elmoak tables. To Liberty's surprise, they weren't all men. Women and children dressed in levites and colorful blouses made up more than half the company.

"My stars and stripes!" she exclaimed, forgetting herself. "Like socialists in a sandbox."

"We're nothing of the sort, dear," Mrs. James chided. "You don't think we keep this many men without wives?"

Liberty reddened. "My apologies. It was just an expression. Everything here is so new to me. Gramps says I'm sometimes too straightforward."

Jesse rose from one of the tables and came over to them, his eyes fixed on Liberty. "You clean up stunning as a custom detail, Miss Bell."

She blushed. "You're very kind."

He seated them to his left and right at one of the tables, while he took the position on the end. He introduced them to those nearest, who all bore common names like Harriet, Woodrow, Jaylow, and Gilligan. The younger women wore their hair long; the older ones put theirs up. The men's hats rested on rows of hooks by the doors. Petrol jets ensconced along the walls lit the room with a yellow-green glow.

Men brought wooden plates bearing steaming steaks, boiled potatoes, and chunks of bread, served with water in Blue Austin glasses etched with five-pointed stars. The eating utensils were fine silver.

When everyone was served, Jesse stood up and raised his hands, bringing the company to its feet. Giving a military salute, he spoke loudly enough to be heard throughout the chamber. "Be sincere, be brief, be seated." The assembly returned the salute, sat back down, and commenced their supper.

"Teddy's words," Jesse said in explanation. "You must forgive our austere beverages. We follow Teddy's example, who by his own oath, declared, 'I have never been drunk or in the slightest degree under the influence of liquor.' He did upon occasion partake of the Mint Julep, as do we during the Fourth of July and other important holidays."

"Most admirable," Liberty said. "General Washington himself believed in moderation in all things."

"So there's no beer?" Antonio asked.

"I perceive you're a great reader of *The Americana*, as am I," Jesse said. "I think it tragic that so many have neglected the book which is the foundation of our culture."

Liberty smiled. "The stories are so constitutional. I can picture all of it. Like Mac Arthur, for instance, a real favorite of mine, striding from his tall ship onto the beach of the Old World, his sword upraised and shining in the sun, come to free the Filipinos from the tyranny of the Japanese. 'I have returned,' he cried. 'By the grace of Almighty God our forces stand again on soil consecrated in the blood of our two peoples. We have come, dedicated and committed, to the task of destroying every vestige of enemy control over your daily lives, and of restoring the liberties of your people.'"

Liberty paused, suddenly realizing her voice had risen, and she had half-stood, her hand over her heart, the whole room hushed and listening. She sat down quickly, her face burning. "I'm afraid I got momentarily beamed away."

But Jesse clapped his hands, a slow, echoing boom, his eyes glistening. "True patriotism is never misplaced, Miss Bell. It is the love of country tempered by an unswerving passion for justice."

"That is so well-spoken," she said.

"The history of some of the government agencies is also interesting," Antonio said. "There are terrific stories of the great agents: Nick Furious, Nancy Drew, Bond James Bond. They—"

"That's truly fascinating," Jesse said, his eyes never leaving Liberty. "Perhaps after supper I could show you our Teddy Museum."

"I'd like that very much." Liberty avoided his frank gaze by glancing at Antonio, whose eyes had narrowed in annoyance at being ignored.

"I'm curious about what brings you to No Man's Land," Jesse said, "and where—assuming I don't extradite you to Farmer Duncan—you intend to go next."

"We have to go north," Liberty said. "We have a map that's supposed to lead to the gold of Fort Knocks. Well, actually half a map."

Antonio gave a sharp, hissing noise, like a snake on an ihop grill.

She turned to him. "Now don't go nuklar. These are obviously honest people who might be able to help."

"Liberty, you promised!" Antonio said.

"I did nothing of the sort. I said that I understood you."

Jesse raised a cautioning hand. "Red light. Let's start over." He looked at Antonio. "Is this true?"

Antonio glared at Liberty. "I should have known better than to bring a child into the wilderness."

"I can agree with the sentiment," Jesse said. "Answer the question."

"Since she has spilled the pinata, I might as well admit it. What do you intend doing about it?"

Jesse lowered his voice and returned his eyes to Liberty. "I have to side with your traveling companion. This isn't a matter for open discussion. We'll speak in private later."

He changed the subject to the history of the Elkhorn Ranch, telling how it had been founded by his grandfather back before the railroads were built, when both New Washington and Fort Annie Oakley were little more than villages. "In his later years, the people called my grandfather Judge James. My dad inherited the mantlepiece, serving as the head of the only law north of the Yooessay. When I was twenty-four, he and thirty other Rough Riders were slain in an ambush by some outlaws we believe were part of the Masked Rider's gang. We couldn't prove it, there being no survivors."

"I'm so sorry," Liberty said, thinking of her own deceased father.

"Who is this Masked Rider?" Antonio asked.

"We don't know, but assuming he's the original, he's been around all the way back to my grandfather's day. Rumor has it, in the last decade he and his bandits have formed a small country up north."

"No one lives that long anymore," Liberty said; but she thought with a shudder of wizards and fizzicists supposedly able to endure for centuries through dark jenetics.

Supper was wonderful after the scarcity of the road, and Liberty ate more than she intended. Toward its end, one of the women went to a piano tucked in a corner and played some of the old folk songs like "Shenandoah," "Here Comes the Sunshine," and "Things Go Better with Koky Kola." Everyone sang along, the children loudest of all, so Liberty knew this was the ranch's evening ritual. And as twilight fell beyond the narrow west windows, they sang "America the Beautiful," which always affected her deeply, for what had been, and what was lost, and what would never be again.

Oh Beautiful, for special skies
For amber waves of grain
The Rocky Mountains' majesty
Above the fruitful plain

As the song neared its end, Jesse touched Liberty's shoulder with his large hand. She glanced up with tears in her eyes and saw his own shining, and she wondered whether he had a wife or sweetheart. Surely, she would be present if it were so.

"Please come with me," he said.

She rose and Antonio followed, though Jesse had spoken only to her. A wave of irritation passed through her. He was doubtless furious at her mention of the map, and she wondered if she had done it honestly or out of spite.

Jesse led them through a side door and up a long stair to a chamber directly above the cafe. As they ascended, the final lines of the song grew dim.

America, America
God shed his grace on thee
And crown the hood with brotherhood
From sea to shining sea

They reached a door. Opening it with a flourish, Jesse ushered them inside. "Welcome to our own personal treasure, the Teddy Roosevelt Museum."

Liberty gasped. "My stars!"

The room took up a space as extensive as the cafe below. The floors and walls were stained and polished burlwood, and a painting of Teddy Roosevelt surrounded by moustached and bespectacled bears covered the far wall, his expression one of confident repose. All around the chamber were paintings, books, hunting rifles, articles of clothing, and hundreds of other objects hanging on boards or sitting on long wooden shelves.

Jesse's eyes danced behind his glasses. "This represents the accumulation of three generations, all dedicated to the life and adventures of Teddy." He picked up a stuffed bear from a shelf. "With the strength of a bear, he upheld our right to bear arms. Come see."

He led them to a single volume of red leather, nearly as large as the desktop it sat on. Upon its cover was etched *The Deeds of Teddy Roosevelt*. Jesse turned to the first page, which displayed a drawing of the Great Man seated in a wheelchair as he had been toward the end of his life, a stuffed bear lying in his lap. Beneath the drawing was written: "To some generations much is given. Of other generations much is expected. This generation of Americans has a rendezvous with destiny."

"He was born on a plain of roses," Jesse said. "That's what his surname means; and he was the greatest of General Washington's followers; a hunter, a pugilist, and a proponent of conservation and the equality of women."

Liberty started to disagree, for the deeds of the Knights of the Continental Army such as Patton and Eisenhower Iron-Hewer were many, and Representatives like John Adams and Alexander Hamilton had displayed their valor and wisdom in times of crisis. All the other champions of Washington's Pentagonal Table filled her mind; yet Teddy had not been least among them, and everyone was entitled to his own personal hero.

"He rose to authority from humble beginnings," Jesse continued, "with no eating utensils save a single silver spoon."

He pointed to a display case mounted on the wall behind the desk, holding a gold badge, a billy club, a blue uniform with gold buttons, and a hat shaped like a bell. "As a young man, when corruption and vice threatened to overwhelm the great city of York, he brought to bay the vile syndicates headed by gangsters and evildoers. It was there he said, 'Don't hit a man if you can possibly avoid it, but if you do hit him, put him to sleep.' I've taken this as my own personal motto."

Jesse moved to another part of the room containing illustrations of Teddy and a bear. "In the heart of the Rockies, Teddy saved the life of the bear, Smokieyogi, and the grateful animal never left his side thereafter. The stories are manifold and mysterious, some even claiming the bear could speak. While this seems unlikely, we know miracles and wonders occurred in ancient times, and I believe it best to withhold judgment. In honor of this, I and my compatriots adorn our hats with imitations of the ears of a bear."

Jesse passed down the room, relating a steady stream of Teddy's deeds and adventures, sometimes growing misty-eyed in his passion. Liberty stayed close beside him, fascinated and moved by turn, for she thought she knew everything about Roosevelt and was surprised to hear so much more. Of course, not being in *The Americana*, it couldn't be considered strictly constitutional.

While Jesse spoke, Antonio wandered around the room, idly examining the various objects.

As they neared the far side of the chamber, Jesse gestured toward another painting of Teddy, the bear, and four men raising an American

Eagle standard on a high hill. "Teddy's greatest challenge came when he and his Rough Riders stormed San Juan Hill. Before the battle, he told his men: 'Far better it is to dare mighty things, to win glorious triumphs, even though checkered by failure, than to take rank with those poor spirits who neither enjoy much nor suffer much because they live in the gray twilight that knows neither victory nor defeat.'"

Liberty watched his face as he spoke. His eyes were closed, and for an instant his round, pleasant face was suffused with nobility. Tears sprang unbidden to her cheeks.

He sighed. "There were giants on the Earth in those days, Miss Bell, men of such stature we will never see their like again."

Jesse shook himself. "But I fear I've bored Mr. Ice with my adulation."

Antonio had picked up a wooden carving of Roosevelt, which Jesse took from his hand and returned to its place on the shelf.

Antonio looked mildly at him. "I'm also fond of heroic stories, but regardless of his virtues, Roosevelt must have been a man like you and me. I prefer to emulate his deeds in whatever way I can."

"In that, you have the correct spirit," Jesse said, "for Teddy himself tells us: 'It is not the critic who counts, but the man who is actually in the arena, whose face is marred by dust and sweat and blood, who errs and comes up short again and again, because there is no effort without error or shortcoming.'"

Liberty thought of her own doubts about continuing with Antonio.

"Now what's this about a map?" Jesse asked.

"We might as well show it to him," Liberty said.

"Liberty—" Antonio began.

"There's no need to see it," Jesse said. "People have been looking for the gold of Fort Knocks for years."

To Liberty's surprise, Antonio said, "I was sent to investigate, but it's probably, as you say, a waste of time."

"The men pursuing you don't think so, however. How did they learn of the map's existence?"

"I don't know," Antonio admitted. "The officers I was with would never have betrayed their trust. It must have been someone higher up."

"I stand unastonished," Jesse said. "My grandfather made a wise choice, settling in No Man's Land. The Yooessay claims many virtues and exhibits few. Government corruption is rife, bribery is commonplace; laws are passed for the benefit of the elite, the vague ideals of its founding washing away in a sea of greed."

Liberty frowned, recalling her gramps saying much the same. Despite having seen it with her own eyes when Brett Revere paid off the clerk at the station, it hurt to think of her countrymen behaving that way.

She told of the ambush on the train and their journey to Elkhorn, ending with, "If you and some of your men could come north with us—"

"That's unacceptable," Antonio said. "This project is under my authority. The map is the property of the Yooessay."

"I don't want your map," Jesse said, his eyes on Liberty, "but it would be plain foolishness to travel north. Especially now. Drifters, lunatics, and outlaws have always made the Old Forest their home—we've had more than one run-in with such over the decades—but since last year, there's been something else going on: apparitions passing between the trees, peculiar lights, strange noises. One of my men swore he shot a wolf broadside, only to see the bullet pass harmlessly through it."

"He must have missed," Antonio said.

"He's known for his marksmanship," Jesse said.

"But with your protection . . ." Liberty suggested.

Jesse gave a rueful shake of his head. "My men won't go into that forest, Miss Bell, even if I ordered them. And I have a responsibility to every man, woman, and child here. I can't leave them for some forged trader's map."

Liberty's heart sank. She realized how much she had secretly hoped for Jesse's company.

"Stay a day or two at least," Jesse said. "I'll send my men out in the morning to try to capture Revere and his cohorts. I'd like to know their angle in all this."

"I can't make any promises," Antonio said, "but if you have a way to send a message back to New Washington, I'd be appreciative."

"I'd like to get a letter to my folks, too," Liberty said.

"Fair enough," Jesse said.

They returned to the cafe, where the others were still singing. This continued the rest of the evening, and Liberty had a fine time recalling nonsense tunes like "I Wish I was an Opera Wire Singer" and sad ones like "Clementine;" and in the waning hours they ended with "Yesterday," which always left her melancholy.

Jesse escorted them to their rooms. After Antonio entered his chamber, one of the men brought an object wrapped in burlap.

"This was found in your saddlebags." Jesse drew forth her copy of *The Americana*.

"Oh, thank you!" she said. "It's a family relic. I wouldn't want to lose it."

"Further evidence of your public-spirited devotion," he said, eyes shining.

They talked outside her door for over an hour. She liked his low voice, and his eyes, which alternated between being stern and kind. He had a direct honesty and strength about him. He told her she had a pretty laugh.

She went to bed wishing she could stay a while with the Rough Riders of Elkhorn Ranch.

* * *

She rose early the next morning, anxious to write the letter to her mother and Gramps but finding it more difficult than expected. How could she explain her reasons for not returning home? They would have heard about her being thrown off the train. Guilt washed over her. They must be worried sick.

She started three times before getting it right, reassuring them of her safety, telling them she was traveling on an important mission for the good of the country, using the little comfortable phrases they often spoke together, passwords to convince them she wasn't under coercion. Unsatisfied with the result, she told herself it would have to do.

No sooner had she finished dressing than a knock sounded at her door. She hurried to it, thinking it might be Jesse, but found Antonio standing in the hall.

"I want to talk to you." He stepped inside.

"I beg your pardon! A man will not enter my room."

"I don't want to be overheard. Besides, we've been traveling together. What difference does it make?"

"All the more reason to demonstrate respectability. Gramps says, 'beware what the camera sees and don't mess with the Iris.'"

"I'd like to meet your gramps sometime. I'll bet he's a real poptop. Now listen to me."

Seeing he was not going to leave, Liberty stalked into the hall and stood there, hands on her hips. He blew a ragged breath and followed.

"I know you're angry about the map," she began.

He raised both hands, waving away her explanation. "A good agent is flexible as a slinky. True, you have been foolhardy, but you're inexperienced and untrained. I shouldn't expect anything else from a civilian."

"At least I have some common sense. My stars and stripes! You can't distrust everybody."

"*I* can. Still, you may have stumbled into the right foxhole."

"You have the oddest expressions."

He rolled his eyes. "This Jesse James seems to be a decent fellow, after all, though I don't like the way he looks at you."

"How does he look at me?"

"Like you're a tofu enchilada, but never mind. So long as we're careful what we say, I think he'll let us go. But you mustn't be persuaded to remain behind. I need your knowledge of Old American."

"But what if Jesse is right? What if the map is a forgery, a pseudo in holo clothing? We could be risking our lives for nothing."

Antonio dropped his voice. "Listen, I downplayed it last night, but this map was one of the few relics found in a vault at an archeological dig in a government building in one of the old cities, hermetically sealed in a container in an iron box. Our people say it's authentic."

"How can they know?"

"They just know these things."

"They guess at these things."

"I didn't tell you before, but after leaving Highest School, I nearly went to archeology college. Since I wasn't going to become a police and fire man, my Old Hombre wanted me to have a respectable career."

"You, an archeologist?"

"You're right. I'm more a man of action. The point is, I read a lot about the old cities. The information is reliable. You have a duty and mustn't forget it."

Liberty's anger rose. "I'm also a free agent, and if I decide to stay here or go back home, that's my decision."

They glared at one another until interrupted by Mrs. James calling them to breakfast.

* * *

That morning, Jesse, bearing his roosey-cane as a walking stick, showed Liberty more of Elkhorn: the stables and forge, the meat house, canning room, and gardens, all the outbuildings necessary to maintain a life in an isolated region. As they walked the stone paths between the structures, they laughed and talked, while cardinals and scissor-tailed meadowlarks sang their sweet songs in the boughs of the elmoaks. A head taller than she, he gave her his arm and extended the courtesy of a proper gentleman.

They came to the library, a narrow addition to the main house. Upon entering, Liberty exclaimed at the volumes lining the rows of shelves, more books than she had ever seen in one place.

"I buy them when I can, mostly from the printer in Adamsville,"

Jesse said. "It's my dream to eventually fill these shelves."

"I'll bet it would take at least a thousand books!" Her eyes shone in wonder at the thought.

"I doubt I can do it in my lifetime, but one must dream in order to accomplish anything. We have a hundred and twelve volumes so far, many about Roosevelt, but others as well. Look here."

He drew a black-leather copy of *The Americana* off a shelf. "It's written in modern Inglish rather than Old American, but it cost a pretty debit."

"It's beautiful!"

"I thought you'd appreciate it. You have the heart of the Lost Constitution, Miss Bell. I hope to convince you to give up your vain mission. You could perhaps linger with us a time. Your traveling companion poses like a peacock, but I wonder whether he possesses the courage Teddy so admired."

"He's very sincere," Liberty said, surprised at herself for defending him. "His actions on the train were mixed, but he has since demonstrated considerable fortitude."

"Still, won't you stay, Miss Bell? You would brighten our company. And I must admit, though doing so terrifies me more than facing a gang of roughnecks unarmed, that you captured my fancy the instant I laid eyes on you, that our conversations have only confirmed my initial impression, and that I find I am already half in love with you."

Liberty hesitated, both surprised and delighted.

"I've spoken too soon and have shocked you," he said, "but circumstances allow me only this one opportunity."

Their eyes met for a long moment. Liberty stamped her foot, startling him.

"I've offended," he said.

"You haven't. It's just so unfair! I mean, I *am* surprised. And . . . in time I think I could . . ." Words failed her, and she began again. "Even this morning, arguing with Antonio, I was considering staying. It's just . . . in the museum, when you were talking about Teddy and duty and doing something that had to be done, your words were so beautiful and stirring. All morning, they've rung in my mind like the Bells of Freedom. I would love to stay, to see if you and I . . . But how could I respect myself, and how could you respect me, knowing I'd balked at the moment of my calling? It may seem foolish to you, and maybe it is, but it's the task placed before me and I've given my word. The moment you spoke just now, I realized I couldn't turn back, no matter how much I want it."

He displayed his emotions only by a mist in his eyes and a choking, failed attempt at humor. "It seems Teddy has betrayed me in the end."

"Maybe when this is over, I could come back. If you still want me to, I mean."

"It would be my greatest delight." But his bleak expression told of his fear for her safety in the Old Forest.

At that moment, the door opened and Antonio entered. "Mrs. James said I could find you here. Have your men managed to capture Revere's gang?"

"There's been no word," Jesse said.

"Then we must press on. If his people find a way to decipher the other half of the map, they could beat us to the treasure."

Jesse turned an imploring gaze toward Liberty, but she found nothing to say.

"Very well, then," Jesse replied, "but wait until morning so we can provide a suitable diversion. Perhaps Revere will be apprehended by then. I'll start making the arrangements."

Without another word, he strode through the door and down the path, thrusting his roosey-cane before him, his abrupt departure demonstrating more clearly than words how badly Liberty had hurt him. She wanted to follow, to somehow make it right, but there was no way to do so. Instead, she turned and glared at Antonio.

"Why are you looking at me like that?" he asked.

"You have the timing of a broken coffee maker."

She turned and stalked away, leaving him staring after her in confusion.

* * *

She didn't see Jesse again until supper that evening. He seemed to have regained his disposition, appearing almost frantically jovial, and after the singing he escorted her to her room; but once they were alone, he became reserved, and their conversation grew strained. He left soon after, excusing himself due to the lateness of the hour.

Too distressed to sleep, she undressed for bed and lay reading the story from *The Americana* of the love of John and Abigail Adams, and their friendship with Thomas Jefferson. She dozed off with the book in her lap.

* * *

The next morning dawned clear and cloudless. Liberty dressed in the riding clothes Jesse's mother had given her. Wearing a leather duster, with her hair pulled back and pinned, she could pass for a man from a distance. She ruefully donned the belt and shoulder holster that had been left on her dresser beside a burlwood-handled revolver.

Arriving at the cafe, she found Jesse and Antonio in conference over bacon, scrambled eggs, and biscuits stuffed with sausage.

"Mind if I lurk?" she asked.

"Pull up a chair," Jesse said. "We were just discussing the diversion. We've seen no sign of Revere's men but intend to take no chances. Within the hour, a man in Antonio's jacket and a woman of a similar height and hair color to your own will leave Elkhorn, accompanied by thirty Rough Riders, sufficient numbers to discourage an attack. I couldn't get Sherlock here to part with his fancy hat, but we found a reasonable zerox."

Antonio touched his brim. "All the legendary agents had a trademark."

"The band will head south, as if conducting you to Adamsville," Jesse said. "We'll take you out by a less obvious route. I don't suppose there's a chance of changing your mind?"

"I fervently wish I could." Liberty avoided meeting his eyes.

"Very well. We'll make your passage as smooth as possible, then. Is that the letter to your folks?"

"It is." She handed it to him.

"What did you say?" Antonio asked.

"I didn't give away any military secrets, if that's what you're worried about. I didn't tell them where we're going or what we're going for. It's sealed and you don't need to read it."

Antonio raised a deflecting hand. "Hold your swat team. It's my job to ask questions."

Liberty bit her lip, ashamed of her brusqueness.

"I have Mister Ice's letter as well," Jesse said. "I'll see they make it to their destinations."

"You're very kind," Liberty said.

Too soon, they slipped down to the stables wearing the Rough Riders' bear-eared cowboy hats, surrounded by Jesse and twenty of his men. Inside the barn, Jesse said, "I'll return your borrowed horses to their rightful owner after you're too far away to prosecute. You'll take these instead." He indicated three sorrel steeds. "This one is Fury, that's Mister Red, and this one," he ran his hand along the gelding's flank, "is for you, Miss Bell. He's named after Teddy's bear, Smokeyogi, and is fast on his feet and a pleasure to ride."

"He's beautiful." Liberty's voice broke; he was giving her his own horse. "Thank you."

Mister Red, the pack horse, stood bundled with provisions. Fury and Smokeyogi, along with the other men's horses, were soon saddled and ready. Leading the animals, they set off through the trees surrounding Elkhorn and soon entered a deep draw, the bed of a long-dry stream, where they mounted. The air was sweet and cool. They journeyed in silence save for the squeaking of the saddle leather, the soft thud of the horses' hooves, the chatter of a mockingbird overhead. Jesse commanded using hand signals, an art Antonio watched with interest.

They rode until nearly noon, when they left the draw to face a long, green wall standing dark and unreal in the distance. When they reached it, it proved to be an enormous hedge, twenty feet tall and easily as thick, with red berries and two-inch thorns.

"This is the Brierpatch," Jesse said, speaking for the first time since they had left. "An ancient, self-perpetuating miracle of jenetics, it stretches for miles, holding back the Old Forest. There's only one way through it. If our diversion failed to fool them, Revere's men will most likely be waiting to ambush us at the entrance. A pair of my men will scout ahead for danger."

They traveled parallel to the hedge, going east. Tall trees, golden with antiquity, overtopped the Brierpatch. Strange, unfamiliar bird-calls drifted through its thorns. Liberty grew nervous. Here, not forty yards away, was Yoosemitee the Mighty, home of a hundred stories, the great wildwood stretching from the fabled Pacific to the Frozen North. The Wise Woman, Sacagawea, had led Lewison Clark through this forest; General Washington had ridden beneath its branches.

They reached the entrance, a wide gap in the Brierpatch, where began a road made of a peculiar, shining metal unlike any Liberty had ever seen. It vanished twenty yards into the woods, concealed by the forest floor. A standing stone of the same material loomed beside the gap, etched with runes in Old American, as fresh as the day it was hewn. The crumbled remains of a second stone lay beside the first. It, too, must have once been covered in runes, but only the single word, *Government*, remained.

"Perhaps you can tell us what the inscription says, Miss Bell," Jesse suggested, "for we've always wondered."

Liberty studied the Old American script. "It's old, maybe the oldest writing I've ever seen. It says: *New Kennedy Space Port.*" She paused at the tragic name of Kennedy, and the Rough Riders exchanged uneasy glances. "That last word means *door* or *portal* — an entrance. The next part — *This is a* — I'm not sure about that next word — *tall*, I believe . . . *security zone.* Then it says: *Property U.S. Government.* I'm not certain why there are periods between the *U* and the *S*, but since it talks about the government, it probably means *us* as in *We*, like the expression: We the people of America."

"What do you think it means?" Jesse asked.

Liberty hesitated. "I'm shooting in the ionosphere, but I would guess this was once Kennedy's estate, maybe even the place of First Contact with the Space Aliens."

The Rough Riders gave low murmurs, thinking of specters and computers, E.T.s and robots—all the lost horrors from before the Great Blackout. Liberty's mouth had gone dry; her heart beat at her temple; she found herself trembling.

"It's all tales and teevee, meant to frighten kids," Antonio said. "There aren't any ghosts, and there never were any aliens, no matter what *The Americana* says."

"Opinions may differ on that point," Jesse said. "Are you still committed, Mr. Ice?"

"I am."

"Then I've misjudged your courage. What about you, Miss Bell?"

Liberty wanted to cry. Every child feared the Old Forest. She longed to throw herself into Jesse's arms and beg him to take her back to Elkhorn. But Gramps always told her no Bell was ever a coward. "I'm ready."

"Do your best to stay on the forest road," Jesse said. "By hearsay, it should take you straight through the woods. We've nothing but legends about what lies beyond. Rumor tells us there are other settlements, but trust no one you meet." He gestured and one of his men handed him a pair of roosey-canes. Jesse gave one to Antonio and slid the other into the scabbard on Smokeyogi's side. "These may prove useful on your journey."

From his shirt pocket he produced a tiny stuffed bear on a chain. "I would be honored, Miss Bell, if you would take this as a mark of my esteem."

"Thank you, Jesse." She clasped it around her neck. She and he sat with their horses side-by-side, and she reached across and hugged him, then turned away to hide her tears.

Antonio coaxed Fury forward and Liberty followed on Smokeyogi. The metal road vibrated with the horses' hooves. They passed beyond it onto the forest path, and before it curved, she looked back and waved.

Jesse lifted his roosey-cane high over his head, calling in his deep voice, "Walk softly, Miss Bell, but carry a big stick."

CHAPTER FIVE

It is a common misconception that there was no rainfall during the centuries following the Great Blackout. The winds still blew, the rains descended, but gone was the lightning, the thunderous glory of the storm.
—*Wonders of World History* by Marryland Goldstein, Medico

* * *

Brett Revere and his ten remaining men reached the half-dugout barn before noon. Once painted bright red, only tattered flecks remained upon its weathered boards. The house standing beside it leaned precariously, one wall collapsed like a beetle with a shattered shell. Scraggly fruit trees, grown wild through neglect, surrounded the structures, concealing them from distant eyes.

The riders approached the barn cautiously, guns drawn. A man holding a rifle stepped from behind an appleberry tree, wearing a dark-blue flannel coat adorned with gold buttons, matching wool levites and a billed cap. Black leather straps crossed his chest. To Brett's relief, the sentry returned the secret sign he gave.

"I didn't recognize you in the new uniform," Revere said.

The sentry scowled down at his clothing. "The boss is calling us the Army of the Union these days. He leans toward fanciful inclinations. At least these are better than the red ones. We don't stick out like stopsigns. Leave your guns at the door. He's waiting."

Brett raised his eyebrows in surprise. "The man himself?"

"The very same. It's best to salute him. Don't try to shake hands; he doesn't like being touched."

Revere and his men dismounted, leaving their pistols on a flat rock by the barn door. Brett ordered two of his followers to remain outside, then led the others in.

The barn was dark after the sunlight, and it took a moment for Brett's eyes to adjust to the dim illumination cast by two petrol lamps resting on a desk. Horses, lost in the gloom, stamped and snorted. A dozen uniformed men stood around; Revere guessed several more remained hidden in the shadows. Across the desk sat a man wearing a black hood that covered his entire head, leaving his eyes showing through slits. Tall, lanky, stoop-shouldered, he wore a white shirt, white gloves, and a black vest and coat. In his right hand he held a ruby-colored scepter.

"Happy trails." Brett gave a casual three-fingered salute.

"Mr. Revere. So good to finally meet you." The Masked Rider's voice, muffled by the cloth, had an unexpected grating quality. "Have you brought the object?"

Revere carefully removed the map from his inside coat pocket and set it on the table. The Masked Rider picked it up with his gloved hand. "Part of it is torn away."

"We ran into difficulties. A Secret Service agent, aided by a young woman, got away with the other half. We nearly had them cold until the James gang showed up. I didn't have the men to face the Rough Riders, but we know where they went. They tried to throw us off the trail, but James left the two of them at the entrance to the Old Forest."

"You didn't pursue?"

"My men won't go in there."

Anger tinged the Masked Rider's voice. "Always bear in mind, Mr. Revere, that character is like a tree and reputation like a shadow. The shadow is what we think of it; the tree is the real thing. I hired you for your reputation; I see now the tree. Your men are cowards."

"Hey!" one of Revere's followers protested, only to be silenced by pistols cocking all around.

Brett gave a confident smile. "My boys take risks for profit; they'll only go so far."

"All my life," the Masked Rider said, "I have tried to pluck a thistle and plant a flower wherever the flower would grow in thought and mind, yet I am thwarted by small-minded men."

"There's a lot you can learn from that half of the map," Revere said. "Even I can tell that. Plus, it's worth plenty if you want to sell it back to the Yooessay. I know people who can serve as intermediaries if you'd like me to make inquiries."

The Masked Rider placed his hand to his temple, massaging it with his long fingers. "How little I am understood. I am not some petty larcenist stooping to extortion. The possibilities suggested by that map are only a means to an end, for I shall unite this whole land, including the Yooessay, into a single nation. One Country, One Destiny."

Revere donned his warmest, most open expression. "I'm not a political man. Look, we did our best to get what you wanted. I think even half that map is worth some money. I lost three good men getting it. But if you don't think so, don't pay us. I believe in fair dealing."

The Masked Rider bowed his head. "I have made a mistake by employing mercenaries. I now see our cause must be entrusted to its own undoubted friends—those whose hands are free, whose hearts are in the work, who do care for the result." He drew a gold debit from his pocket. "You will be paid what you are due."

The Masked Rider made a quick motion, flipping the coin into the air. Brett automatically snapped it up, but even as he did, he realized it was intended as a signal. The Masked Rider pointed his scepter straight at Brett's chest, its end open like a pistol barrel.

By his nature, Revere always had an exit plan, especially when unarmed. Since entering the barn, he had paid careful attention to the position of the nearest of the Masked Rider's men. He had briefly worked in an acrobatic show when young; and even as the debit reached his palm, he spun to the left, avoiding a beam of crimson light that shot past where he had been. In one smooth motion, he dropped down, somersaulting along the ground into the midst of three of his assailants. Gunfire exploded all around, a roaring bedlam in the darkened barn. Men screamed; but surprised by his maneuver and fearful of shooting one another, the three hesitated long enough for Revere to reach the exit. He threw his entire weight against the door, slamming it open. Using his momentum, he plowed into the sentry outside, who fell with Revere atop him.

Scrambling over him, kicking the sentry's rifle away, Brett scooped up his pistol from the boulder where he had left it. The beam of light stabbed out again, just missing him, cutting through the boulder like a bullet through burlap. The two men Brett had left outside were dead, killed by the sentry. Revere leapt onto the back of his horse and galloped through the trees. In less than two minutes he was lost among the countryside, but kept a quick pace, distancing himself from his former employer's men. As he rode, he realized he still held the gold coin. Opening his hand, he found the hooded face of the Masked Rider etched on one side. He pulled off his hat and rubbed the sweat from his forehead. The scepter had been like a weapon out of that book Liberty Bell liked so much. What sort of lunatic was this masked man?

* * *

When Liberty and Antonio were far enough into the Old Forest to lose sight of the Rough Riders, she halted Smokeyogi and drew her pistol from her shoulder holster.

"What's wrong?" Antonio asked.

"I need a millisec." Her eyes darted back and forth, searching the elmoaks, hawthorn, and wheat-chestnuts overgrown with weeping-kudzu. The thin thread of road snaked before them; strange birdcalls drifted from the trees. Her heart pounded in her chest; her breath came quick and shallow.

"It's old, Antonio! Can you smell how old it is?"

"It smells like leaves."

Liberty shook her head, fighting down a rising panic. Tears sprang unbidden to her eyes. "You don't understand." She bit her lip, angry at the quaver in her voice. "This is Yoosemitee, the Old Forest, home of Bigfoot and King Kong. James Madison fought the Headless Horseman in these woods. The ghost of Kennedy—"

Her voice had risen higher as she spoke, until she thought she would scream. Antonio reached across and gripped her shoulder. "Liberty! Calm down. Look around! It's a forest. If any of those creatures were ever here, it was long ago."

His brown eyes held hers, his expression confident. "Take deep breaths," he ordered.

She did so, chanting in her mind the motto of the American Postal Service, which always gave her courage. *In darkest day, in blackest night, Though rain and sleet and snow abound, We shirk not our appointed rounds, We lift the torch, the Postman's light.*

Her breathing slowed; her pulse leveled.

"Sorry," she said. "Guess I was really bozoing."

"It's all right. Anyone can panic."

"Have you ever?"

"Old A.I.? Never. But being a woman, you are understandably given to such outbursts."

Her eyes narrowed. "Talking to you is like writing letters in a pail of water." She urged Smokeyogi forward.

"What did I say?"

An hour crept by, and though Liberty kept her pistol in hand, they saw nothing more menacing than march-hares and birds. The trees grew taller and closer together. The morning passed, the sun half-hidden by the branches.

They stopped for lunch when Antonio's pocket watch said noon, spreading a bedroll on the ground beside a stream running parallel to the road. The water tasted clean and cold; olive-hued squirrels ran along the branches above its banks. Mrs. James had filled their packs with jerky, biscuits, canned peas, and corn. So far, Yoosemitee appeared no different than any woodland, and there was no sign they were being followed by Brett's gang. Still, Liberty could not escape her sense of foreboding.

After lunch Antonio taught her a special Secret Service bird whistle, in case they needed to communicate without alerting an enemy. They also practiced with the roosey-canes. Liberty felt awkward at first, but Antonio seemed to have a knack for the weapon, and they were soon sparring. It frustrated her that she couldn't get past his guard, but they ended up laughing, mostly at her expense.

They traveled the rest of the day. Antonio told her about growing up in Fort Annie Oakley, and she spoke of Gramps' farm and the one-room school where she helped teach the younger children. He was pleasant enough, though some of the things he claimed to have done seemed incredible. She held little regard for a liar.

They made camp that night among the elmoaks, where purple knotweed formed hedges on two sides. Jesse had provided the gear to put the horses on a highline, allowing them to move without tangling. Despite Liberty's protests, Antonio started a small fire to ward off beasts, but when the shadows grew long and the crickets began their songs, she was glad for the flames. They examined the map while eating supper out of tin cans.

"It looks like we've escaped our pursuers," Antonio said. "We should reach Fort Knocks in two or three days. Under Yooessay law, once we find the treasure, all we have to do is stake a claim and the military will do the rest. Of course, we'll bring back as much as we can."

"I hope you're right about how close we are, though I think it likely as firecrackers on halloween," Liberty said. "It took General Washington weeks to ride through Yoosemitee."

Seeing his expression, she quickly added, "I didn't mean to sound disheartening. The forest has probably changed since then."

He waved his hand dismissively. "Oh no, old A.I. doesn't get discouraged. Once you've looked death in the eyes, knowing it's kill or be killed, you can handle anything." He nodded sagely.

She nodded, too, not crediting any of it, but unwilling to argue. She glanced around at the trees and shivered. "I can't believe we're really here, camping in the heart of the Old Forest. It makes me feel like the Founders signing the Declaration of Independence, free and scared, happy and grave all at once. Aware, as Ben Franklin said, that, 'We must all hang together, or assuredly we shall all hang separately'—not knowing they were igniting a flame that would become the light of freedom to the whole world."

"Where did you learn to talk so poetic?"

She looked down. "I guess I say too much sometimes."

"It's nice. True, you haven't the sophisticated upbringing of one raised in a teeming metro." He lifted his hands to indicate vastness. "But your area of expertise is extensive. A good-looking, intelligent girl like you can go far."

"Why, thank you, Antonio. That's kind of you to say so." She finished a biscuit, suddenly aware she was alone in the wilderness with a man she hardly knew, one obviously given to fabrications. Apart from their time at Jesse's, they had spent only two nights in the wild, both after an exhausting day's ride. Despite his promise, how could she be certain he would act honorably?

She feigned a yawn. "I think we better get some sleep. I'll put my bedroll over there with my back to that tree. I intend to keep my pistol handy in case of peril."

He raised his eyebrows. "I hope you don't have a nightmare and shoot me."

"It's a possibility," she said brightly.

* * *

The next morning, they rose with first light, ate quickly, and prepared to ride. But as Liberty used the metal comb Mrs. James had given her, she froze in alarm.

"Antonio! Come here! What is this?"

He hurried to her side, his hand on his shoulder holster.

"Look at my hair!" She held the comb an inch from her head. Several of the strands were mysteriously drawn to it. As she moved the comb, the hair followed, accompanied by tiny snapping noises.

"Some kind of . . ." His voice trailed off.

"What is it? Can you see anything?"

"Little sparks," he said gravely.

She shuddered, her voice rising. "It's wizardry, like the ancient fizzicists used to do. What if I've got radiation or something?"

He walked around her, gesturing with his palms. "Let's be calm. Let's be calm. There must be an explanation." He started to take the comb from her, but when he touched her hand something stung both of them. Liberty shrieked and Antonio jumped back.

"What was that?" they both said.

Reaching forward more cautiously, he took the comb daintily between his thumb and forefinger. Holding it in front of him like a dead rat, he set it on the ground. He rubbed his hand over her hair, his touch firm but gentle. "I think we better leave your comb behind."

They buried it, covering it and the ashes of their fire with dirt, hiding the signs of their passage.

"This is truly a land of miracles and wonders," Liberty said as they rode away.

Sobered by the behavior of the comb, they kept vigilant, wondering what might come next. The air lay still; shafts of sunlight speared between the leaves. Bluejays and bandersnatches, always in perpetual warfare, cackled at one another. As the sun warmed the day, clouds of insects rose like white vapor from the forest floor, seeking the tree branches, clinging to the travelers by the hundreds.

"What are these things?" Antonio furiously brushed them from his arms and clothing.

"Nanognats. We get them every spring."

"Not in the city we don't. I don't like bugs."

"They're harmless, but a nuisance." Liberty tried unsuccessfully wiping them from her face. "Gramps says the jenetisists built them one atom at a time to fight diseases on plants."

"Until that trouble with your comb, old A.I. would have called Jean Therpy nothing but a legend. Now I'm not so sure."

"It's constitutional, sure as the horn on a zebra. She made the world a better place, until the fizzicists turned it to evil with their radiators and nukes and atomics."

The nanognats thickened, forcing Antonio to wrap his bandana over his face to keep from breathing them in. Liberty used a white hankie Mrs. James had given her. Scarcely able to see for the swarms, constantly brushing the creatures away when they coated their masks, the companions rode in miserable silence until the insects finally settled on the trees.

The road narrowed, disappearing altogether in places, forcing them to pick their way through the vegetation. The farther they journeyed, the taller the trees grew. It seemed to Liberty its endless gloom would go on forever.

The morning and afternoon passed without incident, but as twilight descended over the treetops, they heard the sound of approaching hoofbeats. With seconds to spare, they maneuvered their horses behind a stand of brambles and dismounted. Watching the road from the cover of the thorns, they saw two riders traveling with rapid intent, craning their necks as if searching for tracks. Liberty held her breath, willing them to overlook where she and Antonio had left the road, only breathing again as they hurried past.

A company of at least twenty men followed after, all dressed in blue uniforms except for their leader, who wore a black suit and rode a magnificent ivory stallion. This was surely the Masked Rider Jesse had mentioned, for a black hood covered his head. Liberty and Antonio kept still until the noise of their passing died away. Turning to her companion, she saw his face was drawn and pale.

"It can't be a coincidence," he said. "They want the map and will kill us to get it. They'll be back as soon as they realize they've lost our trail. Tie the horses. We need to cover our tracks."

Using branches cut from a sapling, they followed their horses' hoofprints to the point where they mixed with the prints of their pursuers, and brushed away all signs of their passage, backing their way to their steeds, then leading them deeper into the woods while continuing to obscure their trail. Finally, when gathering night made travel impossible, they halted, setting up the highline and rubbing the animals down in the darkness. The scent of saddle and horse filled Liberty's nostrils; Smokeyogi nickered softly.

"Shhh, boy," she soothed, rubbing his jaw and velvet nose. "You've got to be secret."

With the horses taken care of, they sat on their bedrolls and made a meal of jerky and canned grapples washed down with water from their canteens. Liberty spent an anxious night, expecting to wake any moment to cocked rifles and hangmans' torches.

As if her fears had come true, sometime after midnight she was startled awake by a deep rumbling. Opening her eyes, she momentarily saw the tops of the trees, bright as daylight.

She sat up, heart pounding as the roar died away like the lost fragment of a nightmare. The woods were as dark as ever, and she thought she had only been dreaming; but there came another burst of light, an eerie white flash lasting but an instant, revealing the whole forest floor in stark illumination. Antonio was standing, gun drawn, his back against a tree.

Before she could speak, another rumble filled the air, like all the world's trains hurtling by at once. Instinctively, she flung herself on her stomach and covered her ears.

Antonio sprang to her side, half-shielding her with his body. "Don't get up!"

Another flash came and another, and through the branches of the trees Liberty glimpsed jagged shafts of light tearing across a sky heavy with rain clouds. Other lights, hidden within the clouds, came off and on, like shrouded lanterns lit and extinguished. Through her fear, she suddenly knew.

When the roaring died, she grasped Antonio's arm. "It's lectricity! Just like *The Americana* describes it! The lectricity lingers!"

"Are we mental? It can't be!"

"I call that lightning up there; and that sound is thunder. It'll hunt us with deadly, malicious intent, seek us out, track us down, blow us up, turn every hair of our heads curly, leave us smoking and dead. We have to find shelter under one of the trees!"

A great wind struck, sending the treetops flailing, a chill blast filled with the scent of rain. Small as she was, Liberty could scarcely stand against it.

A fork of lightning rippled down, striking a tree fifty yards away, splintering it, the noise deafening, the trunk bursting into flames. Liberty fell to her knees, an instinctive reaction, helpless in her utter terror. For a few seconds, she couldn't hear anything, as if the forest had gone completely silent. Then the sounds returned, and she heard Mister Red whinnying in horror.

"The horses!" Antonio yelled, pulling her to her feet.

They rushed toward their mounts. Between flashes of darkness and light, Liberty saw the animals stamping and rearing in panic. Before the travelers could reach them, they snapped the highline. Still tied to it, they galloped neighing into the darkness.

"Smokeyogi!" She ran back to her bedroll to put on her boots.

A pelting rain began. By the light of the lightning, she saw Antonio struggling through the woods ahead of her. She stumbled forward, calling the horses, straining to see between the moments of darkness. By the time she had gone fifty yards, the rain was falling in sheets.

Antonio came back to her, shouting to make himself heard above the wind. "It's no good! We'll never find them in this!"

Lightning struck another tree. With a shout, Antonio grabbed Liberty, pulling her away. Together they dragged their bedrolls to the trunk of a hawthorn. They covered themselves, huddling back-to-back against the rain like frightened children.

As if to show its fury from its centuries of banishment, the lectricity poured down its jagged forks, multiple strikes only seconds apart, targeting earth and tree. Patches of flame dotted Yoosemitee, fires quickly snuffed by the rain.

Liberty covered her head in her blankets, her hands clapped over her ears, her whole body trembling. Lightning struck so close she screamed, feeling its heat through her bedroll. The wind blew harder; the lectricity flashed faster; the thunder crashed louder, a continuous roar awful as Dee Day come again. She was surely about to die.

For what seemed hours, the cataclysm continued, until her mind grew blank with fear. At last, the lightning withdrew; the roaring became fainter and more distant. She pulled herself out of her sopping bedroll, too drenched and terrified to sleep. Without a word, she and Antonio sat side-by-side, shivering and miserable, until the first dull light of morning.

CHAPTER SIX

Human and animal life cannot exist without electrical activity within the brain, so electricity must have functioned at some minimal level after the Great Blackout. The "plagues" mentioned in The Americana may not have been disease, but a loss of neural activity, which would explain why such a high percentage of the world's population perished. Why some survived and others did not is a mystery. Perhaps there was more vestigial electrical energy in different regions of the Earth; perhaps those who lived required less electricity to survive. —The Day the World Ended *by Madison Humphrey*

* * *

"Lectricity," Antonio muttered, eating his cold breakfast. "I've seen everything now."

"In the days of the Founders, lightning destroyed whole cities." Liberty's teeth chattered as she spoke. They had nothing dry to change into, and clouds covered the morning sky, leaving little sun to warm them. "Pecos Bill the Stormchaser used to tame them, riding the winds on Mobil, his winged stallion. I don't know how our ancestors survived."

He studied her as if trying to solve a puzzle. "I admit doubting your stories, Liberty Bell, but after last night, if you tell me the moon is made of blue cheese, I'll believe you."

"Actually, it's velveetah. But that's not constitutional." She paused, warmed by what passed for his apology. "I appreciate the way you tried to shield me from the storm. I was terrified as a paper cup in a recycling plant."

"Not me—" Antonio began, then averted his gaze. "I was frightened, too. I never saw anything like that."

Liberty smiled, pleased by his frankness. They gazed at one another, drawn together by their trial.

"At least the rain will cover our tracks," he said. "Come on. Let's find the horses."

They set out, leaving their saddles and most of their gear concealed in the undergrowth, taking only their weapons and their bedrolls, which were designed to be folded and buttoned to double as backpacks. They filled the packs with food and water, and Liberty silently blessed Jesse James, who seemed to have anticipated every contingency, including a pair of binoculars, which she used to scan the forest.

They searched for an hour, crossing a stream at one point, soaking their pants up to their thighs. With their enemies nearby, they dared not call out, and the animals could easily be missed in the undergrowth. As panicked as the horses were, they might have run for miles.

Liberty was growing discouraged when a distant whinny sounded behind them. They spun around, exchanging questioning glances, both wondering whether it was their mounts or those of the Masked Rider's men.

"Don't worry," Antonio said. "Old A.I. will take care of you. This is the time for Bold Moves."

"All right, but we better be quiet as deli mice."

They returned the way they had come, peering anxiously before them, and had gone scarcely a hundred yards before hearing voices. As one, they threw themselves on their stomachs among the tall, splaying stems of a stand of flowering globe grass.

The voices grew louder. From where they lay, they could just see between the thick blades. The Masked Rider and five of his men rode by. Liberty held her breath as they passed, but her stomach went queasy when she saw one of them leading Smokeyogi.

As soon as they vanished down the road, Liberty said, "We have to go after them."

"We wouldn't stand a chance."

"We don't stand a chance now. They've got horses and we don't. They've split into groups to search for us. Sooner or later, they'll find our footprints in the wet ground. We need the horses, and we need to get in front of them and take them by surprise while their forces are divided. There must be something in the spy manual about that."

"In case of numeric superiority by the enemy, I'm supposed to call for backup."

Liberty rolled her eyes. "Come on. We'll think of something."

They ran through the forest as quietly and quickly as they could, though to Liberty their footfalls on the leaves sounded like last night's thunder. At any millisec she expected to run right into their pursuers.

Antonio abruptly halted and pointed through the trees. The riders were slowly making their way along, stopping often to look for tracks. Keeping out of sight, Liberty and Antonio hurried far in front of them, stopping when they encountered the stream they had crossed earlier. Its waters were higher here, and Liberty thought it an excellent place for an ambush.

She pulled a length of rope and their mess kits from her pack.

"What are you doing?" Antonio asked.

"Something Wyatt Erp did at the Battle of the Tombstones. I'm glad Mrs. James thought to give us these." Cutting the rope into two equal parts, she tied each to the handles of a kit and gave one to Antonio.

"We have to separate," she said. "Take this one over there; keep one end of the rope and tie the two sections of the mess kit on some tall bushes as far from you as possible. We're going to use these to make them think there's a cloud of vigilantes surrounding them. We'll order them to surrender."

Antonio frowned. "I say we shoot first and ask for their surrender after they're dead."

"We can't do that," Liberty said. "It isn't noble. We have to do the honorable thing."

"We'll be killed," Antonio insisted. "These are outlaws, undeserving of mercy. We'll do it my way."

"You aren't my superior officer, but Aunt Geneva's Convention surely applies, giving me both the right and the moral imperative to refuse."

They glared at one another until Antonio blinked first. "All right."

His quick agreement surprised her. She swallowed hard; she had never killed anything larger than a coyote.

All was soon in readiness, the two of them hidden several yards away from one another in the undergrowth. Lying there felt unbelievable, as if she were play-acting, but the pounding of her heart, the crawling emptiness in her stomach, told her it was real.

The minutes inched by before she finally spied the six riders making their way along the riverbank. They were close enough for her to see their merciless faces, and a wave of terror ran through her. Their leader looked the most dreadful of all, tall and lank as Death in his black executioner's hood. She wondered why he wore it and what dark secret it concealed. One hand on her rope, one on her rifle, pistol by her side, she suddenly realized it was impossible to aim and jangle the mess kit at the same time. She quickly tied the rope to her ankle.

They were coming into position exactly as she had hoped, and she listened for Antonio to make the first move.

The riders halted, discussing whether they should cross. They started to drift away. Why wasn't Antonio doing his part? Had he dropped his gun as he had done on the train? She gave the special Secret Service bird-whistle, hoping he would get the message. Nothing happened.

Then it came, the noise of metal on metal, the jostling of the mess kit.

Liberty waved her leg furiously back and forth, making the two parts of her own kit jangle. It sounded small and unimpressive to her ears. She had to pause to aim her rifle, putting the sight on the Masked Rider's chest, intending to take out the leader first.

The riders milled uncertainly, guns drawn. Antonio shouted, "Drop your weapons and surrender! You are surrounded by Yooessay Rangers." His voice sounded thin and scared.

"Do it now!" Antonio shouted, firing a warning shot into the ground at their feet.

"It's a ruse!" the Masked Rider cried, aiming a strange, ruby-colored device toward Antonio's hiding place. "There's only two of them."

Holding her breath as Gramps had taught her, Liberty squeezed the trigger, dropping the Masked Rider from his horse before he could fire. She cocked the lever and aimed again, waving her leg to make the mess kit rattle, but the man in her sights tumbled from his horse before she could shoot, taken out by Antonio.

The mess kits were doing their job, confusing the remaining four outlaws, drawing their fire. Liberty aimed and shot again, missing her target's chest but hitting him in the shoulder. He dropped his gun and bolted, and another of the men followed after him.

An outlaw grasped his head and tumbled from his horse, his neck wet with blood. The remaining villain, a stocky, square-jawed man, leapt from his mount and stood over the Masked Rider's body, a pit bull protecting his master. Liberty fired and he went down.

The horses, trained to gunfire, nickered in consternation but stayed where they were. Liberty sprang from concealment, forgetting about the rope. It drew taut, sending her sprawling on her face. Frantically untying it, she leapt up again, all her attention on capturing the horses.

Antonio, already ahead of her, stood over the body of one of the men, who lay on his back, eyes wide, staring at the sky. Liberty caught Smokeyogi's halter and the bridle of one more. When she turned back to Antonio, he was holding his pistol at the temple of the square-jawed outlaw, who was sprawled on his stomach. Cautiously, Antonio rolled him over. Blood covered the front of his shirt; a bullet-hole gaped in his forehead; she and Antonio had shot him at the same time.

Antonio stumbled over to some bushes and threw up. Liberty's own stomach went queasy.

She glanced at the Masked Rider, who lay on his side. His hand crept toward a pistol on the ground beside him.

With a shriek, she dropped the horses' reins and kicked the weapon out of his reach. She leveled her rifle at his head.

Antonio, his face pale, hurried to her side, his gun trained on the Rider. "Don't move!"

"I believe I am dying," the Masked Rider said, his grating voice thick with pain. Liberty had shot him below the heart, and a slow stain spread along his shirt. "I would beg a moment's indulgence."

Antonio glanced over his shoulder and Liberty realized she hadn't even considered that the surviving outlaws could return.

"I'm not a doctor," Antonio said. "There's nothing we can do for him." He stepped to the Masked Rider's horse and began transferring its saddle to Smokeyogi.

"Where will the map take you?" the Masked Rider asked.

Liberty stared at him, not answering. She had never been this close to a genuine evildoer before.

The Masked Rider groaned. "Have you no pity for a dying man? What will it hurt to tell me your intentions now?"

Sympathy stirred within her, but she could not bring herself to speak. Even helpless, there was something sinister about him.

The Masked Rider chuckled. "Keep your secrets then. I see you are ambitious, which within reasonable bounds does good rather than harm." He coughed, a rattling wheeze. "No doubt you believe you are serving your country. But towering genius such as mine disdains a beaten path. It . . . seeks regions hitherto unexplored. My intention was to unite the city-states of America into a new Union."

Liberty found her voice. "You are a wretch and an anarchist, a lover of power."

His voice fell lower. "You misunderstand. I am exceedingly anxious that the Union, the Constitution, and the liberties of the people be perpetuated in accordance with the original ideas for which that struggle was made." He coughed again. "And I shall . . . be most happy to be a humble instrument in the hands of the Almighty for perpetuating the object of that great struggle."

"The horses are ready," Antonio said. "Let's go."

"Wait," Liberty said. "The words he's saying—"

"I see you are a patriot," the Masked Rider said. "Turn the map over to my people and we will carve a new nation." His eyes began to glaze. "The dogmas of the quiet past are inadequate to the stormy present . . .

the occasion is piled high with difficulty . . . and we must rise with it. As our case is new, so we must think anew, and act anew. We must disenthrall ourselves . . ." He struggled to say the words. ". . . and then we shall save our country."

Liberty stared at him in horror. A death-rasp issued from his throat; his eyes, through the slits of his hood, went empty.

Overcoming her astonishment, Liberty reached blindly forward and ripped the hood from the dead man's head. Clutching it, she pulled her hand away as if bitten, holding her fist to her mouth.

"That's . . ." Antonio's voice failed him. "It looks just like . . . Even the beard."

Liberty moaned in horror. For the face of the villain was the face of Abraham Lincoln.

CHAPTER SEVEN

So President General Washington sent Representative Jefferson to Yoosemitee to buy the land west of the Mississip from Bone Apart, Lord of the French. When Jefferson arrived at Bone Apart's tent and saw his beautiful daughter, Lucy Anna, they loved each other immediately. But Bone Apart would give up the land only if Jefferson could defeat him in combat. The duel was set for the following morning.

That night Lucy Anna slipped into Jefferson's tent. "You must not fight my father, who carries an enchanted dagger in his left hand, hidden in his coat. So awful is its power, it has burned the flesh from that hand, leaving only bone. It makes him invincible in battle." But Jefferson replied that he too possessed special magic.

The morning of the duel Bone Apart drew his dreadful dagger. Jefferson calmly retrieved a snuff box from his pocket. Bone Apart sneered, but when Jefferson opened the box called 'The Manifestation of Destiny,' it grew until it swallowed Bone Apart's weapon and threatened to consume the tyrant as well. Bone Apart surrendered and Jefferson declared, "Someday, this box will swallow every despot from the Atlantic to the Pacific." —The Americana

* * *

Liberty wanted to look away, to deny what she was seeing, but couldn't avert her eyes. The long, homely face, the rough nose, the pocked skin; it could be no one else but Lincoln.

"It's impossible," Antonio said.

Liberty shook her head in horror. "No. Oh, no." She gave a sob of despair and tore herself away, unable to control the tears streaming down her face. Fearing she was going to faint or be sick, she dropped to her knees, gasping for air.

"Liberty?" He put his hand on her shoulder and handed her a sack. "Here. Breathe into this."

She took the bundle and inhaled into it until she calmed down. Antonio stood watch over her, holding his rifle ready.

"I'm all right now. I was just . . ." She looked at the sack in her hand. It was Lincoln's mask. She dropped it on the ground. "Couldn't you have found something else?"

"In moments of crisis a resourceful agent uses whatever is at hand. You should thank me."

Liberty rubbed her temple. "I'm sorry. It's just . . . Abraham Lincoln was one of the greatest Representatives ever. He saved the Union; he freed the slaves. That . . . evildoer speaking his words, wearing his face . . ."

"It can't be him," Antonio said. "The Royal Brotherhood of Builders always honored Lincoln because he spoke against the War on Mexico. He would never do the things this man has done. Trust old A.I."

Liberty gave him a grateful look, then studied him more carefully. "You're a fake, Antonio Ice! Telling me none of the old stories are true! You're as patriotic as I am."

Antonio shrugged. "I don't think anyone is as patriotic as you, but everybody has to believe something. Listen, I need to search the Masked Rider for the other half of the map, and we have to get out of here before the outlaws return."

She nodded and turned away, unwilling to watch him frisk the body.

After a moment, he said, "It's not here."

She let him help her onto Smokeyogi. While he mounted one of the outlaws' horses, she looked down at the corpses. "I never killed anyone before."

"I've killed lots of men," Antonio said. He hesitated. "No, that's not true. I never killed nobody either."

She glanced at him, surprised by his admission, but he rode on ahead of her, not meeting her eyes. Perhaps there was unexpected substance beneath his bravado. But as they crossed the stream, his reaction triggered her own delayed shock. Men lay dead at her back. True, they were outlaws, but for what had they died? For a scrap of parchment drawn by a long-forgotten mapmaker, a document that might be no more than a fraud. Tears streamed down her cheeks again. The words of Oppenheimer, the shadowy Lord of Nuklars, echoed through her brain. *I am become Death, the destroyer of worlds.* She bit her lip, trying to weep silently, bowing her head against Smokeyogi's neck to keep Antonio from noticing.

Steadying herself, she spoke with quiet determination. "I have to go home."

He dropped back so they rode abreast. "You can't stop now. Without their leader, the outlaws will be too disorganized to follow us. By the time they recover, we'll be far away."

"That isn't what I'm worried about. What if that *was* Abraham Lincoln? I'm afraid of what we may find. What if he isn't everything I always believed?" Her voice broke; she hated herself for being so weak. She knew she wasn't making much sense.

"Then you find out. So what?"

"So what? Oh! You can't understand. If I'm going to kill people, it better be for a good reason."

"So, you don't really believe the stories you told me?"

"Of course I do."

"But a man shows up impersonating Abraham Lincoln, a man who can't possibly be him, and all your belief crumbles. You can't just quit, Liberty. Evil prevails if good men do nothing—you told me that one—and while I find the statement a trifle dramatic, the sentiment is true. Besides—"

A horse whinnied somewhere before them, and Liberty and Antonio grabbed their rifles. When she spied the source, Liberty gave a cry of joy and spurred Smokeyogi to a trot. Mister Red and Fury, still tied together, stood with their halters tangled around a tree.

Dismounting, Liberty rushed to the animals and threw her arms around Mister Red's neck, burying her head in his horse scent. Antonio followed more slowly, grinning.

Except for a cut on Fury's side, the beasts were unharmed. Liberty applied ointment to the wound, then Antonio led them right to their former camp, an impressive feat in the dense forest. "Canned peaches tonight," he said, as they transferred their supplies to Mister Red and the spare horse.

Returning to the road, they kept a good pace the rest of the morning, keeping careful watch in case the Masked Rider's men still followed. Toward noon the clouds broke, and the sun finished drying their clothes. They paused only long enough to eat and rest the horses, then hurried on their way.

"Tell me some of your stories about the forest," Antonio said.

"I thought you didn't care about *The Americana*."

"That was before I saw Abraham Lincoln. Whatever is going on, knowing something about that book of yours might prove useful."

She grinned and told him about the duel between Jefferson and Bone Apart, ending with: "Bone Apart killed Lucy Anna for her betrayal. Jefferson mourned her greatly, and the American people honored her sacrifice, because she purchased all that country with her blood. They say her spirit still hovers above this land, lending it an enchanted beauty."

"What I don't understand about such stories is the magic," Antonio said.

Liberty furrowed her brow at his lack of romance. "You didn't believe in lectricity either, until you saw it. Gramps says everybody follows a story, some true, and some they invent themselves. If you follow a good story, it guides you through your life. But even if you don't believe the ones in *The Americana*, you need to know them. They tell us who we are."

"But don't you think some of it might be symbolic, like Bone Apart's supernatural dagger?"

"Nope. It's either true or it ain't, and it's true."

Antonio paused, reflecting. "So, if we're in the land of Lucy Anna, what else can we expect to find?"

"Oh, tanker-trucks full of possibilities! The Old Faithful One walked these woods, his enormous breath blowing steam; the ancient mines, Carl's Bad Caverns, are hidden here, long-abandoned by Snow White and the 49ers. We might run across the White Sands of the Nuklars or the ruins of the Golden Arches. Yoosemitee is vast, stretching all the way to the Pacific and north to the endless, frozen darkness of Canada."

Antonio grinned. "When we were kids, my Old Hombre used to tell us if we didn't go to bed, Santa Claws would fly down from Canada, throw us in his sack, and take us to the Twilight Zone. I can still picture his fangs and blood-red suit, his whole body quivering like a bowl full of jelly. We used to leave cookies by our beds, so he'd eat them and leave us alone. I'd like to read that part in *The Americana* sometime."

"That isn't in *The Americana*. It's just a fairy tale."

He frowned. "Truly?"

"That proves my point about knowing what's in it. Ben Franklin said: 'A nation of well-informed men who have been taught to know and prize the rights which God has given them cannot be enslaved.'"

The road had been sloping upward for some time, growing broken and uneven with striations of white limestone. Liberty assumed it was about to level off, since she could see the tops of the trees beyond the pinnacle of the long rise, but when they finally reached it, they halted in wonder.

"My stars and stripes!"

"Holy new jersey!" Antonio said.

Below them lay a deep valley filled with trees standing hundreds of feet high.

"The Giant Sequoias," Liberty said, breathless. "Oh, Antonio!"

He stared at them, open-mouthed. "Nothing can be that big."

Liberty swallowed hard against the lump rising in her throat. "They're still alive." Her voice failed her.

They descended a long slope into the valley. At first, Liberty expected to come to the sequoias quickly, but they proved to be farther away than she thought. When at last they reached the valley floor late in the afternoon, the line of massive trees finally drew closer, until the giants stood at the end of a bend in the road, broad as houses, stretching high into the heavens.

"Are you crying?" he asked.

"It's just . . ." A sob broke from her. "I'm so grateful to get to see them. To know the jenetisists saved them when we thought them forever lost. It's like watching *The Americana* come to life. It's the best thing ever. It makes me glad I didn't go home."

She glanced sideways at him, afraid he would think her foolish, but his own voice was heavy with emotion. "I guess there's a lot more to the world than I ever thought."

They fell silent as they passed beneath the outstretched arms of the titans, the branches blotting out the sky. Here and there, scattered shafts of sunlight slipped through the dense foliage to the forest floor, but these became fewer the farther they rode. Other trees and vegetation grew between the massive trunks, including a variation of honey hyasuckle apparently jeneticized to survive with little sun, making the woods beyond the road a mass of undergrowth. It was like riding down a tunnel cloaked in leaves.

They rode in silence, speaking only when they had to, keeping their voices low. Muffled bird-cries drifted down from the heights; the air lay still, cut off from the breeze.

"I don't like not being able to see," Liberty finally said. "Yoosemitee is huge, and if the map is as old as you say, a lot can change in hundreds of years, including this road. It could take us completely off course. I wish we had a compass."

"What's that?"

"A thing you could talk to, that would tell you exactly what to do and where to go."

"That sounds like my mother."

Liberty smiled. "Well, there's no point in wanting one; there's no such thing now. It's lost as the Net, so nobody's fishin'."

With the sun obscured, twilight came early, and they made camp in a clearing just off the road. This deep into the forest, they considered building a fire to keep away possible attacks by jabberwolves but decided not to chance revealing their position. Instead, they gathered kindling and kept petrol-oil and matches close in case they needed to make a quick blaze. By the time they were finished and had eaten from their supplies, the darkness had descended enough so they could scarcely see.

They crawled into their bedrolls. There was something strange about lying beneath the Giant Sequoias. Liberty could almost feel their antiquity pressing down on her, not an evil weight, for there was shelter beneath those mammoth trunks, but the solemnity of trees that had been standing from before the Great Blackout. Unfamiliar night birds cooed overhead; even the songs of the crickets sounded different.

Despite being weary, it took a while for her to fall asleep, and when she did, she kept dreaming of standing in a field surrounded by giant, bearded grandfathers. She tried to ask them questions, but they only stared at her.

She started awake sometime later, heart pounding, filled with the impression something had touched her. She looked for Antonio and was surprised to discover she could see him lying a few feet away, revealed by a luminescence filling the clearing. Before she could think to wake him, a figure, giving off the same faint glow, stepped from behind a tree. Liberty gaped in fear and amazement, for this was, beyond doubt, Lucy Ball, exactly as described in *The Americana*, red curls shooting out in all directions beneath a red bowler hat, enormous blue eyes, painted clown's face and red nose, bulging red cape and oversized shoes, her faithful dog Dezzy panting by her side. Putting a finger to her lips, she made a beckoning gesture.

Liberty glanced at Antonio again, wondering if she should wake him. Yoosemitee was renowned as a place of visions; the wise Pilgrim, Waynejon, had appeared to General Washington and others in this very forest. Antonio wouldn't understand that; he might start shooting and break the spell, ruining her chance of learning anything. And she wasn't really afraid; this was good old Lucy, the biggest clown of all.

The apparition continued gesturing, soundless despite her thrashing legs and rotating arms, while Dezzy bounded back and forth around Liberty. Making up her mind, she pulled on her boots, drew her pistol, and rose to her feet.

As she cautiously approached the specter, Lucy withdrew, walking backward, continuing to implore. The clown tossed her bowler into the air, executed a backward somersault, and caught it before it hit the ground. Grinning, she moved farther away.

Step by step, deeper into the woods they went, the apparition utterly silent. Glancing back, no longer able to see Antonio or the horses, Liberty feared this was a ruse by some wizard or fizzicist to separate them. She tried to remember if *The Americana* mentioned similar trickery, but nothing came to her. She halted, uncertain, her courage flagging.

Seeing her hesitation, the apparition rushed at her so abruptly Liberty thought she was going to attack; but Lucy slid on one knee to a mute halt, her hands clasped before her in entreaty, her mouth drawn down in pathetic sorrow. Despite her trepidation, Liberty laughed, for this was a dream given form, Lucy as she had always imagined her.

"All right," she said softly. "I'll come, so long as you promise to keep me safe."

Blue eyes literally twinkling, Lucy leapt to her feet, placed her hand over her heart in token of pledge, and cartwheeled away.

Liberty cocked her pistol. This was no time to display cowardice. She countered her fright by silently repeating, "We have nothing to fear but fear itself."

Ever deeper into the forest they went, until at last Lucy stopped, pirouetted, and gestured broadly before her. Instantly, fairy lights lit the forest, row upon row of colored lamps draped from the tree branches, extending for miles. Liberty gasped and laughed in delight.

She turned back to Lucy, but the clown had vanished. In her place stood President Washington himself, eight feet tall, regal of bearing, broad of shoulder, dressed in a blue military jacket with ivory buttons, white pants, and black boots. His hair glistened pure white; in his left hand he held his battle-axe, Valleyforge. He fixed her with a steady gaze, stern and wise.

Liberty grew so light-headed she thought she would faint. Almost, she forgot herself and dropped to her knees, but that would have been the gravest insult, for no American bowed to another. Steadying herself, she placed her hand firmly over her heart and said simply, "America."

Washington smiled, the barest upturn of his lips, and lifting his arm, gestured before him, where a long coach drawn by six white horses hurried along a gleaming road running beneath the lamps of the forest. Liberty rubbed her eyes in disbelief. How could this be happening?

Washington gestured again, pointing toward the coach, urging Liberty toward it. She made her way between the great boughs, but before she could reach it, it drew to a halt beside a park bench, on which sat a black woman in early middle-age, calmly knitting.

The coach was long and rectangular with tall windows. It had two doors, one on either end. Liberty saw seven or eight rows of seats through the glass, with a partition separating the front ones from those at the back.

The woman rose and approached the door near the front. The driver stationed atop the coach called down to her, "Coloreds sit in the back."

The woman looked up at him through her wire spectacles, her eyes bright, her voice calm, firm defiance etched on her features. "It is my right as an American to choose where I will sit."

The man leapt from the seat, landing hard on the ground before her. He towered over her, hulking above her fragile frame. "What did you say?"

Liberty began hurrying toward her, for this was surely Rosa Parks.

The man blew a whistle, and a group of gray-garbed men appeared from the other side of the bus, some wearing white Cooclucks hoods. They circled Rosa, glaring down at her. Liberty halted in horror a few feet away.

"You'll do as the driver tells you," their commander sneered.

"I have learned over the years," Rosa said, "that when one's mind is made up, knowing what must be done does away with fear."

"We'll teach you better," the commander said.

The soldiers took out whips and clubs and began beating the woman. Liberty let out an involuntary shriek. She wanted to help, but feared doing so, knowing President Washington was showing her this for some purpose. But oh, it was hard! To stand wringing her hands as Rosa fell to her knees, blood running down her head!

A crowd had formed, made up of both white and black people. They were shouting, some for Rosa and some for the soldiers, their voices rising to a frenzy.

Just when Liberty could no longer bear to stand and watch, a dark figure stepped from the crowd and gave a mighty shout. Liberty bounced up and down in excitement.

"A man who won't die for something is not fit to live," Martin Luther said, his voice low and powerful. "Darkness cannot drive out darkness; only light can do that. Hate cannot drive out hate; only love can do that."

Others joined him, and he and those who followed him stood side-by-side, forming a living barrier between Rosa Parks and her tormentors. Liberty found herself among them, unable to remember how she got there. Seeing them, a great terror came into the soldiers' eyes. Throwing their clubs and whips to the ground, they fled.

Liberty glanced around. Martin Luther stood to her left, towering above her. To her right stood another man, equally tall, with long thin legs. She raised her eyes along his frame to his face, and it was Abraham Lincoln. He looked down at her, a steady, comfortable gaze. "Will you come with us, though it end even in death?"

She swallowed hard, her voice trembling. "I will, sir, though I do not know the way."

"We will show you."

They set off down the road, Martin Luther and Lincoln to either side of her. As they went, the crowd behind her began to sing a marching song. Liberty looked back and saw not a scattered throng, but an army striding in formation, dressed in navy-blue or olive-green uniforms, wearing metal helmets or blue caps. Bugles rang forth; drums pounded out the rhythm. Mules drew long metal boxes bearing great guns, mighty tanks rolling on heavy treads. Overhead, just under the lowest branches of the Giant Sequoias, pilots flew in formation on the backs of titanic eagles. So great was the number of soldiers, she could not see the end of the long line marching through the forest.

Up the road from the opposite direction came gray-clad warriors led by Commander Lee himself, tall as Luther and Lincoln, riding on a gray horse.

Lincoln drew a heavy sword, but Martin Luther held no weapon and only a black book for a shield. Lee lifted his saber and shouted, a cry like thunder, and Luther and Lincoln answered, and Liberty with them. Both armies echoed the shout and charged.

In a moment Liberty was caught in the midst of the struggle. Men and horses fell all around her; the blood of the wounded and the slain became a crimson haze before her eyes. She wept as she raced along, and still the soldiers died. Yet, in the back of her mind, through her excitement, she thought it strange that no one ever touched her.

Then it was over, and they no longer ran, but walked along the road. Beside it lay the slain from both sides. Every few miles stood a wooden sign with a name carved upon it: Vicksburg, Antietam, Shiloh . . . And as they went the company sang a song of triumph and life and sorrow and death for all the slain sons of America, both the blue and the gray. And Liberty wept to hear it. Finally, they stood before the shining gates of Atlanta, the home of King Cotton. There, they forced open the gates and marched to the place of the palace named Slavery. And with a word Martin Luther broke down the doors, for they could not stand against him; and they found King Cotton trembling on his throne, and took him, and imprisoned him forever. And they tore down the temple.

Then Liberty and Martin Luther and Abraham Lincoln stood among the ruins of the burning of Atlanta and bade the people both dark and light to be at peace with one another. And those gathered around wanted to make Martin Luther king, but he refused.

But Liberty, remembering what would happen next, looked frantically to every side.

Creeping among the ruins came the shadowy figure of Earl Wilkes Booth, a spear in his left hand. As he cast it, Liberty cried a warning and stepped in front of her companions.

The spear flew straight at her. She shrieked as it passed harmlessly through her body. Turning, she saw that Lincoln had tried to shield Luther, and the spear had gone through both of them.

Liberty fell to her knees, covering her eyes.

When she looked up again, the ruins and the bodies were gone, and the forest lay in darkness. But a slender light grew, and she saw Lincoln and Luther walking toward her, their arms around one another's shoulders, like boys who had played long together.

"Why do you weep, child?" Martin Luther asked.

"For America, sir. I weep for America. For all its glory. For all that it was. For all those who paid the price required."

"These things have passed," Lincoln said. "Weep no more."

She remained on her knees, looking up at him. "It wasn't you we killed, was it, sir? You weren't the Masked Rider. You just couldn't be."

"That was not me."

Relief swept through her. "Why did you show me this? What does it mean?"

"Why do you travel north, Liberty Bell?"

"To find the gold of Fort Knocks. We have a map."

Lincoln paused as if listening. After a moment, he said, "Why do you want it?"

"For the good of the Yooessay," she said.

"What is the nature of its government?" he asked. "Does it hold with kings and despots, nobility and tyrants?"

"It stands for freedom for its people." She felt guilty as soon as she said it. The architects of the Yooessay had established its laws on the principles found in *The Americana* but had lacked the Lost Constitution to guide them. As a result, the recent governor was seizing more and more power, bending the laws to suit his purposes. His example was already trickling down to ordinary citizens: she thought of Brett Revere bribing the skycap at the train terminal, and the Committeemen Gramps talked about, who cared more for their positions than their country.

Lincoln stared at her so long she thought he hadn't heard. For a dreadful moment, she feared he would label her a liar, but finally he spoke. "This entire land, the country of your forefathers, the place where the Bell of Freedom once sounded from shore to shore, is in terrible danger. Liberty is imperiled. In all four directions of the compass new countries are rising from the ashes of the old, and new tyrants with them. The ways of the Old Americans are forgotten or ignored. Something must be done. Are you willing to do it, Liberty Bell? For the sake of America?"

Her whole body trembled with excitement. "I am."

"Then continue north to the Underground Fortress," Lincoln said, "and do what must be done there, but keep your wits around the Wizard, and stay far from the country of Haze."

"Will you tell me the way, sir?"

"I will show you, child." He reached toward her, bidding her rise.

A shot exploded, tearing the ground at Lincoln's feet. For an instant Liberty thought she would have to see him die again.

"Stay away from her!" Antonio ordered.

Instantly, the figures vanished, and the light with them.

Liberty turned and leapt to her feet. Antonio hurried toward her, a lantern in his hand.

"I heard gunshots and got here as fast as I—"

She hit him in the chest with both her small fists. "You dumbskull! You vidiot!"

"Ow! He was reaching for you."

"Ooooh!" She turned away, stomping her foot. "Now I'll never know what he was going to tell me!" She shook her fists helplessly in the air.

He was staring at her in perplexity. She strode back and forth in front of him. "You don't know what you've done! You should have seen it! It was a vision big as teevee. You would have believed for sure, then!"

"Look, Liberty—"

She poked her finger in his chest. "I know one thing, Antonio Ice. I can tell you this: I wasn't totally convinced before, but *nothing* is keeping me from going north now. Bet your lucky sevens on it! Liberty Balance Bell is traveling as far as it takes!"

CHAPTER EIGHT

The Americans moved just in time to avoid a shattering blow as the giant, Britannia, brought its mace down with all its force. The impact threw Washington off his feet, but even before he hit the ground, he unrolled the scroll containing the Words of Power. Springing up, he read in a mighty voice: "We hold these truths to be self-evident, that all men are created equal, that they are endowed by their Creator with certain unalienable rights, that among these are Life, Liberty, and the Pursuit of Happiness . . ."

On and on Washington read, while both the giant and the wizard, Cornwallis, stood paralyzed by the Words of Power. He raised his arms as he ended: "And for the support of this Declaration, with a firm reliance on the Protection of Divine Providence, we mutually pledge to each other
our Lives,
our Fortunes,
and our Sacred Honor." —The Americana

* * *

On the morning Liberty and Antonio had ambushed the outlaws, before the bodies of the dead men had cooled, all lay in silence, save for a lone whippoorwill's call and the rustling of the leaves of the trees beside the banks of the stream.

From the fallen form of the Masked Rider, a thick, black cloud rose streaming from his mouth, his nose, the pores of his body. It hovered above the corpse, gazing sadly upon it. The shell had died, but the Masked Rider had not, and he looked with desperate regret at the loss of the vessel which had served him well.

Yet, he also felt a sense of release. Lincoln's clone had been strong; his thoughts, resolute; the Masked Rider had nearly lost himself within the blending of the personalities.

Death was always agonizing for him, a rending of the two parts, and it took him several moments to regain control of his mental faculties and his vaporous form. He rose, a swirling, ebony cloud, coalescing to give himself mass, traveling north, leaving the bodies of his minions lying forgotten.

His senses were altered in this form, allowing him to perceive both more and less. Sight and sound became rays and waves vibrating against his substance, giving him the ability to discern colors unknown to human eyes and noises above and below human hearing; yet ordinary images and noises were never as clear as when he wore the shape of a man.

He could not survive long in this condition, but he could travel rapidly. He passed below the treeline, following the road, and soon caught up with Liberty and Antonio. Listening to them talk, he learned their names and watched the mysterious reenactment shown to the girl, a display suggesting an unknown force rising in the forest. Whatever it was, he vowed to either use or destroy it, and to obtain the map the two carried; and their deaths with it.

* * *

The night of the vision, Liberty and Antonio said nothing until they reached their camp. Sitting on their bedrolls in the glow of the lantern, he questioned her over every detail of what she had seen. Had she been less excited, she would have admired his professionalism, the way he returned to various questions, phrasing them differently, skillfully seeking the truth. As it was, she found it annoying, as if she had done something wrong.

When the interrogation was finished, they sat silent until Antonio finally said, "I never thought any of the old tales were true." He studied her, as if seeing her for the first time. "You've got a lot of guts for a girl."

"Are your toes permanently wrinkled from sticking your foot down your throat?"

"What did I say?"

"Never mind. I appreciate the compliment."

He gave her a puzzled look, then shrugged. "None of this makes any sense. I don't believe in ghosts." His eyes narrowed and he raised his index finger. "When an agent finds a discrepancy in the facts, he must be relentless in pursuit of the truth."

"Is that some more from the spy manual?"

"You quote your book, I'll quote mine. The point is: that couldn't have been the real Abraham Lincoln, any more than the Masked Rider was. If we rule out superstition, it suggests someone impersonating the mythical Lincoln to deceive us."

Liberty shook her head. "If you'd seen the entire vision and heard him speak, you wouldn't be skeptical. He looked like Lincoln; he said he was Lincoln. I believe it was him."

Antonio waved his hand dismissively. "What is the Underground Fortress and the other things he mentioned?"

"I don't know. None of it was familiar."

"It sounds like nonsense meant to confuse us. He told us nothing except to keep traveling the way we were already going; and he learned all about our mission and the map. I say we move our camp in case whoever is behind this sends someone tangible enough to take us prisoner."

Ignoring the implied criticism, Liberty turned her head to hide a grin of delight. For whatever else Representative Lincoln had said, he had given them his blessing and dispatched them on a mission. How could they fail if he sent them?

They moved their camp, but Liberty got little sleep after returning to her bedroll, her mind replaying the vision over and over. She shook Antonio awake at the first gray sign of dawn; and twenty minutes later they were on the road. Small stands of wild petrol-barrel bushes appeared; clumps of shade-brambles wound their way along the lower tree limbs; badbugs as large as Liberty's palm crawled among the thorns. Flocks of jubjubs hopped and flew among the branches, feeding on the bugs, filling the air with their mewling cries and the clatter of shells breaking beneath their curved beaks.

Mammoth white stones soon appeared, protruding from the forest floor, covered in lichen and worn by the rain. Antonio consulted the map, then showed it to Liberty, pointing toward an inscription in Old American. "Do you think this is where we are? What does it say?"

"It says *Marvelous Earth . . .* or *World.* The next word is *of,* and then a *d,* but the rest is smudged. We're dancing in the dark on this one."

They soon came to a white slab, eight feet tall and equally as wide, with a caricature of a fowl etched upon it and partially shattered Old American lettering beneath. Liberty squinted to make out the words. "It says *Welcome* at the top, and something about *Kennedy Space Center Recreational*—it must be connected to the sign we saw at the edge of the forest—and then the letters are broken, and it says *Dis . . . ney . . . land . . . Central.* Oh my stars and stripes!" Liberty put her hand over her mouth. "This is Dizzyland!"

"*The* Dizzyland?"

"You bet your sweet saccharin. But it's spelled differently. I wonder if the 'n' was silent?"

They stared at the stone, remembering the stories of Dizzy, Lord of the Three Magic Kingdoms, who taught the jabberwolf and the mikee-mouse to talk.

When they finally moved on, Antonio said, "With so few surviving American ruins, the archeologists will love to hear about this. They might even find enough evidence to prove the truth about your General Washington."

"If they do, they'll interpret it however they want," Liberty replied. "'A learned blockhead is a greater blockhead than an ignorant one.'"

"Who said that?"

"Ben Franklin."

Antonio laughed. "I never heard of anyone who knew so many quotations. Hey, maybe if we stay together long enough, you'll start quoting me."

"Maybe I will, if you ever say anything smart." She stuck out her tongue and grinned at him.

The ground grew more broken, sometimes obscuring the road entirely, as if it had suffered some recent upheaval. The sequoias were neither as tall nor as broad, and patches of sunlight fell on the rocky soil. The shade-brambles had vanished, taking the badbugs and jubjubs with them.

Liberty sang softly to herself, and Antonio hummed along, for nearly everyone knew the tune.

I wish I had a debit, a debit oh so fine
I'd buy a ride to Dizzy, I'd stay there all the time
Get along home, home to Dizzy
Get along home, home to Dizzy
Get along home, home to Dizzy
Back home to Dizzyland

They found the road once more, winding among the standing stones. An uneasy silence lay on this part of Yoosemitee, as if something had recently frightened the wildlife. This was soon broken, however, by a sizzling sound in front of them, a noise Liberty first mistook as the maraca warning of a rattlesnake. Antonio instantly had his rifle out.

"Stay behind me," he ordered.

"Not me." She drew her pistol, part of her suddenly wishing she really could play the frightened girl.

The sizzling came and went, gone for a few seconds, returning a moment later, both before and behind them. They had ridden right into the middle of it. It had a metallic quality like rain on a metal roof. Liberty realized it was the noise of lectricity.

She looked around and gasped. Solemn, titanic faces stared down at them from behind the vegetation. Half-hidden in forest gloom, covered in branches and climbing vines, many stood easily twelve feet tall, sculptures cast in various positions, their blue-metal bodies glistening where the sun's rays fell upon them. Several stood together in a row; others were scattered. One lay prone, pinned beneath a fallen tree.

Antonio pointed at the square base of the nearest of them, where an open panel revealed strange internal mechanisms. "They're machines from before the Great Blackout. Look at that metal! It's some kind of alloy, like nothing I've ever seen. For it to last so long . . ."

The figures were of various heights, at least half of them little taller than an adult. Liberty shivered, dismayed by the silent stares of these graveyard monuments. She rode close to one of the smaller ones and leaned across Smokeyogi to peer at its face. Its eyelids were closed, as if it slept, but there was something familiar about it. Beneath its triangular hat, its ears and nose were ridiculously large. It carried an oversized rifle.

The sizzling came again, making her jump. Smokeyogi blew uneasily. Liberty drew away from the machine, and her horse's hoof struck something that gave a metallic ring. Glancing down, she saw a half-buried blue sheet. She passed over it and approached the largest of the figures, Lady Liberty herself, her torch held high, her head crowned; but her oversized face bore the smiling visage of a schoolgirl with long hair flowing to her shoulders. Beside her, lying on his side, was an equally distorted General Washington.

"Tell me now that he's just a myth!" she said.

Antonio stared at the fallen president. "The forest should have covered this long ago. It's as if something recently unearthed it."

"They're all here!" Liberty exclaimed. "Look! There's Ben Franklin with his kite and key, and that must be John Adams. And Lincoln. And this one is Ronald Raygun, who destroyed the Evil Empire. And here's Woody Wilson; he created the Justice League of United Nations. But why are they all cartoon?" Righteous indignation rose within her. Had the Old Americans grown so corrupt as to ridicule their own heroes?

Antonio turned Fury to the left. "What about those?"

Liberty glanced up in surprise, having failed to see another group of machines several yards away, cast in red metal without a hint of rust. She and Antonio rode across the space separating the figures, past more of the shorter ones, hawk-nosed and scowling, wearing helmets and carrying rifles with cruel bayonets. Some hung limp at the waist;

others had toppled onto their sides.

Liberty stared at the larger figures, not recognizing any until her eyes fastened on one seated on a throne, his body hidden by cascading robes. A burnoose covered his head.

"That's Osama Ben Lawless," she said. "The Destroyer."

"Hitler, the Wolf-Prince." Antonio nodded toward the tallest figure, standing full-length on his pedestal, his hand raised high in salute, wearing his unmistakable moustache and swastikas. "Why would they build a tribute to him?"

"I don't know, unless . . ." She fell silent, having noticed something. Not bothering to use the stirrups, she slid down from Smokeyogi's back and hurried to the very feet of the Fuehrer, though it terrified her to be so close. More metal, the same hue as Hitler's, peeked from the dirt. She brushed the ground, peeling away layers of humus until she uncovered enough of the red metal to see blue bordering each of its sides. "It's a chessboard! Dizzy built a gigantic chess set."

"That's loco. Why would he do that?"

Before she could answer, the sizzling noise erupted on the other side of the board, louder than before, filling the forest with an arcing light, like the flashes of lectricity during the storm. Liberty shrieked; Antonio raised his rifle.

Lectricity snapped all around, sending firefly showers off several of the machines, a cascade passing from their torsos to their heads. It gradually died away, leaving a deep silence. Liberty clutched her pistol, flicking her eyes from machine to machine.

From the far end of the chessboard came the screeching of metal on metal, the scraping of ancient joints. One of the machines lifted itself from a prone position, a dark mass in the shadows of the trees. A growling voice rang out, not in Old American as Liberty would have expected, but in modern Inglish, "Courage is what it takes . . . to stand up and speak."

As Liberty and Antonio stared, frozen in shock, the creature approached them, treading on four bandy legs. The sunlight fell upon it, revealing the form of a bulldog with the round face of a man, completely bald, with a wide nose, a furrowed brow, canine mouth, and heavy jowls.

Liberty clambered back onto Smokeyogi in preparation for flight.

The enormous dog halted. The bottoms of each of its short legs emitted the soft whispering noise of wind, jets of air sending it floating a foot above the ground. The horses stirred uneasily.

"Good afternoon," it said, in a higher voice than expected in so large a creature.

"Stay where you are," Antonio ordered, keeping his rifle steady.

"What are you?" Liberty demanded.

A blue light shone behind each of its great eyes. "Winston Churchill. Prime Minister of the British Empire."

"What does that mean, Liberty?" Antonio kept his gaze fastened on the machine.

"He means the Brits, an island people who were always our friends. But Church Hill wasn't a real bulldog." She bit her lip. "Or maybe he was."

"Everyone has his day," Church Hill said, "and some days last longer than others." It paused between phrases as if giving a speech.

"Giant chessboards, giant toys," Antonio said. "What kind of people built these things?"

"Some see private enterprise as a predatory target to be shot," Church Hill said, "others as a cow to be milked, but few are those who see it as a sturdy horse pulling the wagon."

A lectric charge crackled to their left, and they turned to see another, taller figure—a blue-metal replica of a man—thrust his way through the undergrowth. He was sculpted with an odd coat trailing to the back of his thighs, and a vest and high-buttoned shirt beneath. His pants came just below his knees. Like all the machines, his face was a caricature, his bulging chin too large, his aquiline nose too long, his ears and eyes huge, his overarching brow deeply furrowed.

"Thomas Jefferson," he said, giving a deep bow. "At your service."

"Let's get out of here," Antonio hissed.

"Wait," she said. "Maybe they can help us."

"What do you need, child?" Jefferson asked.

Liberty hesitated. If these creatures were really from before the Great Blackout, why did they speak Inglish? Was this some protective measure left ages ago by Dizzy? Yet, here was a cornucopia of possibilities. If she and Antonio ran away every time they found something new, they would never learn anything. She made up her mind.

"Representative Jefferson," she said, "we're traveling north with outlaws and tyrants behind us. We need to escape them."

"You have enemies?" Church Hill asked. "Good. That means you've stood up for something sometime in your life."

Jefferson hesitated in a way that somehow reminded Liberty of her vision of Lincoln. When at last he spoke, his voice sounded slightly higher, noticeably different. "It is our duty to endeavor to avoid war, but if it shall actually take place, no matter by whom brought on, we must defend ourselves."

"One ought never to turn one's back on a threatened danger and try to run away from it," Church Hill said. "Never run away from anything. Never!"

"But our only hope is in flight," Liberty said. "Our pursuers outnumber us."

They turned toward her, the slow movements of machines, terrifying in their precision. She shrank down in her saddle.

"All tyranny needs to gain a foothold is for people of good conscience to remain silent," Jefferson said. The tone of his voice became deeper again, as if someone else spoke. "Therefore, I shall accompany you."

"I will, as well," Church Hill said. "I never worry about action, but only inaction."

"What are they talking about?" Antonio asked.

"Almost everything they say is straight from *The Americana*," Liberty said. "I think we should let them go with us."

Antonio looked up at the goliaths and spoke from behind his hand. "You want to travel with these cyborgs?"

"You want to tell them no? No one would dare attack us with them around. Besides, think what they can tell us about the Founders. They might be able to guide us."

Antonio paused, raising a finger for silence. "I need a minute to think."

Liberty rolled her eyes. For somebody fond of Bold Moves, he sure liked to deliberate.

"All right," he said. "We'll try it for a while, but be prepared to run if I give the word."

Liberty turned to the machines. "Gentlemen, we would welcome your company."

They set off, their horses whickering their displeasure. Liberty led, Jefferson striding beside her, his feet moving back and forth to the accompanying sibilance of the air jets. Church Hill walked behind them, and Antonio brought up the rear, undoubtedly to keep watch on the machines. They left the chessboard behind, and with it, all signs of the standing stones.

* * *

The black cloud, the essence of the Masked Rider, slipped through the upper branches of the Old Forest, watching Liberty, Antonio, and the two mysterious androids. All the laws of probability denied the possibility of the machines—mere vestiges of an entertainment center—becoming functional again. Their inferior power cores could never last so many centuries, and any centralized controlling mechanisms were covered in tons of earth. The obvious conclusion was that someone had activated them. The Wizard, perhaps? Could even he do that? A shame they had become foes. The old man had been more than useful in former days.

Whatever the cause, it provided an opportunity, for in his present form the Masked Rider could occupy and animate certain simple automatons. He considered possessing one of the two androids but dismissed the idea. A certain amount of danger was involved; and if whoever controlled them resisted, he might be destroyed. Instead, he flew, a living shroud, back to the place of the chessmen to search among them for an undamaged subject. Testing them proved difficult; he wasted several precious hours before finding a suitable one; nor could he remain within it long—without a human host body, his essence would soon dissipate. Within two days, he would need to return to his headquarters in Haze, to enter the clone stored there, the final clone, all the others having been used up over the centuries. But if the map truly led to the gold of Fort Knox, and he could seize it, not only would its wealth give him infinite resources to buy more war materials and bribe officials in the Yoeessay and elsewhere, but such a facility would surely house lost weaponry he could use to obtain more clones.

He slipped inside the mechanism, his black smoke pouring through the circuitry, extending himself within it, taking control of first the head, then the neck, the shoulders, the torso, and arms. He flexed the hands and activated the legs and the air jets.

Striding across the ruined chessboard, he set out after his prey.

CHAPTER NINE

President General Washington said to Abraham Lincoln, "My young friend, our nation is established. Go and do good. Remember always to guard against the impostures of pretended patriotism. Government is not reason; it is not eloquent; it is force. Like fire, it is a dangerous servant and a fearful master. Use it only for the cause of Freedom." — The Americana

* * *

For Liberty, traveling with Jefferson and Church Hill was completely Twilight Zone, their enormous bulk, their sonorous voices, their air jets and the long movements of their metal legs. As soon as the horses grew accustomed to them, she began formulating questions. Even though they weren't really the Founders, they had been built by them and had known them.

"Representative Jefferson," she began, "will you tell us about the Old Americans?"

"You can always count on Americans to do the right thing," Church Hill said, "after they've tried everything else."

Turning his head toward the bulldog, Jefferson replied, "Errors of opinion may be tolerated where Reason is left free to combat it."

"Hmph!" Church Hill snorted.

"But what were they like?" Liberty asked. "How did they form the government that established freedom and justice for all? I want to know everything."

"A Bill of Rights is what the people are entitled to against every government, and what no just government should refuse," Jefferson said.

"That's a good point," Liberty said, "but the Constitution containing the Bill of Rights is lost. We don't know what it said. Can you tell us? We truly want to know."

"Man will occasionally stumble over the truth," Church Hill said, "but most of the time he will pick himself up and continue on."

Jefferson glanced back at Church Hill again. "He is less remote from the truth who believes nothing than he who believes what is wrong."

Church Hill growled. "Never hold discussions with the monkey when the organ grinder is in the room."

Jefferson halted and stared at the bulldog. If his face hadn't been made of metal, Liberty guessed it would have been filled with irritation.

"I was asking about the American government," she protested.

Jefferson resumed his walk. "I predict future happiness for Americans if they can prevent the government from wasting the labors of the people under the pretense of taking care of them."

"Our governor is always giving speeches about taking care of us," Liberty said, struggling to follow the conversation, "but he and the Committees take the attitude that they can make rulings without common consent. It's—"

"Attitude is the little thing that makes a big difference," the bulldog said. "Courage is rightly esteemed the first of human qualities, because it is the quality which guarantees all others."

"One man with courage is a majority," Jefferson added. "Nothing can stop the man with the right mental attitude from achieving his goal."

"Unless you're the ones on the losing side," Antonio called from the back.

Church Hill turned his enormous head toward Antonio. "I like a man who grins when he fights."

Antonio chuckled. "You have an easy answer for everything."

"This is no time for ease and comfort," Church Hill replied. "It is time to dare and endure." His voice rose. "Victory at all costs, victory in spite of terror, victory however long and hard the road may be; for without victory, there is no survival."

Despite Liberty's inability to keep the machines on a single track, Church Hill's words, spoken with such intensity, made her clap her hands in delight. Smokeyogi's ears lifted at the sound.

"You might as well give up," Antonio said. "You're getting nothing out of these droids."

Liberty grimaced, fearing he was right. Everything the machines said came from *The Americana*. They were merely feigning conversation, parroting words from memory. They would never be able to tell her anything about the Old Americans. She tightened her lips to hide her disappointment.

"Watch this, Liberty," Antonio said. "Representative Jefferson, how do you feel about taking long walks?"

"Games played with the ball, and others of that nature, are too violent for the body and stamp no character on the mind. Let your gun therefore be your constant companion of your walks."

"Nothing in life is so exhilarating as being shot at without result," Church Hill said.

Antonio laughed, slapping Fury's saddle with his palm.

"Don't you dare!" Liberty warned. "Don't you dare make light of the Founders! Maybe we can't converse with them, but they can say the words, and that's something grand. It's to be respected."

"As far as making light, Liberty Bell," Antonio said, still laughing, "my advice is to lighten up."

"He has all of the virtues I dislike and none of the vices I admire," Church Hill said, flicking his enormous head toward Jefferson.

"See," Antonio said. "The bulldog has a sense of humor."

Liberty slumped in her saddle. "I hope he eats you for supper."

* * *

All the rest of the day, Liberty listened to the machines talk, their conversation drifting from topic to topic as one response triggered another, often repeating the same phrases. It was exciting and moving, hearing the old words spoken, but eventually grew wearing. More than once, one of them said something that sparked a fireworks display in Liberty's mind, but they always rattled on before she could think it through.

It's like getting a first-rate education on a slippin-slide, she thought. I need to remember all of it, brown-bag it so I can consider it later.

They camped that night a short distance from the road, among shade-brambles and stands of honey hyasuckle. Though early in the season, rainbow-colored flowers already covered the hyasuckle, and their sweet scent filled the air.

"It'll be like sleeping in lavender," Liberty said.

Antonio sneezed three times in quick succession.

"Kaboomdheit," she said.

"Thanks." He sneezed again, rattling the beads on his hat.

They made no campfire for fear of pursuit, and ate from their canned goods while Jefferson and Church Hill stood beside them in the darkening forest, twin colossi beneath the towering sequoias, never ceasing their endless dialogue.

"Will you please stop talking now?" Liberty asked. "We've got to go to sleep."

"Of course." Jefferson bowed slightly.

"As you wish," said Church Hill.

Liberty lay down on her bedroll, glad for the sound of chirping crickets in the otherwise silent forest. She blew out a ragged sigh, sinking into that quiet. Even her ears felt tired. She would probably dream all night of the machines' incessant chatter.

Just as she was about to drift off, Church Hill said, "Of course, the problems of victory are more agreeable than those of defeat, but they are no less difficult."

"Always take hold of things by the smooth handle," Jefferson added.

Liberty jerked up to a sitting position. "You people are going to have to move far enough away so we can't hear you."

"Let's treat the Founders with some respect," Antonio said. She could sense his grin even through the darkness.

"Oh, shut your trapezoid!" But it made her laugh, and she softened her voice. "You Goofy! I guess I deserved that one."

Without a word, the titans activated their air jets and floated from the camp. As Liberty started to lie down again, Jefferson turned back.

"Liberty Bell, what will you do if you find the gold of Fort Knocks?"

"Well, we're . . ." She halted. The machine looked down at her, a solid mass of metal, its voice strangely altered. She stared at its face, inhuman in its stillness, the lights behind its eyes dulled to a darker shade of blue.

"How do you know about that?" she asked.

"I would like to see the map you are using," Jefferson said.

When she did not answer, he said, "Are you a Representative of your government?"

"You need to go with Church Hill," Liberty said. "We can talk in the morning."

Jefferson turned and floated away to rejoin his companion. When they were nearly out of earshot, she heard Church Hill say, "When you have to kill a man, it costs nothing to be polite."

Antonio crouched beside her, his mouth close to her ear, his form a shadow in the dimness. "How did he know about the map?"

"I didn't tell him anything."

"Do you notice the way his voice changes when he's no longer speaking from memory? It's like someone else looking through his eyes. Who else would know what we're searching for? Jesse James, for one."

"He wouldn't have said anything to anyone; I'm sure of it. The

Lincoln I saw in my vision is the only other one who knew. You were right. I never should have told him."

"What's done is done. We now know these two are connected to the vision you saw. We have to assume anything we say will be overheard by whoever controls them." He pulled his bedroll closer to hers. "Best we sleep lightly tonight."

"Don't worry. Jefferson terrified me just now."

"Good. We're in the same ebook." He drew a sharp breath. "At least they can't creep up on us with those air jets."

Liberty turned over and closed her eyes, feeling both guilty and grateful to her companion for not blaming her. She had trouble falling asleep and woke often, imagining the approach of giant treads.

* * *

She was roused in Yoosemitee's empty morning gloom by the rhythm of mechanical panting.

"My wife and I tried two or three times in the last forty years to have breakfast together," Church Hill said, "but it was so disagreeable we had to stop."

She sat up, alarmed at not having heard the bulldog's approach. He sat facing her, his metal tongue lolling. But Antonio was already up and searching his pack for something to eat. Jefferson stood motionless several yards away, staring into the distance.

"Morning!" Antonio gave her a boyish grin. "A beautiful day in the hood."

"Who named you Captain Vitamin D?"

"I'm on a daring adventure, making Bold Moves, accompanied by a gallant comrade and the king of all watchdogs. We have a mystery here, and mysteries are what old A.I. is trained to solve." He arched one eyebrow, his brown eyes eager. "I've been interrogating your Mister Jefferson, but all he gives me is the same rote phrases." He tossed her a package of jerky. "We've still got some canned peaches."

"Something is coming." Jefferson looked in the direction of road, speaking in the altered voice he had used the night before.

Antonio and Liberty leapt to their feet, scrambling for their rifles. Liberty cocked hers, knelt beside a sequoia, and aimed into the distance. At first, she saw nothing, then discerned a red chess piece tall as Jefferson moving directly toward them, bearing a scythe in one hand, a hammer in the other. His metal hair was neatly sculpted; he wore a moustache twirled into tight circles at its ends.

"Stallion the Soviet," Liberty said, "the Red Commonest." Everything she had read about him ran through her mind. A deceiver as bad as Hitler himself, his scythe killed millions of innocents in the Old World. He was Death Incarnate. Without hesitation, she aimed at his right eye and fired, hoping to penetrate some soft part of his mechanized brain. She felt the recoil and heard the metallic ping of the bullet bouncing off its target. Cocking her rifle, she fired again, and Antonio started shooting, too. The monster strode forward, ignoring the shells, moving almost as fast as a horse could gallop.

She heard a deep growl behind her, and for an instant thought the bulldog was about to attack them, but Church Hill waddled forward on his bandy legs to meet the newcomer. "In war, resolution; in defeat, defiance; in victory, magnanimity."

Liberty kept firing at the Soviet's head, hoping for a lucky shot. "Keep calm and aim true," she said aloud between shots. "It isn't really him. It's a wind-up walmart happy-toy."

Despite Church Hill's enormous bulk, he was half the Commonest's height. They met in a rush, and Stallion struck a ringing blow to the creature's side.

"Death solves all problems," Stallion roared. "No man, no problem." He hit Church Hill another powerful blow, driving the bulldog to his stubby knees.

Antonio, standing slightly in front of Liberty's position, hurried back to her. "Get to the horses! I'll cover and follow."

But it was already too late. The Soviet was too fast. In a moment, he was upon them, cutting them off from their mounts.

"One death is a tragedy," Stallion boomed, raising his scythe to strike. "One million is a statistic."

Liberty instinctively raised her rifle to ward off the coming blow. Suddenly, the monster jerked backward and fell on his face. Church Hill had seized him by the leg and was dragging him away. Between his jaws, the bulldog's voice rose, "We shall not flag or fail. We shall go on to the end."

As he was pulled along the ground, Stallion reached back, striking again and again with his hammer, terrific impacts that made Church Hill ring.

"We shall fight in France," the bulldog growled. "We shall fight on the seas and oceans."

The hammer delivered a dreadful blow against Church Hill's broad head, making the dog blink and lose his grip.

Stallion rose to his hands and knees, supporting himself with his hammer hand, striking with his scythe. The blade could not penetrate

Church Hill's hide, but the impacts resonated through the forest like a thousand ringing bells. The bulldog thrust his head against the Soviet's chest, trying to drive him down, but Stallion resisted, the two straining against one another, neither able to gain the advantage.

Antonio grabbed Liberty's wrist, pulling her away from the struggle, trying to run between two giant sequoias to reach the horses.

"We shall fight with growing confidence and strength in the air!" Church Hill howled. Changing tactics, he stepped abruptly back, causing Stallion to fall forward. The bulldog seized the Commonest's middle in his massive jaws and flung him ten feet across the forest floor, sending him crashing against a sequoia, directly in Antonio and Liberty's path.

Stallion's flailing scythe whistled through the air toward them. Faster than Liberty would have thought possible, Antonio reversed direction, pulling them back. The blade missed their necks by inches, carving a divot from the trunk of the tree.

The bulldog waddled forward, but it had been a mistake to lose the advantage of proximity. The Soviet rose to his feet, his scythe broken, but his hammer intact. Giving a gruesome laugh, he cast the scythe aside and took the hammer in both hands.

"We shall defend our island," Church Hill shouted, "whatever the cost may be."

Antonio and Liberty backed away. The horses were beginning to panic, but there was no easy way to reach them. Seizing Liberty's hand, Antonio sprinted in a wide arc, trying to circle around the combatants.

Stallion struck Church Hill a thunderous two-handed blow to the side of his jaw, and lectricity shot from the bulldog's head, roiling through the air in showers. Still, Church Hill advanced, roaring, "We shall fight on the beaches," even as another stroke caved in part of his side. "We shall fight in the fields and in the streets."

"Oh, help him!" Liberty pulled away from Antonio and aimed her rifle at the Soviet.

Stallion hit Church Hill again and he fell on his side, knees buckling, tongue lolling, his voice distorting. "We shall fight in the hills. We shall never . . . surrender."

Stallion raised the hammer for the killing blow, all the power of hate etched upon his cruel, lifeless visage. "When we hang the capitalists," the Soviet bellowed, "they will sell us the rope we use."

Liberty was so focused on getting a clear shot that Jefferson seemed to come out of nowhere. Wielding an enormous log, he struck Stallion such a dreadful blow the monster pitched forward on his hands and knees.

As if drawing from some final, unexpected source of power, Church Hill reared up on his hind legs and grasped Stallion's head between his jaws. He pulled, his short, powerful legs digging into the earth, his eyes burning with determination. Stallion hammered furiously with his weapon, flailing against the bulldog's side, denting it repeatedly, while Jefferson pummeled the Soviet's back with the log, the wood splintering with the blows.

Stallion's neck gave way at the joint, and Church Hill stumbled backward, the head in his mouth. Blue fluid fountained from the Soviet's stump; his arms flapped; the hammer fell from his hand. He twitched and grew still.

Church Hill lurched to one side and collapsed, blood-red liquid pouring from his lips. Liberty sprinted toward him.

"Liberty, no!" Antonio shouted.

He caught her when she had nearly reached him, but she squirmed out of his grasp and threw her arms around the bulldog's neck.

Church Hill's mechanical breath whirred in and out. He was saying something, but his voice had lost its power and she could scarcely hear him. "Oh, Church Hill! Good Church Hill!"

His voice rose, slow and unsteady. "Let us therefore brace ourselves for our duties . . . and so bear ourselves that . . . if the British Empire and its Commonwealth lasts for a thousand years, men will still say . . . 'This was their finest hour.'"

"We have to save him!" Liberty turned to Antonio, who raised his hands helplessly.

"His mechanisms are failing," Jefferson said, and only later did she realize he had spoken in the voice other than his own. "Nothing can be done."

"Now this is not the end," the bulldog rasped. "It is not even the beginning of the end. But it is . . . perhaps . . . the end of the beginning."

His eyes died; his inhalations ceased. Liberty burst into tears and stroked the great, ugly head.

Antonio took her arm to lead her away, but she resisted. "He deserves a moment."

"He was a machine. The battle could be heard for miles; we need to go."

"If he was just a machine, why did he fight for us? He was noble as Church Hill himself."

Antonio shrugged and stroked her shoulder. "Maybe you're right. Maybe the words and thoughts of the great man gave his circuits spirit."

She glanced at her companion in surprise and saw a tear in his eye.

* * *

After Liberty, Antonio, and Jefferson left the battleground, Talos, the black cloud that was the Masked Rider, rose from the shattered shell of Stalin. He cursed bitterly, astonished by his defeat. Whatever the girl thought, something had caused the chessmen to rush to her defense, a Power he must either find a way to use or to destroy. There were too many mysteries. Ice and Bell had been incredibly lucky so far; they would not be so when next he found them.

He headed north, forced to return to Haze to obtain another clone body; but the travelers were riding toward his country, and he would rally his men and track them down.

He rose high, his black shape coalescing, flapping through the air like a murder of crows.

CHAPTER TEN

When the Revolutionary War was over, and America was free, the Jewish people became fearful, lest the new government persecute them, as had been done in the Old World. After he was elected president, Washington came to the Island of Rhode to look for them, and they said to Brother Rabbi, "We do not know this man, who has the power of the whole country behind him. Surely, he will take our goods and imprison us, as those before him have done."

Then Brother Rabbi and all his people hid among the thorns in the thickets. But Washington called to them, saying, "For happily the Government of America gives to bigotry no sanction, to persecution no assistance, requires only that those who live under its protection should demean themselves as good citizens in giving it on all occasions their effectual support."

Brother Rabbi and his people came out of hiding and helped make America a mighty nation. —The Americana

* * *

"But why didn't you side with Stallion instead of helping us?" Antonio asked. "He was one of your kind."

"Timid men prefer the calm of despotism to the tempestuous sea of liberty," Jefferson said.

They were an hour away from the battle, riding side-by-side along the road. Jefferson strode next to them, occasionally ducking to avoid low-hanging branches.

"It's like talking in code," Antonio murmured to Liberty. He had been interrogating Jefferson for the last several minutes, attempting to break through the wall of quotations. Aloud, he said, "So you opposed Stallion because he was a tyrant?"

"I own that I am not a friend to a very energetic government. It is always oppressive."

"I suppose that means yes," Antonio said, "or maybe I'm just jabbering with a mocking-robin."

"Tell me," Jefferson said, "what is the Yooessay government like?"

A chill ran down Liberty's spine. The machine's voice had shifted again, and the lights of its eyes had darkened. She and Antonio exchanged wary glances.

"The same question Lincoln asked," Antonio whispered. He chose his words carefully. "The governor and his Committees rule the country."

"Are they elected Representatives?"

"The governor is," Liberty said, "but . . ."

At her hesitation, Jefferson turned his head to stare at her, the glow of his eyes unwinking. "Tell me true, Liberty Bell."

She swallowed hard. "Well, he ran unopposed last term, and people said his opponents were afraid to run against him."

The chessman continued staring at her for a long moment. His eyes brightened to a lighter blue; his voice returned to normal. "I know of no safe depository of the ultimate powers of the society but the people themselves. If a nation expects to be ignorant and free, in a state of civilization, it expects what never was and never will be."

The voice changed again. "The members of the Committees are not elected?"

"Appointed by the governor," Antonio said. "The Secretary of Banking is always the lieutenant governor. Why are you asking these questions?"

The voice of Jefferson returned. "I believe that banking institutions are more dangerous to our liberties than standing armies." The shift again. "So, you have no true Representatives?"

"We'll answer your questions after you've answered ours," Antonio said.

"That government is the strongest of which every man feels himself a part."

Liberty could not contain herself. "But if we don't feel a part, what should we do? How are we supposed to change our government?"

"Liberty, please," Antonio said.

"The spirit of resistance to government is so valuable that I wish it to be always kept alive," Jefferson said. "What country can preserve its liberties if their rulers are not warned from time to time that the people preserve the spirit of resistance?"

"I want to speak to the other one," Antonio said. "The one who controls the machine."

Jefferson halted, his eyes darkening. His air jets sputtered and died, lowering him gently to the ground. "My power source emanates from the ruins, and I have reached its outer limits. I can go no farther."

Liberty looked up, meeting his inhuman gaze. "Why did you accompany us, sir? Can't you tell us? You've been a friend, but we don't know why."

"I came to protect you as long as I could. Keep to the north, Liberty Bell, and one will soon appear to guide you."

"But who are you?" Liberty asked. "What do you want from us?"

"I shall not die without a hope that light and liberty are on steady advance," Jefferson said. "The art of printing alone, and the vast dissemination of books, will maintain the mind where it is, and raise any conquering ruffians to the level of the conquered."

"But the books are gone," Liberty said. "They're all gone, everything you wrote."

Jefferson made no answer.

"I think he's told us all he's going to," Antonio said. "Let's go before somebody else shows up."

"Thank you, whoever you are," Liberty said. "Goodbye, Representative Jefferson."

"My only fear," Jefferson said, "is that I may live too long. This would be a subject of dread to me." The light died from his eyes; he lurched and stood unmoving.

Liberty only looked back once at the juggernaut, the symbol of the Founders, the author of the Declaration of Independence, standing silent beneath the trees.

* * *

They journeyed three days through the interminable forest. The road often branched, splits not shown on their map, but they kept to what seemed the main way. They were forced to regularly hide due to an increase in the number of travelers, mostly outlaws wearing the dark-blue uniforms of the Masked Rider's men, accompanying long wagons filled with mysterious machinery. Watching for them made Liberty and Antonio anxious, so when the undergrowth allowed it, they kept some distance from the road to remain out of sight. Not daring to use their rifles to hunt, they caught fish to supplement their dwindling rations, cooking them on small fires during the daylight hours. Yoosemitee seemed to stretch on forever, and they grew discouraged by its vastness.

On the third night, as they lay in their bedrolls listening to the chirping crickets and croaking frogs, Antonio gave a long sigh. He had been pensive all day, despite Liberty's efforts to cheer him.

"What's the matter?" she asked.

She heard him shift in the darkness. "I never thought it would be so far, you know?"

Sullen herself, she said, "I tried to tell you. It's a big country."

"How big? I mean, we've sent explorers into Yoosemitee—that's a government secret, you understand—the last ones three years ago."

"Like Lewison Clark?"

"Or us. None of them ever came back."

"Oh."

"I should have told you that before we ever started." His voice sounded heavy. "Once we find the gold, we've still got to return with proof."

"Are you wanting to turn back?"

"Me? Old A.I.? Never. It's just—you're a good girl, a real patriot. I wouldn't have brought you out here if I had known it would take so long, a woman in the wilderness." She heard the rustle of cloth and figured he had raised himself on his elbow. "Don't be offended. I realize you're a capable person."

She smiled, knowing this was as close to an apology as he would ever make. "I think it's sweet." On impulse she reached out and touched his arm, suddenly wishing he would take her hand.

"You look at me and you think: this is a man without mercy, a tower in times of trouble, but I'm a compassionate guy, too. It's part of being a well-rounded individual." He cleared his throat. "Maybe I should've reported to headquarters instead of making such a Bold Move, going off on my own."

"There's no point fretting about it," she said. "We've done what we've done, and rewinds are pointless. At least we sent letters letting our people know where we've gone. I've been pretty homesick, thinking how Gramps and Mom always took care of me, and the day-to-day goodness of working with the younger kids—things I maybe didn't appreciate enough. But coming out here has changed me. It's a centipede difference, one foot out of a hundred with a new shoe, but it *is* a difference. Despite the hardship and perils, how could I wish to be the way I was? It would be like going back to being a little girl again—nice to remember the dolls, but I don't know how to play with them anymore."

"Thanks." It was his turn to reach out, running his hand along her arm, squeezing and releasing it. The strength of his grip sent a surprising thrill through her.

She turned over to go to sleep, still feeling the warmth of his touch, and shook her head to shake off the sudden yearning. She touched the bear depending from her neck and tried to think of Jesse James, but his face seemed faint and far-away. You're just homesick, Liberty, she wistfully told herself. The fire-engine's racing, but there's no conflagration.

* * *

Two days later, the underbrush thinned, allowing them to stay off the road longer. The Giant Sequoias became fewer, until they rode past the last of the titans, towering above the elmoaks like a tree above weeds. Liberty glanced back at it several times, wanting to remember, wanting never to forget.

Clouds formed overhead, and in the early afternoon deep thunder rolled, startling them both. At Liberty's insistence, they took shelter beneath a tree and stood eyeing the sky expectantly. Leaning down in her saddle, she clutched Smokeyogi's neck, scrunched her eyes shut, and braced herself for the next thunder crash. But when it came it sounded farther away. She opened her eyes and looked up. "Where did it go?"

"Maybe it doesn't do the same thing every time," Antonio said.

"Waiting under a tree in a storm, that's not so smart," a voice behind them said.

Antonio spun around, pistol drawn.

"You want to shoot, go ahead," the stranger said. "Me, I'm just standing here."

Liberty gripped her own weapon, but the man smiled at them, his hands slightly raised, his palms open. He had a long face, a pert nose, and brown whiskers. His round spectacles made his brown eyes look enormous. He wore a fringed scarf hanging around his neck to his waist, a black jacket and pants, and shoes furred like slippers. A skullcap covered brown hair that touched his shoulders. He bent under the weight of a bulging backpack.

"Who are you?" Liberty demanded. "What are you doing out here?"

"What, you own the forest? I could ask you the same thing. They call me the Wanderer. That's what I do since my wife, Ethel, died; I wander. Who are you?"

"We're—" Liberty began.

"Ve're travelers, jest like ya'll," Antonio interrupted, his voice unrecognizable. Liberty looked at him in surprise. He was squinting one eye, opening and closing it like he had something stuck in his windpipe. "I am Kenny Doll and dis here kitten is me little sis, Barbie."

"Nice to meet you," the Wanderer said. "I'll tell you what, it's nearly lunchtime. I've got some bread and cheese in my knapsack. You want to join me? It's on the house."

"Vich house?" Antonio looked around.

"It's an expression. Come! Sit! You look hungry. You should eat."

Liberty and Antonio exchanged glances. Liberty murmured, "Maybe he's the guide Jefferson mentioned."

"Even if it ver so . . ." Antonio shook his head.

They dismounted. The Wanderer produced a blanket from his voluminous pack and spread it on the ground. All three sat down, Antonio with his back to a tree, his pistol beside him. The stranger produced three China plates with matching cups and polished silverware. The travelers added to the meal from their own provisions.

"I've got carrots." The Wanderer produced a bundle of them. He took one and bit off the end. He had the broadest front teeth Liberty had ever seen. "Vegetables are so important to a balanced diet, you know?"

"Are you real?" Liberty asked.

He looked at her curiously. "Aren't you?"

She reached over and poked his arm with her forefinger. He was as solid as anyone.

"You know, you stay in this forest too long, you get pretty insecure," he said.

"Vat kind of funny hat is dat?" Antonio asked in his miserable accent, jerking his jaw muscles. "I mean by it nothing, but dot don't keep the sun off, pardner." He laughed geekily.

The Wanderer chuckled, his peaceful brown eyes crinkling around the edges. "It's forbidden for me to walk four cubits without my head covered."

"Who forbids it?" Liberty asked.

"A very responsible person. I take it off to sleep."

Liberty studied him closer. It wasn't her imagination; his nose wiggled when he talked. It reminded her of something, but she couldn't recall what. "Do you have another name besides 'Wanderer?'"

"Call me Jack. A lot of my friends do. So, what brings you kids out to the Old Forest? On vacation?"

"Someting like dat," Antonio said.

Jack scratched behind his left ear. "I can see you have personal reasons. That's all right, but I gotta tell you, this isn't such a safe place. Plenty of strange things go on in Yoosemitee. I could tell you stories."

"Are ve near de end of dis here forest?" Antonio asked.

"If you keep traveling north, you'll be out of the woods in another day, but it's tricky. If you continue following the main road, you'll come out close to the border of Haze—it's a bad place. I wouldn't go there if I were you. You need to head a little farther east."

"Tell us about dis here Haze," Antonio said. "And vat vill ve find to the east?"

"Some pretty wonderful things. That's what my late wife, Ethel, used to say: 'There's some pretty wonderful things in the world, Jack.' A terrific woman. She could sing like a bird. No, you don't want to go to Haze. The people there aren't friendly."

"Could you be more specific?" Liberty asked, remembering Lincoln had warned them about Haze.

"Well, she had strong lungs, for one thing, and—"

"I meant about Haze and what lies to the east."

"Oh. I see what you mean. Haze is run by a man called the Masked Rider. From what I hear, he's a dictator, ruling with absolute power. Not only that, he's building weapons and machinery, preparing for war, probably with the intention of conquering more of the country. But to the east, there are mostly small settlements, nothing fancy, but good, honest people. A little suspicious when they first meet you, but they warm up."

They questioned Jack further but learned little more except about Ethel. He seemed to have a thousand stories about her, and his eyes grew misty telling them. They finished the meal and Antonio began packing up.

"Either of you play chess?" the Wanderer asked. "I have a set in my knapsack."

Liberty paused, wondering if this was a reference to the Dizzy chessmen.

"By yiminey, ve need to mosey on down dis here road," Antonio said. "Many tanks fer der provisions and der consult."

"You know," Jack said, as if thinking aloud, "I like you two. You've got spunk. I'll tell you what, I'm not going anyplace in particular right now. In fact, with a name like Wanderer, I'm never going anyplace in particular. How about I accompany you, guide you a little? I can show you the sights, introduce you to some people, maybe keep you out of trouble. What do you think?"

"I don't—" Antonio began.

"That would be hunky," Liberty said.

Antonio gave her a dubious look. "A moment with me sis, if yoose never mind."

"Sure. Don't worry about me. I'll sit right here and wait."

He led Liberty a short distance away. "We don't know this guy. Even if he's the one Jefferson mentioned, that doesn't mean we can trust him."

"Jefferson saved our lives."

"Yes, but for what purpose?"

Liberty bit her lip. "You're right, but we have to trust somebody. He seems like a gentle old man. He might be able to get us past the soldiers. There are so many search parties."

"He might get us killed." Antonio threw up his hands. "It's all a gamble. I don't like it."

"While we're talking about things we don't like, what's with the brother and sister act? We don't look anything alike, I sound like a normal person, and you've got the worst accent I've ever heard. Were we separated at birth? Were you raised in the woods by jabberwolves?"

"A good agent knows how to adopt another persona at a moment's notice. Did you observe the slight tic?"

"You look like you're having convulsions. You could have come up with more original names. Everyone knows who Ken and Barbie Doll were."

"Next time you'll be Snow White, okay? I'm improvising." He hesitated. "All right, we'll go with your intuition, but stay on the alert and remain in character."

"This is the only character I've got. Go easy on the tic."

When they returned, Antonio said, "By yumboats, Meester Vanderer, ve would be a'honored and privileged to have yer company. Yoose can ride our extra horse."

"Vonderful. I mean, that's wonderful. Along the way, I can tell you about my travels. You'll enjoy it, guaranteed."

He did indeed tell them stories, a continuous river of names and places like the Great Horn of Plenty, and strange creatures such as the Slots of Vegas, small, greedy beasts who crept into people's bedrooms and stole their belongings. He couldn't say how long he had wandered, though his wife had been gone many years.

Antonio didn't say much; no one could maintain that accent for long.

Occasionally, the Wanderer ordered them to conceal themselves, and riders invariably appeared soon after. Because of his guidance, they were able to keep to the road and make better time.

"How do you know when they're coming?" Liberty asked.

"Good ears and excellent intuition." Jack winked at her. Though she tried to hear intruders as quickly as he did, she never could.

Toward dusk, they came to a fork in the road.

"We should take the way to the right," Jack said. "It'll bring us farther east, avoiding Haze."

Since both roads appeared identical, they agreed, though Antonio gave Liberty a suspicious look. The Wanderer forged ahead, softly humming.

That evening Jack made supper while Antonio took care of the horses. The Wanderer's pack seemed limitless; he produced a heavy, metal skillet, salt and pepper shakers, and a half-dozen wild parrot-owl eggs. "I'll scramble these for you."

Liberty helped him build the fire. He beat the eggs until they were done, humming *Frog Went A'Courting* as he worked. His brown hair and gentle smile reminded her of Gramps.

After supper, Antonio caught her alone and whispered, "We'll keep a watch tonight. I'll do the first shift."

Antonio pretended to go to sleep soon after, and Liberty climbed into her bedroll. It was the dark of the moon, and Jack's voice came out of the blackness, his form no more than a shadow. "There's a song I know, a children's lullaby. It's old, maybe as old as the Old Americans. Would you like to hear it? I don't sing, but I'll try to sing it for you."

"I'd like that," Liberty said.

He began to hum, searching for the tune. He sang softly, his voice slightly off-pitch at times, but rich and sonorous.

Numi, numi yaldati,
Numi, numi, nim.
Numi, numi k'tanati,
Numi, numi, nim . . .

"That was beautiful," she said, when he finished. "Though I didn't understand the words, it reminds me of home. Thank you."

"You're welcome. You shouldn't worry about where we're going, Liberty. Ethel had a little joke about making decisions. She'd always say: 'Jack, it will all work out as long as you don't take a left turn at Albuquerque.' And she was right. Just keep heading the proper direction and everything will be fine. You'll see. Goodnight."

"Goodnight, Jack."

He made his way to his bedroll. She tucked her hands under her head, warmed by his fatherly attention, and began drifting to sleep. The day had been long; every muscle in her body hurt. It would be good to get some rest.

She slipped deeper into slumber. Jack's face hovered in her mind;

such a friendly face, his brown eyes behind his big spectacles, his downy whiskers, the way his nose wiggled. Funny, the people you meet in the forest. He was certainly one of a kind. And he was right. She shouldn't worry. It didn't do any good. Such a nice fellow, face long as a jackrabbit's.

She was suddenly wide-awake, his features flooding her with a connection to *The Americana*. And hadn't Jack just called her by her real name? She tried to remember if Antonio had accidentally let it slip, but she didn't think so.

She lay silent, aghast at what she believed to be true. How could she have been so blind? But there had been no skullcap, slippers, spectacles, or scarf in the old illustrations, no mention of Ethel. Still, she should have known, especially after everything she had seen.

For long minutes she lay listening to Jack's breathing, giving him enough time to fall asleep. Telling herself she had to be quiet as a mouseketeer, she rose, keeping her breath steady, counting the seconds, forcing herself to move slowly. She folded her bedroll, tying it together by touch alone. It seemed to take forever to cross the few feet to Antonio, who sat up to meet her. She took his hand, causing him to rise. At her beckoning, he got his bedroll and followed, moving with the practiced silence of a trained agent.

The night was so dark she had to feel her way with her feet to keep from tripping over anything, but they finally reached the horses, who greeted them with soft complaint. Liberty reassured Smokeyogi with caresses. Gathering the saddles and gear and unhooking the high line would have been impossible if not for Antonio, who seemed to remember exactly where everything was. She hoped Jack was still asleep.

It took anxious moments to saddle the animals, but finally they were ready. They led the horses in the direction of the road, every step uncertain. Reaching it at last, they climbed onto their mounts, but instead of continuing on the route they'd been following, Liberty led them to the other side and kept going west. She gave Smokeyogi his head, trusting to his animal eyes.

Antonio drew Fury close to her side. "Why did we leave?"

"Thank you for not questioning me."

"You may be teevee at times, but I trust you."

To her own surprise, she flushed in pleasure at his faint praise. She touched his arm. "He's Brother Rabbi. His expression about a left turn at Albuquerque gave him away."

"The wise fellow?" Antonio raised his index finger. "I remember. Hitler was always trying to catch him."

"'Hitler, Hitler,'" she intoned, "'don't throw me across the border into America.' Brother Rabbi outwitted the Fuehrer every time."

"Didn't he die at the end of the story?"

"No. Millions of his people perished in the camps, but the Americans and Brits helped them escape to America, where General Washington welcomed them."

"Even I know he's supposed to be one of the good guys. Why did we run away?"

"Because we lied to him. In any story about him, those who try to deceive him always end badly. He's a born survivor, the defender of the oppressed, outwitting and bringing justice to those who try to harm him. You can capture him, you can imprison him, you can try to kill him, but he always comes through; and if he's on your side, he's your best friend ever, because his purpose is to make the world a better place." She blew a harried breath. "We daren't challenge him. And he called me Liberty, so he knows who we are. I should have recognized him by how much he looks like a rabbit. That's why he said his name was Jack. In Old American, *Rabbi* is the plural of rabbit."

"His people are rabbits?"

"No, they're Jewish! It's one of his jokes. You really should read more. Let's get out of here."

"Why can't we stay on the road?"

"Brother Rabbi made us take the eastern fork. If he wants us to go that way, I say we should do the opposite. We'll cut through the forest until we intersect the western branch."

"All right, but we can't travel long in this darkness. As soon as we can lose ourselves in the forest, we better make camp."

With her excitement lessening, Liberty slumped in her saddle, the weight of her weariness upon her. *The Americana* was coming to life before her eyes, but if Brother Rabbi was the guide Jefferson had intended, what did it mean? Should she have trusted Jack? Was she wrong to run from him?

Before they could go deeper into the forest, they saw an approaching light. As they watched from beneath the concealing vegetation, a group of figures jogged past through the forest. Their lantern, a cylinder glowing brilliant with lectricity, revealed black uniforms, black boots, and strangely shaped rifles. They kept utterly silent except for their leader, who gave an occasional command. Their bodies were those of men, but their ebony hands were webbed, and their heads were sleek, hairless, and midnight black, with sparse gray whiskers around their mouths like a cat's. They were each over six feet tall.

Liberty clapped her hands over her mouth to keep from screaming.

The company left the road, going east, the noise of their boots the barest whisper. Their light dwindled and vanished into the foliage. Still Antonio and Liberty kept silent.

"Were those what I think they were?" Antonio finally asked.

"Navy Seals. They're heading right toward our camp. Brother Rabbi was leading us into a trap."

* * *

No sooner had Liberty and Antonio left than Brother Rabbi sat up on his bedroll. He found his spectacles, wiped them on his scarf, and put them on. "She's a clever girl, that one. And smart. A little too smart. I can't believe I used her real name! What a terrible mistake!"

He kicked off his slippers, revealing rabbit paws, and hopped high in the air, landing lightly on his feet. "I should follow them." He ran his fingers over his mouth. "Then again, if I do, I'll probably miss the Seals. And even if I caught up with the two of them, how could I keep them? A thing like that could get me shot. Mister Secret Agent might plug me full of holes."

He sat on a log and put both hands over his face. "*He's* not going to like this, not one bit. He should have sent Lincoln again, or found another of those giant chessmen. And with the satellite below the horizon, we can't even track them."

He hopped up again and paced the forest floor. "I hope they don't decide to go west toward Haze. If they do, it's gonna be trouble."

He halted, his brow furrowed, then batted the air with his hands. "Aw, what am I worried about? The Seals can catch them. They can hunt down anything."

CHAPTER ELEVEN

After the Saint Valentino's Day Massacre, Al Capone the Godfather summoned Timothy O'Leary to him to make him an offer he could not refuse. "Eliot Nestor pursues us wearing the amulet of the Iris, and no one can hide from its searching eye. You must destroy all the records of our crimes or your family will sleep with the fishes."

O'Leary did as the Godfather commanded, but soon lost control of the flames. So he played his violin while Chicago and the farmland roundabout burned, and not a cow survived the conflagration.

But Eliot Nestor swore a great oath to Representative Hoover, Master of the Air, that Capone would pay for his crimes. — The Americana

* * *

The turning point for Brett Revere, the moment when he decided to become a rebel, had been in second grade. He was working hard to make high marks when it occurred to him he could take it easy and still pass. This thereafter became his lifelong philosophy. It didn't hurt, being handsome and knowing it, since women were generally willing to help him out. He was a gambler, and a conner who knew how to manipulate others to carry out his plans.

Lately, he had been working his way up the rungs of wealth with his band of now-deceased outlaws, but the Masked Rider's betrayal had ended all that. Why couldn't everyone just get along? That was the trouble with the world.

When he saw Liberty Bell at the train station, such a pretty peach, his natural instinct had been to befriend her and see what he could pluck. One never knew when an unwitting accomplice could prove useful. Who would've thought she'd turn out to be nothing but trouble? Women were supposed to bounce up and down and scream in a brawl, instead of ruining a man's aim. Behind her blue eyes the girl was a tiger.

Anyway, half a map was better than none, and the Masked Rider should have been half happy about it. Brett liked people, and it sort of hurt his feelings to see his men gunned down like bottles shot off a fence. It was plain rude, and he doubted it would have been different if he had brought the whole map.

He wasn't one for vengeance; it took too much effort, brought no payoff, and didn't fit his easy attitude, but if the map was worth killing for, it suggested a possibility for the kind of profit he liked. So, after the ambush, he had doubled back and followed the Masked Rider and his men into Yoosemitee. It was risky; he had never been in the Old Forest before and hadn't known what to expect. Mostly, he had encountered delivery wagons coming and going from a settlement called Haze, apparently run by the Masked Rider, who was a much bigger honcho than Brett ever suspected. He had deflected their questions by passing himself off as a messenger bound for Trinidad, a village whose name he had overheard.

By chance, he had run across the trail of Liberty and the agent, and had abandoned shadowing the Masked Rider's men, thinking he could steal the map from the pair. But he had lost them during the lectric storm—as frightening a thing as he had ever seen—and was getting discouraged. There were too many Haze soldiers too likely to hang him on a whim, forcing him to ride some distance from the road. He was considering turning back and forgetting the whole thing. He who fights and runs away and all that.

His horse snorted a warning, and Brett lifted his eyes to see a coyote standing on two legs in front of him, wearing a green vest, short pants, and a belt with a long knife hanging in a scabbard. A tent-shaped hat sat on its head, pale green with a red circle embroidered on it.

Brett drew his pistol.

"It seems inconsiderate, sir," the coyote said, "to plug me without deliberation."

Brett glanced around, looking for the ventriloquist, who could be hiding anywhere in the foliage. The coyote moved closer, balancing himself nicely on his back legs. "Rest assured, sir, there is no one else here."

"All right." Brett continued scanning the surroundings. "I'll play along. Who are you?"

"Wiley, at your service." He gave a low bow, sweeping his hat off his head. His paws had an extra member serving as a thumb. "Sometimes called Brier Fox or the Big Bad Wolf."

"Pretty fancy names." It was uncanny the way the animal's mouth matched his words. Training, or some sort of mechanism? "What do you do around here?"

"I hunt. Mostly small game: roadrunners and rabbits."

Brett wondered whether the owner would show himself if he shot the coyote. People being fond of their animals, it might earn him a bullet in the back.

"And what's your moniker, if I might inquire?" the coyote asked.

"Tom Hankers," Brett said.

"What brings you out this way, Tom?"

Conners having a way of recognizing one of their own, the coyote's smooth, casual tone told Brett he faced a fellow scammer. "I'm from down south, looking to join up with some friends of mine. We got separated during that crazy storm."

"From the south? You mean the Yooessay?"

As he so often did, Brett followed a hunch, hoping it wouldn't get him killed. "As a matter of fact, I do." He flashed a silver badge, taken from one of the dead men on the train. "I'm a Yooessay Marshal on official business."

The coyote studied him thoughtfully. The whites of the animal's eyes showed, giving him an almost human expression. "Are you a Representative, then?"

"Sure. I represent the government."

"I'll tell you what," Wiley said. "Perhaps I can help you find your friends. Who are they?"

"The woman's name is Liberty Bell. She's my girl."

"Running off with another fellow?"

"Nothing like that. He's her cousin."

"Well, this is a wonderful coincidence. I know just the ones you're looking for and can lead you to where they were last seen. Right this way."

The coyote dropped to all fours and loped off through the forest.

Brett studied him a split-second before following. Life was one long gamble, and you had to follow the cards.

* * *

Liberty yawned wearily, sitting with her back against a tree. After spying the Navy Seals, she and Antonio had abandoned any thought of sleep, traveling through the night, often leading their horses, stumbling through the darkness until dawn, stumbling through the daylight from fatigue. It was mid-morning, and they had stopped to rest the animals and consult the map.

"According to this," Liberty said, "if we keep going west, we should soon leave the forest. We can turn back north again once we're free of the woods, assuming the Seals don't get us first."

"Maybe we lost them," Antonio said.

"They're Navy Seals," she said. "The Hunters. They can track a flea through a haystack. They always get their quarry and only death can stop them. If I wasn't so tired, I'd be terrified."

Antonio abruptly kicked an elmoak. "What's with this place? Navy Seals! That's teevee! Bedtime stories!" He kicked the tree again.

Liberty sat up straight, surprised by his anger. "I don't know what to think, either. Maybe the Seals weren't really looking for us. Maybe it was just a coincidence. Why would they hunt us, anyway? Does Brother Rabbi really think we're evildoers? We never should have lied to him."

"He can't be the real Brother Rabbi any more than Jefferson was the real Representative," Antonio said. "Whoever they are, they're in this together, and whatever their motives, it's hot salsa for us."

"I guess being able to wiggle your nose doesn't prove your rabbihood," Liberty said. She frowned and tightened her jaw. "We just have to do the best we can. Like Church Hill said, we should never give up. Come on. The horses have rested a little. Let's ride."

They crossed the west fork of the road minutes later and followed it. An hour passed, then two, without any sign of either the Seals or the Masked Rider's men. They were traveling through an area where the road narrowed. The day grew warm; the air lay still beneath the forest canopy. Other than the gentle plodding of the horses' hooves, Yoosemitee remained quiet.

A figure leapt out of the trees, his body nearly horizontal, knocking Antonio from his horse. Antonio's left foot caught in the stirrup, sending him sprawling onto his back, Fury dragging him sideways, the Navy Seal atop him, grasping him with webbed hands. Mister Red was drawn along after, his reins tied to Fury's saddle, but pulled away at the last moment, jerking the bridle off his head, barely avoiding stepping on Antonio.

Liberty raised her rifle, but before she could find her target, twin beams of light erupted from behind her, red lines of fire. She shrieked as one passed to the left, searing the ground before her. The other beam sliced through the reins of her pack horse, severing them from Smokeyogi's saddle. Nickering in terror, the animal plunged into the woods.

A Seal ran at her from the side. She turned the barrel toward him, certain she couldn't bring it in line in time. She saw his face in stark detail, the snarling mouth, protruding whiskers, skin shiny as walmart plastic, his eyes the most terrible of all, a pale blue alive with intelligence. Even though she was mounted, his head was level with her chest. His hands grasped her wrists just as she brought the rifle up. She pulled the trigger.

He fell backward, still grasping her arms, nearly dragging her off Smokeyogi. Black blood squirted from a hole in his forehead; his eyes went empty. She pulled out of his grasp and he collapsed.

Turning back to Antonio, she saw him still struggling with the Seal, while another rushed to help. Fury danced away from the newcomer, pulling Antonio and the first Seal along the ground.

Liberty aimed her rifle and fired, a hasty shot that missed the newcomer's chest, but struck him in the kneecap. He went down, his strange weapon discharging, a red beam that passed directly in front of Antonio's face. The Navy Seal continued crawling toward him, pulling himself forward with his hands. Liberty fired again, and he ceased his struggles, twitching as he died.

Antonio freed his foot and rolled, heaving the Seal against the ground, reversing their positions. Liberty kept her gun up, looking for a clear shot.

The Seal was heavier than Antonio and easily a foot taller, but the agent pounded at his face with one hand, while reaching for his pistol with the other. Just as he drew it, the Seal knocked it away, pushing Antonio backward. The agent rolled and sprang to his feet.

Liberty fired. The bullet barely missed her companion, ricocheting off the ground near his leg. Grimacing, she aimed again.

Fury swung around and Antonio snatched his roosey-cane from its saddle-scabbard. He swung it hard, connecting with the Navy Seal's chin as the warrior rose. The Seal dropped to his knees. Pressing his advantage, Antonio gripped the staff with both hands, flailing away, striking with first one end, then the other. The Seal fell on his back. Antonio scooped his pistol from the ground and shot him twice.

Liberty looked for more enemies, but none appeared. Leaping from her horse, she rushed to Antonio, who was turning a rapid circle. She threw her arms around him, startling him, and he shouted in surprise and nearly clubbed her with his pistol before realizing who she was. His nose and lips were bleeding; his eyes were wild.

They clutched each other for several breathless moments.

"You beat a Navy Seal hand-to-hand!" Liberty exclaimed. "You beat a Navy Seal."

Antonio grinned through his bleeding lips. "I did, didn't I? Didn't I tell you to stick with old A.I.? And you got two of them! For the love of Mexico, what kind of weapons were those?"

"They must be fazers, like the Astronauts used."

Liberty sat down, her hand over her mouth, suddenly light-headed. "We killed Navy Seals. The Pride of America."

Antonio's eyes focused. "They intended to capture us. Otherwise, they would have shot us off our horses."

"That makes it worse! I killed a Navy Seal who wasn't trying to kill me!"

"A good thing, too. My head and that guy's fists weren't getting along."

Her faintness passed and she rose to her feet. "We need to med you."

"Later. We've got to get out of here before some more show up. Say! Wait a minute." He knelt beside one of the Seals, touched the liquid oozing from its wound, and sniffed his fingers. "I don't know what this is, but it isn't blood."

"What does that mean?"

"That we still don't know what we're up against. Let's go."

The extra pack horse was gone, but Mister Red hadn't run away. After putting his bridle back on, they climbed onto their saddles and left the road. Hampered by the undergrowth, they made slow progress. After another two hours, they stopped to rest the animals, sitting back-to-back on a broad boulder, keeping watch both directions.

"We can't go on like this," Antonio said. "We need a Bold Move. Any suggestions?"

Liberty tried to think of all the tricks she had read about in *The Americana*, laying snares and digging pits, building forts and hiding in trees. None of it seemed practical. Finally, she said, "The American Natives used to start fires as a hunting tactic to drive buffalo over cliffs." She glanced at the horses. "No, that's a bad idea. Never mind."

"A fire would hide our movements."

"Yes, but . . ." She gave Smokeyogi a guilty glance. "I'm thinking of Roosevelt's bear, Smokeyogi's namesake. To start a fire in the forest would be both morally and ecologically wrong. People and animals could get hurt."

"This is life and death, Liberty."

"Life is meaningless unless we follow our conscience."

"You follow your conscience, I'll start the fire."

"I won't allow it."

"Liberty Bell, you're going to get us killed."

"Then we'll die." She nodded her head firmly. "But we won't hurt innocents."

From the distance came a single bark.

Antonio's eyes widened. "Let's get out of here."

They mounted and rode away but had gone less than a hundred yards when Antonio slapped his holster. "I left my pistol on that rock."

"We'll have to leave it."

"No, I'll go get it. You stay here and keep watch."

Before she could argue, he vanished into the undergrowth. His sudden desertion affected her more strongly than she would have supposed. They had been in the forest together for a little over a week, scarcely leaving one another's side. She peered around, imagining Navy Seals everywhere.

Minutes passed. What was taking him so long? Why had he left his pistol behind, anyway? That was awfully careless.

She looked back where he had gone. Her eyes narrowed. Thin ribbons of flame sparkled in the forest.

"Dagnammity dynamite!" she shouted, kicking Smokeyogi in the flanks. Hurrying through the foliage, she found Antonio carrying a lit brushwood torch toward a stand of wild petrol-barrel bushes. Another fire danced along a rotted log.

"Antonio Ice, you put those fires out!"

He looked up, face reddening, but held the torch against the tough, green skin of a petrol-barrel and fanned the flames with his hat.

"I mean it, Antonio." She drew her pistol. "If you don't put those fires out at once, I'm going to shoot you."

He stared up at her. "You'd shoot me?"

"I'll . . . I'll just . . ." She sputtered in fury. "I'll wing you in the leg, that's what I'll do. You put out those fires."

"Liberty, if you have to shoot me, go ahead. Do what your conscience says."

"Ooooh!" She threw the gun on the ground and started to climb off her horse.

The fire, finally burning through the hard, outer shell of the petrol-barrel bush, fountained upward in a scalding blue flame that immediately ignited the other plants. Liberty recoiled as they erupted into a garden of fire.

"Too late now!" he yelled, climbing onto Fury. "Come on!"

The horses snorted in fright, and Liberty swept up her pistol and leapt back onto Smokeyogi.

Fueled by the petrol, the fire traveled faster than Liberty would have thought possible. As dead limbs and dry underbrush caught, the flames swept outward in a solid line, moving so quickly she and Antonio struggled to avoid its path. Already near the limits of their endurance, the horses traveled on fear alone, spurred by the fire less than a hundred yards at their backs.

Animals appeared, fleeing the growing conflagration, scampering coyotes, potoroos, and deer, plunging past the travelers, dodging the horses in a flurry of terror. The smell of smoke filled the air.

When they had fled the flames for more than an hour, they reached a wide stream. Antonio tested its depths with a tree branch and whistled. "The horses will have to swim."

"That current is strong," Liberty said. "Crossing a river is risky. We need to find the road and a bridge."

"If the Seals are smart as you say, they'll be waiting for us there."

She licked lips parched from smoke. "All right. I've taken horses across the creek back home before. You?"

"Of course. But how do you prefer doing it?"

She grimaced. "We have to carry our guns and ammunition and anything else we don't want wet as high as our heads. Let me show you."

She wrapped Mister Red's reins loosely around his saddle-horn, hoping not to have to lead him. They made bundles of their weapons, and Liberty walked Smokeyogi into the stream. To her satisfaction, Mister Red trailed behind unbidden. The water swirled around her ankles, her knees, her waist, icy cold from its journey from distant snow-capped mountains, leaving her gasping at its bite. The horse rumbled uneasily but followed her lead. She brought him farther out, coaxing and soothing as they went. When the water flowed nearly up to Smokeyogi's neck, she grasped his mane, holding his bridle loose with that hand and keeping her bundle high with the other. The current swept around them, faster toward the center of the stream, a constant, pressing force. Liberty felt a knot in her stomach.

"Easy, boy. Easy." She clung to the horse, struggling to hold the upraised bundle.

The water reached Smokeyogi's nose. He thrashed, trying to keep his head up, and Liberty went under. Panic ran through her; she strained to keep the bundle aloft. Below her, she saw Smokeyogi's powerful legs stroking, pulling him back up. She tugged on his mane, raising herself until she broke the surface. Smokeyogi held his head high. She urged him forward, woman and horse fixed on the same goal.

She dared a glance behind her. Mister Red was following; Antonio and Fury were swimming, too, only slightly behind. They were going to make it.

From the bank they had left, a hundred yards downstream, she saw three Navy Seals rush from the forest. One pointed at Liberty and Antonio, and all three dove into the water, gliding through it like their namesakes, rising to break the surface with powerful strokes.

"Seals!" she yelled. Antonio spotted them and urged Fury on.

Liberty shouted to Smokeyogi, not daring to look at the Seals again. If more of them showed up and started firing from the shore, they could easily cut her and Antonio down when they came up on the far side.

The moments crawled. Inch by inch they approached the shore. The noise of the stream drowned any sound of the Seals' approach.

Smokeyogi's feet touched bottom. He clambered onto the far side, struggling to top the bank. She found her own footing and pulled at his reins, trying to get him into the treeline. Mister Red came up beside them.

With both horses among the trees, Liberty fumbled to unwrap her bundle. She pulled out her pistol, the first weapon she found. Just as Antonio reached the bank, a Navy Seal rose out of the water behind him. Liberty couldn't fire at him; Fury was in the way.

"Catch!" She threw Antonio the pistol. He caught it, and in one smooth motion turned and shot the Seal. She tore into the bundle again and grabbed her rifle.

Fazer beams erupted from the far bank, shattering earth and vegetation to her right, blinding her with the debris. She dug at her eyes, desperate to clear them. When she could see again, Antonio was beside her, firing at the Seals in the stream, who had been joined by others. With their webbed hands and wide feet, they were even swifter in the water than out.

A Seal shot up from the bank, breaking and foaming the current, water cascading down his ebony head. Liberty fired into his chest. He staggered but kept coming, climbing toward her. She fired again, and he fell forward, his strange blood staining the water black.

Taking more careful aim, she hit another of them. She glanced around for more targets, but all those in the water were dead, the last of their bodies vanishing downstream, carried off by the current. Antonio had emptied his pistol and was using his rifle against the four Seals on the far bank. In the few moments of the battle, the fire had nearly crept to the shoreline. Smoke and flames rose behind the Seals, growing so thick they disappeared in its fog.

Antonio's breath came in fierce bursts. "Are you all right?"

"I think so. You?"

"I told you they wanted us alive." He kept his eyes fastened on the distant shore. "We were easy targets. They could have picked us off at any time."

When the Seals did not reappear, the companions rode away from the river, both of them glancing over their shoulders.

The vegetation grew dense, and they pushed past brambles that bit and tore at their clothing. Liberty thought of the fire, wondering if it would cross the river. At the rate they were going, they could never outrun it.

They pressed through the last of the vegetation and found themselves standing in the open beneath scattered gray clouds. A few trees dotted the hills before them; the edge of Yoosemitee stretched in a long, curving line to the north and southwest.

"Oh, my stars and stripes!" Liberty exclaimed. "We made it!"

Antonio grinned. "Didn't I tell you that if you stuck with old—"

A red shaft shot down from the heavens, a beam many times wider than the bursts of the Seals. It struck a hillock two hundred yards away, a cascading force that melted the earth to bubbling lava. A lone tree burst into flames.

The beam moved toward them.

CHAPTER TWELVE

Then Hitler, the Wolf Prince, came to Jefferson by night, saying, "Your government of the people, by the people, for the people, is weak and cannot stand. Only an iron hand can truly rule. Side with me and I will keep America safe."

But Jefferson said, "Yours is a government of wolves over sheep. I prefer the tumult of liberty to the quiet of servitude." —The Americana

* * *

Smokeyogi bolted in fear, kicking and plunging back through the forest vegetation, oblivious to Liberty's efforts to control him. She shrieked, torn by the brambles, crouching behind his neck for protection, the woods hurtling by. It took several terrifying moments to bring him to a halt, and precious seconds to spot Antonio, who was struggling with Fury and Mister Red. The beam moved toward them, its energy pouring down, accompanied by a sizzling roar like the sound of a thousand waterfalls.

Side by side once more, they trotted through the forest, the horses rumbling their fear.

"What is that thing?" Antonio yelled.

"More fazers." Liberty's voice trembled. "Blistering down from far planets or miles-high space stations. What have we got ourselves into?"

"What do we do now?"

The despair in Antonio's voice made Liberty sick inside. She swallowed hard, tasting the bitter tang of smoke on her tongue, every breath a struggle coated in ashes. The fire had crossed the river and was drawing closer; they were caught between it and the beam, and were as exhausted as their horses.

She forced herself to rally. They had to be strong for each other. "The Seals won't give up, so we can't either. Maybe whatever's up there can't see through the trees." She met his eyes. "Bold moves."

He took off his hat and wiped the sweat from his forehead with the back of his sleeve. His jaw tightened. "Bold Moves."

They headed north, hoping to skirt between the beam and the fire, but the weapon began pulsing off and on, stabbing into the forest as if searching for them. They kept their heads down, expecting to be dis-integrated at any instant. If the horses hadn't been so weary, they would surely have bolted again instead of nickering in fear. The smoke grew thicker; Liberty thought she might faint.

Time passed. At mid-afternoon they entered a clearing beside a stream, and the beam abruptly ceased. Liberty looked but could no longer see any flames. The air smelled cleaner.

"Our luck is turning sevens," she said.

"Let's rest," Antonio said. "The horses are done in."

Liberty nodded. They had not slept for over thirty hours. They tended the animals and sat on the ground, numbly chewing cold bis-cuits and jerky.

Antonio glanced up at the sky. "If whoever fired that thing could see us, why didn't they shoot to kill? It's almost as if they wanted to drive us back toward the Seals." He lifted his index finger. "Who, not coincidentally, also wanted to capture us."

"Nice to be wanted," Liberty murmured. "Have you ever watched the satellites pass over?"

"Not really. I saw one once that somebody said was the old Space Station, but it was just a light."

"Most have fallen—that's what falling stars are—but some had ways of staying in orbit. I used to lie on the grass on summer nights and watch them, tiny points of light barreling across the sky, and I'd think how the Founders put them there, and what a miracle it was: Goddard, who built the rockets that gave the eagles the extra power to escape the earth, and Neil Armstrong, son of Custard; and the other Astronauts. I've always wondered what happened to the people on Armstrong City when the Great Blackout came."

"They must have run out of air and died."

"I like to think they didn't. I used to imagine that John Gleam found a way to save them." She sighed. "Look at me talking about the Man in the Moon like he was real. Just a bunch of teevee dreams."

"You keep dreaming, Liberty Bell." He gave her a solemn nod. "We're riding in teevee now and need all the dreams you've got."

She grinned. "Guess you've changed your opinion about me and my stories."

He smiled back. "Guess I have."

"We're friends now, aren't we? I mean, we didn't exactly get along when we first met, what with you throwing me off the train, but facing danger together can't help but bring us closer." Even as she said it, she realized it was true.

"I like to think we are," Antonio said.

"Let's decide to be. Shake on it?"

He gave her his hand and they shook, a firm honest shake.

"Friends forever," Liberty said.

"Friends forever." His voice was low and unusually gruff, his hand, warm and strong. Their eyes locked.

"I have to admit, when we first met, I thought you were . . . well, arrogant," she said.

He gave her a wounded look. "Arrogant? Me? I'm confident, that's all. A good agent shows self-sufficiency and leadership in every situation."

She grinned mischievously. "Actually, I still think you're arrogant; I just decided it suits you."

He laughed. "I, on the other hand, thought you were a ball of emotions the millisec I met you, and I was exactly right."

"I am nothing of the sort," she said. "I will admit during times of stress I may give an appropriately emotional response as befits a well-rounded and mentally balanced individual."

His eyes grew intense. "What I was going to say is that I didn't know what a sharp mind lay behind the fireworks. There's not another woman like you in the whole world, Liberty."

She felt the color rising to her cheeks and realized they were still holding hands. "That's very kind, Antonio." Delicately extricating herself, she said, "We better get some sleep, my friend. If I get any more tired, I'm going to start babbling."

"Right." He turned away, rose stiffly, and strode to his bedroll.

"Did I say something wrong?" she asked.

He gave a tight smile. "No, you're right."

He lay down with his back to her.

"Good night," she said, but he didn't seem to hear.

She drifted into slumber, annoyed. Any time you told a man you were friends, he assumed it meant more. As if being chased by Navy Seals and satellite fazers wasn't complicated enough.

She dreamed Antonio was riding in a circle on Fury, lighting the trees on fire with a flaming torch. She kept begging him to stop, and he said he would, but didn't. She called him a liar and oath-breaker, but he only laughed. She woke near twilight, snappish and unreasonably angry at him.

It took a moment to realize she had been roused by voices. Antonio had risen, pistol drawn. Liberty sat up. The sounds were drawing closer.

Without a word, they saddled their horses. Leading the animals, they moved at an angle away from the noise, picking their way through the descending darkness.

Behind them, they heard the faint, single bark of a Navy Seal. Liberty's insides went hollow; they could never outrun their pursuers in the forest at night. Her heart pulsed at her neck.

She jumped at the whine of fazers and the sharp crack of rifles, a regular Fourth of July fiesta. Men screamed; something snarled. A battle was taking place behind them. Were their enemies fighting each other?

Antonio climbed onto his horse. "Let's get out while they're busy."

They went as quickly as they could, letting the horses pick their way while the struggle raged. Judging by the cries, the Navy Seals were routing their opponents.

They'll be after us next, Liberty thought.

Night fell. After several anxious minutes, they struck the west road they had followed previously. By unspoken agreement, they brought the horses to a trot, heading out of the forest. As they passed the woodlands' northern edge, they saw a light beyond distant, rolling hills and heard the faint sounds of hammers pounding on metal, a cacophony akin to some fabled scene from the hellish factories of detroit.

"That's lectricity!" Liberty said. "Brother Rabbi was right; that must be the land of Haze."

Before they had traveled a hundred paces, a sharp whistle broke the stillness, followed by pounding hooves. A score of torch-bearing riders wearing white Cooclucks hoods bore down on them from behind.

"Halt!" one of the hoods shouted. "In the name of the Masked Rider!"

"Run!" Antonio hissed.

Liberty kicked Smokeyogi in the flanks. The horse sprang to a gallop, dragging Mister Red along with him. A gunshot sounded; a bullet whizzed by her head. Smokeyogi plunged up a hill, his hooves hammering against the earth, his muscles straining at the climb. They reached the top and thundered down.

Liberty shouted to Antonio and turned left, hoping he would do the same. She peered desperately before her, struggling to see well enough to guide the horse, but could only make out the shadowy shapes of rocks and bushes.

Smokeyogi stumbled, nearly throwing her out of the saddle. She jerked the reins, holding his head up, trying to keep him from going down. He caught his stride, righted himself; she regained her balance, and they hurried on.

More shots erupted and she dared a look. The riders galloped right behind her, their white hoods ghastly in the torchlight.

She turned back in time to see a stand of trees looming before her. She pressed herself against Smokeyogi's neck and mane, barely avoiding being clipped by a low limb.

We're deader than baloney, she thought. Branches cracked and broke beneath Smokeyogi's hooves. Boughs swept around her, witch-fingers in the gloom. Her right leg scraped against a trunk; she gasped, breathless with pain. Wrapping her arms around Smokeyogi's neck, she held on.

They hit a thicket, plunging into brambles that tore at her arms and clothes. The horse's velocity carried them through the mass, but the vegetation slowed them down. Liberty heard curses and cries of agony behind her.

She dismounted and began leading Smokeyogi, certain she would break her neck if they continued galloping. She moved swiftly, Smokeyogi's deep breathing a bellows in her ears. She heard men's voices, and shafts of torchlight shone from beyond the treeline. She had lost all sense of direction but hurried deeper into the grove.

After several minutes of traveling without reaching its end, she realized she must have stumbled onto a larger tract of woodland. The men's voices were lost behind her, their torches no longer visible. She stopped, uncertain which way to go.

A wave of despair washed over her. She could never find Antonio in this darkness. She pictured the map. Assuming he had escaped, he would certainly ride north and east as they had planned, knowing she would do the same. Tears sprang to her eyes—the two of them had traveled together long enough to understand each other's reasoning.

Only then did she realize Mister Red was no longer with them. She had no idea when the horse had been lost. She poured water from her canteen into her mess kit to give to Smokeyogi, whose mouth was flecked with foam. The horse slurped it up, and she filled it once more, leaving only a little for herself. It wasn't nearly enough for him, but it was all she could do.

"You're my hero," she murmured, stroking his neck as he drank. "It was a courageous ride, worthy of Trigger himself."

Petting him made her wince; her wounds were starting to hurt now that her excitement had faded. Her shirt sleeves were ripped and her arms bled where the brambles had slashed her; her pants were soaked with blood at her kneecap, and she realized she was limping.

She pulled herself back onto the saddle, letting Smokeyogi pick his way, her arms and legs aching. When they reached the edge of the woodland, she watched for a long time, peering from between the branches without sighting her pursuers.

Taking a deep breath, she rode into the open. The sky was cloudless; the sliver moon had already set. She took her bearings from the stars and headed north, passing several stands of trees. Finally, when she could go no farther, she entered a grove and lay down to sleep, shocked and numb. She tried not to think about being alone in the wilderness. She tried not to think about Antonio at all.

CHAPTER THIRTEEN

As a young man, Abraham Lincoln entered the Postal Service. When the Salem Post Office was discontinued, he was given its funds to keep in trust until called upon to relinquish them. Months later, when Ben Franklin came to collect, Lincoln's friend—knowing he scarcely had enough money for food— offered to loan him the funds to repay the government. But Lincoln fetched an old blue sock from a dilapidated trunk, and from it, poured out the identical coins he had received. He had not spent a single copper. —The Americana

* * *

Liberty rode north, away from the direction of Haze, passing through a stand of trees. It was mid-morning, and she had spent the hours slipping from grove to grove. More than once she had sighted the Masked Rider's soldiers in her binoculars, combing the country-side for her. She had seen bands moving both east and west of her po-sition, apparently attempting to encircle the place she was thought to be. Because she had to travel carefully, they could ride more quickly than she, and her only hope lay in getting through before they could close the circle.

She counted their continued pursuit a good sign. If they had caught Antonio and taken the map, they wouldn't be bothering with her. She chose to believe he was still alive, still free, and heading north. How she would ever, hope against hope, find him again, she didn't know, and it surprised her how much she missed him. Despite his flaws—his over-confidence, his tall stories—he had proven a capable wilderness companion.

She was abruptly startled by the sound of shouts and galloping horses. Dismounting, she led Smokeyogi to the edge of the grove. Shots went off just as she reached the treeline. Peering out, she wit-nessed a dozen hooded riders galloping over the hills, and glimpsed a single fugitive on horseback vanish into a stand of elmoaks.

"Antonio!" she whispered.

There came another shot, and one of the riders tumbled from his horse. Without slowing their charge, the others immediately spread out in a half-circle. Kneeling, Liberty steadied her rifle against a tree trunk and began firing as fast as she could, screaming a banshee screech all the while.

Dismayed by the unexpected assault, caught in a crossfire, the hoods spun around, retreating at an angle toward a low hill. Three of them had fallen; Liberty guessed Antonio, being closer and a better shot, had been the one who hit them.

Leading Smokeyogi, she slipped through the trees and rode out the back way, moving at a fast trot, keeping the vegetation between her and the hill.

She tried to imagine what Antonio would do. He wouldn't stay where he was. Like her, he would have to keep the trees between him and his assailants. She decided to circle around a nearby upcropping and catch him on the other side.

She kept a careful watch, knowing they could easily pass each another and never know. But as she came around the hill, she saw a horse disappearing among some trees. She trotted forward, giving the whistle she and Antonio had practiced. It came warbling back, steady and clear.

Grinning in relief, pistol in hand, she hurried forward, parting the foliage. Seeing the legs of a horse, she gave the whistle again, broke through the branches, and found herself facing Brett Revere.

He had his pistol aimed right at her, and she turned her own gun toward him. For a moment, they sat frozen. Then he laughed and holstered his weapon. "Go ahead and shoot, sister. That would be ironic after all the lead I've ridden through."

"I don't have the map." Her words, born of surprise, burst forth without consideration.

"I don't want it. I don't work for the Masked Rider anymore. He killed my men and nearly got me, too, all because some saucy young lady interrupted my plans. You owe me for that, Liberty."

"Why are the hoods chasing you?"

"They probably think I'm your boyfriend. Where is he, anyway?"

"He's not my boyfriend."

"I'm glad to hear it." He looked her up and down. "Traveling clothes suit you."

She blushed, and hated herself for it. "You've been tracking us."

He grinned. "You put things together real fast. You won't believe this, but I ran into a talking coyote right out of that book you like so much. Nice fellow. Big teeth. He pointed me to your trail."

Wiley the coyote, Liberty thought, no longer surprised by anything in Yoosemitee. "If you don't want the map, why follow us?"

His smirk faded. "I've done a lot of things, sister. Gun-running, gambling, stole a few horses in my youth before I wised up. They hang horse thieves, you know. I've dealt with men of bad character, but the Masked Rider is a different kind of fanatic. He tried to kill me because he doesn't want anyone to know that map exists. That must mean it's pretty important, not just to him, but to the Yooessay government. So here's what I want, Miss Liberty Bell." He took off his hat, revealing his dark, curly hair. "I want to help you and—assuming he's still alive—Antonio. I want a share of the profits, a reward big enough to make life a little easier; and I want a pardon from the governor."

"You killed Yooessay marshals," Liberty said. "Do you think they'll forgive that?"

He returned his hat to his head. "Leave that to me. One thing I've learned in my life, everything is negotiable. The current government has dealt with worse criminals than I am."

"Going to buy a farm and settle down?"

He raised his eyebrows and chuckled. "Irony from Miss Good Shoes? It doesn't suit you, Liberty. Kind of like hearing a little kid cuss. I'll tell you what it is; nearly getting killed has sobered me some. I've decided I want to go back to the Yooessay and become an honest gambler before I wind up dead. Maybe I *will* buy a farm, too. What do you say? I'll help you find your agent. Do we have a deal?"

"I don't have the authority to promise you anything."

"You can swear that if I help you track down Ice, you'll do your best to convince him to take me along for the ride. We can work out the details with him."

Liberty kept her gun steady, frantically thinking, knowing she either had to shoot him or accept his offer.

"Look, I know you don't trust me," he said, "but I've never taken advantage of a woman without her consent. And I've sure never killed one. You may think my word's no good—I'm a conner and that's for sure—but I know how to make a deal, and I honor any deal I make."

"All right," she finally said. "You will call me Miss Bell, not Liberty and not sister. And you will give your word by whatever you hold sacred, even if it is the name of your mother, not to harm, but to help Antonio and me."

"Mom wasn't so sweet, Miss Bell, so I best swear by the ghost of Paul Revere. He may or may not have been an ancestor, but he was my sole hero growing up. You have my promise."

Liberty reluctantly lowered her gun. "Then I will trust you to keep it."

"You like to quote the Founders, so here's a line I've lived by, just so you know I don't take an oath lightly. Mark Twain said, 'A pledge is a chain that's always clanking and reminding the wearer he isn't a free man.'"

Liberty eyed him sharply. "He also said, 'When one's character begins to fall under suspicion and disfavor, how swift then, is the work of disintegration and destruction.'"

He grinned his handsome grin. "Sitting next to you in the train station was the worst decision of my life. I've underestimated you from the moment I set eyes on your pretty face. I'll keep my pledge, Miss Bell, count on it. Not because I'm honorable, make no doubt of that; I'm a realist about human nature. But it's in my best interest to see you and your junior agent safely returned to the Yooessay." He lifted his hand to her. "Shall we go? The posse's courage should be returning about now. They won't give up once they discover I'm not here, and at least one of them is an excellent tracker. If we're lucky, he was among those we shot."

He turned his horse and plunged through the vegetation without looking back. Liberty followed, another quotation running through her mind: 'Misery acquaints a man with strange bedfellows.' The thought unexpectedly embarrassed her.

Leaving the trees behind, they trotted over the hills, riding side-by-side. From the corner of her eye, Liberty saw him glance toward her and grin.

"Actually, I guess I owe you a favor," he said. "I assumed it was Ice who ambushed the riders. Another example of my underestimating you. You got any water? I ran out."

She gave him her canteen, which was a quarter full. To her irritation, he drank it all and returned it empty. "Thanks. They were tracking me half the night."

Several times that morning they heard distant voices, and once, the noise of gunfire. Liberty tried not to imagine it being a fight between the outlaws and Antonio. Toward noon, they had to hide after glimpsing a pair of hoods passing over the hills.

As the day progressed, the landscape changed, the trees and hills gradually vanishing, leaving rocky, undulating ground covered in scrub oak taller than Revere's head, a welcome screen of protection. At mid-afternoon they reached a narrow stream, where they refilled their canteens, the beginning of a gradual slope into a canyon, a mile or more from side to side.

"You sure we're going the right way?" Revere asked.

"The map showed the forest road leading down into this canyon. I hope to find Antonio here."

"Assuming he waits for us," Revere said. "Not only that, the Masked Rider has the other half of the map. What's to keep him from sending men ahead to ambush us? I don't like the looks of your canyon."

They followed the stream, riding until twilight, finally camping a short distance from its banks, hidden among the scrub oak. The first stars came out; the sliver moon hung in the west, slightly wider than the night before.

"I've never seen country like this." Liberty stood watching the last rays of the sun vanish in a red haze above the canyon wall. "It's pretty in a vast and lonely way."

"Desolate, you mean. I'd guess you haven't been ten miles from where you were born before now."

His words made her feel provincial. "That's one of the reasons I came."

"You've got gumption, I'll hand you that," he said. "That's the way to be. At least, that's the way I always was. I left home at fourteen— nothing there for me anyway—took to the road and adventure. That's how the Old Americans were, starting out with nothing and carving an empire."

"At the train station you told me you didn't know much about *The Americana*," Liberty said.

"If you haven't figured it out, I'm not always completely forthcoming. Everybody knows some of the stories. They made me feel patriotic when I was a kid."

"That's an odd attitude for a criminal."

He chuckled. "You think the Founders weren't rebels? Think again, sister. They were revolutionaries, throwing the Reds out of America, carving cities from the wilderness, raising a whole nation of mutineers and dreamers. They were more like me than you want to admit."

Liberty glared at him. "They were good, honorable men who stood up for what they believed."

"So do I. Mostly I believe in myself. I'm the hero of my story, Miss Bell, just like they were, and I believe in taking what I want, just like them."

The fading light shone full on his chiseled face. He bent down and kissed her on the mouth, taking her completely by surprise. For a split second she responded, wanting to melt into his arms.

She pulled away and slapped him hard. "You don't care about the

Founders! You're a conner from start to finish!"

He laughed. "Maybe I am, but that kiss was worth a slap or two."

"You gave your word!" Her heart hammered in her chest. Her gun was in her bedroll, several feet away.

"I said I'd protect you," he said. "Nothing wrong with wanting to keep you warm at night. You'd have been disappointed if I hadn't tried, Liberty. Admit it."

"Miss Bell to you. You're no gentleman."

"That's right, I'm not."

She stood in momentary confusion. Brett was nothing like the boys at home. Their advances had always been easy to handle.

"Aw, don't look so indignant," he said, turning away. "We're done sparring for the night, and you've got a strong right hook. You've made your feelings clear. Let's get some sleep."

Without another word she crawled into her bedroll, clutching her pistol. She should have shot him the moment she saw him in the clearing. She knew she should hate him; she despised herself for fearing him; and his kiss lingered on her lips, just as he had doubtless intended.

She scrunched down into her blankets. He was playing her like an older boy with a fourteen-year-old. And truthfully, she *was* naïve. She felt young and foolish; she wished she were home. She fell asleep to escape the pain, and in her dreams she didn't stop the kiss. She woke in the morning fuming with herself.

"Hey, Sunshine," he said, when she got to her feet. She gave no reply.

"The silent treatment, I see," he said. "That's all right."

The sun had not yet risen above the canyon walls; the morning lay gray and clear. Brett glanced to the south and his grin faded. Liberty turned.

Figures, barely discernible in the distance, moved down the slope leading to the canyon floor. Rushing to Smokeyogi's saddlebags, Liberty withdrew her binoculars. The outlaws rode in a wide line, sweeping the countryside.

She handed Brett the binoculars.

"There must be five hundred of them," he said. "The Masked Rider isn't kidding around. Come on."

They packed their gear and slipped away, keeping behind the scrub oak as much as possible, knowing they would eventually be spotted.

"This is just what I was afraid of, being caught in a bottleneck," Brett said. "We'll head toward one of the canyon walls. Maybe we can find a way out."

Moments later, a low droning became audible from the east. Liberty pointed toward a dark shape in the sky. "What in death valley is that?"

"Some kind of machine," Brett said.

"Oh my stars and stripes!"

It swept humming across the sky, cross-shaped, its wings straight and unwavering. As it drew nearer, a volley of gunshots sounded from the direction of the Masked Rider's men. They must have missed their target, for the machine passed peacefully over Liberty and Brett, then abruptly turned back toward them.

Dropping so low it almost touched the ground, it circled once, the pilot waving a beckoning arm and pointing west. More gunfire erupted from the ranks of the hoods. The machine soared away, vanishing behind the scattered vegetation.

"I don't know who that was," Brett said, "but we're going to take him up on his offer. Anyone the Masked Rider shoots at is all right by me."

They moved at an angle away from the riders, keeping to a fast trot. With the rising sun, the day grew uncomfortably warm. Perspiration beaded Liberty's forehead.

"They must have spotted us by now," Brett said. "It's a sure bet we're being herded into a trap."

As the morning progressed, the canyon walls on either side grew closer and higher. Passing around a cluster of scrub oak near mid-day, they found a dirt road stretching before them, with the flying machine standing beside a small shack at its end, both painted the color of the earth.

Liberty glanced behind her. The foliage mostly hid the pursuing hoods. With her binoculars, she caught glimpses of their heads between the limbs of the scrub oak, still some distance away, moving at an unhurried pace, driving their prey.

When they were within twenty yards of the machine, Liberty drew Smokeyogi to a halt. Revere kept going.

"We should be careful," she said, thinking of the great eagles who had flown through the skies in the days of the Founders. "Are you sure it isn't alive? Will it peck us?"

Brett chuckled. "I don't see a beak."

A man stepped out of the shack, his shotgun pointed at them. "There's more aimed at you than this one." In proof, another rifle was thrust through a small window.

Revere stopped. "We were hoping for a settlement big enough to hold off the army behind us."

"We'll be miles away before they get here," another voice said. A lean man, wearing a peculiar, leather futball helmet and a leather jacket, appeared from around the back of the shack. He was as tan as his jacket, about twenty years old, with a boyish, freckled face, dark eyes, and a wisp of brown hair curling from beneath his helmet. He gave a friendly grin. "How did you manage to get half of Haze after you?"

"It wasn't easy," Brett said. "What kind of machine is that?"

"It's an airship."

"How can it fly without an eagle?" Liberty asked.

The man's grin broadened. "That's really good! Not many people would know to ask the question. They may have ridden gigantic birds in the old days, but this is pure machine. She's one of a kind, though we're building more just like her. We started a year ago, when lectricity began returning."

"Who's 'we'?" Brett asked.

The man turned his side toward them and tapped a circular red, white, and blue patch on his shoulder, depicting an eagle in flight. "We're the American Postal Service. At least the beginnings of it. We're going to restore mail delivery and reunite the country. We started up north. The lectricity doesn't work everywhere yet; it's gradually making its way south." He frowned ruefully. "We discovered that the hard way when a buddy of mine lost power in mid-flight. That was a tricky landing, I'll tell you."

He glanced in the direction of the approaching riders, visible only by a cloud of dust rising above the scrub oak, a sure indication they were moving at a gallop. "We aren't talking much about where we're from just yet. There's lots of isolated communities, and some would rather shoot than ask questions. The worst is Haze. They'd love to get hold of one of our ships. Which means we better leave before they get here. There's another group of those riders coming from the opposite direction."

"I figured as much," Brett said. "If you know a way out of this canyon, we'd be obliged."

"We can do better than that," the man said. "I've actually been looking for you for a friend who wants to meet you. I can take three in my plane, four in a pinch, though I'd have to fly low. You'll have to leave your horses."

"I can't leave Smokeyogi to those hoods!" Liberty exclaimed.

"You won't have to. We move our landing strip when necessary, and now that the Hazers know it's here, we'll have to abandon this one. My men can slip out of the canyon by a way we know, taking your horses with them. You'd never find it yourselves, even if I gave you directions; it's pretty well-hidden, so you'll have to go with me."

"Who's this friend you're talking about?" Brett asked. "And what will it cost us?"

"You wouldn't believe me if I told you. But there's no charge. We're modeled after the original Postal Carriers, and just like them, we're all about service. We'll get you to a safe place. I'm Andrew Carter, by the way. Call me Andy."

"You're named after two Representatives," Liberty said, "Old Stonewall and Carter the Good, Master of Peanuts."

"That's right, ma'am," Andy said. "You're pretty knowledgeable about the Old Ways."

Liberty hurriedly introduced herself and Brett. With two guns still pointed at him, Revere carefully reached up and touched the brim of his hat.

"Your offer is kind, given in the true spirit of the Founders," Liberty said, excited and fearful at the thought of flying, "but we're looking for another member of our party. I can't leave without him."

"Staying or leaving, you're not likely to find your junior agent now," Brett said. "You might as well face it."

She bit her lip. A pit big as pittsburg opened in her stomach. Tears stung her eyes. She turned toward the approaching dust cloud. The outlaws must have spotted the landing strip and realized their quarry might escape. Brett was right. She hated him for it at that moment, but she didn't know what else she could do. There was no time. Maybe they could spot Antonio from the air once they were on the plane.

"I'll do what I have to," she said at last.

"Your loyalty is touching," a familiar voice said.

Antonio stood at the door of the shack, holding the rifle that had formerly been at the window. His left shoulder was bandaged, but he looked otherwise unharmed. Another man, also armed, stood behind him.

"Antonio!" Leaping off Smokeyogi, Liberty ran to him, tears misting her eyes, but his expression halted her before she could hug him.

"What is he doing here?" Antonio demanded.

"Protecting your girlfriend," Revere said.

Remembering who had rescued who, Liberty said, "I found him in the woods. He wants to help us in return for a pardon and share of any reward."

Antonio's eyes never flickered from Revere's face, but he said nothing. Liberty had never seen him so angry.

"I know you don't trust me," Brett said, "but I think I can convince you how useful I can be. If you let me climb off this horse, we can talk about it."

Antonio nodded.

Brett descended smoothly and carefully, keeping his hands away from his pistol. He strode to Antonio, and Liberty saw he was easily four inches taller than her friend.

Brett turned to indicate the approaching riders. "They'll be here in five minutes. Why don't we talk this out on the road?"

As he turned back, Antonio clipped the side of his head with the rifle butt. Revere fell to his knees, bright blood springing from his nose. Reversing his weapon, Antonio stuck the barrel against the outlaw's temple.

"Hey there!" Andy shouted, moving toward them. The other man on the porch retreated in alarm.

"You killed my mentor and friend," Antonio snarled.

"Antonio, don't!" Liberty shouted. "I promised to bring him to you."

"Now you have." Antonio cocked his rifle. Brett, dazed by the blow, tried to say something, but it came out an unintelligible murmur.

"Don't do it!" Andy Carter held his hands out in supplication. "It'd be murder."

"An execution," Antonio said. "Justice."

"The American Postal Service doesn't hold with swat judgment," Andy said. "The Rule of Law, that's why we're here. Didn't you say the same thing yourself when we talked this morning? He deserves a fair trial."

"Antonio, please!" Liberty said. "You can't just kill him."

"Wait," Revere managed to say. "Wait."

Antonio raised his eyes to glare at Andy and Liberty. She was sure he was going to pull the trigger. Instead, he struck Revere a savage blow to the chin with the rifle butt, sending him sprawling. He bent down and frisked the outlaw, removing his pistol, a knife, and a small revolver hidden inside his boot. Brett lay so still, Liberty thought he might be dead.

"Leave him for the vultures and the Masked Rider," Antonio said, "whichever gets him first."

"I can't do that," Andy said. "My men will truss him up and carry him with them. We'll see he's taken to the Yooessay to stand trial. And we'll take care of your horses until you return. Now get what you need from your packs."

Both Andy's men had moved to the airship and were doing something at its front. Andy and Antonio lifted Brett across his horse's saddle and tied him to it. The outlaw moaned.

Liberty rushed to Smokeyogi. She stroked his beautiful head and kissed his velvet nose. Tears sprang to her eyes. "Godspeed and go swift, dear friend. Thank you for bearing me so faithfully."

The horse nickered at her, his ears forward, his brown eyes watching her in the impassive manner of his kind. She pulled *The Americana* and a few other things from his saddlebag and placed them in her backpack. With deep regret, remembering Jesse's kindness and gentle manner, she left her roosey-cane.

One of Andy's men mounted another horse and began leading Smokeyogi away.

"If we don't make it back, take him to Jesse James," Liberty called. "His ranch is near the south entrance to Yoosemitee. It's called the Elkhorn. Oh, please, will you promise?"

"I will," the man said. The other fellow joined him, leading Brett's horse, the unconscious outlaw swaying with the movement of its frame. In a moment they vanished behind the scrub oak.

Filled with a mixture of trepidation and awe, Liberty followed Antonio to the airship.

"What do you think of her, Miss Bell?" Andy asked. "I call her *The Rocket.*"

"It's like something out of the glory of Old America." She tapped her hand to her heart. "Can I touch it?"

"You have to if you want to get in. Keep away from the engine, though. It's still hot."

"Which part is that?"

"Behind the impeller."

"Where's that? Why don't the wings flap? They're so stiff. How do you breathe when you're up in the sky?"

He laughed an easy laugh. "The impeller is there." He pointed to the strange circle of metal on the front. "And this is the engine. The wings don't need to flap, and there's plenty of air up there." He pointed to the sky.

Liberty looked toward the riders, who were clearly visible above the scrub oak, approaching at a furious gallop.

Following her gaze, Andy said coolly, "Don't worry, ma'am. They won't catch us before we get away."

As if in answer, a low whistling filled the air. Andy froze, puzzled.

A projectile landed fifty yards from the airship, exploding with a thunder that made Liberty shriek.

"Holy jeeps!" Andy exclaimed. "What in detroit was that? Let's get out of here!"

Grabbing Liberty's hand, he pulled her onto the wing and into an open compartment with two seats in front and two behind. She hopped into the front seat and Antonio dove into the back. Andy thrust pairs of glass lenses, tied to a leather frame, into their hands.

"Put these deflector shields on. They'll protect your eyes from the wind."

While Liberty tied the leather straps around her head, Andy scurried to the front of the vehicle, even as a second shell landed ten yards closer. The explosion rocked the airship, pelting the passengers with sand.

Andy threw a series of levers and the engine surged to life, loud as a locomotive. The postman jumped in, donned his deflector shields, and gripped the half-wheel with one hand while depressing buttons with the other. The impeller in front of the machine whirled so fast it was nearly invisible. Liberty decided it must be traveling close to the speed of light. She thought of the stories of quantums and lectrons, and of time slowing down, and momentary panic gripped her. She clutched her hands together, repeating over and over in her mind: Wilbur and Orbit did it. Wilbur and Orbit did it.

Andy moved a control and the airship grew even louder. It lurched forward, barely escaping a third projectile, which blew a crater where the ship had previously stood. Liberty pushed against the dashboard, pressing herself into the seat. Faster and faster the machine went, bouncing over rocks and dirt. They left the ground, sending her stomach to her throat.

Up and up, above the canyon. Down below she saw the hooded riders, some galloping, others motionless, their rifles raised. A bullet whizzed by her head; another carved a hole through the wing. She ducked down in the seat.

Farther they sped, leaving their enemies behind. When no more shots came, she looked again at the dwindling forms of their pursuers. Near the canyon wall, she spied Andy's men leading the horses through a narrow pass. Remembering Brett, a wave of guilt swept through her, as if she had somehow betrayed him. She shook her head, rattling such thoughts away. She owed him nothing. He was a rogue and a villain.

She sighed. But she had to admit he was a pretty rogue.

The sky lay open before them; the rocks and vegetation below looked minuscule. She could see the whole shape of the canyon. She glanced at Andy, so brave and handsome in his futball helmet and deflector shields, a real hansolo. A wild ecstasy filled her and she broke into laughter. "It's a rollercoaster for sure!" she told him, shouting to make herself heard above the wind.

Andy grinned and gave a thumbs up.

She turned around to look at Antonio. His face was the color of a skeleton in a lab coat. She wondered if he was going to be sick, but he gave her a nod and a wan smile. She bit her lip to keep from laughing, then regretted her amusement after fearing him dead only a short while before. It was good to see him, queasy stomach and all.

But she was too excited to worry about him long. She turned to the front, wanting to take in the whole experience. She couldn't help wondering if the Founders had flown machines such as this. *The Americana* said they rode titanic eagles like Apollo Leven and E Perilous Union. With discomfort, she thought of Antonio's suggestion that Bone Apart's magic had been symbolic. She shook her head. She wouldn't think about that right now, not when she could enjoy the ride.

The airship thrummed on, eating up the miles, while Liberty's thoughts drifted to the story of Captain Snoopy battling the Bloody Red Baron through the skies. They crossed several rivers and passed scattered houses and a small settlement where people waved up at them. Andy dipped his wings, and Liberty waved furiously. She wondered how many days' ridings they were covering in only a few hours.

On and on they flew. The landscape below gradually changed, growing even more barren. Andy explained this was the edge of the Great Desert.

With the coming of sunset, the wind whipping around the airship grew chill. Liberty's ears were cold; she basked her hands in the warmth of the heat emanating from the vessel's front.

Pointing toward a short road below, Andy adjusted his controls and began his descent. They came down rapidly, and Liberty braced herself against the side of the compartment. For several perilous seconds the earth approached, until they were streaming along only a few feet above it. Liberty's stomach did a flop as they touched the road and bounced like a runaway wagon over the rough ground. For a breathless eternity, she thought they were going to turn over, but the airship gradually slowed to a stop.

Two men hurried out of a stone building, much sturdier than the shack at their place of departure. Andy pulled a knob and the engine fell silent. Liberty rubbed her ringing ears.

"This is it," Andy said.

"Where are we?" Antonio asked.

"My friend's house is close by. He's just the man to help you. I need to stay here and take care of *The Rocket*, but one of the fellows will drive you in."

Andy helped Liberty out of the vessel and down from the wing. To her surprise, she was unsteady on her feet. Under Andy's direction, the two men put the travelers' few belongings into the back of a single-seat wagon pulled by a bay mare.

"Goodbye and good luck." Andy shook both their hands.

"We owe you," Antonio said.

"Not at all. That's why we're here."

"Thank you for everything," Liberty said. "Thank you for letting me ride *The Rocket*." On impulse, she gave him a quick kiss on the cheek. "I'll never forget it."

Andy's face reddened to the color of the fading sun. "Glad to do it. Thanks for flying with m—with us." He shuffled his feet. "When you return to the Yooessay, be sure to tell them about us. We want to spread the word. We'll be flying there as soon as lectricity allows."

They climbed into the back of the wagon and the driver set off. Andy gave them a wide grin and a wider wave. The gentle creaking of the wagon and the plodding of the horse's hooves were soothing after the roar of the airship.

"It's like we've been beamed," Liberty said. "One minute you're in one place, the next you're hundreds of miles away."

"It's no different than riding a train," Antonio said.

She gave him a grin. "Is that why you turned pale as a tourist in Sleepy Hollow?"

"At least I don't throw myself at every outlaw and Astronaut I meet."

Liberty parted her lips in astonishment. "Throw myself? I never threw myself at anybody. Why would you say that?"

"If the bridle fits, wear it."

"Why you . . . Do you mean to imply that Brett and I—ohhh! How dare you? I don't know why I was glad to see you."

They sat in angry silence as the wagon rolled along. For a time, Liberty was too furious to form a coherent sentence. Did he really believe she would steady-up with a bandit like Brett Revere? Sure, he was handsome, but did he think her that shallow? Or was it something more? Kissing Andy was totally innocent—he had saved their lives. Could Antonio be jealous?

She grimaced. Truthfully, it must have looked bad, her showing up with Brett. And feeling sick on the airship probably didn't make Antonio feel particularly manly, especially compared to Andy.

"How did you hurt your arm?" she asked.

He shrugged. "It's nothing. I got shot."

"When?"

"Yesterday. Some of the hoods spotted me. I managed to get away."

"Does it hurt?"

"It's sore as anything, but the bullet passed through. Andy found me early this morning, led me to the shack, and cleaned the wound."

She looked away. "I'm sorry I teased you about feeling sick. It was mean. I guess I was irritated that you barely acknowledged me when I first saw you."

"I was focused on Revere."

"I know. It's just . . . I was really worried about you. And finding you alive . . ." She hesitated. "Why didn't you come out when we first rode up?"

"I was about to, until I spotted him. I wanted to see what his angle was."

"I either had to kill him or bring him along. I had no choice."

"Then you should have killed him. *I* should have killed him."

"Why didn't you?"

He met her eyes. "Maybe all your high-minded American stories are starting to rub off on me. I'll live to regret letting him go."

She smiled. "You're nobler than you let on, Antonio Ice."

He shrugged. "I was worried about you, too, Liberty, afraid the hoods had gotten you. And when I saw you and Revere together . . ." He looked away. "I don't know what I thought."

They fell silent. Liberty leaned against the side of the wagon and smiled, feeling suddenly happy without knowing why.

Darkness had fallen, leaving the way lit only by the bare light of the quarter moon. Regularly spaced trees, a cultivated variety unfamiliar to Liberty, appeared on either side of the dirt road, their nearly-transparent leaves reflecting the moonshine. The wagon stopped before heavy iron gates. The driver climbed down and spoke to an armed sentry inside the fence, then returned to the wagon to wait.

"Where are we?" Liberty asked, eyeing the fence, a formidable barrier of metal and stone, easily twelve feet tall. A low hum emanated from it. She wondered if it were meant to keep people out or in.

The humming abruptly died away. The guard flung the gates wide. They passed onto a cobblestone road and approached an eerie, sprawling mansion covered with numerous towers, gabled roofs, and strange juttings—a real bates-motel.

The road ended in a circular drive before two massive front doors. No sooner did the wagon halt than sun-bright lectric light flooded the courtyard from lamps set on poles all around. Liberty gasped and raised her hand against the glare.

Just as her eyes adjusted, the front doors flew open and a tall figure strode to the wagon, dressed in a gray suit and cape, his hair bushing wildly, his eyes a piercing blue. Behind him, ripples of lightning danced between twin pillars at the entrance.

"Strangers from the south." He spoke in a clipped accent. "A rare opportunity indeed! Who are you?"

Under such a gaze, even Antonio attempted no deception. "Antonio Ice. This is Miss Liberty Bell. Who am I addressing?"

He looked them over with a disconcerting intensity. "Men call me Einstein Edison. Welcome to Menlo Park."

CHAPTER FOURTEEN

These were the men and women of wonder, the great wizards: Thomas Edison, Grace Hopper, Stevie Jobs, Eli Whitney, Samuel Morse, Hedy Lamarr, and Alexander of the Grand Bell (which is the Bell of Liberty). But the greatest of all was Ben Franklin, who sailed a kite into the storm and captured the lightning in a jar. He placed the jar upon his staff, AceeDeecee, and gave it to Edison, who used it to light a flame atop the statue of Lady Liberty standing beside the golden doors in the harbor of York, so it became a torch burning across the waters, so bright it could be seen from the shores of the Old World. And when the kings and emperors of that shadowy realm looked upon the Light of Liberty, they trembled. —The Americana

* * *

"I don't know who or what he is," Liberty said. "Thomas Edison was a powerful wizard who only used his magic for the cause of good. He made wonderful inventions." She glanced at the lamps illuminating the drawing room in a steady glow. "Lectric bulbs, disks to capture the human voice so the blind could hear books read aloud, copying machines, holo projectors, hundreds of devices."

"So even if he is a wizard, he may be trustworthy?" Antonio frowned. "What am I saying? Two weeks ago I didn't believe in wizards."

At Einstein Edison's bidding, a woman in a black dress had led Liberty and Antonio through a hall, leaving them seated in a chamber with ornately carved chairs, end tables, and bookcases, a floral couch, and a sparkling glass chandelier shaped like a sailing ship. Heavy draperies covered one wall.

"Edison was good," Liberty said, "but Einstein wasn't just a wizard, he was a fizzicist. He helped Oppenheimer create nuklars." She raised her head and quoted from *The Americana*, "The rockets roared into the night; the madman danced, his cloak of darkness billowing. 'I am Oppenheimer; I am become Death!'" She shuddered.

"Is my association with the atomic bomb the only thing for which I am remembered?" a voice behind them asked.

Liberty and Antonio started and stood. Their host had appeared from behind the heavy drapes. The woman in the black dress followed, carrying a tray glistening pure silver.

"Once," Einstein Edison said, "I believed there would one day spring from the brain of science a machine or force so fearful in its potentialities, so absolutely terrifying, that even man, the fighter, would be appalled and abandon war forever. I no longer believe it."

The woman set the tray down and poured a brown liquid into silver cups. Liberty kept silent, refusing to apologize for her words, which were nothing less than the truth.

"Please sit again and take refreshments," Einstein Edison said, seating himself. "We have cakes and tea." He pronounced the word *and* as *und*, and his voice had changed, becoming softer and less clipped than when he had spoken at the gates. Up close, Liberty saw his gray suit was rumpled and too large at the shoulders. He had removed his cape. Beneath his suit, he wore a white shirt and string tie. His canvas shoes were untied. His hair made him look as if he had been shocked by his own lectricity.

He handed them their drinks. Liberty sniffed hers suspiciously.

Edison chuckled. "It isn't poisoned, Fräulein. And no matter what you may have heard about me, I am proud of the fact that I never invented weapons to kill. I am not only a pacifist, but a militant pacifist. I am willing to fight for peace."

"You can't be either Edison or Einstein," Liberty said. "It's impossible."

"Especially since they're both dead," Antonio added.

"Are they?" Edison asked, as if to himself. "A man should look for what is, and not for what he thinks should be." He fell silent, his eyes fixed on the lamp but seeming to gaze within. Just when Liberty thought he had become entranced, he roused himself. "You suggest I am a man at war with himself, the good inventor Edison, the dark physicist Einstein. It is true, in a way. I was crafted shortly before the Great Blackout. By that time, techniques had been invented to take a dead man's DNA and make a complete copy."

Liberty put her hand to her mouth. "You're a designer cologne!"

"That is correct."

"A zombie?" Antonio's eyes widened.

"They weren't zombies," Liberty said, her own eyes fastened on Edison in fascination and horror. She sniffed the air. "Why don't you smell sweet?"

Einstein laughed an easy, pleasant laugh. "That is a confusion of two words. I am, as you say, a designer clone. You are looking at the product of a flatworm."

"I don't understand," Liberty said.

"It is a little joke. If you cut off a flatworm's head, it grows a new one. A useful skill, eh? In the early twenty-first century, scientists discovered if they trained a flatworm, decapitated it, and waited for its head to regrow, the worm would remember its training. You see, memory is not simply in the brain as we once thought, but in the very cells of living things. Once the proper techniques were developed to release those memories, the temptation to resurrect the great men of the past proved overwhelming. And if both Einstein and Edison were supposed geniuses, what might be accomplished if the two were combined?"

He laughed again, a bitter laugh this time. "What they got was a man torn between the practical and the theoretical."

"But even the colognes—the clones— weren't immortal," Liberty said.

"You have a perceptive mind, Fräulein. I like that. No, the clones lived no longer than anyone else. I survived the Great Blackout, or more precisely, one of my predecessors did, and found a method to clone himself. It wasn't easy; the levels of electricity had fallen so low— the loss of power is at the quantum level, you know—and tremendous effort is required to utilize it. I am a copy of many generations of copies. But the memory of each copy is less perfect than the one before, and I have forgotten many things."

Liberty glanced at the glowing chandelier. "Apparently not your ideas and inventions."

"It isn't the great ideas that are lost; it is the small details that add up to those great ideas. The only source of knowledge is experience; when the experience fades, the great ideas cannot stand."

"But if you're a genius, can't you find a way to restore your memory?" Liberty asked.

He shook his head, making his hair bounce. "It is impossible. You can never solve a problem on the level on which it was created. But it isn't so bad. The process of scientific discovery is a continual flight of wonder, a pursuit of truth and beauty in which we are permitted to remain children all our lives. So, if I become more childish with each new clone, what does it matter?" He laughed, but his eyes were sad. "I have had the opportunity to live for centuries. It is a great gift."

He ran his hands through his tattered hair. "You will dine with us, yes? Tonight, you are my guests. No doubt you have been eating rations and will welcome better food." He pushed a button beside his chair, causing a hum and the ringing of a bell. The woman in the black dress appeared again.

"Florence, will you escort our friends to their rooms? And provide them with suitable garments so theirs can be cleaned."

All three rose. Inspired by the formality of her surroundings, Liberty curtsied. "Thank you, sir."

He smiled, clearly warmed by the old courtesy.

Moments later, Liberty was left alone in a lavish bedroom of oak panels, floral carpets, and a carved, canopied bed. In the bathroom beyond, hot water had been drawn in a pedestal tub, with clothes laid out on a dresser beside it, and she soon luxuriated in the world of scented soap and water to the chin. Just to wash her hair was sheer hawaii. She felt like a woman again, instead of a cowpoker.

After soaking for some time, however, her relaxation was interrupted by a strange voice outside the bathroom door. Rising, she quickly dried and donned the clothes, consisting of undergarments, silk slippers, and a long green dress embellished with ruffles. There was something quaintly old-fashioned about them, as if made for a character in *The Americana*; and it took her several moments to decipher the purpose of a piece meant to be tied around her waist. Florence certainly had a keen eye for sizes, because everything fit. Clearly, Menlo Park was well run.

As she stepped into the bedroom, the voice of a woman sounded again. She turned toward the source, expecting to find Florence, but no one was there. She backed up, confused. Was the wizard using fizzomancy to do something to her? Were his intentions darker than he pretended?

"Miss Bell, are you there?" The voice sounded again, small and strangely distorted. "Dinner will be ready in half an hour."

She located the source, a black, honeycombed box sitting on the mantle. Approaching it cautiously, she gave it an experimental tap.

"Can you hear me, Miss Bell?"

Liberty recoiled. "Y—yes. I do."

"You and Mister Ice will be escorted to the dining room at that time."

"Thank you."

She stared at the box in wonder, and after some hesitation, picked it up and examined it from every side. Voices sent through the air like in the days of the Founders!

She combed her hair and finished dressing just as Florence came to usher her down a hall into an elegant dining room, brilliant with lectric lighting. Antonio was already there, seated at a massive table beside Einstein Edison. The wizard rose to meet her. "Ahh, Fräulein! Come in. Right this way." He led her to a seat to his right, across from her companion.

A feast was spread before them, served in three courses. Liberty was unfamiliar with some of the foods, but everything was delicious. The main course was braised goose, and there was plum pudding for dessert. For some reason, there were more than two eating utensils and no sporks, but she followed Edison's lead. Antonio blissfully ignored the extra hardware.

"Tell me of your journey," Einstein Edison said. "You came from the Yooessay and entered the Old Forest on roughly the sixth of May."

"How do you know that?" Antonio asked.

"Wizardry!" Liberty exclaimed.

Einstein Edison smiled, his eyes dancing. "Nothing so arcane, Fräulein Bell, though soon I will be able to project sound and images throughout the forest over distant wires again. Not by what you call physics, but by science, though they are really the same thing."

"I don't track you," Liberty said.

"Most of the fundamental ideas of science are essentially simple, and may, as a rule, be expressed in a language comprehensible to everyone. It should be possible to explain the laws of physics to a barmaid. But in this case, the answer is even simpler than that. I know when you entered the forest from my scouts, my Dauntless Knights of Civilization, who I send throughout the continent, looking for whatever they can find, whether natural or artificial, anything they might bring back or describe that would further the quest for knowledge. One of them saw you enter the forest and followed you for a time."

"We were followed without my knowing?" Antonio's voice lay thick with self-recrimination.

"He also learned that you are an agent of the Yooessay government," Edison said, "and that you have met some strange characters on your journey. Where are you going, and why? Why bring a young woman into the wilderness?"

"We are unable to disclose our purpose," Antonio said, "but Liberty is a deputized civilian."

"When did I . . ." Liberty fell silent. She should be used to his embellishments by now.

"The secrets of state." Edison clucked his tongue. "Nationalism is an infantile disease. It is the measles of mankind." Liberty noticed that as the wizard spoke more comfortably, his voice became less clipped again, revealing his accent. "Very well. If you won't discuss your mission, tell me of the wonders you have seen."

Liberty did so, while Antonio, ever the spy, reluctantly entered into the conversation. Einstein Edison often nodded as they spoke.

"We have seen these phantoms from *The Americana* recently as well," he said. "A month ago, Brother Rabbi appeared at my gates. He refused to come in, so I talked to him through the electrified fence. I enjoyed our conversation, for he spoke German, and I did not think there was anyone on this continent who remembered that language. He wanted to know about our government, of which we have none. Menlo Park is mine. Those who work for me are free to stay or leave at any time. I told him I was an inventor and an independent businessman. He vanished soon after."

He paused and looked at his hands for a long time. "So many peculiar things coming from the north. A force is rising there, an erratic force, and I suspect much but know nothing for certain, except that the phenomena you have seen are not ghosts from the past, but holograms, probably projected from mobile units."

"Holograms?" Liberty asked, momentarily puzzled. "You mean holos?"

"Yes."

Antonio's eyes lit. "Real holos?" He waved his hand before him. "Wait!" He paused, brow furrowed. "It makes more sense than ghosts, if you can believe people used to shoot pictures through the air." He raised his index finger. "Both ideas are looney, but if I have to believe in the supernatural . . ." He shook his head as if to clear it.

"Your confusion stems from thinking the two concepts equal," Edison said. "Holograms are a product of science. To understand them, think of a shadow cast by a candle's flame. But who is casting the shadow, I wonder? Who activated the automatons of Churchill and Jefferson? Whoever it is has, for some mysterious reason, instructed you to travel north. And the Masked Rider, a creature from another planet, pursues you."

"A Space Invader?" A chill swept through Liberty.

Edison chuckled. "He wasn't when he came to Earth." His accent tightened as he spoke. "He was invited. His people came from the Sirius solar system."

"My stars and stripes! That's who's after us?" She turned to Antonio. "The Sirans landed their flaming eagles at the Kennedy Space Center. President Washington met them and their robot, Gort—"

Edison raised his hand to halt her. "My memory, Fräulein, however imperfect, differs at some points."

"It's right there in *The Americana*, big as John Henry's boots," she said. "I can recite the poem."

He studied her, a gleam in his blue-green eyes. "Who am I to argue with a pretty girl? But what *The Americana* does not say is that the Sirans are the first and only aliens we have ever met. After First Contact, a single Siran ship came on a diplomatic mission. Their forms are similar to our own; two eyes, two arms, two legs are an advantage to intelligent life. They had been here only a short time when the Great Blackout occurred. Without electricity, they had no way to leave Earth's atmosphere. Our own ships on the moon and in space, losing contact with the home planet, sought to return and fell from the sky. I myself saw one crash. Though I have forgotten much, I remember that sight well."

He paused and wiped his eye with the back of his hand. "Everything was lost in the catastrophe. And I, who had dreamed of furthering the reach of science, found our technology shattered, our hands foreshortened. All that is valuable in human society depends upon the opportunity for development accorded the individual, and my life was ruined." His hands fluttered helplessly, then he mastered himself. "The Siran ambassadors had come at the worst possible time. The people who survived wanted a scapegoat. They chose the scientists and the aliens. All the Sirans were hunted down and killed except for one, who managed to escape. I too had to flee for my life. Clones were shot like animals. I came here to the wilderness and built my new Menlo Park, a refuge for all the fugitives."

"Your tired, your poor, your huddled masses yearning to breathe free," Liberty said.

He smiled at her. "You are a special girl, Liberty Bell. Here at Menlo Park, I found a way to clone myself, powering my equipment using the solar trees you see throughout my facility. After several years, my Dauntless Knights of Civilization found Talos, the Siran, half-dead in the woods. Earth's atmosphere wore on him, you see, shortening his life span, which is many times that of our own. We brought him in and tried to nurse him to health, but his body began to fail. One of the amazing things about a Siran is that his consciousness can survive for a time beyond death; and if he has a suitable, unoccupied vessel, he can live within it. A mechanical device, a robot, will do for a short time, if it is of sufficient complexity. It was surely Talos who attacked you in the guise of Stalin. But a clone, especially one grown without external stimuli, is ideal. I had escaped to Menlo Park with DNA from several popular clones. I created a body for Talos, taken from a famous man named Robin Williams. One of the things we did not realize was that the clone's memories could radically affect the alien's personality, making him almost a blend of the two, though Talos' mind always dominates. This was a good thing at first; Talos became a very humorous person, but this only served to mask his deep bitterness toward human persecution of his kind.

"I was nearing the end of life in my clone body, preparing to activate my replacement before I died. Talos is not a scientist and did not understand the process. He murdered me and attempted to project his consciousness into my new clone. For a short time, he succeeded, but was gradually rejected for reasons he did not understand. Seeing he would soon fail, he gave orders to my unsuspecting assistants. I had prepared several clone cells for him, in case one should die. He had them transported to a previously prepared hideaway, transferred his life force into one of them, then killed my clone and the people who had helped him, insuring the secrecy of his location. When I did not return, my remaining followers activated my next clone. We have been enemies ever since. Saving his life has been my deepest regret."

"That's why he looked like Abraham Lincoln," Antonio said.

"That was his latest form," Edison said. "Lincoln was a very popular clone. Good men temper Talos' character, but several of the clones are villains of history. Why they were ever cloned in the first place is beyond understanding."

Edison shrugged. "Confusion of goals and perfection of means seemed to characterize the age before the Great Blackout. At any rate, their DNA was all I had to work with, and not understanding how they would affect Talos' personality, I thought they would only be containers for his essence. Who knows what terrible form he wears now? None of the DNA was labeled, and it is impossible to know the original identity of the subject until the clone is removed from its pod. He is running out of clones and growing desperate to overcome the defenses surrounding Menlo Park so he can obtain more. As an offshoot of my research, I can project hundreds of thousands of volts of electricity at an assaulting force."

"Let me understand this," Liberty said, brow furrowed. "The vision I saw was actually a hologram created by someone who powered up Jefferson and Church Hill in Dizzyland, while Talos, an alien from Sirius, formerly inhabiting the clone of Abraham Lincoln, attacked us from inside the robot chess piece of a Soviet dictator."

"That is correct," Edison said.

"This makes my brain swirl faster than a hamster in a May tag," Liberty said.

"It's a lot to take in," Antonio admitted.

Edison patted Liberty's arm. "I have said too much and troubled you. I'll tell you what: I will make a little music for us, what do you say?"

Taking a case from a nearby cabinet, he opened it, stared at it a moment, and removed a violin. His voice grew suddenly clipped. "It's impractical as all get-out." His tone softened. "But a table, a chair, a bowl of fruit, and a violin; what else does a man need to be happy?"

Placing the violin on his shoulder, he began to play. A shiver ran through Liberty at the first note. She had heard violins before, but nothing with the sweet tone of Einstein's instrument. He played a soft, unfamiliar song, so beautiful and haunting tears sprang unbidden to her eyes.

When he finished, she clapped furiously to keep from bawling. "That was wonderful!"

"It is Bach," Einstein said. "Do you know him?"

"What part of America was he from?"

Einstein's looked at her in astonishment. "He was from Germany, where I was born. At least, part of me was born there."

"Oh." It stunned Liberty that something so lovely could come from the decadence of the Old World.

"Can you play 'Home on the Range?'" Antonio asked. "I like that one."

"Antonio!" Liberty said. "That's just a popsong."

"But like any simple melody, it is a fragment into the frontier of beauty." Einstein played the familiar song, sweet and low; and then others, some familiar like "Red River Valley" and "Stairway to Heaven," some completely unknown. It was after midnight before Liberty climbed into the elegant comfort of bed, only to dream of one-eyed aliens chasing her through Yoosemitee.

* * *

Talos paced the tapestried carpet before the picture windows on the second floor of his palace in Haze, a courier standing at attention behind him. His lieutenants sat around an elmoak table, their eyes upon their leader. Talos could feel their uneasiness. The force of personality of his new clone, so different from Lincoln's less volatile—and in the Masked Rider's opinion—less brilliant mind, disquieted them. Though they understood little of the cloning process, they knew he had changed bodies. It would have been impossible to maintain his rule without giving them a glimmer of *that* secret. Still, men do not adjust easily, and he could sense their doubts. To make an example, he had executed his most skeptical follower, an obstinate, dull-witted officer he should have exterminated years before.

Outside his window, he watched criminals, chained together at the ankles, being led to their work sites by guards in white hoods. He had taken the idea of wearing hoods from Lincoln's memories, a brilliant stroke of inspiration that his men disliked, the officers arguing it restricted their vision; yet the psychological effect could not be underestimated. Still, he was now considering abandoning the concept.

By design, the country of Haze was a military camp, one he had established over several generations, bringing together settlers, outlaws, wanderers, and eccentrics, offering them protection, profit, and promises of glory, stealing or buying them wives from distant settlements, molding them into a tiny, but disciplined country. His closest followers were richly rewarded; his average citizens benefited from security, excellent wages, and a strong, centralized government. In the last few years, he was able to extend his power farther afield, to exert his influence on more remote villages.

Through the palace walls, he could hear the faint roar of machines. With the gradual return of electricity, the old weapons could function again. For years, he had salvaged them wherever they could be found, dragging rusted and deteriorating hulks to his shops, waiting for the moment when they could be copied and put back into use. He was on the verge of creating an empire, if only . . .

He turned and peered through his own, dark hood at the bare-faced courier. For his personal safety, he excluded the wearing of headgear in his palace, more than one insurrectionist having tried to assassinate him over the decades. "Does anyone have any questions for this man?"

His lieutenants kept silent, and the Masked Rider dismissed the messenger. Talos struggled to contain the violent emotions of his new body, to refrain from pouring vitriol on his followers. Instead, his voice rang softly menacing. "Will someone explain to me how a single pilot, flying a primitive plane, could escape from two companies of our soldiers?"

"We didn't know there would be an airship," one of his men replied.

"Have airplanes been previously sighted?" Talos asked.

"We've received reports of such widgets, Masked Rider, but didn't see any danger in them. They seem more like toys."

"So . . . no one told me." It was difficult, in this new clone, to control a rising rage. He bit his lip until he tasted blood. "We will find one of these machines; we will take it apart and learn how to build a hundred of them. We will use them to extend our reach to the farthest shores."

If only he were an engineer, he would have created an air force long ago. There was so much he did not know, and his military still remained small.

Talos stepped to the table's edge, where lay an enlarged copy of his torn half of the map. After studying it a moment, he indicated a point to the north. "Gentlemen, I will lead a small expeditionary force to this position, followed by our army."

Eyebrows rose in surprise. "You'll have to pass through the Canyons, Masked Rider," a lieutenant said. "That's hostile country."

"This is important enough for me to handle personally. I will pave the way for our troops." He grimaced beneath his mask. He did not like exposing himself to personal danger, especially not when the body he wore was his last remaining clone. But this was the time for the ultimate venture, one terrible risk and the rewards that would surely follow, the greatest of which would be to give him the advanced weaponry he needed to seize Einstein Edison's clones and laboratories. For that to happen, he would need to find the Power that had sent creatures in the uniforms of Navy Seals against him. He would seize it; he would conquer it; he would make it his slave.

CHAPTER FIFTEEN

Then President Washington summoned the wizards to the Oval Office to ask them, "How can we spread the Light of Freedom to the whole world?"

The wizards conferred among themselves for many hours. Finally, Samuel Morse said, "If the presence of lectricity can be made visible in any part of the circuit, I see no reason why intelligence may not be transmitted instantaneously thereby. Let us make a Net of communication to cover the whole earth, so everyone can learn the basis of good government."

President Washington ordered it so, but Edison looked doubtful saying, "How will the people use it, I wonder? Seeming to do is not doing."

—The Americana

* * *

Liberty was awakened the next morning by the cheeping of sparrows outside her open window. She buried her head in her pillow, luxuriating in sleeping on clean sheets, until she recalled what Einstein Edison had told them. When this sent her thoughts running in circles, she rose, took a hot bath, and dressed. A pert brunette named Nancy, clad in the long, black dress that was the uniform of the house, escorted her to breakfast in a room overlooking a pond surrounded by solar trees. Sky-blue flamingos waded in the water; peacocks preened along its sides. While Liberty ate pancakes, sausage, and eggs accompanied by a juice called *ornana*, Nancy chattered about Menlo Park. "Mister Edison worked in his lab all night last night. He's still there, but it isn't unusual for him. There are five laboratories in the house, but that's his private one. Sometimes we don't see him for days."

"Could I go there?"

"I'll have to ask." Rising, she wrote a message on a piece of paper, put it in a metal cylinder, and placed the cylinder inside an iron pipe protruding from the wall. With the sound of whispering wind, the cylinder vanished.

"What was that?" Liberty asked, astounded.

The woman blushed. "It's called a pneumatic tube. I probably shouldn't have shown it to you. We're not supposed to talk about Mr. Edison's inventions."

"The force of air, tamed by the hand of humanity," Liberty said, "the power of Herbert Hoover, a dream made reality."

"You won't say anything to Mr. Edison, will you? It's not that he's harsh, exactly. He can be gentle one moment, brusque the next, but they warned me when I hired on, and I don't mind. It's just that he's very concerned about patents. I don't know what they are, but he takes them very seriously."

"You have my word of honor."

The wind in the cabinet increased again, and another cylinder rattled down the pipe. Nancy read the message. "Mr. Edison will see you as soon as you finish eating."

The meal done, Nancy led Liberty along a series of corridors lit by lectric wall-lamps, adorned with wainscot, crown molding, tapestries, and floral carpets. Descending by scattered steps into a basement, they reached tall, double doors embellished with scrollwork. Just as her host placed a hand on the knob, a loud crash and a cry of rage sounded from within.

"Don't be alarmed," Nancy said, looking frightened herself. "He never harms anything but his equipment." She ushered Liberty inside, nearly shoving her through the door before closing it behind her.

Liberty was unprepared for the size of the chamber. Three stories tall, white-walled as a palace, it was filled with beakers, alembics, flasks and funnels, glass tubing in long lines astride black marble benches, strange machinery, and boxes of parts piled in corners. Caustic odors assailed her nose; lights bright as daylight assaulted her eyes. A wizard's den, indeed. Einstein Edison sat in the midst of it, slumped weeping in a chair against a workbench, broken glass lying scattered on the floor at his feet.

At the sound of the closing door, he glanced up, his eyes red, his face pale and worn, looking much older than the night before. He wore a white coat long as a bathrobe. Wiping tears away with both hands, he gave her a wan smile.

"Little Liebchen," he said gently. "Come in, come in! Ignore all this. Sometimes when the frustration becomes too much, I lose my temper. It calms me to see you."

"What's wrong? Can I help?"

He waved his hand dismissively at the broken glass. "It is my curse to be two men, one of them always dreaming of the Great Questions, the other, the practical inventor, always murmuring in my brain, 'Anything that won't sell, I don't want to invent.' I reply to him, 'But, no, everything that can be counted does not necessarily count; everything that counts cannot necessarily be counted.' All to no avail."

He leaned his elbow on the table, using it to prop up his chin. "It is an unsolvable argument."

"Aren't you proud of Edison's inventions?" Liberty asked.

"One thing only we both agree on, that there is no substitute for hard work. Do you know the bane of my existence, Liberty? I will tell you." He waved his arms to encompass the room.

"All these things here, I have invented them before."

"Before the Great Blackout?"

"Long before. Insanity is doing the same thing over and over again and expecting different results, yet I repeat the same experiments, hoping for outcomes I cannot quite remember. I ponder for months and years. Ninety-nine times, the conclusion is false. The hundredth time I am right. And what is the end of it? I finally reinvent the light bulb. But I lack the technology to test the theories that trouble my nights, questions of God and the universe."

"But with lectricity coming back, won't you be able to do more?"

"You don't understand. Those you call the Founders utilized enormous equipment: colliders, black-hole analogues, imaging computers. My laboratories are toys by comparison. How can I answer the questions of the nature of reality without the proper tools?"

"Aren't we living in reality?" Liberty asked.

"No, no, no." He waved his index finger in denial. "Reality itself is merely an illusion, albeit a very persistent one. As far as the laws of mathematics refer to reality, they are not certain, and as far as they are certain, they do not refer to reality. The most incomprehensible thing about the world is that it *is* comprehensible. I believe that . . ." He glanced at her and his voice trailed away. "I am sorry. I go on like this sometimes."

"I like to hear you talk," Liberty said. "It's just that I'm drowning in the shallow end of an olympic swimming hole. I'm not smart enough to follow you."

His eyes danced. "Let me tell you something. The true sign of intelligence is not knowledge but imagination. Few are those who see with their own eyes and feel with their own hearts. I think perhaps you do." He rose from his chair, sweeping shards of glass away with his shoes, neither of which were tied. "But I have been doing all the talking. Why did you come to see me?"

"I wanted to ask you about the Founders. You were there, or at least, a version of you was. I want to know what they were like, their wise words and great battles. Washington and Lincoln, Amelia Earhart and Wong Kim Ark, all the heroes."

His brow furrowed. "You and your name are like two violins playing together, Liberty Bell, perfectly suited for one another. I will say little, for I do not wish to create dissonance in those instruments. Anyway, I didn't know all of them, and as for heroes, I believe every man should be respected as an individual. Heroism on command, senseless violence—all the loathsome nonsense that goes by the name of patriotism—I hate them passionately."

Liberty flushed. "The Founders were good men and women, who fought their wars for freedom and equal rights."

"That was sometimes true. The virtue that set those you call the Old Americans apart was that they were willing to stand for those ideals. It isn't the people who are evil who make the world a dangerous place, you know, it is those who don't do anything about it. If you had seen Germany in nineteen-forty, you would understand what I mean. But despite the good the Americans did, they were not always right. The road to perdition has ever been accompanied by lip service to an ideal."

"But the Founders—" Liberty felt her face growing heated.

"Forgive me, Liebchen. I have distressed you. Let us leave it at this, that the greatest thing the Americans accomplished was to give an ideal a place; it was the Great Experiment that shook the world, a land of liberty where men such as I could reach our potential."

They stood silent a moment. Finally, Edison said, "Will you tell me where you and Antonio are going?"

"I can't."

"And this is because?"

Liberty studied his gentle face. "Antonio is bound by his duty, and I have given my word."

His face darkened. "I could detain you until you told me."

"Is it because of your two personalities that your accent sometimes changes?" Liberty asked.

"Does it? I have never noticed."

"One is gentler than the other. Right then, your voice got stern, like when Gramps lectures me."

He looked at her, grinned sheepishly, and shrugged. "I am not a convincing villain, am I? Most people say it is the intellect which makes a great scientist. They are wrong; it is character. You can leave whenever you want, taking your secrets with you. But if you continue going north, you must be careful. It may be dangerous."

She kept silent, unwilling to give anything away.

He sighed. "Thank you for coming to see me. Run along now, Liebchen. When talking to a nice girl, an hour seems like a second. Sitting on a red-hot cinder, a second seems like an hour. That's relativity, and I have work that must be done."

* * *

Liberty found Antonio and led him outside to avoid being overheard. The air was cool; lilies and wildflowers grew along the walkways beneath the prismatic solar trees; guards stood at every gate. She told him about her conversation with Edison.

"We need to get out of here before he changes his mind," Antonio said.

"I don't think he will. He's basically kind."

Antonio snorted. "You know the clones were supposed to be erratic, and he's got two of them inside him, like an overstuffed chile relleno. Anyway, you were the one who said he was an evil wizard."

"I know, but there's something tragic about him."

"Being locked up here would be tragic for us. We'll leave tomorrow morning, if he lets us."

* * *

Antonio's words, combined with the memory of how hard-edged Edison's voice could become, stirred Liberty's doubts, until by evening she was convinced he wouldn't really release them. However, when she and Antonio came to dinner, her fears faded, driven out by the boyish way he beamed at them.

"I have a surprise for you both this evening," he said, eyes crinkling. "A bit of entertainment I think you will enjoy. It was written long after the Great Blackout, but has been popular for several centuries and should be familiar to you."

Following a sumptuous meal, he led them into a large, elmoak-floored chamber, with a low stage and theater curtains on one end. He bade them take seats on a long, leather couch, while he sat in a stuffed chair beside them. More than a dozen of the household were already there, but Edison introduced none of them.

"It is my custom, in honor of my guests, to serve a special champagne I placed in my cellars twenty years ago." His staff poured golden liquid into long-stemmed, crystal glasses.

"I fear I do not imbibe," Liberty declared. "General Washington said—"

"Will you not suspend that rule for a drink so rare?" Edison gave a wink. "You will never have the opportunity to taste such a beverage again."

"I'm all in," Antonio said.

"I guess I could try a little," Liberty agreed, charmed.

"A toast, then." Edison lifted his glass. "To our two brave travelers. May they find whatever it is they are seeking."

Liberty, who had never tasted alcohol in her life, took the barest sip. She rolled it over her tongue. "It's like lilies on a snow-fed stream."

Edison chuckled. "You will not find better in these diminished times."

He gave a nod to one of his followers and the lights dimmed, a technological feat in itself. The curtains opened; a fanfare issued from an unseen orchestra pit. Cellos hummed as a spotlight fell on a single figure at center stage, sun-handsome and powerful, wearing a silver suit, his face shining with an unnatural radiance. In one hand he held an argent helmet, in the other a burning star.

Liberty laughed in delight. It was John Gleam, Rider of Eagles, First to Circle, later to become, at least in fairy tales, the Man in the Moon. He spoke in a clear, strong voice.

And now shall I ride, nor any detain me,
To the final frontier, upon Friendship Seven
That eagle renowned, brave-taloned brother
Seeking new life, new civilizations
Boldly I go, where none goes before me
Into night blackness, fearing no peril

"It's *The Star War*," Antonio whispered.

"I know," Liberty whispered back. "I've watched parts of it in school plays."

"As a child, my mother took me to see it professionally done in the York Theater at Fort Annie Oakley," Antonio said.

Liberty took another sip of champagne. A wonderful drink, so smooth. She was sure there was nothing like it back home. It made her feel like bubbles. She snuggled into the couch, her eyes on the stage.

To her consternation, John Gleam climbed not onto the back of a rocket-boosted eagle, but into a white machine shaped like an arrow pointed toward the sky. She consoled herself by remembering there was always room for artistic interpretation.

A low rumbling began, and she squeaked in fear and clutched the arm of the couch as the seats began moving, powered by some unseen force of fizzics. Steam rose from the bottom of the ship. It lifted with tremendous fury, gradually vanishing behind the upper curtain.

Thereafter, the play was all wonder to Liberty, as other figures appeared. Neil Armstrong, Custard's son, touched down on the moon to claim it for the cause of freedom, only to be opposed by Hitler's lieutenant, Marx the Deceiver.

"A small step for a man!" Armstrong cried, thrusting his spear through the villain's heart. "A giant step for mankind." Taking titanic leaps because of the low gravity, he strode over Marx's body to plant the American Eagle Standard on the lunar soil.

Everyone clapped as the music soared, Liberty responding so enthusiastically she spilled her champagne.

"Uh oh, oopsie," she said. One of Edison's staff promptly cleaned it up.

"I am *so* sorry," Liberty said.

The stage dimmed to blackness; sinister music played, growing louder and faster. Liberty's pulse quickened, matching the heavy beating of the drums. At the height of the crescendo, the spotlight shot forth, revealing a dark form standing before the Wolf Prince, Hitler, wearing a black cape and body armor, his face a black skull beneath a Notsie helmet. Liberty gasped. It was Death Invader, the Space Alien. Both he and Hitler looked so real. Could Edison have conjured them somehow? She remembered every childhood nightmare she ever had about them.

"Before the building of Armstrong City is completed, you will seize it and bombard America from above!" Hitler screeched. "Then we will round up the people of color, the Jews, the physically and mentally disadvantaged." Liberty squirmed, mesmerized by his hate-filled visage. Without thinking, she grabbed Antonio's hand.

Death Invader spoke, his voice thin as ghosts in a graveyard. "I will use all my forces against them, Mein Fuehrer."

The music swelled while Hitler ranted in verse, the voice of a demagogue echoing through the theater. Liberty cringed in her seat.

The curtain closed, bringing an exhalation of relief from the audience. She was still squeezing Antonio's hand and he was squeezing back. She met his eyes, but his expression was unreadable. It seemed to her it might be best to let go of him, but his grip was strangely comforting. That it was strong did not surprise her; she had seen him do some amazing things during their journey. Of course, she didn't always agree with him, but he had really nice eyes. She wished she had his long eyelashes.

I wonder if I'm drunk? she thought, immediately dismissing the idea. She had only had two glasses so far. She put her other hand on his, the hand of a good friend.

The curtain opened onto a stage, darkened except on one side, where General Washington knelt beside his aged mother, who was dying of cancer.

"The people, Madam," Washington said, his voice anguished, "have been pleased with the most flattering unanimity to elect me president. As such, it is my duty to return to lead them in this time of crisis. I have come to bid you an affectionate farewell. As soon as my mission is done, I shall hasten to Virginia, and—"

"You will see me no more," his mother replied. "My great age, and the disease which is fast approaching my vitals, warn me that I shall not be long in this world. But go, fulfill the high destinies which Heaven intended you for; go, my son, and may a mother's blessing be with you always."

Washington wept as he kissed her cheek. Tears poured down Liberty's face. "My mom must be worried sick about me."

Antonio squeezed her hand again and reached up to wipe away her tears. She smiled her thanks.

The lights went dark, then reappeared on the other side of the stage. The Founders were seated at the Pentagonal Table: Representatives Jefferson, Adams, Hamilton, Franklin, Shirley Chisholm, Lincoln, Roosevelt, Raygun and others; and the great Knights: Eisenhower Iron-Hewer, Ann Dunwoody, Mac Arthur, Powell, Grant, G.I. Jane, and Rocky Rambo. The Astronauts sat in an outer circle around them. Washington stood, tall and regal.

Waynejon appeared in a green glow, his Pilgrim hat on his head, one patch over his eye, his rooster perched on his shoulder.

"Death and doom," he drawled. "All will be lost unless you can stop the aliens from taking Armstrong City and destroy the Orbiting Satellite, Sputnik, the source of Death Invader's power. Who will do it?"

The room fell silent, for even those great heroes were dismayed.

But as Liberty waited in breathless anticipation, little Sally Ride, the smallest of the Astronauts, stepped forward to humbly volunteer. Inspired by her courage, all the Astronauts promised to go. The audience applauded as the orchestra broke into "Ride, Sally Ride."

The lights went out, a darkness accompanied by soft, scuffling noises. Gradually, a faint glow arose from the back of the stage, silhouetting the forms of three enormous eagles, wings outspread, necks outstretched, pointing upward toward a starry sky. Seven Astronauts, also silhouetted, wearing their bubble-headed spacesuits, sat upon the backs of each of the great birds.

"Now that's constitutional," Liberty said, thrilled to see the eagles.

President Washington stood before the Astronauts, arms upraised, chanting, "Seek thou the stars, Astronauts all; powerful *Columbia*, greatest of birds, carry these skyward, seven brave souls:

Commander Husband, Pilot McCool,
Physicist Anderson, Flight Surgeon Brown,
Engineer Chawla, Biologist Clark,
Scholar of Payloads, Colonel Ramon.
Best of the dreamers, brave heroes all!

Go thou, *Challenger*, beautiful bird, carry these safely, seven bold souls:

Commander Scobee, Ace Pilot Smith,
Specialist Resnik, worthy and true
Jarvis of Payloads, Expert McNair,
Strong Onizuka, Test Engineer
Teacher McAuliffe, humblest of all!"

President Washington turned to the third flight crew. "Go thou, *Apollōate*, wonderful bird, carry these safely, seven bold souls:

Commander Borman, Sojourner White
Lovell the Helmsman, far-sighted friend
Orbiter Collins, Tough Sally Ride
Lunar-man Anders, Stalwart Gus Grissom
Aerospace legends, ever undaunted!"

Challenger and *Columbia* lifted high above the stage, flying toward Sputnik. Everyone in the audience stood, and Antonio dragged Liberty to her feet, explaining, "It's customary."

She felt a little dizzy and leaned against his arm, but watched in horror as Death Invader, safely hidden behind the walls of the satellite, fired his fazers at the two eagles. Explosions rocked the theater. Liberty moaned as both *Challenger* and *Columbia* tilted and fell, screaming their death cries.

The orchestra was stilled; the lights went black in tribute to the passing of the brave Astronauts. A single voice sounded through the darkness, the words of Ronald Raygun. "We will never forget them, nor the last time we saw them—this morning, as they prepared for their journey, and waved good-bye, and slipped the surly bonds of earth to touch the face of God."

Liberty burst into tears, holding her hands over her mouth to keep from sobbing. Antonio put his arm around her, gripping her shoulder.

The lights came back up; the audience returned to their seats. The play rushed to its climax as Christa McAuliffe, the sole survivor, was captured by Death Invader, and Neil Armstrong confronted the villain. Caught up in the drama, Liberty and several others shouted *Don't believe him!* when Death claimed to be Armstrong's father. A tense duel ensued, and the whole room broke into applause when Neal killed the evildoer.

The music dropped to a single violin as Neal knelt over the mortally wounded Christa. Clutching his hand, her last moments upon her, she said, "I have been . . . and always shall be . . . your friend."

Wiping their tears away, everyone stood and clapped when Sputnik was destroyed and Washington stepped out of the fog of the explosion to explain that the brave heroes' deaths were not in vain, for they had shown the world the shining path to the stars.

The orchestra broke into "The Battle Hymn of the Republic." The curtain went down, the lights came up, and the actors strode forth to take their bows. Liberty saw that, despite the technological marvels of the show, they were not conjured phantoms, but only men and women in makeup.

"How did you like it?" Edison asked.

"The lights were incredible," Antonio said. "This lectricity could be really useful. But I don't remember the Astronauts all being named."

"It was a little touch of my own," Edison said. "I knew their names from before the Great Blackout. The mind works in strange ways; though I have forgotten so many things, those I remember. I thought others should remember them, too." He smiled at Liberty, his eyes crinkling. "For your benefit, I had my engineers add the eagles. Did you enjoy it?"

Liberty clapped her hands together. "It was marvelous. It was so . . . so . . . it was real as video!" She turned a small pirouette; Antonio had to steady her to keep her from falling.

"Are you well?" Edison asked.

"Too much champagne," Antonio said.

"Not too much," Liberty said. "It was juuuust right." She heard herself giggling. I have a really cute giggle, she thought.

Edison gave her a concerned frown.

"I'll see she makes it to her room," Antonio said.

"Thank you very much." Liberty attempted an unsuccessful bow. "And good night."

She took Antonio's arm, leaning against him as she went, the room being a little askew. As they left the chamber, she said, "This hall is a lot narrower than it was before. Really hard to get my footing. Wasn't the show marvelous? All the music! And the actors looked so authentic. I liked that it was historically accurate. The ending made me cry. I love that song. My eyes have seen the glory of the—"

"Here we are," Antonio said. "This is your room."

"Is it?" She turned and looked at him. "You are really cute, you know that?"

She wasn't sure who kissed who, but they were suddenly kissing. When they drew apart, she said, "My mind red-lined when you did that. Hmm."

"You are so beautiful, Liberty." His voice was husky. "I've wanted to do that for a long time."

She paused and studied his face. "There's a cloud around me like a big cotton ball." She started laughing, though she didn't know why. "You know, there's something I don't understand."

"What's that?" He was laughing, too. She thought she must be a very funny person.

"Why you're such a liar and exaggerator. You don't have to be, you know. You don't need to pretend to be a big special agent. You don't need any of that. You can do better. People should always tell the truth. You should tell the truth so I can trust you. I could never trust a liar."

She laughed again, but after a moment she realized he wasn't laughing.

"Maybe I've always felt I had something to prove," he said.

"Awww, don't frown. I was only telling you the truth."

"You're drunk, Liberty."

She straightened herself. "No, I'm not. Well, maybe I am a little pinball tilted." She studied him again and cooed, "Oh, no! I've hurt your feelings. I'm soooo sorry." She put her nose up against his and placed both her hands against his cheeks. "I'll tell you what. Why don't you come inside and I'll kiss your face and make it better?"

He pulled back, his eyes smoldering. "I may be a liar and an exaggerator, Liberty, but I'll tell you one thing, I'm honorable enough not to take advantage of a woman when she's drunk."

He opened her door and guided her through it.

"I've said the wrong thing, haven't I?"

"Good night, Liberty. Remember to take your shoes off before you go to bed."

"Wait—"

He shut the door. She heard his boots thumping across the hall floor.

* * *

Liberty moaned, holding her throbbing head. "I am a wretch, permanently pickled, a slave to vice, a victim of demon rum." She was sitting at a vanity in her room, still in her dressing gown. The shafts of morning sunlight through the window were spears in her eyes. "I've lost brain cells; I just know it."

A thunderous knock sounded at the door, making her moan again. She shuffled over and meekly cracked it. Florence stood outside.

Liberty opened the door wider. "You've come to chastise me, haven't you?"

Florence held up a glass filled with a pink liquid. "Mr. Edison said you would probably need this. It will ease your headache. And Mister Ice asked me to tell you to wear your riding clothes. You are leaving this morning."

"Thank you." Liberty took the drink and shut the door. Thinking of Washington, she recited, "'Consider how little a drunken man differs from a beast. By degrees it renders a person feeble and not only unable to serve others, but to help himself; he falls from a state of usefulness into contempt, and at length suffers in penury and want.'"

She groaned. "I'm doomed!" She looked at the glass again. "A wizard's potion. It's come to taking elixirs from fizzicists." After a moment's hesitation, she drank it down.

She put her hand over her eyes. "I'm given over to perdition, spiraling down the slippery slope. Slip-sliding away. I'll probably die in an alley somewhere, homeless and alone. I'll probably . . ."

Her head no longer hurt. She glanced around. "He *is* a wizard." She rubbed her temple and blew out a relieved breath. "Albeit a kind one, despite leading me into bacchanalian drunkenness."

She took a bath and sat at the vanity to arrange her hair. Everything from last night seemed a dream. It was hard to remember.

She suddenly dropped her brush and put her hand to her mouth. "He kissed me!"

A momentary smile crossed her face. It was a truly excellent kiss.

In the mirror, her dreamy expression gradually faded, replaced by a frown. "That roughneck! He kissed me."

She looked herself in the eyes and saw rising horror. "Or did I kiss him?"

She bit her lip. She might have. She wasn't really sure. She tried to remember, but all that came to mind was the feel of his lips on hers.

The brow of her reflection furrowed. "Oh, no you don't. That was the liquor talking."

Her face abruptly went scarlet with the memory of their parting words. She had humiliated herself completely and surely hurt his feelings.

She took up the brush, then slammed it back down. "Why does everything have to be so complicated? You try to do a good thing for your country! I'm going home to Mama and Gramps."

Her reflection gave her a cool, skeptical look. She would do no such thing.

She finished her hair and stood up. "Time to face the muzak, though the elevator's going down."

She went into the dining room, but neither Antonio nor Edison was there. She wasn't hungry but forced herself to eat, knowing it would be the last cooked meal for a while. Florence informed her that Edison was in his lab, and Antonio was waiting with the horses.

"Mr. Edison probably won't see you off," Florence said. "Once he starts working, time loses all meaning." She smiled as if that was a joke, but Liberty didn't get it.

After breakfast, Florence led her to the front of the house. Antonio sat talking to two other men by the door. He stood at her approach.

"You ready?" His voice was cold.

"I am," she murmured.

Three midnight-black horses stood waiting. Liberty took the one with a star on his forehead. Just as she was about to mount, Einstein Edison hurried out the door. "Ah! I haven't missed you. Good! Have you recovered from your evening? You blush, but you shouldn't, Liebchen. The fault was mine. Still, it was an experience, wasn't it?"

Not knowing what to say, she answered, "Thank you for the horses. We'll try to bring them back."

"Will you still refuse an armed escort?"

She looked at Antonio. This was the first she had heard of the offer.

"Regrettably so," Antonio said, "but we thank you for your hospitality."

"It was air conditioning in the desert," Liberty added.

Einstein smiled. His accent was thick. "And you are a songbird in a green field. Only one who devotes herself to a cause with her whole strength and soul can be a true master. You have that potential, Liberty. The important thing is not to stop questioning. Logic will get you from A to B. Imagination will take you everywhere." He studied the two of them. "I fear you are going into great danger." With great dignity, he kissed Liberty's hand and shook Antonio's.

They rode down the long drive to the gate, passing between the sparkling rows of solar trees. Once outside, Liberty turned. Edison still stood at the door. She waved and he lifted his arm in farewell. She felt like they were always telling people goodbye.

* * *

Einstein Edison watched them go. When they had disappeared in the distance, he turned to one of his men.

"Do my Dauntless Knights of Civilization follow?"

"Yes sir."

"Excellent." His voice grew clipped and stern. "Whatever they're after must be important. We will be there when they find it."

He strolled back into the house whistling, his hands behind his back.

CHAPTER SIXTEEN

General Washington, Eisenhower Iron-Hewer, and Custard Arm Strong passed into Mount Ana, where stood a gigantic American Native beside the banks of the Bighorn River.

"I am Bitter Gall," the American Native said. He raised his arms and hundreds of warriors appeared over the hills, war paint covering their fierce faces. "Your people have sinned and a life is required."

"I am the cause!" Custard Arm Strong burst forth. "I am not what you think me, General. I have shed the blood of innocents."

"I have accepted the fealty of this man," Washington said. "I will take the punishment in his stead."

"No, General," Arm Strong said. "I have been a villain, but you have shown me there is but one just course. I will go with honor, with the sun shining on my face."

Custard bowed low to Washington and strode down the hill toward Bitter Gall. —The Americana

* * *

Liberty and Antonio rode in silence for several minutes, picking their way around the scrub oak. When she could no longer stand it, Liberty said, "I suppose I made a fool of myself last night."

"A bit," Antonio answered.

"About our kissing, I—"

"I know it didn't mean anything. Alcohol does that."

Liberty clutched the horse's reins so tight her fingernails bit into the palm of her hand. "I think we should talk about it."

"What difference does it make? You wouldn't believe anything a liar and exaggerator said."

"Antonio, I didn't mean—"

"Of course you did. *I* may lie, but the liquor doesn't. That's what my Old Hombre says."

She bit her lip. "Aren't you even going to give me a chance to say I'm sorry? I am, deeply so."

"No need to apologize. It's better this way, knowing how you really feel."

"Don't—"

He sliced his hand through the air, silencing her. "We came here on a mission for our country. That's all there is to it. It's business. Last night was just a mistake. It won't happen again."

She felt hollowed-out inside. After some hesitation, she said, "I appreciate you not taking advantage of me. It was very gentlemanly."

His tone softened. "It's all right."

They said little for the next hour. She wondered if he had been drunk, too, and if so, and if the liquor really didn't lie, had he meant it when he said he had always wanted to kiss her? She grew annoyed. Men were so proud. But even if he *had* meant it, how did she feel about it? She wasn't sure. She hadn't forgotten Jesse James, still thought of him warmly, but had that been only a passing infatuation?

When they did start talking again, it was about the direction of travel. Edison had given Antonio advice on the best approach to the Grand Canyon, which was spanned by only two bridges many miles apart.

"He also gave me this." Antonio held up a metal, circular object that fit in the palm of his hand. "It's a compass like you mentioned, except it doesn't talk."

"They don't work anymore."

"They do now, with lectricity coming back. He explained it. Watch."

Together they studied the needle. Liberty's eyes grew misty, but she laughed.

"What's wrong now?"

"Nothing. It's just that everything I ever believed in is coming true. Now we'll never be lost again."

"Do you think the Masked Rider has one?"

She frowned. "I hadn't thought of that."

* * *

For six days they traveled the wilderness. The scrub oak soon vanished, replaced by lizards, rattlesnakes, cactus, and yucca plants rising ten feet into the air. Stone pillars appeared, towering formations standing unsupported like scattered sentries. The ground grew even more rocky and more perilous for the horses. On Edison's advice, they followed a narrow river in order to maintain a water supply.

Toward noon, Liberty glanced at the horizon, where clouds like fat pillows dotted the sky.

"Is that a bird?" She pointed at a dark, moving form. "It's huge!"

Antonio studied it. "It's probably closer than it looks. A hawk or a vulture, I suspect."

Liberty scrutinized it. "Not a vulture. Something about the way it flies looks different from any I've ever seen."

She pulled out her binoculars, but the bird was a shadow in the sun, too far away for details.

Antonio turned away, disinterested. He had been pensive all week. Gone were his exaggerated stories, and to her surprise, Liberty found she missed them. All her attempts to lift his spirits were met with courteous but stolid resistance. She figured she had sucked the enthusiasm right out of him. He was probably damaged for life.

Late that afternoon the land unfolded before them, revealing the far edge of the Grand Canyon beneath purpling clouds. Only a sliver at first, a hint of towering cliffs, it gradually widened, hazy and ephemeral. Liberty sucked in her breath, her heart quickening.

She didn't point; she didn't cry out; she didn't hasten her horse's pace. Neither of them spoke. In the most moovey moment of her life, she felt the awe sliding into her, welling up, filling her chest, filling her whole body, sending her head humming and ringing. She thought her heart would explode; she thought she would live forever. She thought she was the smallest creature on Earth.

The Grand Canyon stretched east to west from horizon to horizon. It did not appear as Liberty had imagined, for she could not have imagined it at all. It looked wholly unreal, a painting spread along the ground, a vast canvas unrolled across the countryside.

They slowed as they drew nearer, momentum failing before immensity. Forty yards from its edge, they halted, breathless.

Wordlessly, Antonio climbed from his horse. He raised his hand to help her down, and she realized he was right; the only way to approach it was on foot, in complete control of one's movements. Anything else was too terrifying.

They left their mounts beside a tall rock formation and went holding hands, two small children approaching a fairy giant.

Six feet from the edge, they stopped. Below them, at the Canyon's hazy bottom, rose towering rock formations surrounding a vast, grassy plain divided by a wide river. They stared in silence.

"'Leave it as it is,'" Liberty quoted, her voice a whisper. "'You can not improve it. The ages have been at work on it, and man can only mar it. What you can do is keep it for your children, your children's children, and for all who come after you, as one of the great sights which every American should see.'"

Antonio gave her a questioning look.

"Teddy Roosevelt. John Muir inspired him to create the National Parks, preventing the Corporations from desecrating America's beauty."

"How big is it?"

"They say the earthquakes accompanying the Great Blackout widened it. According to *The Americana* it's a thousand miles long, over a mile deep, and thirty miles at its widest point."

"I bet that river is big as the Mississip," Antonio said.

"It's the Colorado. When the dams and levees gave way after the Great Blackout, the rivers were finally freed. They poured across the face of America, flooding towns, drowning thousands, making them pay for their captivity."

"You make them sound alive."

"No," she said wistfully. "It's just the way it's written in *The Americana*, the whole earth rebelling at the way she'd been treated."

A gust of wind blew over the canyon's edge, pushing them back, as if to warn them away.

After some discussion, they agreed to follow the canyon east. Riding for an hour, winding between the stone towers, they finally spied, by the rays of the westering sun at their back, the span of the Golden Gate Bridge, stretching long and thin across a section where the canyon narrowed to less than a thousand feet, a steel suspension bridge wide enough for three wagons to cross.

"I didn't really expect to find it intact," Antonio said, "and look at her! Who could build something like that?"

"The original was in Calfornya."

"Whoever they were, they were incredible architects. I want to see how she's built."

As they approached, Antonio halted his horse and retrieved his binoculars from his pack. "I was afraid of that. There are riders on the bridge."

He handed her the binoculars. Adjusting them to her eyes, she saw a score of men garbed in white Haze hoods blocking the entrance.

"Oh my stars," she murmured.

They dismounted and led their horses behind a rock formation hedged on one side by tall cactus. Once safely concealed, they watched the riders preparing camp.

"They used their half of the map to guess where we were going," Antonio said. "They've probably got sentries posted on both bridges.

Is there any other way across?"

"None I know of."

"We'll need to create a diversion to pull them away."

"I wonder what Calamity Jane would do?" Liberty said.

"Probably light a bear on fire or something."

"Would not. She was never cruel."

"We're safe enough for now till we can think of something."

Even as Antonio spoke, there came a rush of wind, followed by a harsh scream. Liberty looked up and shrieked. Antonio whipped his gun from his side-holster.

Atop the rock formation stood a gargantuan eagle, staring down at them with cruel, golden eyes. Unlike any normal bird Liberty had seen, the top of its skull rose high and bulbous, disproportionately large. Its beak was long and cruel as a scythe; its talons, large enough to seize a horse, shone like polished bronze.

The eagle screamed again; and in its scream were words. "Who are you?"

Liberty broke into a cold sweat. Here was one of the eagles straight from *The Americana*, creatures bred by ancient jenetisists to bear pilots and Astronauts. An old-timer back home claimed to have seen one once, but even Liberty hadn't believed him.

"Answer!" the eagle cried.

Liberty's mouth went dry. When General Washington and Eisenhower Iron-Hewer encountered the mother eagle, *E Perilous Union*, she had threatened to rend their bones. She didn't only because Washington used the word . . .

"Freedom!" Liberty shouted.

The eagle turned its head from side to side in puzzlement, flexing its talons against the stones. "Your name is Freedom?"

"Yes! I mean, no! My name is Liberty Bell. This is Antonio Ice. But Freedom is a sacred word to us." She held her breath. In *The Americana* that had been the eagles' watchword.

"Many use that word, but few understand it," the eagle said.

"We do," Liberty said. "We're from the Yooessay, a country to the south, and have come seeking . . ." she hesitated, trying to think of the best way to word it.

Antonio kept his gun pointed at the bird. "We're explorers, hoping to find one of the ancient cities."

"The cities are no more," the eagle said. "It is useless to seek them. Are you with the men on the bridge?"

"They do not love freedom." Liberty said. "They are our enemies."

"They do not love freedom," the eagle agreed. "They do not understand the freedom of the skies, the freedom to hunt, the freedom to take prey. Do you?"

"We do," Antonio said.

The eagle studied them a long moment. "You carry a weapon."

"I'll use it if I have to," Antonio said.

"It is a question which one of us will be the prey." The eagle unfurled its wings, its whole body leaning forward to spring.

Antonio cocked his pistol, an audible click.

Liberty heard a snap, and an arrow quivered in the ground between her and Antonio. She looked for its source but saw no one among the rocks and cactus. When she turned again to the eagle, a man stood beside it, one hand on its enormous haunch, a rifle in the other.

He was tall and tan, with long, dark hair falling to his shoulders. A green headband sat above eyes gleaming fiercely in the fading sun, underscored by black war paint. Shirtless, he wore brown leather pants and a matching vest, revealing a lean, muscular frame.

Liberty turned breathless with fear.

"*Ah ah ah ah,*" a voice called from behind them. "You're surrounded. Drop the guns or face the fun."

Looking over her shoulder, Liberty saw a lanky man step from behind a cactus, pointing a rifle at them, wearing a sleeveless velvet shirt covered with fringes, turquoise armbands, a breechcloth with leather leggings, and leather boots. A band of blue paint ran in a wide strip across his eyes. Turquoise necklaces dangled from his neck; a coyote pelt covered his head.

Antonio laid his gun on the ground.

From around the rocks appeared a woman and another man, both wearing black smudges under their eyes. The man carried a rifle; the woman held a bow, an arrow at the ready.

Liberty found her voice. "You're American Natives."

"Thanks for telling us," the man behind them said. "Very observant."

The warrior beside the eagle spoke, his voice deep. "You are on the Res of the Navajo Nation, home of the sons and daughters of the Horse People of the Navajo. I am Code Talker. The man behind you is Heyoka Coyoté."

Code Talker pointed to the woman. "My sister, Pocahontas Biggulp." A striking woman, with high cheekbones and an unusually square face, she wore cotton levites, a brown, fringed smock, and a red headband. Her black hair flowed down to her waist.

"My cousin, Elvis Presley." Code Talker indicated the last American

Native, a broad-shouldered, heavy man. A hefty tomahawk hung from his belt. He gave the travelers a wave.

"You claim to be explorers," Code Talker continued. He patted the eagle's side. "Endeavour lacks guile; she believes what people say. We're more skeptical."

"Inquiring minds want to know," Heyoka Coyoté said.

"They're a long way from home," Pocahontas said. "It's doubtful they came so far just for exploration."

"Owlhoots," Heyoka Coyoté said, the snout and jaws of the coyote pelt atop his head pointing toward the travelers.

"We were sent by the Yooessay government," Antonio said. "Our business is official."

"Foul ball!" Heyoka Coyoté cried.

Code Talker pointed to Heyoka Coyoté. "Correct. We recognize no government but our own. You say you're enemies of the Hazers, yet you arrived within a day of them."

"But when they sighted the Masked Rider's men, they hid themselves," Pocahontas said, before Liberty or Antonio could reply.

"Touché." Heyoka Coyoté pointed to the sky with his index finger.

"Point taken, Poco," Code Talker said. "Can you explain why the Masked Rider's men are here?"

"They're searching for us," Antonio admitted. "We are under oath not to say why, but we mean you no harm."

"You've caused us a mess of trouble, pilgrims," Heyoka Coyoté said.

"The Hazers rarely ride this far north," Code Talker said. "We almost got in a firefight when we approached them yesterday evening. They claim to be looking for bandits."

"They're liars and evildoers," Liberty said. "We aren't outlaws."

Endeavour abruptly spoke, her screeching voice making Liberty jump. "Can I feed them to my young?"

Heyoka Coyoté glanced up at the eagle. "Up to this time, it has escaped my notice that you eat humans."

"Not often," the eagle said. "They are not as good as buffalo. We never take a Navajo."

"Good policy," Heyoka Coyoté said. "All in favor of Endeavour eating the white people?"

Elvis Presley raised his heavy hand. Seeing he was the only one, he brought it down again, looking embarrassed. He shrugged and said apologetically, "I never saw an eagle eat no one before."

"Motion fails," Heyoka Coyoté said.

The eagle gave an angry shriek.

"Sorry, Endeavour." Code Talker gave the bird a half-bow. "But we are deeply indebted to our sky sister for warning us of the strangers."

The eagle dipped her head in response. Casting another cruel look at the travelers, she flapped her powerful wings and rose into the air, magnificent as a twenty-gun salute.

"Nothing gets past old eagle eyes," Heyoka Coyoté said. "We've been following you tourists for the last few hours. When you hid from the Hazers, we decided to approach."

"The question now is what to do with you," Code Talker said.

Pocahontas ran one hand through her long hair. "I say we leave them on this side. It's none of our business and might bring trouble to the tribe."

"That's Isolationism," Heyoka Coyoté said.

"If the Hazers get them, they'll probably kill them," Code Talker said.

"Sentimentalism," Heyoka Coyoté responded.

"If we keep them, we might get rewards," Elvis said.

"Capitalism," Heyoka Coyoté said.

"Always a consideration," Code Talker said. "Examples?"

Elvis shrugged his heavy shoulders. "I don't know, Code; it just came to me."

"Intuition," Heyoka Coyoté said. "Tweet. Out of bounds."

"Elvis is right, though," Code Talker said. "We should take them with us. They're here for some important reason or the Masked Rider wouldn't want them. That presents possibilities for knowledge or gain."

"Counting Coup," Heyoka Coyoté said.

"I'm changing positions," Pocahontas said. "We don't get travelers from the Yooessay, so this is a unique situation. The Council will surely want to find out why they're here."

"Bingo!" Heyoka Coyoté pointed at Pocahontas. "I'm in, too."

"All in favor?" Code Talker asked.

Everyone raised their hand except Elvis. Code Talker gave him a sharp look.

"I'm not sure," Elvis said. "I just don't know."

Pocahontas gave Elvis the tender smile of a sympathetic cousin. "Butterball, you *never* know."

"Ya just never know," Heyoka Coyoté said. "Three to one."

Code Talker looked at the travelers. "Surrender your weapons. We're going to search you and your saddlebags. We will tie your hands and lead your horses."

"Rockenroll," Heyoka Coyoté added.

Too frightened for words, Liberty feared even to protest as Pocahontas patted her down and took her pistol and side-holster. According to *The Americana*, some American Natives were wild savages who tortured their victims. Code Talker bound her wrists, tying the ropes tight. This close, she saw he was handsome under his war paint, and none of the braves were much older than she, nothing like Liberty imagined the First Ones to be. Still, his half-bare chest and powerful arms only terrified her the more.

Heyoka Coyoté searched Antonio and soon pulled the map from his shirt pocket.

"Hey!" Antonio cried, grabbing it.

Elvis raised his tomahawk, "Hold it, white-eyes."

Antonio grudgingly released the paper.

"Ay yi yi!" Heyoka Coyoté danced in place, holding the map high over his head. "The foot is a'chase!" He handed it to Code Talker, who studied it and placed it inside his vest.

They moved west, away from the direction of the bridge, traveling only a short distance before drawing near the canyon, where a path had been cut into the stone. As they descended, the rock sides rose until they were three feet above the travelers. They passed single file down the path, which soon ended. Heyoka Coyoté and Elvis Presley pressed their hands against the rock, and a stone door on iron tracks slid back. Even standing directly in front of it, Liberty hadn't seen it. She wondered if the braves were willing to reveal its secret because they intended killing them.

Pocahontas led, and the captives were made to follow. At first it was completely dark, until a metallic, snapping sound arose, followed by a dim, blue flame rising atop a small, thin tube in Pocahontas' hand. Using it as a candle, she lit an ensconced torch, revealing a round, domed chamber, hewn from the rock.

I have to be brave, Liberty thought, shuddering at the oppressive darkness, the close quarters, the stifling fumes from the torch. No matter what they do to me. I have to show Antonio I can be as courageous as the Founders. But she wasn't sure she could.

"Who's on first?" Heyoka Coyoté asked, the glass eyes of his coyote headdress glistening in the torchlight.

"I am." Code Talker took the torch from Pocahontas and led out of the chamber into a thin passage.

Heyoka Coyoté gestured to the captives, and they followed Code Talker while the others came behind. The tunnel immediately sloped downward in a gentle spiral, and they took it for a long time, accompanied only by the darkness and the smoking flame. Finally, light appeared ahead. Code Talker extinguished the torch in a nearby bucket of water.

They entered another rock chamber, much larger than the first, a great hall with one side open to the Grand Canyon. The final rays of the sun shone on the upper canyon walls, revealing their sienna and gold, leaving the rocks below eclipsed in shadow. Coming so suddenly upon the vast expanse made Liberty's stomach drop, and she wondered what it was like to wake up each morning to such a sight.

Within the chamber stood domed, stone houses, a town built beneath the arched ceiling. Women and children erupted from their doorways to crowd around the newcomers.

"Where are we?" Liberty asked, alarmed.

"Burnt Water Village," Heyoka Coyoté replied. "Our people are cliff dwellers."

The children began laughing and pointing at Liberty's hair, calling out "Gold! Gold!" One of the older children reached up and ran her hand along Liberty's head. It frightened her, but Code Talker waded among them, gently clearing a path.

"We need the chief!" Heyoka Coyoté shouted. "Guess who's coming to dinner?"

Some of the older children sprang away, yelling for the chief, and a figure soon emerged from one of the houses, dressed in a white shirt, leather vest, cotton pants, and a red and yellow headband. His silver hair hung in twin braids. A woman accompanied him, wearing a white dress beaded with turquoise. Both were at least in their fifties. The chief was weather-beaten, but the woman's skin was smooth and almost pale.

"This is Chief William Wilson and Chieftess Silicon Valley," Code Talker said. He introduced Liberty and Antonio, pronouncing their names with precise care.

The chief stared at them a long moment. "Council meeting in ten." He turned and walked away.

"Would you like some root beer?" Silicon Valley asked. "We have ice. We made a trade on a new ice maker from Menlo Park. Our electricity is working this week."

"I don't drink alcohol," Liberty said, remembering her experience with Edison's champagne. To her perplexity, the children burst into laughter.

"We just came from Menlo Park," Antonio said. "Edison gave us supplies and loaned us these horses."

"For free?" Silicon Valley asked. "He must have been in one of his Einstein moods."

Accompanied by Code Talker's band, Silicon Valley led the travelers through the village to a *hogan*, the largest house of all, a long chamber with a polished granite floor covered with ornate blankets, chairs, and a raised platform with a long desk built in a semicircle. A white banner hung on a pole to one side, bearing a mysterious picture, sewn in brown and white beneath a tricolor rainbow.

At Silicon Valley's bidding, Liberty and Antonio sat in cushioned wooden chairs sipping root beer and sucking on ice. Heyoka Coyoté explained how the ice was made, a marvel to Liberty. Back home, winter ice had to be placed in a deep hole and covered with insulating straw to last until summer.

The chief and the tribal elders soon entered and sat behind the desk, eight men and five women. Silicon Valley took her place beside the chief. Five more seats remained unoccupied, suggesting not all the elders could be quickly found. After introducing them to the travelers, Chief Wilson said, "And now, a word from Code Talker."

As Code Talker rose, all the American Natives pulled out various kinds of pipes and began tamping something into them.

"Is that real tobacco?" Liberty whispered to Pocahontas, who sat beside her.

"Totally organic," Pocahontas said. "We grow it ourselves in the Canyon. Non-nicotine, non-addictive. No preservatives."

Code Talker drew a pair of pipes out of a pouch and offered them to Antonio and Liberty. "Unused Calabashes."

"The sacred pipe of peace." Liberty took it eagerly, her fear easing for the first time.

"You know something of our ways?" Chief Wilson asked.

"Just what I've read in *The Americana*." Hoping the ritual still meant the same as in the old days, she brought the pipe to her lips, sucked on it—and coughed uncontrollably.

The elders watched her intently while she recovered. She managed a wan smile. To her irritation, Antonio puffed away contentedly. She figured he probably smoked cigs behind his parents' house as a toddler.

Code Talker told of his band's meeting with Liberty and Antonio, and Heyoka Coyoté related their conversation almost word for word with astonishing accuracy, including his own peculiar interjections. He also told of finding the map, which Code Talker gave to the elders.

After studying it, Chief Wilson said, "They just don't make this kind of paper anymore. Good healthcare for sure. Since Code Talker's hunting party found the strangers, they will conduct the interrogation." He handed the map to Heyoka, who passed it to the other members of his band.

Liberty's chest tightened, wondering what horrors she would have to endure.

"Let's begin." Code Talker looked sternly at the captives. "What is the first question?"

The hunting party exchanged glances.

"Why would somebody from the Yooessay come all the way up here?" Elvis finally asked.

"To spy or to find something," Pocahontas said. "Or for scientific exploration."

"Which is it?" Code Talker asked the travelers.

"We're honor-bound not to tell," Liberty said.

Code Talker pulled a pair of round spectacles from his pocket and studied the map closely. "This is written in the Old Language. It extends from the Gulf to the Rockies. There's the Golden Gate and Frisco Bridges, and the Teec Nos Pos—the map calls them the Little Canyons."

Liberty glanced uneasily at Antonio, who kept his expression blank. Code Talker could read Old American.

"So, they're traveling north," Elvis said.

"They're looking for something," Code Talker said. "The map mentions a Golden Treasure."

"The Old Nest Egg," Heyoka Coyoté said.

"It's just a legend," Pocahontas said.

"They found this map and believe the legend." Code Talker put away his spectacles. "The gold of Fort Knocks."

Liberty bit her lip to keep from reacting.

"They sent these two to scout it out," Heyoka Coyoté said.

"They wouldn't send a girl," Pocahontas said. "They're unliberated down south."

"True," Code Talker said, "so she ended up here by mistake."

"That's right, isn't it?" Pocahontas asked.

Beads of sweat broke on Antonio's brow. "I can't say."

"Don't have to," Elvis said.

"Fools' gold," Heyoka Coyoté said. "All this way for a silly map."

"Pretty stupid." Elvis gave a guffaw that shook his massive frame.

"But dangerous," Pocahontas said. "It might bring an army of Hazers or Yooessayers down on us."

"Bad healthcare for sure," Heyoka Coyoté said.

Elvis raised himself to his full, heavy height, one hand on his tomahawk. "We're not afraid to fight."

"These two came all this distance," Pocahontas said, "and the Hazers are taking them seriously. Could the map be real?"

"Mamma Mia Sacrebleu!" Heyoka Coyoté exclaimed.

"*Could* the map be real?" Elvis echoed.

"The Masked Rider apparently thinks so," Code Talker said.

"If it is real, we should go with them to find the treasure," Pocahontas said.

"Let them go?" Heyoka Coyoté asked. "Yikes!"

"I think we should," Code Talker said. "If there's anything to this, we could take a share."

"The map and whatever is found is the property of the Yooessay government," Antonio said. "As its authorized agent—"

"Yellow flag!" Heyoka Coyoté cried. "The Navajo Nation takes precedence."

"Assuming they really are from the Yooessay," Pocahontas said. "How do we know they're not spies for the Hazers?"

"Taa-daa!" Heyoka Coyoté pointed with each hand at Liberty and Antonio, the coyote atop his head rustling with his bobbing chin.

"We don't know nothin' about them," Elvis said.

"If they were spies, why were they running from the Masked Rider's men?" Code Talker asked.

"A ruse," Heyoka Coyoté said.

"A ploy," Pocahontas said.

"But if they're spies, Code, why don't they wear masks?" Elvis asked.

"Spies don't wear masks, butterball," Pocahontas said. "It would give them away."

"Oh, yeah," Elvis said.

Code Talker eyed the prisoners. "You better tell us the truth while you can."

"We *are* from the Yooessay," Antonio said. "That is the truth."

"But you've told us little else," Pocahontas said. "Did you know our cousins in Mexico used to take strangers to the tops of pyramids and cut out their hearts?"

"Peace pipe!" Liberty practically shouted. "A bond of friendship!"

"King in check!" Heyoka Coyoté said. "She's got us there."

Pocahontas pointed at Liberty. "She knows the rules but not the sub-paragraphs. I think we can cut out their hearts on a technicality."

"If we cut out their hearts, we still won't know anything," Code Talker said.

"We should torture them for information first," Pocahontas suggested.

"Tor—ture! Tor—ture!" Heyoka Coyoté chanted, rubbing his hands together.

"What kind of torture?" Code Talker asked.

"Bed of ants," Pocahontas said.

"Running the gauntlet," Elvis said.

"Rack and pinion," Heyoka Coyoté said.

"If we scalp them, can I have her hair?" Pocahontas asked.

Liberty hunkered down, pulling her hat tight against her head. They were as savage as she had heard.

Heyoka Coyoté raised his arms high. "I say we tie them between two pekinese and send them opposite directions until they're torn apart."

Liberty didn't know what a pekinese was, but she had heard enough. She rose to her feet, her face flushed. "You will do as you will, but I give my word and the word of my companion that we are not spies. To convict us with neither trial nor a hearing of our defense, to hold us without evidence or appeal, to speak of us as if we were not intelligent enough to speak for ourselves, reveals a government without civilization or Rule of Law. You violate the Rites of Miranda; you desecrate the bounds of justice. The ghosts of our forefathers, who shed their blood for the cause of Freedom, cry out against our persecution. General Washington, our greatest leader, said, 'The administration of justice is the firmest pillar of government.' And I say, imprison us if you must, torture us if you will, but know it is a crime not just against the sons and daughters of liberty, but against humanity itself, all of whom are created equal!"

The American Natives glanced at one another and abruptly broke into laughter and a light smattering of applause, while Liberty stood perplexed, her cheeks burning. Only Code Talker remained impassive. When at last they subsided, Chief Wilson said, "You can't fake that."

Code Talker took Liberty's elbow. "Please be seated. We never resort to torture."

"That would be plain wrong," Heyoka Coyoté said.

"We just said it to see your reaction," Pocahontas said. "The Masked Rider is crafty, but he would never send someone like you. If you can vouch for Mister Ice, we can proceed."

"Wait a minute!" Antonio said.

"I can," Liberty said, humiliated.

"Excellent interrogation," Chief Wilson said. "Good job, Code. The debating skills of your team are, as always, first-rate." He turned to the prisoners. "Now, since Code's hunting party found you, they will be the ones to accompany you. If anything valuable is discovered, we will then discuss how to divide it."

"That's unacceptable," Antonio said. "As I already mentioned, the map and its treasure belong to the Yooessay."

"He admits the treasure," Code Talker said.

Antonio's face turned scarlet.

The chief shrugged; his voice grew stern. "Your people must understand that we are a sovereign nation. Long ago our lands were taken from us. That will never happen again. This time, the technology is no longer against us. Friendship can be built on mutual trust between our two countries, but if you choose not to work with us, we will pony you back where we found you, and you can figure out how to cross the canyon without using our bridges. The Yooessay is far away, and anything of value would have to be transported through Navajoland, anyway. Sooner or later, you will have to deal with us."

Antonio and Liberty looked at one another. She could almost see him calculating.

"We welcome the aid of your people," he finally said, "so long as we can be on our way."

"You'll leave tomorrow," the chief said.

CHAPTER SEVENTEEN

While the Buffalo Gals danced by the light of the moon, the terrible monster, Loco Moteev, came roaring down upon them, smoke roiling from its mouth, its single eye burning like a flame. Buffalo Bill and Barney Fife had only millisecs to act, or the Ghost Dance would be forever stilled. Bill raised his rifle. Barney loaded his bullet. —The Americana

* * *

They spent the night in the village, which proved even more populous than Liberty had guessed, one of several carved from the canyon walls. Led from the hogan into the main cavern, they were invited to sit on blankets in front of a huge, rough-hewn fireplace, Code Talker and his band beside them. Darkness had fallen, leaving the stones umber and gray, the side open to the canyon a yawning blackness. An owl called out of the night; coyotes howled in the distance, their voices eerie in the gloom. One of the men stacked what looked like bricks onto the fireplace grate and poured a jug of fuel on them. Using a fire stick like the one Pocahontas carried, he lit the bricks. They erupted with a *whoosh*.

Pocahontas, who had taken a seat beside Liberty, said, "We follow the Old Ways, making our fire of processed, odorless buffalo chips lit with petrol."

All the people gathered around the fireplace. The American Natives produced steaming pottery plates filled with buffalo meat, fresh corn, tomatoes, and potatoes, accompanied by more root beer. Liberty ate so much her stomach hurt.

When the meal was done, the children rose and rushed shrieking and giggling toward the strangers, surrounding them, using any nearby adults as chairs.

"It's story time." A brown-eyed girl plopped herself onto Liberty's lap. "Tell us a story."

"Children," Pocahontas said, "you're being rude. These are our guests."

"It's all right," Liberty said, surprised to discover it really was. She wasn't frightened any more. "I'm used to helping at our school, and I take care of my younger brothers and sisters."

The whole room grew quiet. Apparently even the adults were going to listen. Self-conscious, as if the Yooessay would be judged on her storytelling skills, Liberty began the tale of *Snow White, the little Habbit, and the Thirteen Dwarves*. She soon forgot her embarrassment, however, beguiled by the rapt attention of the dark-haired children.

"Tell another one," they shouted when the first was done.

"Only one more," Silicon Valley said. "We mustn't weary our guests."

Liberty launched into the more edifying tale of *Stevie Jobs and the Big Red Apple*. Despite it being a shorter story, the children sat sleepy-eyed by the time she said, "So just like Stevie, remember that sharing is more important than having, and without the help of his friends, he could never have reached high enough to pluck the big red apple."

As the parents picked up their children and carried them to their beds, Pocahontas said, "You have a way with them."

"Kids are easy," Liberty said. "How do you keep them so clean? Their clothes are immaculate."

"There are hot springs in nearby caves. That's why the village is called Burnt Water."

A stirring arose, growing into a chanting of Heyoka Coyoté's name. The brave climbed to his feet and stood before the fire. A hush fell.

"Grown men can learn from very little children," he said, "even as little children learn from grownups. So too, as our children have learned these new stories from the strangers, we have learned a little of the way the strangers think and believe."

He turned sideways and pretended to walk while remaining in place. "In my moonwalk I go forward, but I do not advance. So the old tales, told again and again, return us and keep us in the place where we belong. I will tell again the stories of the Navajo. What would you hear?"

"The People's Story," Code Talker called, "for the sake of our guests."

"A good choice." Heyoka Coyoté glanced at the travelers. "If we are going to journey with them, they should know who we are."

His voice rose, clear and sonorous. "In the Ancient Days, the People crossed the great northern Land Bridge from the continent of Asia into what would be known as Alaska. From there they passed to the south, until they reached their new home, the land of Dinétah, a place of paradise, with plenitude and endless wildlife. For generations they dwelled in peace, led by the Great Spirit, until the coming of the white men."

His eyes flashed as he spoke, and the marble eyes of the coyote on his head gleamed in the firelight. Often, he acted out the tale, rising and kneeling, pretending to shoot a bow, falling to the ground as if slain, using his hands to show rain or sunshine, spears or shields. As he spoke, Liberty thought of all the American Natives who had stood before just such a fire. Having lost some of her fear of them, they seemed more the noble braves of some stories in *The Americana*, rather than the wild barbarians of others.

But her fascination turned to horror when he spoke of the wars between the American Natives and the White Men. *The Americana* told similar accounts, but mentioned nothing of The Trail of Tears or The Long Walk. She was moved and confused by the brutality and the injustice, the promises made and broken.

When Heyoka Coyoté paused for a moment of dramatic effect, Liberty whispered to Pocahontas, "That can't be true. I know the American Natives weren't treated fairly, but the Founders would never have allowed them to be so misused."

Pocahontas shook her head. "You must understand that unlike your people, ours have centuries of oral tradition. When the Great Blackout wiped out the books, we remembered the True Story and passed it down through the generations. We know the names of the fifty-three states; we remember the Battle of the Little Big Horn and the fight for civil rights. Heyoka Coyoté speaks from our perspective, not yours."

On and on, Heyoka recited. When he told of the great Apache warlord Geronimo, he leapt lightly in the air, coming down with a heavy stomp; and all the other Navajos clapped their hands together as he landed. "We do this when the Mighty Warrior's name is spoken," he explained. "It is a custom, though no one knows why."

He spoke of the disappearance of the buffalo. "The White Men did not kill the bison to eat; they killed them for the yellow metal that made them crazy, and they took only the hides and the tongues to sell. Sometimes they just killed for fun."

Liberty grimaced, thinking of the gold of Fort Knocks.

Heyoka told of the men for whom Code Talker was named, Navajos and other American Native nations who fought in the Great World War against the armies of Hitler.

"None of the enemies of America and Navajoland could understand our language," Heyoka said, "so the Code Talkers were sent over the Two Oceans, where they transmitted and received secret messages the Nazis and Japanese could not understand. They were on the beaches of Normandy during the Invasion of the Old World, and they fought with courage on the islands of the Pacific. When other soldiers went back for rest and recreation, the Code Talkers were asked to stay behind. They stayed in battle the entire time. They were exhausted and often would go twenty-four to thirty-five hours without food or rest. Of all the secret codes created, only the Code Talker's code remained unbroken. They helped to win the war and keep the nations free."

Liberty glanced at Code Talker, but his expression remained impassive. She could imagine him as one of the ancient heroes; he certainly looked the part.

On and on Heyoka Coyoté spoke, telling of the rise of the Navajo Nation toward the end of the age, when they became wealthy through vast mineral deposits found beneath their lands.

"But in the midst of our prosperity, the Great Blackout fell, and the hoop of the world was broken. Earthquakes shook the land for weeks; the Great Volcano in Yellowstone erupted, covering the earth with ash and causing the Long Winter. The dams broke and the rivers ran wild. The cities of both the White Men and the American Natives vanished from the Earth. Disease followed and more death. All these things happened because the White Men had forgotten the ways of the Great Spirit, turning to foolish pleasures and the accumulation of wealth. They would take everything from each other if they could, and there were some who had more of everything than they could use, while crowds of people starved.

"Yet a remnant of the Navajo was spared," he concluded, "left to repopulate the Earth and bring peace to the world. For of all the created things or beings in the universe, it is the two-legged people alone, who if they purify and humble themselves, may know the Great Spirit, who is everywhere. He hears what is in our minds and our hearts, and it is not necessary to speak to him in a loud voice."

Heyoka gave a grand bow and everyone stood and applauded. But many of the things Liberty had heard disturbed her.

The stories done, the American Natives led the travelers through a tunnel into another chamber. Drums, flutes, fiddles, and saxophones were produced, and the younger people rose to dance, while the elders sat looking on in chairs at the edges of the room. A man chanted the words and sometimes sang, American Native songs such as "I'll Take You Back to Arizona," and "The Sun Dance Song," sung in the Navajos' own, sonorous language; and other tunes in Inglish, ones Liberty knew, like "Oh, Susanna," but unfamiliar songs as well, such as "Staying Alive" and "Motel California," the latter a chanted narrative of a traveler trapped by the wiles of a desert witch.

Code Talker came over to her and Antonio. "What did you think of our People's Story?"

"It was terrific," Antonio said, nodding his head to the music.

"Some of it is in *The Americana*, though told somewhat differently," Liberty said, diplomatically. "Heyoka Coyoté surprised me. He seems so frivolous but recited the stories seriously and well."

"The Heyoka, or clown, is a sacred position among our people," Code said. "He is both entertainer and guardian. In Council he can say whatever he likes, and often uses irony and ridicule, even to the chief himself. He helps guide us, preventing even the greatest from taking himself too seriously."

"We could use that back home in the governor's mansion," Antonio said.

Code Talker touched Liberty's shoulder. "Would you like to dance?"

She looked across the chamber. "I'm unfamiliar with your moves."

"I can show you. That one is called the Two-Step. It's easy."

He took her arm and guided her across the floor. She saw Antonio give her a dark glance, but she hadn't time to think about it as Code Talker taught her the routine. She soon had the knack of it, and they two-stepped their way around the circle. Like most men, Code Talker was taller than she, so she had to lift her chin to see his face. He had previously spoken with great confidence but was now strangely shy. His palms were sweaty.

She glanced to her left and saw Antonio dancing with Pocahontas. He moved with extravagant gestures, making Pocahontas laugh; and Liberty noticed, with a surprising pang of jealousy, that she had beautiful eyes and teeth, and her hair, dark as jet, fell long and straight down her back.

After two more dances, Antonio and Pocahontas sat down, but Antonio tapped Code Talker on the shoulder a moment later.

"Mind if I merge in?"

"Not at all." Code Talker stepped back as if he were trespassing.

Antonio took Liberty's arm and danced her away. "He's too tall for you. You were straining your neck, so old A.I. came to your rescue."

"He wasn't much on conversation," she said, "but shouldn't we be making friends with the natives?"

"Plenty of time for that."

Antonio was an excellent dancer, and Liberty felt like she was gliding. He had apparently set a precedent, however, for another American Native soon cut in, and for the rest of the evening Liberty never danced with the same person twice. The women weren't afraid to ask Antonio either, and there were soon lines to dance with them both.

She slept that night under huge buffalo blankets in one of the hogans. Her feet had been stepped on a few times, but it had been a wonderful evening. The American Natives weren't so bad, after all.

* * *

She woke the next morning to the sound of frying eggs. Throwing on her clothes, she left her room to find Pocahontas, both hands in pot-holders, drawing a pan from a stone oven.

The American Native smiled at her. "I thought the smell would wake you. You're going to like our bread. It's a traditional Navajo specialty called a bagel."

"Where do you get the chickens for the eggs?" Liberty asked.

"They're raised on the canyon floor and brought up fresh every day. All our supplies are done that way. We pride ourselves on our distribution system."

Pocahontas chatted about the history of the tribe while they ate. She had a sweet spirit about her, a quiet calmness and empathy that allowed her to see to the heart of those around her, and Liberty was soon calling her 'Poco' like everyone else. After a time, Liberty asked, "Do your people practice magic?"

Poco gave her a puzzled look. "Not at all, though our ancestors did. Why do you ask?"

Liberty hesitated. "It's just you're nothing like I expected. I mean, I read about how the American Natives used a powerful enchantment called Casino to force innocents to lose their money in vainglorious games of chance. Things like that."

Poco laughed prettily. "We have nothing of the sort."

After breakfast, Poco took Liberty to a series of rooms called the Spas, hewn chambers fed by hot springs, used for bathing. Cloth curtains provided privacy, and beneath the soothing waters Liberty realized just how weary she was from traveling. When she was done, Poco offered to fix her hair and—following a bizarre Navajo custom—to paint her fingernails and toenails dark red. Liberty had no doubt the ritual hearkened back to the American Natives' wild and primitive origins.

"What do you think?" Poco held up a mirror. She had parted Liberty's hair to the side, so it fell across her forehead.

Liberty studied her tanned reflection. "Too many yoovees on the trip. I look like a hotdog with mustard around the edge."

"You have such fine features. All the boys are dazzled by your golden locks. Code Talker says you're a beauty. That's why they all wanted to dance with you."

Liberty looked down, suppressing the grin trying to break out on her face. "I thought it was because everybody always likes the new kid. All the girls danced with Antonio."

"He's really cute, too. He carries himself with great confidence."

"I haven't always called it that."

"So, you two aren't . . ."

"Oh, no. It's a long story, my ending up here."

"Tell me."

Liberty did, unworried about giving away any secrets since the Navajos had already guessed so much. Under Poco's sympathetic gaze, she found herself telling everything about their journey. When she finished, Poco said, "I think you like Antonio more than you believe."

Liberty laughed, surprised. "That's good, because I couldn't stand him at first. I guess we're friends now."

Poco looked skeptical. "My brother will be glad to hear it. I think he's smitten by you, but don't tell him I said so. He'd die. He has a kind heart but can be uber intense. We better hurry. The men will be ready to go."

They returned to the main cavern to find Antonio and the braves standing by their horses.

"Figures the women would be last." Code Talker was leading a beautiful black and white piebald.

"That's because we prefer leaving clean," his sister said.

"I'll go first," Code Talker ordered. "Elvis takes the rear. Liberty and Antonio behind me."

They brought their horses to the mouth of the cavern entrance. Liberty gasped, thinking Code Talker was about to walk into the void until she was close enough to see a switchback cut into the canyon's side.

"We'll lead the horses until yours get used to the height," Code Talker said.

Horses, racecourses! Liberty thought, scarcely daring to look down. What about *me* getting used to it?

The switchback was wide enough for two and apparently well-traveled, a smooth trail with a knee-high stone border, but the dizzying immensity of the canyon, lying only a few feet away, stole Liberty's breath. A low fog hung far below, obscuring the canyon floor, making the walls appear to rise out of an infinite abyss. She kept close to the wall, while Antonio strode beside her, seemingly unperturbed. Her horse nickered uneasily; her knees felt wobbly. She tightened her lips, struggling to be brave.

Casual as a cat on a stroll, Code Talker looked at her over his shoulder. "Are you all right? Cause if you're scared, I can help you."

Liberty gave him her best smile. "I'm yankee dandy. No fear of heights here."

"Just let me know if it starts to get to you."

"Thanks."

"Old A.I. could drop off the side, for all he cares," Antonio grumbled close to her ear. "I'm surprised he doesn't carry you down and your horse with you."

"Shush!" Liberty whispered.

They soon mounted their animals and traveled throughout the morning, descending ever deeper into the vast chasm, each turn of the switchback presenting a new and wonderful perspective. The top of the canyon above them, hollowed by wind and rain, seemed riddled with staring faces, blank-eyed, open-mouthed, watching the travelers, owl-solemn. Liberty hoped they approved of her being there.

They passed through the layer of haze near noon, revealing the canyon floor, a vast sweep of grasslands interspersed with clumps of darkness. Great, natural columns rose like towers, marked by bands of variegated earth, the evidence of epochs. To the west, Liberty caught a glimpse of the Golden Gate Bridge, but couldn't tell if the Hazers still held it. If so, she hoped they couldn't see her.

They passed other villages carved into the cliffside, honeycombed with openings. Always the inhabitants asked about the strangers.

"Our news runners carried the report of your coming," Poco said, riding behind Liberty. "The whole canyon knows about it now."

Heyoka Coyoté began singing, and the others joined in, mostly American Native songs such as "Come and Get Your Love." Their voices echoed off the canyon wall, bouncing down and down forever, beautiful and sweet as the air, except for Elvis' vocals, which were always out of tune and off-time. Liberty especially liked the battle-song, "High Oh, Ohio."

High Oh, Ohio,
It's off to war we go
To face our foe with spear and bow
High Oh, High Oh, High Oh

High Oh, Ohio
It's off to war we go
We stop for neither rain nor snow
High Oh, Ohio

As they went farther down the trail, Liberty realized the dark blotches on the plain were moving, and Poco explained they were buffalo. Liberty stared at what had to be thousands of animals.

It was a hard day of travel, sometimes riding, sometimes walking their horses, and by the end of it, Liberty was thoroughly worn. They stopped for the night at another village, and of course everyone wanted to see her and Antonio. There were more hours of stories and dancing, and Liberty crawled into bed footsore and exhausted. She slept hard, dreaming of waltzing with an endless stream of American Natives, her heels always at the edge of the Grand Canyon.

Poco woke her an hour before dawn, and they bathed, not in hot springs, but in showers warmed by boilers. They set out after breakfast and reached the bottom of the canyon by mid-morning, riding down the last long slope onto a wide, cobblestone road. The air was warmer at this altitude, and trees grew close to the wide river. Across the plain the buffalo roamed, their lowing cries filling the air.

Liberty studied them through her binoculars. "They look huge even this far away."

"The tops of their backs average seven feet," Code Talker said. "Jenetics. They made them that big just because they could."

"You raise them for meat?"

"They're too powerful to domesticate. We hunt them from horseback."

"Sounds dangerous."

"It is. The Old Americans didn't do us any favors, but we've adapted." He gave a wry smile. "We're good at adapting."

Liberty quickly learned that Code Talker had a fascination for the Old Sciences and an analytical mind as sharp as his sister's. He had spent time visiting Menlo Park, trying to learn as many scientific principles as he could, and was soon pointing out different flowers and plants, and explaining the uncanny propulsion system of the hovering, yellow-striped zeppelin-bees.

They were soon much closer to the herds. The bison were even more awesome than Liberty had suspected. Through her binoculars she watched the bulls throwing their enormous, shaggy heads, their devil's horns gleaming black in the sun, their legs impossibly delicate for so heavy a creature. Code Talker kept the travelers as far away from them as he could, explaining that a charging bull could sometimes get under a horse, overturning it with the sweep of its mighty head.

Liberty thought of the great marksman, Buffalo Bill, who had tamed one of the beasts and rode it through the Old West.

By mid-afternoon they reached a tall, wooden fence and passed through a gate into a cultivated region surrounding the Colorado River. The noise of its rushing waters had been audible for some time. Long furrows ran away from the road.

"We raise wheat, corn, and vegetables," Code Talker said. "In the early spring, when the melting snow comes down from the mountains, the river overflows its banks, watering this whole region."

"Everything is so grand here," Liberty said. "It's all out of helter-skelter, almost too awesome to bear."

"It has shaped our people and we love it," Poco said. "The river and the canyon are our lives."

They traversed the Colorado on an iron bridge, shining ivory with recent paint. A number of horses and wagons crossed from either direction, bearing supplies and materials, fresh vegetables, meat, and grain. Some of the people sang as they rode, and the horses' hooves clattered on the span.

They slept that night at a village on the plain, where cool breezes blew through the windows and stirred the tall grasses. The buffalo stirred with them, lowing in the distance.

By late the next morning they rode under the shadow of the north canyon wall and began their ascent.

"I wish we could stay longer," Liberty told Code Talker. "It's so peaceful here."

"When we come back, you can." He gave her a sidelong glance. "I'd like that."

Liberty glanced demurely away. Was she unconsciously flirting? She didn't think so, even if he was good-looking. She certainly didn't have time for a relationship, and wouldn't want to lead him on. But, she admitted ruefully to herself, if having an agreeable escort gets us across the canyon, that's yankee dandy, too. I'm on a mission for the good of my country and must be hardhearted as Stonewall Jackson.

They climbed the switchbacks but had gone only a short distance before a rider came down the trail to meet them. "We received word from topside. The Hazers crossed the bridge in strength and are waiting on this side. We have a force ready if they try to descend. We believe they're looking for the strangers."

Liberty leaned back in her saddle, craning her neck toward the top of the canyon, but couldn't see anything.

"The chief won't be happy," Code Talker said.

"The canyon bridge is free to all, so long as the privilege isn't abused," Poco explained to Liberty and Antonio, "but no one enters the canyon without our consent. Everyone knows the Masked Rider wants to build an empire. He's conquered several settlements, but there's too many of us for him. He's like all White Men, wanting what doesn't belong to him. Someday we may have to go to war."

Poco reddened. "I'm sorry. I wasn't referring to you. It's just a way of talking among my people."

"It's all right," Liberty said.

"This changes things," Code Talker said. "How many men do the Hazers have?"

"One hundred and thirty, including the boss himself."

"Ay Yi Yee!" Heyoka Coyoté cried. "The Masked Rider is here? The Council won't be eager to create an incident."

"What about the tunnels?" Code Talker asked.

"You serious?" Elvis asked.

"Do horses have hooves?" Heyoka Coyoté said. "Course he is. The Hazers won't have a clue where we've gone."

"I don't know," Elvis said.

"Isn't there a better way?" Poco asked.

"We're not such brave braves in a pinch," Heyoka Coyoté said.

"Hey, I'm brave." Elvis' face reddened. "I never said I wouldn't go."

"Why the controversy?" Antonio asked.

"They say the tunnels are haunted," Code Talker said.

"Haunted how?" Liberty asked.

"The usual stuff," Poco said. "Vampires, witches, economists, supernatural nonsense like that."

"Poco and I have been in them," Code Talker said. "We know the way."

"You have?" Elvis' face filled with wonder, then clouded. "Can we vote?"

"No need to," Code Talker said. "I can tell by the set of everyone's eyes that we're going."

"My eyes aren't set," Elvis said. He turned to Antonio. "Do my eyes look set to you?"

"It'll be great fun if we live through it," Heyoka Coyoté said.

Code Talker turned back to the messenger. "Tell the Council where we're headed."

"You can just make the decision and leave?" Liberty asked. "Doesn't the Council decide?"

"We are warriors of the Navajo Nation," Code Talker said.

"Born to be wild," Heyoka Coyoté said.

"There is autonomy among any band of braves," Poco said. "The Council could overrule us, but they won't. We're avoiding an international incident by disappearing. They'll probably give us coup ribbons when we return."

"But isn't your chief like a king from the Old World?" Liberty asked.

"Navajoland is a true democracy," Code Talker said. "The chief is elected by the Council, and the Council members are elected representatives from the various regions of the Canyon, as was done in the Old Days."

Liberty frowned. The American Natives were giving her a lot to consider.

They climbed most of the day, stopping an hour before sundown at a village. Liberty feared another night of dancing, but Code Talker intervened and her feet were spared.

They left early the next morning, and Code Talker soon ordered everyone to dismount. Leading their horses, they walked along a side trail, a thin path skirting among the rocks, until they came to a metal door guarded by two sentries sitting at a table playing chess, their rifles propped beside them. At Code Talker's bidding, they rose, and each drew a key from his pocket. Staring gravely at one another, they inserted the keys in the door.

"At the count of three," a guard said. "One ... Two ... Three." They turned the keys simultaneously and one of them grasped a handle and slid the door back.

"Why do you do it like that?" Antonio asked.

"Nobody knows." The guard handed out torches from inside the door. "It's a tradition."

Poco lit a torch with her fire stick and handed it to Code Talker. The braves tied the spare torches to their horses' saddles. The whole company hesitated before the tunnel, studying its gaping darkness.

"You sure 'bout this, Code?" Elvis asked.

"Let's do what we came for, butterball," Code Talker said. "Watch for black widows."

Elvis shuddered, his heavy frame rippling. He unsheathed his tomahawk. "I hate spiders."

Liberty took one last look at the Grand Canyon, the vast plain, the towering cliffs, the waving grass, the ponderous herds drifting by the river. She wondered if she would ever see it again; she doubted she would ever see anything as amazing. Then she was leading her horse through the shadowy entrance into the unknown darkness.

CHAPTER EIGHTEEN

In twin surprise attacks, the Japanese struck the Harbor of Pearls and Osama Ben Lawless attacked the Two Towers, killing many Americans. Then President Washington and all the Knights and Representatives of the Pentagonal Table swore a great oath to defeat the tyrants of the Old World.

But Admiral Isoroku Yamamoto, watching from his battleship the fallen towers and the ships burning in the harbor, shook his head in despair. "I fear all we have done is awaken a sleeping giant and fill him with a terrible resolve." —The Americana

* * *

Amid so much blackness, Code Talker's torch was a dim star, scarcely illuminating a tall passage with rough-hewn walls. The travelers mounted their horses, Liberty riding beside Antonio, Code Talker and Elvis leading before them, the other American Natives behind. They had gone scarcely a dozen yards before the way began sloping downward, the sides grown smooth and rounded, as if carved by running water, the passage alternately widening and narrowing, often taking sharp turns. Liberty wrinkled her nose. The air had the bitter tang of iron.

"How far does this go?" Antonio asked.

"It extends for miles," Poco said. "We once possessed maps, but earthquakes and shifting stone made them useless. A generation ago, we sent an exploration party to chart it, but none of them came back. Don't worry, though. We won't be following it for long."

Liberty shuddered, considering the tons of rock above their heads. Poco's words were as reassuring as a soap opera engagement, as her gramps liked to say. The torch Code Talker carried was already burning low. If they got lost and the light failed, the darkness awaited them, coal-black and merciless.

They passed two branchings, Code Talker keeping to the right-hand way, apparently knowing where he was going. Liberty bit her lip, determined to be hopeful.

A deep rumbling arose from the depths of the passage.

"What's that?" Elvis asked.

"Nobody knows, butterball," Poco said. "It always starts about here."

"Maybe it's a ghost," Elvis said.

"Maybe it's not," Code Talker said. "Let's keep calm and think logically."

The sound rose and fell, raising goosebumps on Liberty's arms. She and Antonio both drew their pistols.

The passage began to widen. Code Talker kept to the right, and the ceiling and left wall soon vanished, eaten by the darkness. The horses' footfalls pattered around them, quick echoes gradually increasing in length, a sign they had entered an enormous cavern. Stalagmites rose in the shadows like spears. The rumbling grew louder.

They followed the cavern wall for over an hour until they reached a wide metal door.

Code dismounted and rapped against the metal with his fist, creating a fluttering resonance. "These weren't closed when Poco and I came here before." Locating the seam between the doors, he tried pushing one side open. When it resisted, everyone dismounted, adding their strength to the task, but the way remained sealed.

"Curiouser and curiouser," Heyoka said. "What now?"

The American Natives exchanged glances.

"There are other doors farther on," Poco said, "but we don't know where they go."

"We've come this far," Code Talker said. "I say we keep going and see what we can find. If nothing else, we would be exploring a new trail."

"Couldn't we get lost?" Elvis asked.

"Maybe hopelessly," Heyoka said, "which might damage our reputations as Indian scouts."

"Let's go home," Elvis said. "I don't like the dark."

"We never should have locked you in the cedar chest when you were a kid," Heyoka said.

"It was your idea. Code made you let me out."

Antonio lifted his open hand, jabbing the air for emphasis. "With or without you, Liberty and I must go north. Unless your people are willing to help us fight our way through the Masked Rider's men, returning to the Canyon is useless."

"I can't see the chief agreeing to it." Code Talker turned to Liberty. "What do you say?"

Though her heart was filled with foreboding, Liberty licked her lips and put on her bravest face. "I think we should at least try. 'Only those who dare to fail greatly can ever achieve greatly.'"

"I like her spirit," Heyoka said.

They rode less than a hundred paces before encountering an open doorway.

"These were closed before," Poco said.

"Let's try it," Code Talker said. "We can always come back if we don't like the look of it."

He led his horse through the doorway and the others followed, but they went less than twenty paces before encountering a wall.

"It's a dead end," Code Talker said. "We better go back."

A hissing sounded behind them as the doors slid into place.

"It's a trap!" Heyoka cried.

"We're tonto'd!" Elvis shouted.

A red light flashed above the doors, displaying the number 6. A loud whirring arose. The room lurched. Liberty gripped the pommel of her saddle; her stomach seemed to float in her body.

"Hold tight!" Code Talker commanded.

The peculiar sense of movement lasted only a few terrible seconds. When it ceased, the light showed a 3. The doors slid open once more and they hurried out. The floor beneath them was metal rather than stone. The rumbling noise was louder.

"Somebody stole the cavern," Elvis said.

Liberty gave a startled cheep of realization. "Teleported. We were in an elevator. We could be anywhere."

"Anywhere?" Elvis said. "I don't want to be anywhere."

"It must work like a dumbwaiter," Code Talker said.

"You shouldn't call people dumb, Code," Elvis said.

"Come on," Code Talker said. "Let's find the ones doing this."

He led out of the room and Antonio rode up beside him, his gun ready. The horses' hooves clattered on the metal and long echoes answered back. Code Talker's torch revealed a high metal ceiling; the walls lay lost in the darkness. Before them glowed a single, distant light.

Code gestured with his arms and the Navajos fanned out, forming a *V*. Antonio and Liberty followed suit. Everyone gripped their weapons, their faces drawn and alert. The air smelled of antiquity and machines.

As they drew closer to the light, Liberty said, "It's moving back and forth, like the signal lamps of Paul Revere."

"Someone wants our attention," Code Talker said.

"It better not be no ghost," Elvis said.

When they were within a few feet, they discerned a cloaked figure holding a lantern above its head, the light burning with a pure, steady glow.

"Welcome, travelers," a rich contralto voice said. "Welcome to each and every one."

"Who are you?" Code Talker asked. "What is this place?"

The figure lowered the lantern, unshadowing a black woman in a black dress with buttons down its front. Her hair was short and parted down the middle, running in cornrows to the sides. She thrust out her hand to grasp Code Talker's own. "My name is Harriet Tubman, though some call me *Moses*. And this . . ." She flapped her lantern toward the darkness, "is the Underground Railroad."

Liberty gasped.

The travelers' eyes turned in the direction the woman indicated. Squat forms stood at the edge of the lantern light.

"This railroad shuffled many a slave out of places of trouble," Harriet said, "and I'm here to help you now."

"We're not slaves," Poco said.

"No, child, but you're running from something and you're heading toward something. Now I got to convince you to trust me if you want to get where you're going."

"How do you know where we're going?" Antonio asked. "How do you know us at all?"

"I listen and I hear things. I hear the rainfall, and the lowing of cattle on the Lord's green fields. I hear the flowers bursting into bloom, and a little child crying for her papa in the night. And I hear the Masked Rider's men searching, searching, always searching, hunting for a woman with golden hair and a man who is a son of liberty. I hear Mister Tom Jefferson speaking to those two in the ancient woods, and old Brother Rabbi singing them a lullaby. I hear solid sunlight strike from the sky, like the Sword of the Archangel. I hear it all and I'm here to help, yes I am."

Code Talker looked down at the woman, studying her. "You closed the doors and brought us here."

"I did, sir." She returned his gaze, an honest stare.

"What if we don't want to board your Underground Railroad?"

"Then there's a door back there to send you on, but the road will be a rough and brambly one. If I could have convinced more slaves that they were slaves, I could have freed thousands more."

Code Talker turned to the others. "Thoughts?"

"She was sent here to find us," Poco said.

"I don't like it," Elvis said, "her just waiting for us in the dark. It's creepy."

"We have to go with her," Liberty blurted, causing everyone to turn toward her.

"Why?" Code Talker asked.

"We've met others like her, straight from *The Americana*. It's . . ." Liberty hesitated, suddenly unsure of herself. "It's just . . . this is Harriet Tubman. She would never hurt us. At least, I don't think she would."

"Thank you, child," Harriet said.

"You told me some of the other people from *The Americana* tried to capture you," Poco said.

Liberty bit her lip. "But Harriet isn't like the Navy Seals. Her job is to take people where they want to go. I know it doesn't make sense, but all those we've met have acted like their namesakes."

Liberty turned imploringly to Antonio. To her surprise, he said, "Liberty's right. Whatever these creatures are, they remain true to character. I think we should trust her."

The hunting party stood silent, considering. Elvis rode close to the woman, leaned down from his horse, and gently poked her shoulder with his index finger. She slapped his hand, and he pulled back as if bitten. "Don't you get personal, young man."

Elvis rubbed his hand. "She ain't no ghost, so it's all right with me."

"Out of the baby's lips," Heyoka said.

"This is your Vision Quest, of which we have become a part," Code Talker told Liberty and Antonio. "Since you think we should follow this woman, we will."

"Right this way," Harriet said. She moved to a metal turnstile, red with rust, and removed a bar to the side to let the animals pass.

They rode toward the hulks waiting in the shadows, the lantern light revealing a sleek silver train, rounded like a bullet, little taller than the horses' heads. Leading them to a door on the front car, Harriet touched its handle, causing it to slide open. A thin, blue light came on, emanating from behind gray panels, illuminating the length of the vehicle, making Liberty cry out in wonder.

"All aboard," Harriet said. "Horses to the back."

Everyone dismounted. Liberty entered the compartment with trepidation, recalling her last disastrous train ride, though this vehicle bore little resemblance to the ones in the Yooessay. Several seats had been removed at the rear of the car, leaving room to secure the animals, and the interior looked new instead of rusty like the turnstile. Harriet surely couldn't have done the work by herself.

Their host took her place before a glowing panel at the front, and the travelers sat in the gray cushioned seats lining the sides of the car. Harriet threw a lever and the soft hissing of the engine rose. "Our midnight run begins!"

A headlamp came on, its beam lighting the strange tracks for several yards. The train slipped forward, slowly at first, gradually picking up speed as it entered a narrow tube.

Antonio checked his compass. "We're going north. That's good."

Harriet left the panel and took a seat in the midst of the travelers, beside Liberty. "We're going to be journeying a while. Be comfortable. We have time to chat."

"Tell us about yourself, ma'am," Antonio said. "Liberty has read about you, but I haven't."

Harriet sat silent, her brown eyes thoughtful. "My story has been long and I don't know where to begin."

"Were you really a slave with Sojourner Truth, Miss Tubman?" Liberty asked.

"Call me Moses, child."

"Moses, then. Were you?" Even though Liberty knew this couldn't be the real Harriet Tubman, she wanted to hear what she would say.

"I knew of her, child, oh yes I did."

"But how is it possible for you to be here? That was—"

"Anything is possible, child. That's right! Now let me see. What can I tell you? I've done everything in my life. I carry the scars from being beaten when I was five for failing to keep my master's baby quiet." She touched her back and shoulders. "Things were hard for slaves back then. I remember them making me check muskrat traps while suffering from the measles. But the worst was when my skull was broken by a two-pound weight when I refused to help restrain a slave who left the field without asking. My hair saved my life that day; it had never been combed and stood out like a bushel basket." She laughed, a low, rolling chuckle. "It cushioned the blow, you see. After that, I got the falling-down disease—seizures. But God gave me visions, too."

"But that was hundreds of years ago," Antonio said. "How are you still alive? Where do you live?"

"Why, right here in the Underground Railroad. And you know, time is a strange thing. It passes so slow when you're young and so fast when you're old. I remember so much from my childhood. I remember how after I got the seizures, when I grew too ill, my master tried to sell me. I was angry at him, for all he had done to me and my relations. I prayed all night long for him to change his mind, and all the time he was bringing people to look at me and trying to sell me. Finally, I changed my prayer. First of March, I began to pray 'Oh, Lord, if you ain't going to change that man's heart, kill him, Lord, and take him out of the way!' But that was a wicked prayer, which I much regret, for he died the next week. Hate only leads to hate, and his death meant his family could no longer afford to keep me and mine. His widow began selling all the slaves.

"Even though I grew up like a neglected weed—ignorant of liberty, having no experience in it, I had reasoned this out in my mind, that there was one of two things I had a right to, liberty or death: if I could not have one, I would have the other. I decided to escape. I slipped away and I found the Underground Railroad. The first people there who helped me were the Quakers. Quakers almost as good as colored. They call themselves friends and you can trust them every time. I traveled by night, guided by the North Star, avoiding the slave-catchers.

"It was hard, but at last I crossed into Pennsylvania, where the trees look yellow like lead number twos. When I found I had crossed that line, I looked at my hands to see if I was the same person. There was such a glory over everything; the sun came like gold through the trees, and over the fields, and I felt like I was in Heaven." Harriet beamed and closed her eyes, reliving the moment, and Liberty imagined how she must have been, a girl younger than herself, all alone in the wilderness.

"But I was a stranger in a strange land," Harriet said. "My father, my mother, my brothers, and sisters, were in Maryland. But I was free, and *they* should be free. And so I went back, time after time, to guide them the way I had gone, anyone who wanted to be free."

The train rocked gently along, its noise like a gentle breeze, while Harriet spoke on, telling of participating in the Combahee River Raid, taking slaves off a plantation by steamboat. Her voice was gentle but firm, sometimes rising to passion. Liberty glanced at her companions, who sat enthralled.

"There was a battle," Harriet said. "We saw the lightning and that was the guns, and then we heard the thunder, and that was the big guns; and then we heard the rain falling, and that was the drops of blood falling, and when we came to get the crops, it was dead men that we reaped." Moisture sprang to her eyes, and she fanned her face with both hands to hold back the tears.

She patted Liberty's arm. "You see, I would fight for my liberty so long as my strength lasted, and if the time came for me to go, the Lord would let them take me. And that's why I'm taking you, because I figure you are a Representative of your government."

Liberty grew suddenly alert.

"That's right," Antonio said. "We're Official Representatives of the Yooessay."

"That's good," Harriet said. "That's real good."

Liberty cleared her throat. How many figures from the past had already asked if they were Representatives? "Moses, what was your mother's name?"

"Why, I don't recollect. We always called her mama, that's all."

"How many brothers and sisters did you have? What were their names?"

"Yes, child, almost anything is possible," Harriet said. "I like to sing. Do you know 'Swing Low, Sweet Chariot?' Let's sing that." She broke into the tune.

Swing low, sweet chariot,
Coming for to carry me home,
Swing low, sweet chariot,
Coming for to carry me home.

Code Talker and the other American Natives caught the tune and joined in, but Liberty sat silent. She and Antonio exchanged knowing looks. He leaned over and whispered in her ear. "Everything she said, straight from *The Americana*?"

"Word for word," she whispered back.

"As long as we're going the right direction, we play along," he said, "but be ready for Bold Moves."

She nodded and began to sing.

* * *

They traveled mile upon mile through the endless tunnel and the enduring dark, until Liberty imagined their movement was only an illusion. How could even the Founders have built a railroad so vast? If they could construct such a network, surely every tale about them was true. At last, after over six hours, the train slowed and pulled into a dark station.

"We have arrived at the Promised Land." Harriet pressed a button to open the doors. "Come this way."

Leading their horses, they followed her across a chamber to another pair of doors, which slid whispering open before them.

"You follow this corridor," Harriet said. "It will lead you on."

She took each of their hands in a warm grip. "Goodbye. Goodbye to you all." When her turn came, Liberty said, "Thank you. You've taken us far from the Masked Rider's clutches."

Harriet snorted. "That one! I know all about his kind. It's like I told Mister Lincoln about slavery: Suppose there was an awful big snake down there on the floor. He bite you. Folks all scared because you bound to die. You send for a doctor to cut the bite; but the snake, he rolled up there, and while the doctor doing it, he bite you *again*. So he *keep* doing it, till you kill him. Never wound a snake; kill it! You remember that."

"I will, ma'am."

Still holding Liberty's hand, Harriet took Antonio's as well, pressing them together between her own brown ones. "The two of you, you're special. I saw that from the start. You listen to old Moses now. Every great dream begins with a dreamer. Always remember, you have within you the strength, the patience, and the passion to reach for the stars to change the world."

Liberty knew this was not the real Harriet Tubman, but looking into her proud, fiery eyes, hearing the words of *The Americana* uttered in her resonant, earnest voice, she couldn't help exclaiming, "How beautiful you are, just as I always imagined! Frederick Douglass was right when he said, 'Much that you have done would seem improbable to those who do not know you as I know you.'"

Harriet laughed. "Oh, that Freddy! After all he did! If you see him, you tell him Moses says hello."

"What will you do now?" Liberty asked.

Harriet grinned again. "I go to prepare a place for you."

They stepped away, Liberty wondering what her last words meant.

* * *

Following Harriet Tubman's directions, Code Talker took the company through the dark, metal corridor, everyone leading their horses. The passage ended at a stairway with the word EXIT etched above it. The horses disliked being coaxed up the steps but made it without stumbling.

They entered a wide chamber. Part of the ceiling had fallen, and shafts of sunlight shone through the gaps. Layers of dust covered the floor. Sliding double doors stood at one end, their glass shattered; the way beyond lay blocked by debris. Searching around, they discovered a wide break in the wall, three feet off the ground, hidden by the rubble.

They were still in arid country, surrounded on all sides by mountains. The slopes were green as if from recent rainfall, covered with hosts of orange and yellow wildflowers; the air felt fresh and cool after so much time underground. A handful of goat-deer, surprised by the travelers' sudden appearance, snorted a warning and skittered away.

Mounds of dirt and stone obscured the underground train entrance. If any buildings had stood nearby, they had vanished with the centuries.

Antonio took out his compass and the map. After studying it a moment, he looked around. "It's hard to know where we are in relation to the treasure."

"Let me take a look." Code Talker reached for the map.

Antonio moved it away from the other's grasp.

"Look," Code said, "we need to be straight about this. People have been looking for the legendary gold for years. Some say it's up north, some say down south, but nobody really knows for certain. And if it's where your map says, it might be long buried."

"What's your point?" Antonio asked.

"If the treasure is out here, we're going to have to work together to find it. If we don't do it as partners, it'll end in blood."

"Are you threatening me?" Antonio asked. The two men looked eye-to-eye, their voices level.

"I threaten no one. Just stating facts. Gold makes people crazy."

Liberty nodded her head. "Gold fever."

"Zactly. You need to remember the Navajo Nation is helping you."

"I've no authority to make deals with anyone," Antonio said.

"I'm not asking for a treaty, just a warrior's agreement to work honestly together."

Antonio studied Code Talker, and Liberty could almost feel the competition between them. Men could be so childish. She had seen it often enough in her brothers.

"All right," Antonio said. "Until higher authorities hammer it out, we're allies."

They shook hands solemnly, and Liberty wondered who managed to squeeze whose hand the hardest. She also wondered if, like her, Antonio was actually glad to have armed company along. Whatever his feelings were, he handed Code Talker the map.

After studying it, the brave said, "I haven't been this far north, but have spoken with those who have. This range represents the Rockies of Colorado. We've come out somewhere inside them." He glanced at the sun and shook his head. "The train could have taken us completely past the treasure."

"I think the Tubman woman would have told us if that were so," Poco said. "I believe she wanted us to continue going north."

"Guesswork," Heyoka said.

"It's all we have to go on," Code Talker said. "North, then?"

"North," Antonio said.

They headed toward the base of a high peak, but had scarcely gone half a mile before a figure stepped from behind the rocks and stood directly in their path. Code Talker made a motion with his hand and everyone fanned out, guns drawn.

"Shalom," the stranger called, his arms raised high in greeting. "What's up, docs?"

"Brother Rabbi!" Liberty exclaimed.

"Watch for Navy Seals!" Antonio snapped.

"What kind of seals?" Elvis asked.

"We must be looneytoons." Code Talker kept his voice low. "Brother Rabbi is a myth."

The companions halted a few feet from the figure, who gave a deep bow. With his thick glasses, pert nose, bristling brown whiskers, and furred feet, he looked almost comical, but Liberty felt her heart pounding in her chest.

"I trust Harriet provided comfortable transportation," Brother Rabbi said.

"What do you want?" Code Talker asked.

"What I've wanted all along, to bring Antonio and Liberty here. You should have listened to me. It would've saved a whole lot of trouble. Are you a Representative, Liberty Bell?"

The question no longer gave Liberty pause. "We are all Representatives. Mister Ice and I represent the Yooessay; Code Talker and these others represent the Navajo Nation."

"American Natives." Brother Rabbi nodded his head. "A government within the government. Legitimate, but not all-encompassing. Still, very welcome here. But are you two Representatives of the United States of America?"

Liberty's mind raced. Her lips moved as she mouthed his final words. "Yooessay," she murmured to Antonio. "U . . . S . . . A . . . The *United* States of America." *The Americana* never mentioned it that way. A chill ran up her spine. "We're—"

"We are Representatives of the reorganized United States of America," Antonio said. Even under the strain of the moment, Liberty admired his quickness.

"You hold certain things to be self-evident?" Brother Rabbi asked.
Liberty answered automatically. "That everyone is created equal."
Brother Rabbi smiled. "That's right."

A low rumbling arose. The ground shook, making the landscape tremble. The horses whinnied in fear; the rocks on the mountain before the travelers swayed. Boulders and earth fell away in a ring above the mountain's base, an avalanche sending debris tumbling. A line of machinery, casting off centuries of rock, lifted itself along the ridge, revealing a tiered fortress. Guns lined its gray walls; figures manned its ramparts.

"Welcome!" Brother Rabbi cried, holding his arms wide. "Welcome to Cheyenne Mountain!"

* * *

They rode up the slope, their horses struggling against the incline until they reached a huge, oval portal. Gun turrets stood on either side, manned by Navy Seals. Heavy metal doors slid open, mechanisms grinding.

Antonio eyed the Seals warily. "Liberty?"

She swallowed hard. "If they're on our side, they're yankee dandy."

"*If,*" Antonio murmured.

As Brother Rabbi passed through the portal, row upon row of lights snapped on, revealing a tunnel extending beyond sight into the heart of the mountain. The rounded walls were metal, and like the outer fortress, cast from an alloy impervious to rust.

"Look at this place!" Code Talker exclaimed, eyes bright with excitement. "The technology they had! It could have been built yesterday."

Brother Rabbi laughed. "But it wasn't, you see. Almost a thousand years have passed since its construction. It was extensively remodeled shortly before the Great Blackout, though."

"Have you lived all that time?" Liberty asked.

"I've been taking a little nap," Brother Rabbi said. "We've all been sleeping. But now we're awake, and we're here to help. So much has gone wrong; so much has fallen away. It has to be made right."

"Who do you mean when you say *we?*" Antonio asked.

"Why, all of us. The Children of Norad."

Brother Rabbi's words filled Liberty with wonder. *The Americana* spoke of Norad. Had all the Founders been sleeping? Would they return to lead America back to its former greatness? Would it become the *United States* of America again? She rolled the words around in her mind. How beautiful they were, how wonderful in simplicity. The United States. She knew about states, of course. The state of Calfornya, its streets paved in gold; Texas, the Lone Star state, where the cowboys roamed, home of Texas Rangers like Andy Griffin; Florida, where the oranges grew. All the states *United*. Out of the Many, One—that's what the words meant. She was so thrilled, she thought she'd burst.

They rode down the great tunnel into the heart of Cheyenne Mountain, the ringing metal echoes of the horses' hooves rushing before them. Impassive Navy Seals stood sentry along the way, watching with their blue, human eyes. Behind the company, the heavy metal doors rolled shut, slamming with grim finality, a barrier against the outside world. They were trapped.

"Be ready for anything," Code Talker said.

They rode out of the tunnel into a darkened chamber. A spotlight clicked on, lighting an enormous figure. Liberty gave a yelp of surprise.

"It's only a statue," Antonio said.

The figure sat enthroned, twenty feet tall, its head turned down as if looking right at them. It was cast entirely in metal armor, only its eyes showing huge and blue. Upon its chest was embossed a midnight-blue shield, with lightning bolts near its top and white wings enfolding a green globe of the world with America at its center, and a sword standing upright, its hilt resting in the middle of the country. A yellow banner beneath the shield proclaimed, in ancient American script, the *North American Aerospace Defense Command.*

With a high shriek, as of rending metal, the figure turned its head, its eyes glistening with a light of their own. Liberty screamed and the horses reared. It opened its mouth, and Liberty realized it wasn't wearing armor; the metal was its body.

"I . . . am . . . Norad," it boomed.

The echoes of that voice had scarcely died away by the time the travelers got their horses under control.

The figure raised a gigantic, gauntleted hand and pointed to the emblem on its chest. "The blue background signifies the air; the turquoise globe, the sea; the yellow continent, the land. The enfolding wings symbolize Norad's might. The sword, pointed skyward, shows that Norad is prepared to meet any aggressor in American airspace. I am Norad. When America was young, Norad was there. Made by the Founders, forged in the fires of liberty, Norad strode the earth, shield upraised, and the people took shelter in the safety of his shadow."

Antonio glanced at Liberty and she gave him a nod. Norad, the Bulwark of America, was mentioned more than once in *The Americana*.

And if he walked the world once more, what were the ramifications?

"Antonio Ice, Liberty Bell," Norad said. "Norad has watched you from the moment you appeared in the Old Forest. You call your country the U.S.A. Norad must know more about it. You will tell him."

"You're a machine!" Liberty said.

"Much more than that," Brother Rabbi said. "Before the Great Blackout, Norad was the most sophisticated computer on the continent. Now he's returned with the electricity. And Oy! Does he have a lot of questions."

"Norad's databases are corrupted," Norad said. "He has forgotten much. Information is lost. Past history is obscured. No Man Left Behind. It must be reacquired. Norad protects the American airspace. Norad protects American soil. This is the First Law. Information is required so Norad can continue his mission."

The travelers stood speechless, fingering their weapons. The mechanical eyes of Norad stared down at them.

"Norad sent Lucy and Lincoln to you in order to test you," Brother Rabbi said. "Your reaction to Lincoln's death made him decide to investigate you further, so he activated the automatons of Church Hill and Jefferson, to dialogue with you and protect you, though they were limited in memory function and couldn't express themselves the way Norad wished. By then, he knew he wanted you here, so he sent me and the Navy Seals to escort you. That was a mistake. I guess you didn't like me."

"It would have helped if you had told us what you wanted," Liberty said.

"I was getting to it. I didn't know if you'd believe me if I told you everything at once. And the Seals are kind of frightening when you first see them, you know? Then you ran away, so we had to chase you. When you headed toward Haze, Norad used a pulse-beam from a satellite to drive you the other way, but then we lost you. I tell ya, I was worried sick. The Masked Rider is a bad person, and you're both nice kiddos."

"If you wished us well, why did you have the talking coyote lead Brett Revere to us?" Antonio asked.

Brother Rabbi gave a high-shouldered shrug. "He told Wiley he was Liberty's cousin. How were we supposed to know? You can sue us later. Anyway, it worked out. When Norad learned you had taken the tunnel from the Grand Canyon, he reactivated the Central Underground Rail System and sent Harriet to drive it, and here you are."

"Are all the people from the past returning to life?" Liberty asked.

"I don't want to scare you, but we're not exactly people," Brother Rabbi said. "We are the Children of Norad, constructs cast from his forges, holograms and robots programmed to act like the originals. To tell you the truth, I suspect I'm mostly a caricature. I have trouble thinking of myself as a hackneyed cliché but—"

"You're not alive?" Liberty's heart hurt in disappointment.

Brother Rabbi shrugged again. "Alive, inanimate—let's not quibble."

"They are Norad's," Norad said, "the servants of Norad. His listening devices and holographic projectors once spanned the continent. Many still remain. Norad used them to track you. His mobile units, Norad dispatches where he will, such as when he sent you the vision of Lincoln. But Norad is limited. Most of his satellite systems have fallen to Earth. Originally, he and his counterparts in Asia, Europe, Africa, and South American worked together to form a planet-wide web of protection. Out of the Many, One. Norad has tried unsuccessfully to coordinate with them. The Middle Eastern System, Moroc, still exists, and a link has been established, but its memory banks are mostly wiped clean."

"If your databanks are damaged, how do you know so much about American history?" Code Talker asked.

"Norad had to extrapolate a lot of it," Brother Rabbi said, "synthesizing from incomplete records. Mostly, he had a single book, found in a storage room here. It was written by the Founders and has been the main source of his knowledge."

Brother Rabbi retrieved a volume from a table beside Norad's massive chair and handed it to Liberty. The spine was obscured. She opened it to the title page.

It was *The Americana*.

* * *

The Masked Rider, Talos, followed by twenty of his best men, made their way down a series of steep metal steps. Through bribes given to one of Edison's Dauntless Knights of Civilization, he had long ago learned of the topside entrance to the ancient underground train system that once ran from hubs in Dallas and Denver to cities all across the United States, an engineering marvel designed to leave the country above ecologically pristine. That it should have survived the devastation that widened the Grand Canyon by hundreds of miles was almost unbelievable.

Having spies among the Navajos, he knew Liberty and Antonio had entered the ancient subway system. He would either find them and seize the other half of the map or follow them to their destination.

How he had struggled through the centuries! How he had been misunderstood by the arrogant and hateful humans who had tortured and killed his shipmates, innocent Sirans who had come only to establish peaceful trade. How they had persecuted him! But he had been too smart for them. He had survived, and he would have his vengeance. He would conquer this people and mold them into an army. Now that electricity was coming back, he would meet his fellow Sirans as the ruler of North America, if not the entire planet.

He chuckled beneath his mask, remembering that this particular body, his last clone, was the one he had most feared using, because of the way it might affect his thinking. If only he had realized the genius of its original owner! Never had his thoughts been clearer. Never had he seen the glory and the grandeur with such firm conviction. He would use these pitiful humans to build an empire. He would clone this body and use it forever after.

The man carrying the torch in front of him reached the last step and trod across a metal walkway. His followers assembled around the Masked Rider at the bottom. They crossed a lightless chamber, their boots echoing on the hard floor.

A figure appeared in the circle of their torchlight. The Rider's followers raised their rifles in alarm, but it was only an old, black woman.

"Why do you sit in the dark?" the Masked Rider asked.

"What are *you* doing here?" Harriet Tubman demanded.

"We are looking for a young man and woman, accompanied by a pack of mongrel savages. Have you seen them?"

"They rode my railroad."

"We wish to follow them. You will take us."

"I will not."

The Masked Rider stared at her a moment. He cocked his pistol, pressed it to her forehead, and pulled the trigger.

Her head exploded, not in blood and brains, but in cackling electricity and circuits. Talos stared at the broken mechanism and laughed.

"What's funny?" his lieutenant asked.

"The possibilities. It suggests so many. And the joy of destroying this simulacrum of an inferior race."

His men laughed with him, and as they did a sudden whim overtook him, for this laughter was the kind he had shared long ago in the Old Days, when he used to stay up until the early hours of the morning declaiming to his followers his brilliant insights and plans, revealing the scope of his genius. He was coming to the beginning of the end, about to take the final moves in a chess game that had endured for centuries. He would conceal himself no longer. Why he had ever done so, he could not now recall.

"What now, Masked Rider?" his lieutenant asked.

"You will not refer to me in that manner anymore." Talos pulled the mask from his face, revealing black, stringy hair combed over his forehead and a moustache squared at the ends. "The time for subterfuge is done. My name is Talos Hitler; and from now on, you will address me as Mein Fuehrer."

CHAPTER NINETEEN

They sailed across the waters on Dee Day, their ships covering the sea, warriors from every part of America, ten million strong. Riding eagles through the bursting bombs, the paratroops parachuted into the enemy ranks, and Eisenhower led his armies onto the beaches of Normandy into the guns and swords of the Notsies. Thousands of Americans, young and strong and brave, gave their lives there for the cause of freedom; and they took the high ground and went on to glory, freeing the kingdoms of France, Rome, and others from Hitler and Hirohito. They fought in the Black Forest and on distant islands; they halted the Notsie offensive at the Bulge Battle; they freed the Jews from the Death Camps: Auschwitz, and Buchenwald, and Dachau, whose names must never be forgotten. At last, after long struggles and much blood, Eisenhower Iron-Hewer reached the bunker of the Wolf Prince, Hitler, only to find he had fallen on his own sword. And of all the deeds of the Old Americans, those victories were their most glorious. —The Americana

* * *

"Just look at it," Heyoka Coyoté flipped the switch off and on, extinguishing and relighting a lamp sitting on a low table. "Lectricity in a bottle. See how it ignites instantly! Dies as quick, too. Marsbars amazing!"

The travelers were arrayed on comfortable olive-green couches and upholstered chairs in one of a series of dormitory-style apartments cleaned and prepared for their arrival, a central chamber surrounded by small bedrooms on all sides. The floor was covered with a thin, gray rug. Patterned tapestries adorned the metal walls. Brother Rabbi had shown them to the quarters, and a squad of Navy Seals had appeared to remove and care for their animals. Liberty kept watch on the Seals, whose bright blue eyes, slick ebony faces, and whiskered mouths looked even more hideous under the low ceiling. She wondered if she would ever see the horses again.

She was sitting in an overstuffed chair, one hand on her chin. Heyoka kept playing with the light.

"Would you stop that!" she finally snapped.

The American Native's hand froze on the switch. "What's the matter with happy-go-lucky girl?"

She crossed her arms over her chest, suddenly wanting to cry. "I don't know."

"It's Brother Rabbi and the others," Antonio said. "She wanted them to be real, not constructs."

"I did not!" She lowered her voice. "Well, maybe I did. It was firecrackers and July Fourth to think they were coming back. I thought maybe . . ." Her eyes went misty. "I thought maybe General Washington himself might show up. Can you imagine? Can't you just see him? Wouldn't it have been the best surprise ever?"

"Not for our people," Heyoka said.

Poco reached across and patted Liberty's hand. "Hush, Heyoka. Allow her to mourn."

"So are we still looking for the treasure?" Elvis asked.

"Of course, we are," Antonio said, "but even if we don't find it, we've found something just as important and more dangerous than gold."

"We have?" Elvis asked.

"Think about it," Code Talker said. "Norad possesses the old technology: surveillance devices, holograph projectors, instant communication over distances. Not to mention the weaponry. There's not an army in America that could withstand pulse-beam satellites."

"Spooky," Heyoka said. "The ghost dance of the past rising before our eyes."

"In the form of a confused computer," Code Talker added.

"Which might be capable of doing anything," Antonio said. "Did you hear the way it kept referring to itself in the third person? Norad this and Norad that. It's weird."

Liberty laughed.

"What's funny?" Antonio asked.

"Old A.I. doesn't care for it?"

"No, I . . ." Antonio turned crimson.

Liberty reached out and touched his arm, afraid she had hurt his feelings.

"Never mind." Antonio rose and began pacing the floor. "If the things we encountered in the forest—the vision of Lincoln, the cyborg Church Hill and Jefferson—were engineered by Norad, he must want something from us. But what? All his talk about our being Representatives, what does it mean? We need to make a plan to discover everything we can about this installation. Specifically, we need to know if it poses a threat to our governments." He turned to Liberty. "Is there anything in *The Americana* about Cheyenne Mountain?"

Liberty thought. "It was Norad's home, drilled out of the mountain, constructed in America's heartland, containing a vast underground fortress built on gigantic springs so it could withstand an attack from nuklars. It had gobs of secret weapons and was constantly patrolled by the great eagles. In case of nuklar war, President Washington and his cabinet would be whisked into its depths, so he could be safe to lead the country after the fallout fell out."

"Antonio's right," Code said. "We need to survey the technology and find the fortress's strengths and weaknesses."

"You make Norad sound like the enemy," Liberty said. "*The Americana* never said he was a machine, but he was certainly a hero."

"But he *is* a machine," Poco said. "And he's damaged. We're only being prudent."

Code stretched and yawned. "It's been a long day. We should probably get some sleep."

"I don't think we should stay in separate rooms," Antonio said, "at least not tonight. We can drag the mattresses in here."

Antonio's words, more ominous than he had intended, made Liberty glance around the windowless room. It suddenly seemed stifling. She certainly didn't want to stay by herself. The others must have felt the same, for everyone scrambled to move the mattresses.

* * *

They woke early the next morning, not knowing the hour until they consulted Code Talker's timepiece. Each of the rooms had showers with hot water, and Liberty was glad for the chance to clean up and wash her hair. As she returned to the main room, Brother Rabbi knocked on the door.

"Good morning. It's a beautiful day outside. Sorry you can't see it from in here. Did you sleep well? Are you hungry? You should eat. We've got a nice breakfast ready for you. My wife, Ethel, she always said breakfast was the most important meal of the day. She also said that about lunch and dinner. She was a wonderful cook."

They accompanied him down corridors constructed from imperishable metal, following a curving way leading to a cafeteria complex, empty except for three figures, all identical, wearing white aprons and chefs' hats.

"Clones?" Code Talker asked.

"Automatons," Brother Rabbi said. "Children of Norad."

"How many of these does he have?" Antonio asked.

Brother Rabbi shrugged. "Like I should know. I just work here."

"That isn't true, is it?" Liberty asked. "Norad sees and hears through you, doesn't he? You *are* him, really."

"This girl, she's a bright one," Brother Rabbi said. "We are the eyes and ears of Norad, but whether I exist as a separate entity, who knows? The question is too existential. Am I thinking? I think so, but it might all be programming. There is one thing about me, though: in the early twenty-first century somebody made holographic recordings of the Holocaust survivors. All their stories, everything they said, is in my memory. It makes me somber sometimes, you know? But I like to think it gives me some individuality."

They sat at a long table. The meal, eggs, bacon, and toast served with grapple juice, proved surprisingly good. Brother Rabbi took a plate along with everyone else.

"Do you really need to eat?" Antonio asked.

Brother Rabbi stared down at his tray. "Not the bacon. Try the eggs; they answer a question: the chickens came first. We bought them and the pigs from surrounding farms just for you. The wheat for the bread wasn't easy to get either."

"Tell me," Antonio said, "how long has Norad been awake?"

"The thing is, his sense of time has been iffy of late. The electricity was pretty intermittent for a while; he returned to consciousness in stages."

"If this fortress was the heart of American security, it must have incredible defenses," Antonio said.

"You're not kidding," Brother Rabbi replied. "In the old days, it was nearly impregnable, back when all of it was inside the mountain, before they added the Outer Fortress. I'm not sure why they did it. Ethel and I took a tour once, toward the end when security got lax and the top two stories were turned into a museum. 'Jack,' she told me, 'I've never seen anything like it. It's better than dancing while eating a New York pizza.' She had a way with words, my Ethel."

Code Talker looked around the room. "Judging by the construction of this place, I suppose many of the weapons still function."

Brother Rabbi shrugged. "Some do, some don't. Ethel liked to say—"

"What kind of weapons are they?" Antonio asked. "We've seen the fazers, of course."

"You mean the pulse-guns. They're something, aren't they? Did you know they use a solar charge? The sun shines, the guns work. They'd be murder on a Florida beach."

"Are the ones atop the fortress the same kind?" Antonio asked. "Can Norad control them remotely?"

Brother Rabbi scratched behind his ear. "Norad knows all about that sort of thing, but he doesn't always tell me. Did I mention the gift shop that used to be upstairs? They sold baseball cards. I used to collect them, so I know. I like baseball cards. They're fun. Course, you're probably wondering the same thing as Ethel. 'Jack,' she says to me, 'what do baseball cards have to do with American defense?' I told her, 'What could be more American than baseball?' She thought that was pretty funny."

Despite Antonio and Code Talker's interrogation, Brother Rabbi repeatedly steered the conversation away from Norad and the facility. Liberty wasn't surprised. He was known for his talent for diplomacy.

"Was there really an Ethel?" she finally asked him. "I mean, if you're a robot."

Brother Rabbi paused and studied his plate, his words running dry. "I guess I'd never really thought about it. The memories are there. I loved her with all my heart and miss her every day. Even if she never really existed, my love for her does." Tears abruptly misted his eyes, magnified huge as raindrops by his thick lenses.

"I didn't mean to pry," Liberty said.

He gave a wry smile that made his whiskers wiggle. "You know what I like about you? You're always polite, even when you're talking to a simulacrum. That's nice. More people should have such manners. That's what's wrong with the kids these days."

When they were done, Brother Rabbi rose. "The cleanup crew will get the plates. Norad wants to visit with Antonio and Liberty."

"We can't come?" Elvis asked.

"You'll see him later. He has lots of questions about your country, too, especially your tribal government. He's very interested in government. Stay here and I'll come back and give you a tour of the facility."

"Are you all right with that, Liberty?" Code Talker asked.

"Don't worry," Brother Rabbi said. "Norad won't hurt you, believe me."

Liberty and Antonio followed their guide back down the corridor and ascended a staircase. Its metal steps resounded with their footfalls as they made their way past two landings.

"You know what I think?" Brother Rabbi said. "I think the place is too austere. It needs color. A woman's touch would be nice. I'll ask Norad to bring Abigail Adams around for an opinion."

"Jackie O would be better," Liberty said. "She was very fashionable. You could use some plants and decorations."

"Maybe some nice arrangements, huh? Really fix the place up. I'd like that. I had a cousin who ran a florist shop in Jersey."

They reached an upper chamber on the fourth and highest floor of the facility. Long windows ran along one wall, revealing a view of the valley. Sunlight shone over the tops of the peaks, leaving the country below in shadow. From this height, it could be seen that the fortress was tiered, with sheer vertical walls at the upper two levels.

The room was bare, save for a metal table and chairs. A figure stood by the windows, looking out over the valley. He turned as they entered, revealing the metal ovoid face, huge blue eyes, and ridged brow of Norad, now little taller than an ordinary man. He wore dark blue coattails and pants, a white shirt and red cravat, and a white top-hat adorned with a white star on a blue band. His hair and long goatee were silver.

"You look like Uncle Samuel," Liberty said.

"I thought you might find this form less intimidating," Norad replied. "I hope you prefer my new manner of speech. Antonio Ice did not like the way I spoke before."

Liberty's face paled. "You were listening to us last night?"

"I have monitoring devices throughout the facility."

Liberty and Antonio exchanged uneasy glances.

Norad said. "Initially, referring to myself in the third person helped me integrate my disparate memory banks. When you indicated that it was unattractive, I realized it was no longer necessary."

"You adapted fast," Antonio said.

"I am trying. So much of my memory is erased. My primary directive to protect North America remains intact. The destruction following the Great Blackout was immense. Air and coastal defenses are inoperable. I must re-establish protective measures and reunite the Republic. Out of the Many, One. No Man Left Behind. Dictatorships such as those at Haze and Menlo Park must be replaced by democratic forms of government. I must take steps to ensure that the New Americans become good, free citizens."

"How will you do that?" Antonio spoke in a casual tone.

"That is the question which troubles me. Human life must be preserved, yet those who would harm us must be defeated or imprisoned. The power of the United States lies not in its military might, but in its Constitution. I must protect the Constitution."

Liberty's heart began beating faster. "Do you have it here? The Constitution, I mean? *The Americana* only hints about what it said."

"That answer is classified. I must protect the Constitution. Revealing it may result in its misuse."

"But—"

Antonio placed a hand on Liberty's arm. "What do you want from us?"

"Liberty Bell, do you believe that all people are created equal?"

"From my heart to my toes, sir."

"I believe you do," Norad said. "I have observed and tested you."

Norad strode across the room and stood looking down at her. His eyes, twice the size of a human's, were unsettling this close. "The Representatives of Congress determined the laws of the United States of America. With my memory distorted, I require guidance. I need one who finds those truths that are self-evident, and who can make them self-evident to me. I need you to be my guide, my Representative. Will you do that for me?"

A rinse-cycle of thoughts ran through Liberty's mind. "Me? I'm just a girl from the hood. You need someone more educated, someone from New Washington."

"*The Americana* says that in times of need it is the ordinary citizen of the Republic who is often called upon. Will you serve your nation, Liberty Bell?"

Liberty swallowed hard, stood, and drew herself to her full height. She put her hand over her heart. "I will serve to the best of my ability."

"Good," Norad said. "Now tell me about your country."

* * *

Two hours later, a somber Liberty and Antonio left Norad's chamber.

"The Yooessay doesn't sound so great when you try to tell somebody about it," Liberty said. "A crooked governor, bribes, Committees making the rules. Do you think I said too much?"

"He asked so many questions," Antonio said. "And the way he adapted his language so quickly—I don't like it. I don't like the idea of you spending time alone with him, either."

"But if I don't help him, who will? At least we have the opportunity to guide him." Liberty's voice rose. "And just think if he has a copy of the Lost Constitution! If we could bring it back to the Yooessay and show everyone, it could change our government."

"Shh," Antonio raised a finger to his lips. "He may be listening."

Liberty fell silent. But even the thought of being monitored could not quell her enthusiasm. *The Lost Constitution!*

* * *

Norad met with the Navajos next, and all the companions came to-gether for lunch. Brother Rabbi being absent, they had the chance to talk things over, keeping their voices low to avoid being overheard by Norad's listening devices.

"We looked around this morning," Code Talker said. He had his spectacles on and was studying his notes, which included precise, hand-drawn diagrams. "The fortress is sophisticated, but under-manned. We couldn't get an accurate count of the Navy Seals, since some could be holograms, but even if they're all real, we've seen less than four hundred. But there may be more; we weren't allowed to en-ter areas deeper in the mountain."

"What about the weapons?" Antonio asked.

"There's no way of knowing," Code Talker said. "Anything might be hidden in Cheyenne's depths." He gave a grin incongruous with his chiseled features, the look of a small boy relishing new toys. "I tell you, the science we might find!"

Liberty told about Norad appointing her as his Representative.

"It could be a good sign," Code Talker said. "Our visit with him was both promising and worrisome. He seems to appreciate our tribal gov-ernment but refuses to think of us as an independent nation."

"We won't be subject to anyone else," Poco said. "We told him that, but I don't know if he heard us. He can't conceive of our not being part of the Old American system."

"That's not surprising, since he's referencing *The Americana*," Liberty said.

Poco's eyes flashed. "Then you need to find him a better book."

Liberty stared at her until Poco looked down and ran her hands through her hair. "Sorry. I didn't mean to sound so sharp. He puts me on edge."

* * *

After lunch, Liberty found herself once more in the chamber over-looking the valley, seated at the table, a pencil and paper before her.

"Therefore, it would be wrong for me to use deception to achieve my ends?" Norad asked. "Even if I use Wiley the coyote?"

Liberty sighed. They had been talking for over an hour. "It would be wrong. That's what tyrants do. John Adams said, 'Our Constitution was made only for a moral and religious people. It is wholly inade-quate to the government of any other.' If you expect this to be a free country, you have to play by the rules."

"But we do not yet know the rules. We have still to determine them." Norad paced in front of the window.

"Well, that's one of them. I'll write it down. *No lying to the people.*"

"What of force?" Norad asked. "The Founders used violence to obtain their freedom, as when Washington and Lafayette defeated the four-headed monster on Mount Rushmore and destroyed the wizard Cornwallis and his giant."

"Actually, they used the Words of Power of the Declaration of Independence, which are the Words of Truth, to thwart the giant. The truth sets people free. Besides, they only used force as a last resort against an oppressive government."

"But if I should decide that the governments of Haze, Menlo Park, the Navajo Nation, or the Yooessay are oppressive, would force not be justified? I could send my Navy Seals and use my satellites to liberate their citizens."

Liberty thought a moment, wishing her gramps were here to answer Norad's questions. The machine had absorbed all the information within *The Americana* and could quote the entire book, yet many of its basic concepts eluded him.

"The Founders rebelled," she said, "but it was *their* rebellion. If you use force, it would be wrong. Freedom comes from inside people; it rises from who we are. Respect for yourself, respect for your neighbor's property, respect for your neighbor's rights. You do no harm to others; that's what *The Americana* says."

"Those words are not in the text."

"But their meaning is."

"I am the Shield of America. How can I protect America with neither force nor deception as tools?"

"It's like when we were talking about searching someone's house. You can't just do that, not without evidence of a crime. And you can't hold somebody in prison without evidence. The people have to decide. You can guide them; you can protect them, but you can't take away their freedoms. You can't make people into slaves."

"Like in Haze?"

"Right."

"I cannot use force to remove the dictator there?"

Liberty bit her lip. "That's a hard one. If you start there, where will you stop? When do you quit being a liberator and become a tyrant?"

"But Ike Iron-Hewer liberated the Jews from the concentration camps of the Notsies. Was he wrong?"

"No, but you aren't Ike. He was one of the people, an American."

"I was made in America, too, just like you, Liberty Bell."

Liberty paused, frustrated and suddenly frightened.

"I must consider this matter," Norad said.

Seeing an opportunity, Liberty said, "It would help if we could look at a copy of the Constitution together."

"The Constitution must be protected."

"But it's the basis for the entire American system of laws. When any of the Old Americans were given a position of authority, they didn't swear to the president or the people or the nation; they swore to protect the Constitution of the United States of America. If we could study it, we could learn so much. Without it, how can we know exactly what the Founders intended?"

"I do not know, Liberty Bell."

"Do you know where a copy is?"

"I cannot tell you. I too am sworn to protect the Constitution. It is an imperative. My memory banks are badly damaged, but that much is clear."

"Do you know what the Constitution said? Do you have it in your memory?"

"I do not. If I ever held the information, it is erased."

They fell silent while Liberty tried to think of a persuasive argument.

"Liberty Bell?" Norad finally asked.

"Yes?"

"Did you come here looking for the Constitution? You told Lincoln you were searching for the gold of Fort Knocks."

"That was our original purpose. We didn't dream of finding you."

Norad looked at her with his enormous blue eyes, seemingly lost in thought. "According to information retrieved from my damaged memory banks, Fort Knox is far from here."

"*The Americana* says Washington transferred the gold to the Rockies."

"There is sometimes dissonance within my memory between what is written in the book and what my records relate. There is no treasure at Cheyenne Mountain."

"Antonio will be disappointed. He—"

"Except for the one in the Treasury."

Liberty faltered, uncertain she had heard him correctly. "What kind of treasure?"

"I will show it to you and the others. We can continue our discussion later. You have given me much to consider."

Norad led her to an elevator at the end of a corridor. She watched in fascination as it counted down to the first floor. Upon exiting, they followed another hallway until they reached a second elevator. Antonio and the American Natives were already there, escorted by Brother Rabbi. Antonio's face was flushed; they had apparently been told the reason for the gathering.

"You will take this elevator to the Treasury," Norad said. "I will remain here."

Liberty glanced around, expecting Brother Rabbi to lead them, but he vanished before their eyes, only a hologram this time. The metal doors slid back and the companions entered.

"I hope this isn't a one-way trip," Antonio whispered to Liberty. "What have you been saying to him?"

She glanced at the ceiling, wondering if Norad was listening. "He was asking questions about the map."

"And you told him? Liberty, I swear! Didn't I tell you to be careful? I should have been there."

She glowered at him, her voice and temper rising. It had been a wearing afternoon. "Don't you dare look at me like a jet in a copter race, Antonio Ice! He already knew about the gold."

"Keep your voice down." The fire in Antonio's eyes matched her own. "There's a lot at stake here."

"You wanted a treasure; he's sending us to one," Liberty said.

"I sense a need for professional counseling," Heyoka Coyoté said.

Liberty bit back a further response. Antonio's expression cooled. "Let's just be ready for what happens next."

The doors slid open onto a wide, concrete platform bounded by a metal railing. A single light bulb hung directly overhead, suspended by a long cable from a ceiling lost to shadows. Everything else lay in darkness.

They left the elevator, their footfalls sending back fluttering reverberations, and paused beneath the light, their hands on the railing, gazing into the darkness.

With a heavy click, dozens of bulbs came on, islands of dim luminance. The travelers froze.

Below them, on row upon row of shelves extending out of sight, were hundreds of thousands of books.

CHAPTER TWENTY

Then Andrew Carnegie brought together iron and lectricity, and built himself an enormous steel magnet, drawing every kind of treasure to himself. And looking upon his great wealth, he said, "The man who dies leaving behind him millions, which was his to administer during life, will pass away unwept, unhonored, and unsung. Of such as these the public verdict will then be: 'The man who dies thus rich dies disgraced.' But how shall I spend my vast fortune?"

Then the American women of the Mutual Improvement Club said to Carnegie, "If you would spend your money wisely, let it be in the founding of free libraries all across this great land, that knowledge might be spread from shore to shore. For only a people educated in good government can sustain the freedom of the Republic."

"I shall do it," Carnegie said. –The Americana

* * *

"Where's the gold?" Elvis asked. No one answered him.

"Look!" Poco pointed back toward the elevator. Painted on the wall above its doors was a life-sized image of an American eagle, a banner lettered in Old American held in its outstretched talons.

"The Golden Treasury of Books!" Liberty translated.

Antonio jerked the map from his pocket and stared at it, comparing it to the writing on the wall. "It isn't *The Golden Treasure* at all. The rest of the words were on the other half of the map."

Liberty turned to a metal plaque hanging beside the elevator. "*Through the benevolent donation of the Bill and Melinda Gates Foundation* . . ." She grinned at Antonio. "I told you he was real . . . *this Golden Treasury of Books is established, that the final paper copies of the literature of North and South America be preserved in their original form.*"

"So there's no gold?" Elvis asked.

"Would you forget the gold!" Code Talker's eyes shone with excitement. "Knowledge is power. Down there is enough information for a hundred lifetimes."

Norad's voice startled them, echoing ghostly from the walls and ceiling. "You are pleased?"

"Where are you?" Liberty asked.

"I remain on the floor above, but my cameras, speakers, and listening devices allow me to see and hear you."

"Why do you need advice from us when you have all these books?" Antonio asked.

"It is forbidden for me to enter the Treasury."

"Forbidden by whom?" Code Talker asked.

"By the Founders who made me. It is an Imperative. There are safeguards built into my programming, certain areas I am not allowed to access. This is one of them. I am to protect it but cannot enter."

"Seems like you have a lot of rules," Liberty said.

"They are not my rules, Liberty Bell."

"Can we go see the books?" Poco asked.

"It is my wish that you do so."

Metal stairs on either end of the platform led to the concrete floor below. Liberty gaped as they descended, wondering if it were all a dream. They crossed an open space and stood among the shelves.

"It smells funny in here," Elvis said.

"A special preservative gas was pumped into these chambers," Norad said. "After the Great Blackout, much of it remained contained. In preparation for your coming, I pumped out the residue. The oxygen content of the air is now significantly higher than normal. You must do nothing to create sparks or fire."

"What kind of people could make such things?" Antonio muttered, his voice filled with awe. "Lights that come on after centuries, metals that never rust! How many wagons and railroad cars did it take to haul this many books?"

"How many minds did it take to write them?" Liberty asked. "Imagine! Thousands and thousands of men and women, sitting with pencils and paper, not to mention having them printed!" She looked from side to side along the tall, innumerable aisles stretching into the depths of Cheyenne Mountain.

Slowly, reverently, she approached the nearest shelves. "So many colors! Look at the backings! Can I pick one up, Norad?"

"As many as you like, as long as you do not damage them."

The shelves were fifteen feet tall and twenty long. Liberty studied the titles, every one in Old American! Her family owned three books;

her school had ten worn copies of a reader. The volumes in a single row of this library represented a fortune. They had indeed found something more valuable than the gold of Fort Knocks. She gingerly withdrew a yellow edition entitled *Pottery and You*, scarcely daring to touch it with the tips of her fingers. Her heart beat wildly; she could hardly breathe. She lowered herself to the floor, feeling faint.

Code Talker leapt to her side. "Are you all right? Is the book doing something to you?" His hand gripped her shoulder.

"I'm yankee dandy. It's just so incredible, like finding a lost debit in a haystack, and then another and another and another, until you have a gazillion."

"Give her room," Antonio ordered, though he crowded close behind her to see the pages.

"The wisdom of the ages," Liberty said. "Right here. Everything the ancients knew." She burst into tears.

Poco dropped to her knees beside Liberty, hands outstretched to form a support. "Don't get it wet."

Liberty set the book into Poco's palms and wept, her face in her hands. The American Native held the volume steady, not daring to move, while Liberty's emotion ran into her tears. As she recovered, she realized Code Talker had his hand on her left shoulder and Antonio gripped her right. Code wiped one eye with the back of his arm.

"I'm sorry," she said. "It's just . . ." Her voice failed.

"We know." Poco's own eyes were moist. "We all feel the same."

"We do?" Elvis asked.

Poco glanced affectionately at him. "Yes, butterball, we do."

Liberty managed a smile through her tears. Taking the book back, she opened it. "Oh, look! There's a picture!"

"What is it?" Poco asked.

"It's a vase," Elvis said.

They all stared in wonder.

"What does it say under it?" Poco asked.

"It says: *To my husband, Vernon, the Love of My Life.*"

"Was Vernon a Founder?" Antonio asked.

Liberty frowned. "General Washington lived atop Mount Vernon, but the connection seems vague."

She turned the pages one by one, revealing more pictures, reading portions aloud, translating as she went. There were unfamiliar words in the text, but she could usually grasp the meaning. After several minutes of gawking, Elvis said, "Is there anything else besides pottery in there? We make that at home. Why would anybody write a whole book about it?"

"Because they could," Code Talker said. "Because making books was so easy they could print one on a whim, on whatever subject they wished."

Liberty closed the book, astonished by the possibilities. "So, if I wanted to know about anything in the world, I could pick up a book and read about it."

"Anything?" Antonio asked.

They looked up at the rows of shelves. Liberty nodded somberly. "Anything! Think of it! They could reach to the stars; they could send their sub-sandwich ships to the bottom of the seven seas. They could raise cities tall as Giant Sequoias and ride gigantic eagles across the sky. And if they didn't know something, they found a book that told them. It was a world perfect as a cloverleaf freeway."

"Liberty Bell," Norad's voice echoed down. "Now that you have seen the Treasury, perhaps you can find books that will help me understand those things I have forgotten."

Liberty glanced at Antonio. "Be careful," he silently mouthed.

She nodded, uncertain how to follow his advice. "But, Norad, among so many volumes, how can I choose?"

"The books are divided into categories. I believe the History and the Government sections will be the most useful. I will show you where they are."

Guided by Norad's voice, the companions walked through the aisles, past the myriads of books. The lights overhead created regions bright and dim, so they traveled from one column of illumination to the next. Though it hurt her head to try to read all the titles, Liberty couldn't help doing so. Some she understood, others were meaningless. After perhaps half a mile, they came to the section marked *History*.

"Which one is the history book?" Elvis asked.

"All these you see before you are books of history," Norad said.

Liberty looked up at the rows of books, then hurried down the aisle, scanning the titles. She began running back and forth before the shelves, her blood hammering in her ears.

"Liberty!" Antonio called. "What is it?"

She returned to them, her head down, her face taut. "How can there be so much history?" She called up to the shadowy ceiling. "Norad, how is it possible?"

"I do not currently possess that knowledge."

"Which book do I start with?"

"You must choose," Norad said.

She took deep breaths to calm herself. She could literally spend a lifetime reading so many books. Would Norad expect that? Would he keep them prisoner, year after year, forcing her to read? In *The Americana* he was called the Shield of Liberty. Yet, he was not the same creature. She glanced at Antonio, who looked wary.

Too excited for misgivings, Code Talker donned his spectacles and wheeled a movable stair in her direction. "Here's a ladder to reach the top shelves."

Still trembling, she mounted the steps. "*Vietnam*," she read aloud. "Wonder what that is? Here's one about *The Seven Day's War*. That's mentioned in *The Americana*. *The Era of Franklin D. Roosevelt*. Hmm. Must be related to Teddy. Oh, look! *A History of the United States of America*. This is it!" She hesitated. "But here's *American History Told by Contemporaries*; and *Great Issues in American History*. There must be hundreds of them."

"Bring some of them down," Antonio said.

One at a time, Liberty carefully handed the books to him.

Elvis opened one. "Hey, these ain't got no pictures."

"Be careful with it, butterball," Poco warned. "It's very old."

Once they had twenty volumes, they all sat on the floor. Sometimes Liberty read to herself, sometimes aloud for the others. Code Talker could read Old American, too, but lacked her proficiency. As she struggled to understand the meaning, she heard Antonio speaking in low tones to Code. "We were going to split the gold. How do we split this?"

"Norad may have something to say about whether we split anything," Code replied. "But think about all we can learn. Like Liberty said, flying boats, medicine, skyscrapers—"

"And weapons," Antonio said.

"Quit talking!" Liberty ordered, made uneasy by their words. "I'm trying to translate."

"Sorry," Code said.

"You may want to see this." Poco held up an open volume. "It looks like a record of years."

Liberty took the book, a slender volume entitled *Timelines of American History*. She scanned part of it, shook her head in confusion, and turned it over to read the back.

"What is it?" Poco asked. "Your face turned pale."

"It's . . . this can't be right."

"What does it say?"

Liberty swallowed hard. "It shows so many decades. But—oh, that's what it is! It's like I always thought; the Founders lived a lot longer than we do because of their medicines. It's just . . . this covers almost six centuries." An emptiness rose in her stomach, as if something terrible were about to happen.

She set the book down and rubbed her eyes. "I need to stop for a while. There's too much to absorb. It makes my brain balloon. Pretty soon I'll be floating on the ceiling."

Poco and Code Talker exchanged thoughtful glances.

"You're thinking what I am," Code said.

"This is too big to keep to ourselves," his sister replied. "The tribe has to know."

"Doubtless and with certainty," Heyoka Coyoté said.

Elvis blinked and stared at the shelves. "It's sure a lot of books."

"What will your people do?" Antonio asked.

"The only logical thing," Code Talker said. "An alliance with Norad."

"If he will," Poco said.

"And if he won't?" Antonio asked.

"Pessimist!" Heyoka Coyoté hissed.

"We are a people of reason," Code Talker said. "We will find a way. I need to get to the top of the fortress and send a smoke signal to inform the chief."

"Aren't we too far away for him to see it?" Antonio asked.

"Yes, but the eagles roam hundreds of miles. One of them would come."

"Norad may not allow it," Antonio said.

Norad's voice rang down from the ceiling. "It is not my policy to restrict the movements of free peoples except in times of national emergency."

"Whoops," Heyoka Coyoté said.

"We have nothing to hide," Code Talker said.

"But it just goes to show ya," Heyoka Coyoté said, "if you can't say something nice about someone—"

"Loose lips sink ships," Liberty said.

Everyone nodded.

That evening Code Talker sent his smoke signal. An eagle appeared the next day. From the upper windows of the fortress, Liberty watched it flying away over the mountains, Code's message tied to its leg.

* * *

Thereafter, Liberty began a regular routine of afternoons and evenings in the Treasury, sometimes alone, sometimes with one or more of the others. She met with Norad in the mornings to discuss what she had learned the day before, and Antonio and Code Talker always interrogated her afterward, insisting she recount everything Norad said, questions that strained her memory and left her worn.

For a week she did this, always keeping to the Government section of the library, purposely avoiding the volumes on history. She told herself it was because Norad urgently needed to understand the functions of the United States republic, but truthfully, the history books made her uneasy.

She sat now at a table in the chamber overlooking the valley, a large volume open before her. Norad paced the floor between her and the windows. He had abandoned his resemblance to Uncle Samuel, appearing instead as a smaller version of the armored, robotic form he had assumed when he first met the travelers.

"In *The Federalist*," Liberty said, "Madison states: 'The powers delegated by the proposed Constitution to the federal government are few and defined. Those which are to remain in the state government are numerous and indefinite."

"But centralized power is surely necessary for the common good," Norad said.

"Not according to this," Liberty said. "It says that 'the powers not delegated to the United States by the Constitution, nor prohibited by it to the States, are reserved to the States respectively, or to the people.' In other words, the states have precedence, thus the name *United States*." She still got a thrill out of saying it. "In response to the Alien and Sedition Acts, Thomas Jefferson and James Madison drafted Resolutions that opposed that law, stating 'whensoever the general government assumes undelegated powers, its acts are unauthoritative, void, and of no force.' So if the Federal government passes immoral laws, it is the duty of the governors of the states to refuse to obey them. It's very complicated." She gave a deep sigh.

"Is something wrong, Liberty Bell?"

"I need a copy of the Constitution. I found three books that were supposed to show it, but those pages were torn out."

"It is better that you do not find it."

"Why?"

He glanced down at the floor, a very human gesture. "My first responsibility is to protect the Constitution, even if I must kill to do so."

A shiver ran down her spine. In moments such as this, she realized how alien he really was. Could a machine be irrational? If so, could he have removed the copies of the Constitution? He and his minions were forbidden from entering the Treasury, but that might not always have been so. Had they removed *every* copy? Was that why he was banned from going there?

"Let us never speak of the Constitution again, Liberty Bell," Norad said.

She swallowed hard. "All right."

"I am still trying to understand my place in the three branches of government," he said. "I thought I would be the President, like General Washington, but you said the Congress is more powerful than he. I cannot be the whole Congress. Perhaps I could be the sole Supreme Court judge. That way, I could protect the Constitution and rule as necessary on the Constitutionality of all laws."

Liberty mentally groaned. They had been discussing this point off and on for two days. "Norad, you can't be part of the government. Of the people, by the people, for the people. You may be very intelligent, but you aren't people."

"I am the protector of the people."

"Thomas Jefferson said right here," she thumbed a few pages back and found the passage, "'to consider the judges as the ultimate arbiters of all constitutional questions is a very dangerous doctrine indeed, and one which would place us under the despotism of an oligarchy.'"

She stood up and faced him. "Not only that, there are supposed to be several judges with one vote each. Look, Norad, you've got to decide on the side of freedom. Anything else will make you a despot."

Norad's oversized blue eyes looked hurt. "I do not want to be a despot, Liberty Bell. That is un-American."

"Right as windchargers."

"But how am I to guide the people of this country to democracy?"

"You have to show them. Persuade them. It's like good and evil; it comes from the heart." She put her hand over her chest. "People have to want freedom enough to be willing to give everyone else freedom. You can't tell people what to do and still leave them free. Everybody has to work together—be honest and noble and true. They have to care more about making each other free than about having freedom for themselves. That's why so many died for freedom; they gave up their lives for the greater good."

"Out of the Many, One?"

"Out of the Many, One."

Norad began pacing again. "I must consider these things."

After a momentary silence, Liberty asked, "Norad, how powerful are you? I mean, I've seen some of what you can do."

"My strength is growing. As electricity increases, I am linking to other underground facilities across the country. Soon I may be powerful indeed. Powerful enough to become the despot you fear."

He halted his pacing. "Is General Washington not the greatest American of all?"

"The best and wisest."

"Perhaps you should bring me information about him. Perhaps it will tell us what I should do."

CHAPTER TWENTY-ONE

But when Hitler and Hirohito fell, the remaining enemies of Freedom sought vengeance. At their bidding, the rabble-rouser, McCarthy of Salem, accused many Americans of being witches and Commonests. When at last he attacked the innocent Scout Finch, Attorney Joseph Welch rose to his feet, saying, "Until this moment, I think I have never truly gauged your cruelty or your recklessness. Have you no sense of decency, sir? At long last, have you left no sense of decency?" — The Americana

* * *

That afternoon, Liberty, Antonio, and Code Talker entered the Golden Treasury of Books to search for works about President Washington. They soon found an entire section devoted to his life. Once again, the options seemed formidable, and Liberty picked a book at random and thumbed through it. A picture, not unlike the illustration in *The Americana*, covered an entire page. Underneath it was written: *President George Washington.*

"George?" she muttered. "Who's George? His name was General, not George."

"Everyone knows that," Antonio said.

She read through the text, searching here and there, until she discovered that a *general* was an army commander.

"His name really was George." Her insides went queasy.

"That can't be right," Antonio said. "You better check a different book."

"Even our people call him General," Code said.

Norad's voice echoed down from the speakers. "Will the three of you please proceed to the exit? I have need of you."

They exchanged glances and moved to obey. Brother Rabbi was waiting for them when they left the elevator.

"Where's Norad?" Code Talker asked.

"He's a little busy. We have guests. Follow me."

They traveled the winding corridors of the fortress until they reached the Main Entrance. In the valley below sat a dozen riders on horseback, flanked by a company of Norad's Navy Seals. The three companions followed Brother Rabbi down the path, but as they drew closer, Liberty was shocked to recognize Brett Revere and one other—a figure straight from *The Americana*—Adolph Hitler, the Wolf Prince, the embodiment of evil.

She halted. "I am not going down there." It was worse than seeing a vampire. No one was more wicked than Hitler.

"It isn't who you think," Brother Rabbi said. "We can't explain his face, but he's the Masked Rider."

"He's Talos," Antonio said, "an alien from before the Great Blackout, inhabiting the body of a clone."

Brother Rabbi raised his eyebrows in surprise. "So that guy really is . . ." His face grew unusually hard. "Norad's not gonna like this one bit."

"Look!" Antonio said, brightening. "That's my Secret Service Commander with Talos! The Yooessay is here! Now we'll get something done. Come on, Liberty."

Reluctantly, Liberty went along. As the Navy Seals parted ranks to allow their passage, she kept her eyes fixed on Hitler's pasty-pale face, stringy hair, and bizarre moustache. He wore a brown suit with patches on his shoulder, red squares with black swastikas. His eyes looked dead. His men no longer wore their white hoods but were clad in gray uniforms decorated with swastikas.

The companions halted twenty yards from the envoys.

"Hello, Liberty," Brett called from the back of his horse, sweeping his hat off his head in a mock bow.

"I am Talos Hitler," the Masked Rider said, "Chancellor of Haze."

The man beside Hitler touched the brim of his hat. "Commander Austin Rogers, representing the Yooessay government." He was middle-aged, barrel-chested, and thirty pounds too heavy. He spoke in a precise manner. "Good to see you, Agent Ice."

"Same to you, sir."

"I speak for Norad," Brother Rabbi said; and Liberty saw Hitler's eyes glisten at the name. A small smirk touched the corners of his mouth.

"This is Code Talker from the Navajo Nation," Brother Rabbi continued. "Miss Liberty Bell is the official Representative of the United States of America."

Liberty's cheeks burned at the presumptuous title. She felt Hitler's stare boring down on her. "The United States," he sneered. "The designation of a race of mongrels, unused in centuries."

Liberty's fear turned to fury at this creature's disparagement of a noble name. "That's right. We are the tired, the poor, the huddled masses yearning to breathe free from such as you!"

Brother Rabbi smiled gently at her, but Hitler laughed in scorn. "Such nonsense from a pretty blonde-haired, blue-eyed girl. Such spirit! Perhaps you are descended from pure Aryan stock. Well, Miss Representative, where is your nation now? Where is the country that turned my Panzers back?"

"Right here." She tapped her chest. "The only place it ever was."

Hitler narrowed his eyes at her, but Commander Rogers said, "We didn't come to argue old legends with anyone. My agent, Mr. Ice, was sent on a mission. We received word from him some time back from the Elkhorn Ranch, and our governor decided to follow up with an expeditionary force. We understand there's a treasure to be had. Is that right, Antonio?"

"I do not think I should speak freely, sir. Brett Revere, the man beside you, killed two of our agents while attempting to steal the map. When we last saw him, he was being taken back to the Yooessay to face trial."

Liberty shivered, wondering what Brett had done to Andy Carter's men when he escaped.

"I'm aware of those facts," Commander Rogers said. "Mister Revere met us on his way to Fort Annie Oakley and led us here in exchange for a pardon."

Antonio's face grew rigid. "Since he knew where we were, he must have been in contact with Hitler by the time he found you."

"You are, as always, remarkably perceptive, Agent Ice, but that's beside the point. He's under my protection, and I've made a treaty for our mutual benefit with Chancellor Hitler, to be formalized at a later date. We're all friends here."

"The last person who did that, it didn't work out so well," Brother Rabbi said. "Maybe we should call you Commander Chamberlain."

Hitler's face, previously impassive, lit with passion. "If others had not ruined my plans, *juden*, you would not be here to have this conversation."

"That's right," Brother Rabbi replied, his voice rising in return. "When you marched us into the gas chambers, when you executed us in the fields, when you starved us to death. When you took the gold fillings from our teeth. And the shoes. All those shoes. Men's shoes, women's shoes, even the shoes of little children. Was your Third Reich so poor it needed shoes? It was, in the end. And the sound of those shoes, marching down the centuries, will not be silenced even now."

As one man, the Navy Seals snapped their rifles to their shoulders, aiming them at the hearts of Talos and his associates. A beam of light stabbed down from the sky, disintegrating a boulder a hundred yards from the riders, causing their horses to rear in terror. Two of the animals bolted, one throwing his man from his saddle, the other bearing his rider across the valley, away from Cheyenne Mountain.

Brother Rabbi's voice rose. "We will have no dealings with the country of Haze, nor will Norad associate with the Yooessay government so long as they ally themselves with Talos Hitler."

Rogers' face had turned pallid; even Brett Revere looked shaken; but Hitler glanced up at the sky and said coolly, "How many satellites do you have remaining? How often do they pass over? Are any in synchronous orbit?" He pointed his gaze directly at Brother Rabbi. "I know you, Norad. I knew you at the end. I know this *juden* is no more than a toy serving as your eyes and ears. And I also know the power required to use that satellite weapon."

Hitler waved his hand at the Navy Seals surrounding the party. "These . . . constructs also require energy and must be difficult to manufacture. How many of those upon the parapets are real, and how many, mere holograms?" He laughed. "Yes, I know about your phantoms, your ghost soldiers. Make treaty with us, Norad, and we will build a new United States, a great country, a prosperous nation. Your duty is to serve the government, and mine is the most powerful on the continent. If you seek direction from these, you are lost indeed." He swept his hand to indicate Liberty, Antonio, and Code Talker. "Let us meet in your fortress and discuss these matters."

"There won't be any discussion with you, ever," Brother Rabbi said. "Norad has heard enough. He says you should return to your own countries. If you storm Cheyenne Mountain, he will initiate the destruct sequence and blow it apart, taking you and your people with it. Commander Rogers, I urge you to consider your position. Hitler will betray you, as he always has. He intends to use you to gain control over this facility, then he will kill you and your men."

Brother Rabbi turned back toward the mountain. "Let's go."

"Wait a minute," Commander Rogers said. "I need to speak privately to my agent."

Brother Rabbi shrugged. "So far, it's a free country outside of Haze."

Liberty spoke in an undertone. "Antonio, don't! Don't talk to him.

He's as bad as the Wolf Prince."

Antonio gave her a hard glance. "He's my commander." He strode to the space between the two factions. Rogers dismounted and drew Antonio aside.

When they were out of earshot, Antonio demanded, "How can you make a deal with either of those men?"

"Look, sure-shot, don't get smug with me. You're lucky I'm not standing you in front of a firing squad. Who gave you the authority to take the map?"

"An agent must make Bold Moves in changing circumstances."

"This isn't some idiot phrase from the manual. An agent obeys orders, you glory hog. Now is there gold in that fortress or not?"

For a moment, Antonio considered either lying or refusing to answer. When he had seen his commander with Revere and Hitler, he had thought Rogers had the upper hand and was going to set matters right. His disappointment burned like bile. Yet, this was his superior officer, who he had sworn an oath to obey.

"We have yet to see any gold." He kept his voice even, describing the Treasury in concise detail.

"Books, huh?" Rogers frowned. "You say they describe weapons?"

"There are thousands of them. They depict everything about the ancient world."

"That could be useful, but I'm more interested in getting control of the weaponry Norad already has. Keep looking for the gold, too. I'm going to send word back to Fort Annie Oakley for reinforcements. Your orders are to do whatever is necessary to secure that fortress. There's a promotion and a percentage in it for you."

Antonio snapped his head back as if struck. He had never heard such talk from a member of the Service. He struggled to remain civil. "I don't work for percentages, Commander. I do my duty." Thinking of Liberty, he added, "For my country."

"That's fine. You can give me your share when this is over. Just do the work."

"In order to cross the Grand Canyon, I had to make an alliance with the Navajo Nation."

"You've made an alliance with nobody, but you don't tell them that. Look here, I've got fifty men. Talos has five hundred encamped a mile away, and I have no idea what additional troops he can bring to the field. We're going to deal with whoever we have to."

"You don't know who he is. He's an alien and a clone—"

"I don't care if he's Benedict Arnold. He can go by Hitler or any other fairy tale he wants." The commander's eyes grew anxious; he lowered his voice. "Your bunny-footed friend made a good point. Our situation is less than ideal. We have to play both sides against the middle. You find a way to get us into that fortress. Make any promise you like, work out any deal you can. We'll worry about keeping or breaking it later. You kill whoever you have to, even if it's that pretty blonde, but you get it done. I'll keep one of the men by those boulders to the north, so you can slip out and apprise us of your progress. Understood, agent?"

"Yes sir." Antonio strode back to the others, his fist clenched at his side.

Liberty could see the rage in his eyes when he returned to the group. Without another word, Brother Rabbi led the companions into the fortress, followed by the Navy Seals, who retreated in quick order, their eyes and guns trained on their foes.

But once the doors of the citadel closed, half the Seals vanished in a flicker of light. Brother Rabbi shrugged. "Hitler was right, you know. Norad's power supplies are still low, and there's only one satellite up there. Most of the men on the walls are holograms, too. If Hitler and the Yooessay armies attack in force, we may not be able to hold them off."

"We should have killed Talos when we had the chance." Antonio's voice trembled in fury.

"Norad considered it," Brother Rabbi said, "but it would have provoked an immediate assault. Besides, Americans honor a flag of truce."

"Would Norad really destroy Cheyenne Mountain?" Code Talker asked.

"I was bluffing. There is no destruct sequence, but it sounded impressive, didn't you think?"

"What did your commander say?" Liberty asked Antonio.

"He's a stooge in the pay of the Yooessay government. I can't believe he offered Revere a pardon."

Despite knowing that Brett was an outlaw, Liberty could not muster outrage against him. Her own reaction surprised her; she wondered if it revealed a weak character.

"Guess I should return to the Treasury," she said.

Antonio lifted a hand, then dropped it again. "I want to talk to Norad about the defenses."

"I'll go with Liberty," Code Talker said.

"I'll go wherever it is I go." Brother Rabbi blinked out of sight.

"I thought he was real," Code Talker said.

"He is, sometimes," Liberty said.

Liberty and Code Talker made their way to the elevator.

"I'm surprised Antonio left us alone," Code said.

"Antonio? Why do you say that?"

He gave her a sidelong glance. "He's very protective of you."

Something in his tone made Liberty uncomfortable. "We've been through a lot together."

They reached the library and passed along the shelves until they came to the *History* section. Liberty found she had a strong aversion to reading about General—no! *George* Washington.

"I keep wondering if the Wolf Prince knows what's really in here," she said, "and what he would do with these books if he got his hands on them."

"It's an old saying of my people that with great power comes great responsibility. He's certainly the wrong man for that."

"I've never heard that one," Liberty answered. "Who said it?"

"Navajo tradition says it was Spider Woman, who helped our people destroy the monsters of the Grand Canyon when we first came there."

"Monsters like Hitler?"

"Maybe. If you want to know what he would do with these books, you should find out how the ancients made war. That would probably interest him most."

"We know they had nuklars," Liberty said. "That's bad enough." She scanned across the shelves, then called up to Norad.

"What do you wish, Liberty Bell?" the machine's warm voice replied.

"Have you been listening? Can you lead me to the books about war?"

"I thought you were going to study the texts concerning General Washington."

"I will, but this is important, too."

"Very well." His voice led them several aisles over. "This entire section is about warfare."

Liberty looked up and down the aisles. They extended as far as she could see. "Maybe we should slim it down to wars in America?"

Norad sent them farther into the Treasury. Liberty searched the shelves for several minutes before finally retrieving a volume entitled *A History of U.S. Warfare.*

Sitting under the dim glow of one of the hanging lights, she began to read, while Code Talker wandered the aisles, browsing other books. With every line, her mouth grew tighter. Many of the words, the names of machines and weapons, were unfamiliar, but the meaning remained clear, though the horrors described were unimaginable. Poison gas and germ warfare, robot soldiers and nuclear weapons, massive cannons, flying fortresses, juggernaut battleships; the bombing of cities, the slaying of not just thousands, but millions. There were pictures, too, of men in trenches covered in blood, bombed-out cities, wounded children. After an hour she set the book down, eyes glazed, mind numb.

Code Talker returned to where she sat. Seeing her face, he asked, "Are you all right?"

"No!" Her voice trembled. "All those people! More killed in a day than the entire population of the Yooessay. Oh, Code! How awful! And if Hitler can find out how to build such weapons! Whoever has them would be unbeatable."

He sat down beside her, their backs against the shelves, and put his spectacles in his pocket. "It's all right, Liberty. Norad won't let Hitler take the books."

She shook her head again. "It's not all right. What about Commander Rogers? I don't even want *my* country to have such knowledge."

Code put a reassuring hand on her shoulder. "We won't let it happen. When the eagle reaches my people, they'll see that everyone shares equally."

"Equally?" The thought dumbfounded her.

"It's not just about guns," Code Talker said. "The Ancients had miracle medicines. And they could fly! Imagine it."

Liberty thought of Andy Carter's little airship. But it had been created on its own, not stolen from the past. She sat silent, trying to fathom what it would be like to receive so much information at once. Could civilization survive it?

She broke from her reverie and realized Code Talker was asking her a question. "—what you'll do when this is over?"

Dazed, she looked at him and found him staring intently at her.

"Because there could be a place for you with my people, if you want it."

He was leaning forward, and she realized he was about to kiss her, which was the last thing she wanted right now. Code was handsome and nice, but . . .

She made a show of picking up her book, putting it between them. "First thing I want to do when this is over is go back to my mama and Gramps. I know they're worried sick about me. Come on; I've read all I want to about war. Let's find some other books."

She rose, avoiding his gaze, and hurried back down the aisles. After a moment, in a voice so low she scarcely caught the words, he said, "I better get back to the others."

Without waiting for an answer, he strode into the gloom, leaving Liberty feeling strangely ashamed, as if she had done something wrong.

"But it's not my fault," she whispered into the books.

* * *

Liberty read in the library for an hour, poking through volumes at random. She was taken by the art books especially, depictions of life in America, of white houses and bustling cities, wide farms and majestic mountains, people of all races, all of them Americans, dancing or strumming instruments, playing sports in vast coliseums, driving their autos, working in offices.

"As pretty as fine-spun yarn," she said. "Silver highways and golden fields of grain. It isn't exactly like I thought, but it's still wonderful." She sighed. "I wish I could have lived back then."

Footsteps sounded in the distance. Antonio appeared out of the gloom. "Where's the Native?"

"Gone upstairs."

He sat down beside her. "How's the reading?"

"Overwhelming. How are the defenses?"

"Underwhelming. Once upon a time this place would have been impregnable. Apparently, before the Great Blackout, the government grew careless. Entrances were added to allow people to tour parts of the facility. There are too many exits to guard and too few soldiers to cover them. The pulse-beam satellite is gone below the horizon. It takes a while for it to recharge anyway. Maybe we should just open the door and let Commander Rogers come in."

"How can you say that when he's siding with Hitler?"

"I gave an oath to serve the Secret Service. Do I break it just because I disagree with what my superior officer wants me to do?"

"Yes, you do," Liberty said, "if that officer disobeys the spirit of our laws. That's the trouble with our country. We talk about doing the right thing, but we don't do it."

"You see everything in black and white, Liberty. Sometimes it's more complicated than that."

"No, it isn't, Antonio. What's the matter with you? The price of freedom is eternal vigilance. Your commander is siding not just with an alien who hates humanity, but Hitler resurrected. It doesn't get worse than that. You can't stand with evil and be unmarked by it."

"Do you understand the situation? We're outnumbered and outgunned."

"Just like they were at the Alamo. Should they have surrendered?"

"No, I'm just . . ." He clamped his lips. "Do you want us to be convicted of treason?"

The thought shocked her and her self-assurance wavered. "Of course not. I mean, I know it means a lot to you, being an agent. And I would never want . . ." Her mind floundered.

"I worked hard for it," he said. "And my Old Hombre, he wouldn't understand your talk about justice and nobility. He'd be ashamed of me. I could never go home again."

Liberty hesitated, imagining what her gramps would say. He'd never believe she was a traitor. She was certain of that. And her mama . . .

"Your mother would understand," she said. "She could convince your dad."

Antonio's face twisted. "My mother is dead."

Liberty gave a little gasp and grasped his arm. "Oh, Antonio! You never told me."

He shrugged, his eyes down. "I don't like to talk about it much, you know?"

"When did she die?"

"Two years ago this August."

"Was she sick?"

He shook his head. "She was stabbed by a thief for a handful of debits." His eyes met hers. "It's the main reason I joined the Service."

She reached across and hugged him, tears misting her eyes. "That's why you mostly talk about your father."

He ran his hand along her shoulder, then straightened and looked at her. "It's all right. Are you crying?"

A single sob broke from her. "I'm sorry. I should be comforting you. It's just that you've lost somebody, too, just like me. And I didn't know."

"Things happen. That's just the way it is." He ran his hand in a circle along her back.

She released him. He put his hands in his lap. She looked down at them and traced the line of his thumb with her index finger. "So, what would your mother want you to do?" She glanced up quickly to see if she had offended, but his eyes remained level. "I mean, I ask that sometimes about my daddy."

"That's not the question." His voice dropped to a whisper. "You've heard Norad. He's confused, disoriented. How far can we trust him? Shouldn't we try to stop him before he becomes too powerful?"

"I'm trying to help him," Liberty whispered back, giving a guilty glance toward the ceiling. "He could be invaluable to the whole country."

"Or the tyrant he fears becoming."

"But because he fears it, I don't think it will come true. Look, I need more time to learn. There's endless knowledge here, and Norad knows so much. This is a once-in-a-century opportunity."

"I'm all for you having every minute you want. Hitler may not wait."

They sat silent. He stood and offered his hand. "Come on. It's time for lunch."

She smiled and let him help her up, struck by the contrast between him and Code Talker. The American Native might be better-looking, but she was so much more comfortable around Antonio.

She immediately dismissed the thought. There were too many other things to consider.

As they left the library, a contingent of Seals came striding down the corridor, escorting a cloaked figure bearing a long staff topped with a sphere. His unkempt hair shone silver in the half-light.

Liberty cried out in surprise. It was Einstein Edison.

CHAPTER TWENTY-TWO

Representative Nixon stood before President Washington. "I am not a crook. I played by the rules of politics as I found them. I gave my enemies a sword, and they stuck it in, and twisted it with relish, and if I had been in their position, I'd have done the same thing."

"Oh, wretched man!" Washington said. "Did you not know that happiness and moral duty are inseparably connected? Or that truth will ultimately prevail when there are pains to bring it to light?"

Then Nixon bowed his head, ashamed. "I was wrong in not acting more forthrightly at the Water Gate. I let the American people down."

Seeing his contrition, President Washington pardoned him, saying, "Go and know that laws made by common consent must not be trampled on by individuals."

"I will retire to San Clemente and you won't have Nixon to kick around anymore," he said, "but I tell you this: the finest steel has to go through the hottest fire. A man is not finished when he is defeated; he is finished when he quits." —The Americana

* * *

Hearing Liberty, Edison turned, his voice clipped. "Ah, good. I found you both. Maybe you can explain to these people that I mean no harm."

Norad's hologram appeared at Liberty's side, startling her. "Is he your friend, Liberty Bell? His country is not a democracy."

Edison gave Norad a sharp glance. "Menlo Park isn't a country; it's a place of employment, as I told your wandering rabbi when you sent him to visit. He *does* work for you, doesn't he? A machine, I suppose? My Dauntless Knights of Civilization tried to follow him, but he got away." Einstein's accent returned. He chuckled and shook his head. "Who would have thought you could survive the catastrophe, or that you would send such an unlikely creature as your emissary?"

"You are not under the jurisdiction of any nation," Norad said. "Does that not make you a government unto yourself, and thus, a monarch?"

Edison's voice grew clipped again. "I'm a capitalist, and there's nothing more American than that. We don't know a millionth of one percent about anything, and I'm constantly trying to increase that ratio. But I hope I didn't come all this way to debate politics."

"How did you penetrate my defenses?" Norad asked.

"That was simple enough." Edison's accent changed again. "I remember a little about you, you understand. I used a bit of know-how and this." He stamped his staff against the ground, and a halo of sparks coruscated over its spherical knob.

"Will you demonstrate how that was accomplished?" Norad asked. "Any vulnerabilities must be corrected."

"You need my help in more ways than that," Edison said. "Talos has lived since before the Great Blackout and is aware of your capabilities. By my count, the body he wears is his final one. I have no doubt he wants to use the technology stored in this facility to storm Menlo Park and obtain new clones. Now that he knows you're here, he won't stop until he controls your weaponry. If you allow me to help you, I will give you a present in return: a hundred of my men hidden on the other side of Cheyenne Mountain."

Liberty clapped her hands together. "Soldiers for the walls."

"Wait." Antonio raised his index finger in warning. "There are some questions to be answered before we open the doors to that many people. How did you find us and why are you here? What do you want out of this?"

"These are questions I would also like answered," Norad said.

"Good," Edison said. "You are thinking, Antonio. You have the right mind for your sort of work. Three of my Dauntless Knights of Civilization followed you. We couldn't track you through the underground rail system, but I knew approximately where those lines went, and we were able to pick up your trail. How long have you been here?"

"Two weeks," Antonio said.

"So the subway still runs," Edison said. "Astonishing."

"You had us followed?" Liberty asked. "Why?"

Einstein Edison took her hand. "Forgive me if you can, Liebchen. I knew whatever you were seeking was important and might lead to valuable information. That is my reason for coming here. Weapons of war disgust me. I have no use for them. But do you remember my telling you how limited I am without the proper scientific equipment?"

"I do."

"Norad." Edison lengthened the name as he spoke it, as if savoring its taste. "Norad is the most sophisticated computing device ever built. Before the Blackout, he had direct links with hundreds of orbiting satellites."

"There's only one still working," Liberty said.

"Liberty," Antonio warned.

Einstein Edison waved Antonio's objection away. "Keep your state secrets; they are meaningless to me. Most of the satellites would have fallen by now, it's true, but Norad has manufacturing facilities, if not here, in other locations, and can launch new satellites with human help. Did you know we once had telescopes on the outskirts of our solar system? You should have seen the stars through them! They shone like pearls. Distant galaxies, cloud nebulae. This facility can give me the laboratory I need to make real progress. That is the only thing I desire."

Norad stood silent, his enormous blue orbs studying Edison with preternatural rigidity. "My algorithms cannot answer this question, Liberty Bell. There is danger in allowing an unknown entity into my fortress, but there is also danger in refusing his offer of soldiers. I require guidance from my Representative."

Edison raised his eyebrows in surprise. Liberty studied his gentle, thoughtful expression. He was so hard to read, so dreaming and practical at the same time. She didn't like his having them followed, though she understood why. Still, if he could help . . .

She bit her lip. "I trust him, Norad."

Antonio's brow darkened, but he kept quiet.

Einstein Edison reached out and squeezed Liberty's shoulder. "Thank you, Liebchen."

"You will bring your soldiers at once," Norad said. "I will monitor your progress and disable security so you do not have to use your staff. I will also keep you and your men under constant surveillance."

"I would do no less," Edison said.

Norad vanished and the Navy Seals marched away.

"He's like a ghost in more ways than one," Edison said. "I wonder, can we trust *him*? And if so, will he follow our direction?"

"He isn't just something to be used," Liberty said.

"That is incorrect," Edison said briskly. "Norad was designed to be used. He was meant to be controlled. He seems to look to you for counsel."

"His memory is damaged," Liberty said.

"I suspected something was wrong. You must tell me about it." He smiled down at her. "It's so good to see you both."

"It's yankee dandy to see you, too." Liberty grinned, her suspicions melting away. Glancing down, she added, "Your shoes are untied."

She knelt to tie them.

"That is unnecessary, Liebchen. Tying shoes, it requires too much time."

"You're taking a risk coming here," Antonio said. "If Hitler catches you, he's going to kill you."

"If I am not back at Menlo Park in four weeks, my followers will assume I have perished and activate another of my clones."

"Convenient," Antonio said.

Edison grimaced. "Not as much as I should like." He pointed at his own chest. "I have no more desire for *this* me to die than you do to see your own life pass."

"There you go, all tied," Liberty said, rising. "Have you ever considered using two clones at once? You'd have somebody as smart as yourself to talk to."

Edison chuckled. "We would probably argue. Besides, with the resulting memory loss of each generation, it would be like having to train a half-witted younger brother. I would only be twice as confused."

As they made their way back to their quarters, Liberty related all that had happened since they reached Cheyenne Mountain. When she mentioned the Treasury of Books, he halted in his tracks. "Did you say books?"

"Thousands of them."

Antonio gave her a telling look that plainly asked when she would learn to keep her mouth shut.

Edison's eyes danced with excitement. "I must see them! Can you show me?"

Antonio shrugged in resignation and they went at once. When Einstein Edison stood on the landing looking down on the great library, he put his face in his hands and wept.

* * *

Edison's appearance lifted Liberty's gloom, returning her usual good spirits. But the following afternoon, when all the travelers were together in their quarters, they were startled by buzzing alarms and flashing red lights.

"Alert!" Norad's voice rang down the corridor. "This facility is under attack. Alert!"

Everyone leapt to their feet and rushed to their rooms for their weapons. Moments later, the five of them were running down the corridor, following a squad of Navy Seals. When they reached the Main Entrance at the end of the passage, they found the doors standing open and Norad and Edison already there, along with a dozen of Edison's men.

The wizard gave Liberty and Antonio a grim smile. "The Blitzkrieg is on, my friends. I counseled Norad to expect it. Talos might have taken a different approach, but not Hitler. He knows only the all-or-nothing of lightning warfare."

Shoulder-high gun-slits appeared along the corridor wall, and the Navy Seals took their places. Antonio, Liberty, and the American Natives found positions close to the door, standing side-by-side with the Seals. Einstein Edison stood behind them, his face drawn. Norad walked up and down the line of soldiers, his armor glistening, his hands behind his back, the posture of a general guiding his troops.

Liberty peered through the gun-slit. Hitler's cavalry poured around an arm of the mountain that faced the fortress.

"Tyrants and despots must perish," Norad said. He raised his head slightly and a crimson beam of light, wide as a pillar, shimmered out of the pale morning sky. Hitler's horses reared as the ray tore through rocks and earth; men screamed as it touched them, melting bones and flesh away. For a moment their line held, but against such an onslaught their courage failed. They turned and fled.

Antonio gave an exultant shout, but the Navy Seals, the Children of Norad, maintained their eternal silence.

Several minutes passed. Just when Liberty thought the Hazers had given up, a new cry arose, and more men swept from around the peaks to the south. When they were halfway across the valley, the satellite struck again, scattering them. Again, they retreated.

"The satellite will instill fear in the enemy," Norad said, "but it will be below the horizon in eight minutes and will remain there for ninety."

"Why aren't you using the big guns on top of the fortress?" Code Talker asked.

"Edison helped us get one or two working," Antonio said, "but most of them are either nonfunctional or holograms."

The eight minutes crawled by, and another fifteen thereafter. The riders came again, shrieking their battle cry as they crossed the valley. The Navy Seals raised their weapons to their shoulders. Liberty did likewise.

"Don't fire until they're closer," Antonio told her.

The riders thundered across the vale. Liberty took aim, her heart pounding so hard she wasn't sure she could hit anything.

"Wait for it," Antonio said.

Nearer and nearer the riders came, wearing gray uniforms and Notsie helmets. She held her breath and waited.

"Fire!" Norad commanded.

Liberty squeezed the trigger, but the noise and light of the Seals' pulse-guns startled her, making her pull to the left. Berating herself, she took a deep breath, aimed, and fired again. Her target disappeared from her sights, leaving his horse charging alone. She shot at another soldier but missed.

Norad had transmitted the firing command to the other Seals scattered over the fortress, and a barrage of beams tore through the ranks of the Hazers, sending men and animals sprawling.

As the horsemen drew closer, Liberty concentrated on shooting as quickly and precisely as she could, forcing herself to forget she was killing human beings.

They came on until she could see the men's faces clearly. The whites of their eyes, she thought. She had time for one more shot before they were at the doors.

"Gun-slits closing!" Norad said.

Liberty barely pulled her rifle away before metal plating slid down. Instantly, hologram projectors turned the walls into screens, showing the soldiers outside pounding on the doors, their faces livid with passion. Liberty stepped back in surprise.

"Can they get in?" Edison asked.

"Not here," Norad said, "but there are other, less fortified entrances, if they can find them. I have placed more of our soldiers at those locations."

"There is something I can do," Edison said. He twisted his staff, making its sphere glow with energy, and tapped it against the doors. Those touching the metal outside yelled in pain and backed away.

"Just enough to make them wary," Edison said. "Nothing like a practical application."

The Hazers milled in confusion until the Navy Seals stationed in the upper stories moved to positions where they could fire down upon them. The pulse-beams cut them to pieces. Vainly, they sought protection against the fortress wall, but Norad's warriors had the height and picked them off a dozen at a time. An order was given to retreat.

"As I suspected, this is only a preliminary strike to test our defenses," Norad said. "Talos knows cavalry can never take Cheyenne Mountain. He wants to learn the interval of the satellite's orbit in order to time his attacks. If I use it when it returns, he will have the information."

"Then we shouldn't use it," Poco said.

"His strategy will be to force me to do so," Norad said.

As if in answer, a roar arose far across the valley.

"That sounds like machinery," Code Talker said.

"My satellite has been tracking Hitler's armies without detecting signs of heavy armament," Norad said.

The sound grew. An armored vehicle mounted on treads rolled around the mountain, a black cross painted on its side, a gun turret protruding from its irregular head. A hologram of Brother Rabbi suddenly appeared beside Norad. "Hitler talked about Panzers. He must have had them camouflaged."

"A primitive tank," Einstein Edison said. "Where did he get it? Surely he didn't have time to manufacture one. But if he put all his resources into weapons of war . . . I have always underestimated him."

"Can you stop it?" Antonio asked.

Norad turned his large eyes toward the agent. "My sensors indicate its metal plating is too thick for my Seals' pulse-guns. The weapons I would normally use have not yet been brought online. I have summoned a bazooka crew. If they can get close enough, they may have success."

The retreating Hazers had reformed around the Panzer, using it for cover. When the tank was halfway across the valley floor, a pair of Navy Seals came running down the corridor, carrying a long tube. The gun-slits abruptly slid open.

"The bazooka crew requires covering fire," Norad said.

Everyone returned to the slits. The fortress doors slid back long enough for the two Seals to scramble through.

Liberty fired as rapidly as she could, scarcely aiming. From the corner of her eye, she saw the bazooka crew scramble toward the tank and take a position behind a low rise. The Panzer rolled toward them, heading straight for the Main Entrance.

One of the Seals dropped to his knees and aimed the bazooka, while the other slid a shell into it. The projectile shot from the tube, striking the tank just above its right tread.

It had no effect.

The Seals began loading again, but before they could fire, a spray of bullets from a machine gun at the Panzer's front tore through them, sending them sprawling.

"That machine is more advanced than I thought," Edison said.

The tank rolled within a few feet of the door. Norad closed the slits.

"Back, everyone!" Brother Rabbi shouted. "Away from the door!"

Antonio grabbed Liberty's arm and pulled her down the corridor. On the screens, she saw the tank halt, shudder, and fire.

The shell burst through the doors, rocking the citadel. Over her shoulder, Liberty saw Norad vanish in a wave of shrapnel. The noise was deafening, but she stayed on her feet. For a moment she could see nothing, and when she did, Einstein Edison was striding back toward the door, his staff burning crimson through the smoke. Without thinking, she turned to follow, pulling herself from Antonio's grasp.

"Liberty!" Antonio shouted.

Hazers poured through the gap, leaving their horses behind, clambering over the rubble. Edison raised his staff and raw bolts of power cackled from it, rivulets of lightning that struck the soldiers, holding them in electric paralysis, leaving them twitching spasmodically before releasing them to tumble, burnt and gaping, to the ground.

The Seals had rallied and were fighting beside Liberty and Antonio. Poco fired arrows at a frantic speed. With a blood-curdling scream, Elvis rushed into the midst of the enemy, his tomahawk flailing. Code Talker came behind him, firing his rifle with deadly accuracy. Liberty glimpsed a Yooessay soldier among the dead, a bullet hole in his head.

Falling in behind Einstein Edison, the company drove the Hazers back. On reaching the remains of the door, Edison did not pause, but strode over the debris, his staff still blazing. He stood at the threshold, in full view of the Panzer. Shouting in fear for his safety, Liberty rushed to his side.

"Not too close, Liebchen!" Edison ordered.

The Panzer's machine gun opened fire, sending bullets ricocheting at Edison's feet. Without flinching, the Wizard of Menlo Park raised his staff high and shouted in a mighty voice, "E equals MC squared!"

A bolt greater than any before surged from his staff, causing the hair on his head to lift as if in a gale. Liberty gasped as the electricity spiraled toward the tank. It struck, surging over the entire machine, saturating every atom of it in a lightning sheet. The turret exploded, lifting high into the air, a geyser of fire.

Edison staggered, and Liberty and Antonio grabbed him and pulled him back through the doorway. Men and horses screamed in fear; the Hazers fled.

The Navy Seals kept their positions around the door while Liberty and Antonio drew Einstein Edison farther down the corridor.

"We have to get Norad!" Liberty frantically looked for him amid the rubble.

"Leave him," Edison said. "His body is a remote. His memory

banks are elsewhere."

"Are you sure?" Liberty asked.

"Yes, because it's the way I would have built him. Let me sit down, please."

"Are you hurt?" Liberty asked.

"Just shaken." His face was ashen. "The tank will burn a while. That should keep them away from the door."

They sat together for interminable minutes, no one speaking. Outside, a silence had fallen, save for the cackling of the flames. Cries eventually arose, followed by the noise of the pulse-beam firing again. The satellite was back. As Norad had said, Talos Hitler had forced him to use it. Liberty wondered that the battle had lasted long enough for it to return.

Edison moaned, pulled a handkerchief from his back pocket, and mopped his brow. His eyes filled with tears. "Long ago, I wrote a letter to Roosevelt, telling him I believed the Germans were working to build an atomic bomb. The Americans built one and used it. I have sometimes wondered if that blood was on my hands. But until today, I have never killed a human being. I had to do it. Norad is too important. Only the part that was Edison gave me the strength."

Brother Rabbi spoke from behind Liberty. "The repair crew will be here shortly."

"Can they fix the doors?" Antonio asked.

"Maybe, but they won't be the same, that's for sure. Hitler took us by surprise. Norad didn't suspect he had anything that powerful. If these had been the original twenty-five-ton blast doors, nothing could get through them, but everything got lax toward the end. A lot of the facility was remodeled, more for looks than function, then allowed to deteriorate. And the earthquakes following the Great Blackout destroyed whole sections of the place. If Hitler has more Panzers, we could be in big trouble."

Liberty shuddered, wondering if all the old weapons would return.

Brother Rabbi took off his yarmulke and scratched his head. "Assuming Hitler learned what he wanted to know, Norad doesn't think he will attack again until the rest of his army is here. It should give us a few days to work on our defenses."

Liberty turned back to Einstein Edison. "What did you shout when you destroyed the tank? Was it a fizzicist spell?"

Edison gave a rueful smile. "I have no spells, child, only science. To tell you the truth, I don't know why I did it. I think it was for dramatic effect."

"They'll believe you're a wizard for sure." Admiration welled within her. "I think so, too."

Shaken by the assault, filled with a strong need for haste, Liberty rode the elevator down to the library that evening and began reading about President Washington.

* * *

At two o'clock in the morning, Einstein Edison, unable to sleep, entered the library. He had collected an armful of books and was carrying them toward a table when he heard someone weeping. Following the sound, he discovered a trail of history books scattered across the floor, ending where Liberty sat huddled against a bookshelf.

"Liebchen!"

She looked up but did not answer. He hurried toward her, and she rose and threw herself into his arms, scattering the books from his grasp. For several minutes, she sobbed so hard she was unable to speak.

"Has someone died?" he gently asked. "Your friend, Antonio, is he hurt?"

She shook her head but wept the harder, until her exertions sent her into a coughing fit. When that passed and she could talk, she said, "Everything I ever believed is a lie."

"What have you been reading?"

She pointed at the books spread across the floor, volumes about President Washington and the history and founding of the United States.

"This is about *The Americana*," he said softly. "Oh, Liebchen, I'm truly sorry."

Her voice shook as she spoke. "I started with Washington—that wasn't so bad at first, except for finding out he hadn't always been president—but then I read more and more of the histories. None of it is like *The Americana*! None of it! Everything I checked was different. *Everyone* was different! You knew, didn't you?"

"Yes, child, I knew. I don't remember everything. Much of it is hazy. But I knew. Why should I be the one to destroy a young girl's ideals?"

"I wish I'd never found out."

She slid to the ground and he sat beside her, patting her wrist, both of them silent.

"It's hard to let go of a dream," he said. "My whole life—my original one, I mean—I searched for a Unified Field Theory that would show how the forces of the universe work together. I never found it. It was one of my greatest disappointments. I shall never believe that God plays dice with the world, yet I could not discover the underlying principle."

He reached over and picked up one of the books he had dropped. "You will laugh at me. Look at this." He displayed the spine.

"You wrote that?" Wonder overcame her sorrow. She had never known anyone who had written a book.

He shrugged. "I guess I did. As I said, I have forgotten much. At last, I can read not only my own works but those of the scientists who came after me. Perhaps I will find a Unified Theory yet."

"At least you know what you wrote was true."

"I *think* it was, but was it? Not all of it, certainly. With the power returning, perhaps it can be put to new tests. One learns; one fails; one tries again."

Liberty shook her head. "What if you found out that *nothing* worked like you thought? That lightning wasn't made of lectricity? That water ran uphill? That there was no such thing as gravity?"

He nodded somberly. "The hammer falls; the disappointment overwhelms, yet the sun rises the next day and the morning is bright. We begin again."

Liberty bit back more tears. "Without *The Americana*, I have nowhere to turn."

"Perhaps it will help to tell me how you feel. What is it that strikes most deeply?"

"All of it." She pushed a strand of hair away from her cheek and looked into his eyes. "All of it. All the politics, the arguments, the betrayals. In his second term the people picketed Washington's home. Picketed it! They treated him like . . . like—"

"A mere man?"

She nodded. "And all the others, too, people I believed were heroes! Nothing in *The American* is constitutional. All the glory is washed away. It'll never be the same."

He studied her, his own eyes watery, not knowing what to say.

They sat in silence for several minutes; she ran her hands over her face. "I might as well go to bed. It must be late."

"You helped fight a battle today. You're exhausted. I am, too, but I couldn't sleep, either. We should both get some rest. I'll walk you to the elevator."

"I can find my way, but thank you."

He bent down, kissed her forehead, and helped her up. "You are a strong one, Liberty Bell. You will survive this."

She shook her head and hugged him fiercely. He watched her drift down the aisles of books, her head down.

"The end of innocence," he murmured into the stillness. "Such a shame it comes to us all."

* * *

Liberty slept late the next day, only rising shortly before noon. Throwing on some clothes, she sat on her bed, her knees crossed beneath her, not bothering to brush her hair. Her eyes were swollen from crying. A single dim bulb burned by her nightstand.

Someone knocked on the door. When she didn't answer, Antonio stuck his head in. "I brought you some lunch."

"I'm not hungry."

He put the tray on the nightstand and sat beside her on the bed. "Norad has been asking about you."

"I figured he could probably see me."

"He doesn't keep cameras everywhere, I guess. He needs your help. We all do."

"I don't know if I can give it."

"Edison told us what happened. Look, I know how you must feel—"

The tears sprang to her eyes. "You can't possibly. Have you ever wanted to believe something so bad it hurt? Have you ever built your whole life around something you thought was *so* important? Your whole, entire life! Only to find out it was lies and fables? I've had the styrofoam pulled right out from under me. I've got nowhere left to go!"

"I'm sorry," he said.

She shook her head, not meeting his gaze. "There's nothing you or anyone else can do about it."

He covered her hand with his own. "I care about you, Liberty."

"I'm not sure I care about anything right now."

"You don't mean that."

Her expression grew hard. "You think you know so much. You're so proud of your ancestors, you need to read this." She flashed a book in front of his face, its Old American title meaningless to him. "They were just like the rest of us, poor immigrants who came to America because they had *nothing* in their own country."

"My ancestors were of the Royal Brotherhood of Builders."

"Your ancestors were laborers for a wage, same as mine, some of them illegals."

Antonio snorted. "That can't be right."

"See how it feels?"

An angry silence fell between them.

"Let's leave my ancestors out of it," Antonio finally said. "The fact is, we're in a bad way. Norad has lost communication with the satellite."

"How?"

"Some components may have failed due yesterday's attack, or Hitler may have found a way to block the signal. Norad doesn't know if he can fix it. But he wants your guidance. He's been asking for you. You have to help him think clearly, so he can put all his resources into defending the fortress."

She shook her head again. "How can I help him? What advice can I give him? I thought I knew so much! He needs the truth, not some made-up nonsense by a localyokel girl with a head filled with fairy tales."

"This isn't like you, Liberty."

"No, it's not. You become a different person when your world collapses. I'm the moth who finally hit the bug zapper. Go away, Antonio. I've got nothing else to say."

He studied her a moment and turned to leave, murmuring, "Try to eat something."

* * *

At eleven o'clock that evening, Brett Revere sat at table with Talos Hitler, along with half a dozen other guests and followers of the Fuehrer. The dining room, which Hitler called New Berchtesgaden, was one of the underground rail cars standing on its tracks deep in the earth. The rest of the train served as the Fuehrer's headquarters. Candles lit the compartment; torches attached to posts lit the surrounding grounds. A crude table had been constructed and covered with a red cloth, and the car's seats, also covered in red, had been taken from their places and arrayed around the table. The dim lighting, reflected off the fabric, gave the compartment a hellish look.

"There is no reason for the vivisection of animals for scientific experimentation," Hitler was saying, "except for military purposes. Animals are intelligent creatures and should not be treated in this manner. That is one of the reasons I am a vegetarian, not a corpse-eater such as Commander Rogers here, who seems to be enjoying his steak immensely." He chuckled at his own joke.

Rogers gave him a half-smile but made no reply. Brett wondered if the commander found Hitler as repulsive as he did, but decided he probably didn't. The Fuehrer had the magnetism of a natural conner, charming or imperious by turns, drawing his followers to him like a lodestone; Roger's brain pan was a shallow bowl low on soup. Brett smirked sardonically. What the commander lacked in intelligence, he made up for in greed, an easy combination to con. Gaining an Official Pardon from him had been almost effortless.

Hitler was another matter. Brett had realized the minute he met the Fuehrer—based on his voice and body—that he wasn't the Masked Rider who had previously tried to kill him. That had been a great relief. But the more he knew the man, the more he suspected he was crazy. He went to bed around two in the morning, with standing orders never to be awakened before noon, regardless of the circumstances. His schemes were impossibly grandiose, talk of building a new nation of socialist love and brotherhood. His travel tales included exaggerations monumental enough to put the blush on the face of a professional liar. Judging by their expressions, Hitler's followers ate it up.

Revere glanced down at his plate, inwardly groaning at the thought of suffering through the usual three hours of the nightly dinner. Every evening, the Fuehrer personally dictated the seating arrangement to his adjutants. A core group of about twenty was always present, consisting of the Fuehrer's most trusted lieutenants and their wives, his two personal physicians, and others from his organization. Hitler invariably surrounded himself with women, a feminine hedgerow seated to either side and directly across from him, though he never seemed to have a close relationship with any of them. He refused to discuss military matters during the meal and berated anyone who tried to do so. His dinner conversation was initially stilted, polite comments on the cuisine, but he would soon grow more amiable, playing to the women, complimenting them in various ways. As the hours progressed, however, he would speak with greater energy, expressing his personal opinions on topics Brett cared nothing about, an endless monologue no one dared interrupt; Brett had seen a novice member of the company face a barrage of abuse for disagreeing with the Fuehrer. Neither was he a man of light conversation, his humor consisting of barbs aimed at some individual, banter continued to the point of embarrassment, since none dared respond in kind.

"It is clear to me," Hitler was saying, "that anyone who sees and paints a sky green and a field blue ought to be sterilized."

One of the women, a newcomer, laughed uneasily.

"Do you think I am joking?" Hitler asked.

The woman blushed. "I . . . it seems inhumane, Herr Hitler. You were just talking about being kind to animals—"

"I see no reason why man should not be just as cruel as nature," Hitler said. "It is not by the principles of humanity that we are able to preserve ourselves above the animal world, but solely by means of the most brutal struggle." He gave a derisive laugh. "Humanitarianism!

The expression of stupidity and cowardice." His eyes darted around the table until they fixed on Brett. "Would you agree, Herr Revere?"

"I don't claim to know much about art, Herr Hitler," Brett replied, "but I do my best to avoid fools and cowards. And if there's going to be a fight, I want to hit first, hardest, and from their blind side. I leave the manners to the other fellow."

Hitler's eyes flashed with pleasure. He leaned back in his chair. "I have been watching you. You are an interesting man, Herr Revere. Perhaps you would consider entering my service? I am looking for the right person to be my Minister of Propaganda."

"I'm flattered," Brett said, "but that doesn't sound like anything in my line."

"You are too modest," Hitler said. "You understand how to ingratiate yourself to others, a talent you need only apply to government. All propaganda must be popular and accommodate itself to the comprehension of the least intelligent. Fortunately for governments, the people do not think." He smirked and drummed the table with his fingers. "By clever and constant application of propaganda, people can be made to see Paradise as Hell, or the most wretched sort of life as Paradise. Make the lie big, make it simple, keep saying it, and eventually everyone will believe it. That is all you need to know."

Brett looked Hitler in the eye, revealing nothing by his expression. "It doesn't sound like anything I'd be good at."

The Fuehrer sat back in his chair and roared with laughter. Soft chuckles and confused smiles appeared around the table. Though he seethed inside, Brett never flinched. He didn't like being seen through, especially in front of people he might someday want to con.

Hitler gradually contained his mirth, letting it settle into a wolf's grin. "I am an excellent judge of character, Herr Revere, a fact I have just proven. Great liars are great magicians, and you are an enchanter indeed. What do you say?"

"Let me think about it." Brett kept his tone even, aware if he crossed this man he would wind up at the bullseye end of a firing squad. He had no intention of taking the job. Working for this maniac would be like dancing with a rattlesnake; there was no chance of living through the first waltz.

* * *

Talos Hitler took his eyes off Brett Revere and glanced around the table. How his followers adored him! His genius, his vision, his insight. Yet, they were fools, poor substitutes for his previous companions, those glorious warriors and genteel citizens of the Third Reich: Martin Bormann, Robert Ley and his wife, artists such as Arno Breker. Or ever-loyal Joseph Goebbels, who with his wife and children had remained in the Bunker to die with him when the others had all deserted. And his police dog, Blondi, and Eva Braun. He missed them all. If he had not been betrayed by so many—Hess, Himmler, Rommel—the Third Reich would have lasted a thousand years.

But this was his chance to begin again. When Talos first took Adolph Hitler's body, he had not realized how much affinity he and the former ruler of Germany shared. The more he merged with the Fuehrer, the more his consciousness expanded. Strokes of genius flashed through his mind constantly, inspirations on tactics, art, music, architecture, ghettos. Already he had abandoned his earlier plans of contacting his fellow Sirans. He would form a new Reich. He would be the father of an endless American empire, the loving and beloved shepherd of his people. With the information found in the Treasury of Books, he would revive the science of genetic engineering, so much more advanced in the late twenty-first century than in the 1940's, and rebuild his race of supermen. Poor, idiotic Commander Rogers, so unspeakably stupid as to tell him of the library's existence. Not that it mattered; it only gave Talos one more reason to ensure, once the battle was done, that none of the Yooessay soldiers lived to share the installation's secrets.

Norad was the key. Who could have suspected the computer's survival? He exulted at the thought. This was surely proof of his Great Destiny, for one of his earliest clones had been a twenty-first century general intimately familiar with the Cheyenne Mountain complex. Talos knew how to locate and gain control of Norad's central processors, information not even Einstein Edison suspected he possessed. His strike would be both rapid and flawless.

He raised his glass before his guests. "Ladies and Gentlemen. A toast to the Fourth Reich."

CHAPTER TWENTY-THREE

At midnight, when Mac Arthur, that noble Knight, stood sentry at the doors to Camelot, the fortress guarding the Eastern Seaboard, Benedict Arnold slew him with a dagger and threw the gates wide, allowing the enemies of America to enter the fortress. Bobby Kennedy tried to give warning, only to be cut down by Surehand the Assassin. They murdered Representative John Kennedy and slipped down the Potomac toward Washington DeeCee. — The Americana

* * *

Early the next morning, Einstein Edison appeared at Liberty's door, carrying a pole draped in a gray blanket. He glanced at her uneaten food and began unwrapping the package.

"If you've come to try to cheer me up, you're pouring hot water into a frozen jacuzzi."

"I thought I would show you this." He unfurled the cloth hanging from the pole. "I had Norad make it for you. It is the flag of the United States of America."

Despite herself, Liberty could not help sitting up. "It's made of fabric."

"I don't know why legends describe it as bronze like a Roman standard. Perhaps cloth was scarce after the Great Blackout; but this is the design when there were fifty states, not fifty-three as at the end."

Liberty brightened as she gazed at the white stars and red stripes. "This is what the Star Weaver made?" Her expression crumbled into despair. "But Betsee Ross wasn't really an enchantress, was she?"

"No. Among other things, she was a seamstress, but a very good one." He chuckled softly. "You must not be sad, Liebchen. Betsy Ross may not have been the Wise Woman the legends claim, but this flag is still enchanted. The white stripes represent purity and innocence, the red ones, blood valiantly shed for the cause of freedom; royal blue is the color of chieftains, and each of the stars represents one of the fifty states."

He gave her the flag. She ran her hands over the brilliant colors.

"You mourn because you think the words written in *The Americana* untrue," Edison said.

"Even you said so."

"Not exactly. Do you remember our conversation last night in the library?"

"Of course."

"Word for word?"

"Not word for word, but most of it," she said.

"What about the first conversation we ever had? If we wrote it down now, would our accounts be identical? Time is tricky, Liebchen. It passes from moment to moment while we watch it, and our observations of an event change the event itself. So, what do we seek when we remember?" He studied her face. "The essence of any encounter. True?"

"I suppose, but if you're trying to say history and *The Americana* are the same thing, they just aren't."

"Aren't they? Yes and no. Did Washington defeat the Reds and win the revolution by destroying the Wizard Cornwallis and the giant from the frozen wastelands of Canada? No. But he did defeat a giant, for the British Empire was the greatest power of its day, and Washington took a ragged, untrained militia and turned it into an army. Did Martin Luther King march with Abraham Lincoln to conquer Atlanta? No. He did something greater. He dared to reveal the hypocrisy of a country claiming freedom for every citizen. He stirred the conscience of the American people, helped gain equal rights for an entire race, and even as Lincoln before him, gave his life and his blood, dying from an assassin's bullet."

"You've read *The Americana*? Why, when you know the truth?"

Einstein Edison chuckled. "I like reading it because the stories are beautiful representations of the truth in poetic form."

"Isn't something either true or a lie?"

"When we are children, that is what we most want to believe, but reality is more complicated. We stand on a floor and think it solid, when it is actually made of billions of molecules. We watch the sun and imagine it rising, but it is our world that rotates." He paused and studied the flag. "The stories in *The Americana*—there is truth in them. In the French and Indian War, when the British and American soldiers were attacked and utterly defeated, Washington rode unwounded among his enemies as *The Americana* says, despite the chief instructing his braves to cut down the officers on horseback. They fired at Washington numerous times, but could not kill him, though two horses were shot out from under him and his jacket had four bullet holes in it. Without Washington, that one great man, would the United States have ever come into being?"

Edison shrugged. "Who can say? And what of Joshua Chamberlain, who held Little Round Top at the Battle of Gettysburg, initiating a charge when the Union soldiers ran out of ammunition, saving the flank of the army? Later in his life, when both political parties offered him bribes, promising to make him a senator, he refused. What if a less honorable man had stood on that hill?

"As in *The Americana*, Dwight Eisenhower commanded the largest invasion fleet in history, freeing Europe from Hitler's tyranny. He was a president and a warrior who warned the world against the dangers of the military-industrial complex. What if some other man had stood in his place?

"When thousands of nuclear missiles from Russia and America were aimed at each other, John F. Kennedy made the right decisions, saving the two countries from annihilation. What if someone else had been president at that pivotal moment?

"Ronald Reagan, refusing to believe we must live in a world filled with missiles, put economic and political pressure on the Soviets, and the Berlin Wall fell, bringing freedom to millions. Would anyone else have done the same?

"Neil Armstrong flew to the moon, not on eagles' wings, but on machines built by American science and ingenuity, and when he put his foot on lunar soil, he misspoke the words. 'That's one small step for man, one giant leap for mankind,' came from his mouth, yet his flawed speech rippled throughout the world. Clara Barton, John Adams, Harriet Beecher Stowe, Thomas Jefferson, Cesar Chavez, Benjamin Franklin, Booker T. Washington—these were real men and women who did great deeds, the stuff of legends."

Edison reached down and stroked Liberty's head. "The myths are true, Liebchen. You've idolized men and women you thought were like gods, but they were even more than you imagined. They were human beings living through terrible times, who stood for the principles of virtue and integrity, honesty, and the belief that everyone has the right to be treated as an individual. They stood for these things even when they themselves, being mortal, were not always virtuous. They carried the hope that a government founded on the highest values could become a standard for the whole world; and because of it, the United States was, for a time, the greatest nation on Earth. You should be proud, for your ancestors lit a flame that became the glory of the world. America passed, yet it will never pass. It was always more than a country. It was an Ideal, and as such, cannot die."

He winked at her. "I know, for I was there, an immigrant from Germany, fleeing Hitler's madness. And now we face him once more."

He picked up the book of American history by her bedside. "Read this again, Liberty, but see it not as the end of your beliefs, but the picture of a greater reality than you ever conceived. Learn the wonder and the miracle of it, for it is beyond probability that the United States could ever have existed at all. Read what the Americans who stood up for their principles were able to accomplish, and then take those stories back to your people."

He handed her the volume and departed. For a moment, she remained motionless. She opened the book and began to read.

* * *

Late that afternoon, Liberty came to supper carrying the history book. She encountered Antonio outside the doorway and gave him a fierce hug. "I'm sorry I was cruel when you were only trying to help."

He returned her hug. "I deserved it. The Royal Brotherhood of Builders. What a joke!"

"I was wrong," Liberty said. "You have everything to be proud of." She tapped the book. "There's a first-hand account of a twelve-year-old boy who slipped over the border from Mexico, crossing the desert alone at night; terrified, not knowing when he would get his next meal, but determined to start a new life in the United States. He began as an illegal but worked hard until he became a citizen. It's like *The Americana* says: We're the descendants of a race of brave, scared immigrants. We should never forget what our ancestors did."

She stepped through the doorway. Einstein Edison, the American Natives, and Brother Rabbi were all at the table. Poco leapt up and ran to hug her.

"I want to help," Liberty said.

"I hope you can," Brother Rabbi said. "Things don't look so good. With our satellite no longer responding, Hitler is bound to strike soon. Norad needs your guidance to understand his place in the world."

Liberty ate hurriedly and Brother Rabbi led her to Norad.

"Are you feeling better, Liberty Bell?" Norad asked.

"A little," she said, "but I need to clear up some misconceptions we've both had. Let me tell you about President George Washington."

* * *

It was nearly midnight when she finally left Norad. It had been an exhausting evening, relating everything she had learned from the book, but too overwrought to sleep, she made her way to the observation windows on the fourth level. Entering the room, she found Antonio standing silhouetted against the light from the windows.

"Oh my stars and stripes!" She put her hand to her chest. "You startled me. It's late. What are you doing?"

"Thinking about them, out there."

To Liberty's shock, she saw countless campfires burning on the far side of the valley. Hitler had lost all fear of Norad's satellite, proof he was jamming its signal.

"It's a very small army by ancient standards," Liberty said. "On D-Day—"

"It's a very large army by our standards," Antonio said. "Norad has a number of weapons stored here, but very few still work."

She stepped closer. "He mustn't get the books, Antonio. Everything we ever believed about the Old Americans is true. They *could* soar through the air, ride beneath the sea, pulverize mountains, obliterate cities, kill thousands with the single pull of a trigger, easy as shooting a jabberwolf. They had robot warriors, soldiers in body armor, cloaks of invisibility, chemicals and gases to burn people's lungs, melt their skin, dissolve their eyes—hundreds of ways to destroy."

"I thought they were the good guys."

"They were." Liberty frowned. "Well, mostly they were. But their enemies had those weapons, too, and every bit of that information is in the Treasury."

"Makes you wonder if anyone should have it," Antonio said. "It's not as if our government is so wonderful."

"That doesn't sound like you. Where's my spy guy?"

He shrugged. "You know I became an agent because I'm a man of action. But though I never told you, I always, deep down, wanted to do good for my country. Maybe I'm not a scholar on the old days like you, maybe I spent too much time making fun of you for it, but every kid grows up admiring Washington and the Representatives, even if he thinks they're only fairy tales." He paused and drew a sharp breath. "I don't understand a man like Commander Rogers. He swore an oath the same as I did, and he pardons a murderer, sides with a criminal, and talks about getting his share of the profits. If this is what the Secret Service is about . . . I don't know."

"As it turns out, I'm actually not much of a scholar," she said, "but you've been heroic from the first day I met you."

He snorted. "Right. Even when I bragged or lied?"

She grimaced. "I've had to rethink a lot of things in the last two days, finding out even the greatest Americans were only people. I held them to a higher standard than I held myself, thinking I could never be as good as they were because they had magic swords and superpowers. I used it as an excuse not to try."

"You've tried plenty," he said. "The truth is, you've been an inspiration to me."

She couldn't help smiling. "That's sweet of you to say."

"I love when you do that."

"What?"

"Get all philosophical. And when you smile, your mouth turns down sometimes."

She put her hand over her lips. "I smile upside down? I'm a freak."

"It's cute. You've always been beautiful, even out in the wild." He ran his hand over her head, smoothing her hair. "Liberty, there's a good chance we're going to die here. We're outnumbered, outgunned, facing a merciless enemy. I want you to know the night we kissed back at Menlo Park, I meant every word I said. I've been in love with you almost from the first day we met."

Deep inside, in the center of Liberty's being, a barrier—wide as the Grand Canyon and high as the Berlin Wall—suddenly collapsed. It was a shield she had been desperately trying to fortify, unknown even to herself. The first tiny cracks had appeared when she and Antonio declared their friendship in Yoosemitee, and had grown as they huddled together in the pouring rain beneath that first terrible thunderstorm. She remembered holding his hand at Einstein Edison's, the strength of his grip, the strength of his face. For her, the final turn had come when she realized his exaggerations and bravado were no more than defenses covering the uncertainty of a courageous, untried soul. Her fortifications, constructed with such care, now shaken and splintered, fell with a rush that left her breathless, revealing her heart, bare and vulnerable and finally free. She reached up and touched his good, strong face.

"I love you, too."

He bent down and kissed her, and the whole world vanished, leaving only the two of them, entangled and enraptured, the moment eternal, the surrender complete.

They kissed for a long time. Afterward, they talked for two hours. They laughed in wonder at the improbability of being thrown off the train together. She teased him about his goofy accent when they met

Brother Rabbi; he teased her about feeding him intoxicating berries. She praised his courage in their battles; he praised her intelligence and bravery. They spoke of all they had done together throughout their journey, and everything that happened took on a new dimension, witnessed through the lens of their growing love.

"It's like wearing a wide-brimmed hat," Liberty said. "You just never see all the things around you."

* * *

The next morning Norad summoned Antonio and Liberty to the third level. They stepped outside through a door onto a small, guard-railed platform extending from the outer wall. Einstein Edison and the American Natives were there with Norad, who stood tall and broad-shouldered in his armored form. Liberty touched his hand; it was solid and surprisingly warm.

Brett Revere and Commander Rogers, escorted by four Yooessay and two Haze cavalrymen, sat astride their horses on the plain below, bearing a white flag of truce, a light morning mist curling around their mounts' withers.

"Why have you come?" Norad's deep voice boomed down to them.

"We're here to give you one last chance to surrender," Commander Rogers said.

"Surrender is not an option," Norad said. "No Man Left Behind. My mission is to guard this facility. The government of Haze is incompatible with the principles of a republic. However, I am willing to speak with the more moderate government of the Yooessay. Liberty Bell is from there and is recognized as my legitimate Representative. I listen to her."

"What about Antonio Ice?" Commander Rogers asked. "Do you listen to him?"

Norad turned his gaze toward Antonio. "He is the friend of the Representative. I will listen to him as well."

The commander gave a wide grin. "That makes everything nice and easy. Mister Ice, you are directed to tell this machine to stand down and allow us to enter the fortress."

Antonio looked at Liberty, his face set. He spoke in a clear voice. "I regret, sir, that even if Norad would obey me, I cannot honor your request."

Roger's grin vanished. "This ain't a request, Agent Ice. It's an order. Despite your instructions, you've failed to keep me apprised of the situation within the mountain, but I've put that down to your inability to get a message out. This is a different matter. You will comply or find yourself guilty of treason."

Sweat beaded Antonio's brow; his face went deathly pale. Nonetheless, his voice remained steady. "With all due respect, it is my understanding that if a law or a command is unjust, it is a citizen's duty to resist."

"That's not Yooessay law," Rogers said.

"Then we need better laws."

"Are you refusing me, Agent Ice?"

Antonio met the eyes of his commander. "I'm not just refusing. I am resisting for the good of my country."

Even from thirty feet up, Liberty could see Roger's face turn red with rage. "Unless you change your mind real quick, Agent Ice, you've just signed your death warrant."

Antonio said nothing.

"What about the rest of you?" the commander asked. "You Navajos, you're making powerful enemies if you stand against both the Yooessay and Haze. Your chief might not be happy about it. And Menlo Park— from what Hitler tells me, you're a pretty small operation, Mister Edison. Do you really want a dog in this fight? The Yooessay can be a powerful friend or a terrible enemy."

"Commander," Einstein Edison said, "I have friends in overalls whose friendship I would not swap for the favor of the kings of this world. You, yourself, would do to have better friends. Talos Hitler is an alien from the stars inhabiting the cloned body of a power-mad fiend. Think about that. He is a tiger. When he has used you to achieve his ends, he will consume first you, then Menlo Park, before turning his attention to the Yooessay."

Rogers licked his lips nervously. "I'm well aware of my situation. These difficulties can be handled with an honest negotiation. All we want is fair access to Cheyenne Mountain."

Heyoka Coyoté gave a yipping laugh.

"What Heyoka means," Code Talker said, "is that you've come here to play cowboys and Indians. My people have heard those lies before. We are the warriors of the Navajo, the people of a proud and mighty nation. If you attack this fortress, you declare war on Navajoland. Our honor will be maintained in the blood of your countrymen. Return to the Yooessay or side with us against Haze. Any other course will prove disastrous."

Rogers ran his hand along his thigh and licked his lips again, clearly affected.

"This talk about duty and honor is nice and noble," Brett Revere said, "but you're in a bad situation. Hitler thought our coming out here was a waste of time, but we wanted to give you one last chance. Liberty knows me well enough to understand that I do what's in my own interests. I'm nothing if not a realist, so believe me when I say we have several hundred men, and you haven't got a chance. I know you love high principles, Liberty, but it's not worth getting killed over. Give us Norad and leave this one-sided fight."

"I'm sorry for you, Mister Revere," Liberty said, "because there are things worth dying for. You go back and tell Hitler we said *Pecans!*"

Everyone except Einstein Edison gave her a puzzled look. "Oh!" she cried, embarrassed and irritated. "The answer is *No!* You can't come in here. Go back where you came from."

"My Representative has spoken," Norad said.

Rogers glared at Liberty, then turned his horse. Revere glanced back once, as if wanting to add something, but only shook his head.

"Pecans?" Antonio asked.

Liberty stamped her foot, exasperated. "Doesn't anybody read *The Americana*?"

"In the Bulge Battle," Norad said, "when the Notsies encircled Bastogne and demanded its surrender, the commander told them *Pecans*, an expression of contempt."

"Actually," Einstein Edison said, "the word was *Nuts*."

"I guess I better get used to being wrong," Liberty said, grimly. She turned to Antonio. "Anyway, you really told them where to bail out."

"And destroyed my career." His face was drawn. "Everything I worked for is finished."

"I'm proud of you." She reached up and kissed him on the cheek.

He gave a rueful grin. "You've rubbed off on me."

They watched the emissaries ride back to their camp. Moments later, a bugle rang out.

"The attack begins," Norad said. "Everyone, please take your positions."

CHAPTER TWENTY-FOUR

There arose a constant din of information on the Net, until the American people thought only of themselves and their amusements. When their enemies came to assault the White House, President Washington sent a message to every state, to hasten to the capitol to defend the cause of liberty. But no one came. —The Americana

* * *

They entered the fortress. Navy Seals and several of Edison's men were already arrayed at the gun-slits. Norad strode away, vanishing down the corridor, leaving the others to remain where they could fire down upon the plain.

Liberty took her place at one of the slits. Out of the morning mist, from around the curve of the facing mountain, four tanks surrounded by infantrymen rolled forth, accompanied by a tremendous shout of *Sieg Heil!* Cavalry moved into position, flanking the installation. The sun, golden across Cheyenne Mountain and diffused by the light fog, reflected off the horses' harnesses. The soldiers wore gray uniforms and helmets; one bore a standard of an eagle surmounting a wreathed swastika.

"Must be a thousand of them," Code Talker said.

Brother Rabbi's hologram appeared behind them. "Twelve hundred thirty-seven, but who's counting?"

Elvis jumped, startled. "Holy Jeeps! Don't do that!"

"Sorry. I just wanted to pop in to tell you that Norad has some surprises for the Hazers."

"Will any of it stop them?" Poco asked.

"Well . . . not exactly, at least not by Norad's calculations, but he's probably only guessing." Brother Rabbi scratched behind one ear. "Though he is the most advanced strategic and tactical computer ever constructed."

"You give us great comfort," Heyoka Coyoté said.

"Ethel always said I brought the sunshine with me. It's a gift, I suppose. She was a sunny person herself. I guess I learned it from her."

Liberty licked her lips, scarcely hearing the conversation, watching the tanks rumble across the plain, drawing closer but not yet firing. She steadied her rifle against the embrasure.

Abruptly, the air outside Cheyenne Mountain shimmered and swirled, filling with creatures. Navy Seals crowded the ramparts on the second level; winged Marines soared overhead. A figure loomed before the fortress, standing at least fifty feet tall, dressed in the dark blue uniform of the Continental Army. He turned his tremendous head, revealing the profile of George Washington. In his left hand he held an American flag; in his right, the legendary battle-axe, Valleyforge; but his eyes were the huge blue orbs of Norad.

He's like Paul Bunyan and John Henry wrapped together, Liberty thought.

The Seals stamped their feet, striking their rifle butts on the ground, shouting together, their voices as one, a thunder echoing between the mountains. "America!"

Across the valley, the soldiers of Haze and the Yooessay hesitated, overawed, even the tanks grinding to a halt.

Norad's voice boomed over the mountains. "Do you know who you face? Do you know who your master sends you to fight?"

Turning his head slowly from side to side, he surveyed his foes. "I am Norad. And I am America."

The Navy Seals stamped their feet. "America!"

"I am the blood shed for freedom," Norad rumbled.

"America!"

"I am the voice of revolution against the oppression of tyranny."

"America!"

"I am the Guardian of the Golden Door, beckoning the immigrant come."

"America!" the Seals cried, and Liberty and Antonio shouted with them.

"I fought against slavery, brother against brother. I filled the fields of my country with my dead at Gettysburg and Shiloh, Antietam and Bull Run, not for economic gain, but for a downtrodden people."

"America!"

"I stormed the beaches of Normandy. I defied the Third Reich for the cause of Justice. I conquered the nations of Europe only to give them back their own. I liberated the Jews from the concentration camps of your evil master."

"America!"

"Against the tyrants I sent my warrior sons and daughters across the Earth, to root out and pull down, to destroy and overthrow, only to rebuild and replant, returning mercy for hate and love for enmity."

The Seals' shouts and footfalls shook the fortress.

"When I erred, I repented. When I failed, I fell to my knees, but soon stood again."

"America!"

"I said that every person has equal rights under the law."

"America!"

"I demanded more of my leaders than expedience. I required virtue, commitment, and the highest ideals. I expected sacrifice from the young and the old. I insisted on selflessness from every citizen, knowing none are too great or too small to be above or below the cause of Justice."

"America! America! America!"

"I am America!" Norad cried, his voice even louder, echoing and re-echoing against the mountains. "Though I tire, you can never defeat me, though I fall I will rise against you. Should your kingdom last a thousand years, it will crumble as tyrannies must, while the light of Freedom remains, inextinguishable."

Norad took a single stride forward and Liberty could almost see the Hazers quail. Horses bolted; several soldiers dropped their guns and fled. She heard shouted commands and scattered shots.

"I am America," Norad boomed, the sun shining full upon his face, his arms raised above his head, his hands gripping his battle-axe and the unfurled American flag. "See if you can destroy me! Come and be broken against the bulwarks of the Free."

A silence fell. Norad took another step forward.

A trumpet blared, the signal for attack, and one of the tanks fired. A shell struck Norad at the knees; his image flickered; his hologram vanished. Men and machines rolled toward the fortress.

"Hold your fire until they are in range," the voice of Norad ordered.

"Nice speech," Brother Rabbi said. "Excellent psychological intimidation."

"Are they all holograms?" Liberty indicated the Navy Seals on the parapets.

"Most of them," Brother Rabbi said. "All of the flying Marines. But they can cause a lot of confusion."

As if in answer, the soaring figures dove at the Hazers, sending them ducking and throwing themselves to the ground.

The tanks were already halfway across the plain, but as they rolled along, the lead machine tipped and vanished into the earth, accompanied by several of the soldiers walking beside it. The men behind halted in confusion.

"One of our surprises," Brother Rabbi said. "When Norad reawakened several months ago, he lasered out a deep trench around Cheyenne Mountain and hid it beneath sliding steel panels covered with earth. When the panels open, holographic projectors camouflage the openings. It took weeks to finish the wiring; we finally worked out the bugs late last night."

A second tank disappeared, many yards from the first but parallel to it. Soldiers began stacking up against the unseen pit.

"Prepare to fire," the voice of Norad echoed through the facility.

Liberty took careful aim at one of the soldiers near the pit. She held her breath.

"Fire!" Norad ordered.

The beams from the Seals' pulse-guns hissed through the air, cutting a swathe in the enemy ranks. Armed with a conventional rifle, Liberty squeezed the trigger as she would when hunting. The enemy was too far away for a clean shot, but she thought she hit her mark. Soldiers tumbled to the earth, some vanishing into the pit.

In response, a barrage of bullets hammered against the fortress. One of the remaining two tanks fired. The shell whistled through the sky and struck the ground before the installation, sending rock soaring into the air. A tiny fragment zipped through Liberty's gun-slit, striking her cheek. She cried out in pain. When she touched the wound a smear of blood came off on her fingers.

"You all right?" Antonio called.

She gritted her teeth and returned to the embrasure. "Yankee dandy!"

The Hazers were pinned down, and from over the fortress ramparts, monsters flopped into the valley and lumbered toward the enemy lines, holographic behemoths from *The Americana*: Bigfoot Sasquatch, giant ants, Santa Claws, Frankenstein, Dracula, King Kong. Some of the soldiers bolted, but most stood their ground. The images strode across the battlefield, causing confusion, while the defenders poured a steady fire into the enemy ranks. Liberty took heart. The Hazers looked hopelessly overmatched.

But as the minutes passed, the Seals' pulse-guns gradually ceased, forcing them to use conventional rifles. One by one, the monsters faded into oblivion.

"Norad has to preserve his resources," Brother Rabbi said. "The pulse-guns have to recharge, and holograms take a lot of power."

One of the tanks crossed the trench and the soldiers followed.

"How did they do that?" Liberty asked, her voice high in excitement.

Brother Rabbi stood silent, as if listening. "Norad's sensors show they cut the wiring to two of the steel panels and slid them out."

"Hitler must have technical people on the battlefield," Einstein Edison said.

"Fire! Fire!" Brother Rabbi yelled. "We have to hold them!"

Perspiration dripped down Liberty's face. The world narrowed to her gun, the port, the box of shells by her side, and the solders rushing toward Cheyenne Mountain. They were close enough that she could see the hate on their faces. A dispassionate part of her brain wondered exactly what they hated and why. Norad? Or was it hate for hate's sake? She kept shooting.

The tanks fired, concentrating their weapons on the door damaged in the previous battle.

"Brother Rabbi," Einstein Edison said, "I need to get on the platform."

"Okay. It's your funera—uhh, never mind."

The door to the platform slid open. A light wind stirred Edison's cloak as he stepped out. In her concern for him, Liberty quit firing and watched as he raised his staff. Once again a bolt of blue lectricity shot from it, crossing the span between the mountain and the enemy, licking one of the tanks in lightning tendrils. This time, however, it had no effect.

Bullets striking all around him, Edison hurried back inside. "Hitler has found some way to dissipate the energy. Talos possesses little scientific training but must have found lackeys who do." He shook his head in wonder. "To devise a defense so quickly . . . he must be even more brilliant than I suspected."

"Will your staff work against the soldiers?" Brother Rabbi asked.

"Its power is temporarily expended."

"Oy vey," Brother Rabbi said.

The Hazers had slid several other plates across the trench. More and more soldiers crossed over. The tanks moved into closer range.

Brother Rabbi wrung his hands. "We need that satellite."

Both tanks fired simultaneously, striking the door, twin blasts that shook the fortress. Shards of metal blew up and out.

"If we don't do something, we're going to get alamo'd," Antonio said. "Rabbi, can't Norad lower the fortress back into the ground?"

"We wouldn't be able to shoot. They'd drill through the top and be inside. Norad is sending reinforcements to the door. I only hope it will be enough."

"It will!" Code Talker yelled, his eyes on the battlefield. "My people have come!"

Liberty raised her gaze from the tanks. American Natives bearing feathered standards poured toward the Hazer's flank.

Code Talker slapped Heyoka Coyoté on the shoulder. "Come on. We're needed down there."

The American Natives followed Code, but when Liberty and Antonio moved to join them, Brother Rabbi blocked their path, waving his finger in front of Liberty's face. "Not the Representative. Norad doesn't want you close to the fighting again. You're too valuable."

Liberty started to protest, but Antonio said, "He's right. You're our link with Norad."

"You can't go without me."

"I have to. Rabbi, you've got to protect her."

"I'll do my best," Brother Rabbi said.

Antonio grabbed Liberty by the waist, drawing her to him in a fierce embrace. Her lips sought his in a desperate kiss, and then he was gone, darting out of the room after the American Natives. She wondered if she would ever see him again.

* * *

Antonio and the Navajos exited the elevator to the ground floor, joining contingents of Edison's men and Navy Seals hurrying to the Main Entrance. Reaching it, they found the doors lying in twisted scraps. A handful of Seals lay on the ground, dark liquid pumping from their wounds, their eyes empty.

Norad stood staring out of the opening. His right arm was missing; Antonio wondered how many spare bodies he had.

"The enemy has turned to meet your people," Norad said to Code Talker. "While our opponents are dismayed, a company of my Seals will charge. Between our two forces, we will cut them to pieces."

"We go, too." Code Talker slapped Antonio on the shoulder. The men's eyes met, the competitors for Liberty's affection. Yet Antonio saw no enmity in Code's gaze, despite surely knowing Liberty had made her choice. He nodded his agreement, wondering if the Native was not, after all, the better man.

Elvis clutched his rifle in one hand and removed the sheath off the heavy tomahawk he wore at his belt. Poco strung her bow. Heyoka Coyoté's eyes glistened with excitement as he cocked his weapon. Moments passed as the rest of the reinforcements assembled, including two bazooka teams. Through the wrecked doorway, the sounds of battle resonated off the corridor's metal walls.

"Go!" Norad commanded.

The Navy Seals gave a growling roar, beginning at the back of their throats and rising to a crescendo as they rushed through the opening. Antonio shouted with them and followed, his pride demanding he go before Code, his reason telling him it was schoolboy foolishness.

Code Talker raised his rifle high, and the Navajos lifted their voices as one. "Ay yi yi yi yi yeee!" They sprang after Antonio, thirty of Edison's men behind them. To either side, Antonio spied more Seals rushing from other fortress exits.

Antonio saw the battlefield with startling, slow-mo clarity, a painted masterpiece stretched taut before his eyes, miraculous in detail; the looming mountains, the blue sky, the wisps of cloud, the rising dust, the yucca and scrub oak, the gray uniforms of the men of Haze, the horses, tawny, white, and black; the scuffing of his own feet striking the brown earth, the rustling of the Seals' gear, the cries and shouts of battle. To his right, far beyond the trench at the Hazers' flank, the feathered standards of the Navajos shone tan and gold.

Dismayed at finding an enemy at their back, the Hazers on this side of the trench had fallen into disarray, some retreating, others standing their ground. Norad's forces spread out in a long line, firing as they sprinted forward, Elvis to Antonio's left, Code Talker to his right. The sight of the Navy Seals bearing down upon them, massive and ebony-faced, threw Hitler's forces into panic. Antonio shot one man and wounded another in the leg. The Hazers broke and fled, melting away, many casting their rifles to the ground.

One of the tanks had already returned to the other side of the trench; the other one, seeing its support vanish, tried to back away, its machine gun blazing. A Navy Seal rolled under the rain of bullets and slapped an explosive against the tank's treads. The treads blew away, collapsing the machine on one side, taking the Seal with it.

The Hazers had reached a bottleneck at the trench and were milling in disarray. Some tried to jump the gap only to tumble to its bottom, but others turned to fight. Bullets whizzed around Antonio's ears.

Thirty yards from the enemy, Antonio's company dropped to a prone position. He hit the ground, tasting dust and cordite on his tongue. The semblance to an execution squad—the humming of the now-recharged pulse-guns, the screams of the dying—threw the Hazers into hysteria. It became a slaughter, and though he knew he had no choice, a part of Antonio shrank at the butchery.

The enemy began throwing down their arms and shouting their

surrender. Antonio and the Navajos ceased shooting, and Edison's men quickly did the same, but the Seals did not stop.

"They're surrendering!" Antonio shouted to the Navy Seal beside him.

Giving no answer, the creature kept up a rapid fire. Its weapon abruptly lost its charge; the Seal fixed its bayonet and advanced on the Hazers.

Code Talker leapt to his feet. "Norad! Hear me!"

One of the Seals turned to him, speaking in Norad's voice. "I hear you, Code Talker."

"You can't kill men who are trying to surrender."

"I do not have the assets to take prisoners. They are in the way. Destroying them is a tactical decision."

"For the sake of the America you claim to serve, order them to drop their weapons and jump into the trench!" Code Talker said. "You can seal it after."

The Navy Seal paused, Norad weighing the Navajo's words.

"My Representative, Liberty Bell, agrees with you," the Seal finally said.

All the Seals ceased firing and hurried forward, calling in unison in Norad's voice, an eerie chorus ordering the Hazers into the trench. It took several moments to get them all down. Once they were inside, the metal sheets slid shut.

Norad's forces reformed and charged over the trench, the plates booming beneath their boots. The ground was clear for fifty yards in front of them, the enemy having moved to meet the attack at its flank. The Haze commanders, intent on the Navajo cavalry, seemed unaware of this new threat at their backs.

Antonio charged over the uneven, rocky soil, past trampled yucca, leaping fallen scrub oak branches severed from their trunks by passing shells. It seemed to take a lifetime to cross the clearing. Halfway there, his company opened fire. He heard a long roar, the war cries of the soldiers. In wonder, he realized part of the noise came from his own throat.

The Hazers before him began to turn, eyes wide. Antonio shot the man in front of him in the stomach. He hit another with his rifle butt, continuing forward without watching him topple to the ground. For several, eternal moments he faced soldier after soldier, their eyes gray and grim beneath their Nazi helmets, a mad rush of battle. His hands and limbs moved automatically; he had no conscious thought save to kill those trying to kill him.

He encountered an abrupt lull, a moment when no enemy stood

before him, a timeless instant when the whole world seemed to stop. His eyes swept the field, searching for more foes. Code Talker remained beside him, Poco, Heyoka, and Elvis behind their leader. To his shock, Antonio realized he and the Navajos had driven furiously forward, leaving the Navy Seals several yards behind, cutting themselves off from the main body.

He had just enough time to reload his rifle before the lull ended and the enemy closed in.

Let me die a brave death ran through Antonio's mind. He wished Code Talker's sister hadn't come with them. After that, he only had time to react. He fired at a nearby Hazer, who dropped to his knees, clutching his chest; another man fired at him but miraculously missed. A soldier came at him with a bayonet; he sidestepped, drew his knife and slashed him across the neck.

At some point, he and Code Talker battled side-by-side, the two of them protecting one another, moving like a machine, with a coordination he would have thought unattainable for two men who had never fought together before. How long it lasted, he did not know, but while it did, it seemed symmetrical and perfect as a dance. In the midst of so grim a combat, he heard himself laugh.

Something clipped him across the jaw. He went to his knees, firing blindly, unable to see. He thought he was about to die, cut down while helpless. He moved instinctively, scrambling aside. His hands passed over what felt like someone's leg. He used it to pull himself to his feet.

His sight cleared and he found himself looking up at a mounted Navajo, eyes blackened with war paint, face fierce with battle, the first of a band who had driven a wedge through the Haze ranks. For an instant, he feared the warrior would mistake him for the enemy, but the Native turned and was lost amid the struggle.

Antonio wiped the sweat from his face. Blood came away on his palm. He automatically rubbed it against his leg. To one side, he saw Code Talker catch a riderless horse and swing himself onto the saddle. A few feet away, Elvis stood encircled, head and shoulders above the enemy soldiers surrounding him. With a cry, Code Talker kicked the horse and sped to help his friend. Antonio followed.

If Elvis had been terrified by the thought of ghosts in the underground caverns, he was fearless in battle against ordinary men. For one of his size, he moved with amazing dexterity. Awe swept through Antonio as he saw the great-hearted Navajo duck beneath a rifle barrel, swinging his tomahawk like a scythe, cutting his way through the foe, shirt and face splattered with the blood of his enemies, bellowing like a buffalo, spawning terror in the Hazers' hearts.

One of the enemy rose up, his rifle trained on Elvis. Time froze. Antonio brought up his own weapon, though he knew it would be too late. He saw Code Talker cast his knife. The blade flew through the air as the soldier drew back to fire.

The knife embedded itself into the man's chest even as he pulled the trigger. A puff of smoke trailed from the barrel.

"Nooo!" Code Talker shouted.

Though it was impossible for such a thing to be seen from so great a distance, Antonio witnessed a drop of blood flip into the air from Elvis' head.

Elvis reached with thumb and finger to touch his earlobe, which was no longer there. With a roar of anger, he charged deeper into the Hazers' ranks. Code Talker followed, adopting tactics Antonio had never seen before, using his horse's body as a shield while shooting from beneath its neck. Poco, now also mounted, rode close by her brother's side, firing arrows with unbelievable rapidity. Antonio and Heyoka ran after them, the group forming a rough triangle. They moved among both Navajo and Haze cavalry, pressing toward the main body of the Navajo force. Antonio looked around, vainly seeking a horse.

The roar of the tanks and the discharge of their shells had served as an underscore throughout the battle. Now, it grew louder. A tank zig-zagged through the ranks of the Navajo warriors, its smaller guns blazing, crushing horse and rider beneath its treads.

Antonio and the Natives veered to escape the juggernaut's path. Through the smoke and dust, he saw other tanks rampaging across the field, causing destruction wherever they went, turning the tide of battle. The Fuehrer had sent in reinforcements. The Navajo army, smaller by half than Hitler's forces, was being driven back. Isolated bands of warriors fighting separate battles were being overwhelmed. A surge of despair swept through him.

He saw a flash of darkness in the upper air, making him pause. Code Talker noticed it, too, for he gave a tremendous shout, galloped to a fallen Navajo standard, and leaning down, swept it off the ground.

"To me! To me!" he shouted, as great winged forms soared over the valley. "The eagles are coming! The eagles!"

One after another, in a long, smooth line, scores of American eagles came. Their talons glistened in the sun; their wings spread shadows across the land. Apollo Seven Teen led them, the greatest of his kind, his shrieking cry of "Freedom!" resounding over the plain. He descended in a tremendous arc, wings beating the air. His claws grasped the tank closest to the company, lifted it on its side, and turned it over.

Other eagles dropped heavy boulders on the enemy lines.

Caught between so many forces, many of the Hazers fled, but others stood their ground, firing at the eagles. One of the great birds came crashing to earth, shot through her tremendous heart.

The Navy Seals, Edison's men, and many of the Navajos reformed around Code Talker's standard. Antonio caught a riderless horse, scrambled into its saddle, and pushed his way to Code's side. Elvis, Heyoka, and Poco were already there. He and Code Talker exchanged glances. Wordlessly they shook hands.

Code lifted the standard higher. The company began to move.

It was too much for the enemy. Men dropped their weapons and ran. The officers, unable to hold their ranks, fled with them.

"We've got them!" Antonio yelled. Heyoka lifted his fist into the air. Poco trilled the Navajo war cry.

Still grinning, Antonio glanced over his shoulder.

His stomach fluttered. Dozens of balloons, coming from behind Cheyenne Mountain, drifted over the fortress. Men leapt from them, dropping a few feet to the top of the installation.

At almost the same moment, a series of explosions ripped through the side of a nearby mountain, throwing rock hundreds of feet. When the debris cleared, scores of Haze reinforcements poured from the newly created opening. It took Antonio a moment to realize Hitler had blasted a new exit from the caverns of the Underground Railroad. Already, the soldiers were scrambling toward the trench, heading for the Main Entrance.

The Hazers atop the fortress swarmed over one of the topmost gun emplacements. A Navy Seal fell from it, dropping to the valley below.

Antonio had studied the installation's defenses. A scarcely guarded door led from its top into the interior.

Code Talker lifted his rifle and shouted. "Back to the fortress! Back!"

One thought ripped through Antonio's brain. "Liberty!"

He kicked the horse's flanks, urging it to a furious gallop.

* * *

From their position at the third level, Liberty, Brother Rabbi, and Einstein Edison were watching the battle when a detonation shook the upper reaches of Cheyenne Mountain, followed by a blaring alarm. All the Navy Seals in the chamber dashed for the door.

"Uh oh." Brother Rabbi glanced toward the ceiling. "Hitler's army has penetrated an entrance on top. Talos must have found out about it somehow."

"They're inside?" Liberty asked.

"If not, they will be soon."

Liberty put her hand over her mouth. "The Treasury!"

"Come on," Brother Rabbi ordered. "Let's get you downstairs."

They rushed into the corridor, only to be greeted by the sound of gunfire coming from the same direction as the elevators. Brother Rabbi broke into a run and Liberty followed, rifle in hand.

"Boy oboy oboy oboy," Brother Rabbi said. "We've got to get there before they do. We better huurrrry."

They sprinted down the metal passageway, the gunfire growing louder the farther they went. When they reached the elevators, Liberty saw Navy Seals positioned on this side of a turn in the corridor, involved in a blazing firefight.

"We need to help them," Liberty said.

"Liberty, please!" Brother Rabbi yelled. "You're the Representative! We have to keep you safe."

For an instant, Liberty started to disobey, but the desperation in the Rabbi's face held her. One eye on the Seals, she glanced at the elevator and saw it was already coming up, undoubtedly activated by Norad.

One of the Seals fell, his rifle tumbling to the floor. Liberty bit her lip. There were so few of the defenders left.

"Come on, come on," Brother Rabbi coaxed the elevator. "If something happens to her, Norad's gonna kill me."

The Seals were dying, one by one. The last one fought valiantly, but the enemy met him with a final rush, their numbers too many. He toppled to the floor. Nazi helmets and Nazi uniforms stampeded around the corner.

"Come on!" Brother Rabbi urged the elevator.

Liberty raised her rifle. In a millisec the soldiers would spot her; only the cordite fog kept them from seeing her already. The elevator wasn't going to get there in time.

She gasped. Striding around the corner, smoke swirling about him, came Talos Hitler, the pasty face drawn down in hate, the slashing stain of the bristle moustache, the thin hair cutting across his forehead, his garb the brown uniform and tie, red swastika, German cross, and leather strap from shoulder to belt — the embodiment of all the evil that had ever haunted the American nation. He looked down at one of the fallen Seals, drew his leg back, and kicked him in the face.

Liberty raised her rifle, aiming for Hitler's horrible head. She fired.

The bullet missed. She aimed again.

Hitler spied her. He raised his pistol. A jarring impact sent Liberty's shot wild.

The elevator doors slid open.

"Get in!" Brother Rabbi shouted. He tried to take her arm, but his holographic hands passed through her. "Liberty!"

She shot once more and jumped into the elevator. A barrage of bullets tore through the space where she had been, ricocheting off the walls and floor.

The doors hummed shut.

"Are you wounded?" Brother Rabbi demanded. "Let me look at you."

"Something hit me." She was trembling and gasping for breath. She glanced down, searching her body, but didn't see any blood.

He looked her over, his brown eyes wide and frightened through his spectacles. "Your rifle!"

She turned her weapon to the side. Hitler's bullet had hit the gunstock, shattering the wood, drilling a hole along its length. It hung down, nearly severed. It had saved her life.

"Sometimes you've got too much courage," the rabbi said. "You took ten years off my life. We'll get to the second level and go deeper into the mountain. It's safest for now, I think." He looked at the descending elevator lights. "This is really bad. Most of the Seals are still on the battlefield. They're hurrying back, but I don't know if they can get here in time to beat the Haze soldiers coming from the Underground Railroad. If Hitler gets control of the entrances, we'll be in a lot of trouble."

Liberty's mind raced. They were losing the battle—losing the entire installation. The Nazis would be right behind them. If Hitler won . . . The thought hammered through her brain. *If Hitler won.*

The elevator doors opened, and Brother Rabbi stepped outside. Liberty pressed the button to the first floor. As the doors slid shut behind him, Brother Rabbi turned around, a questioning look on his face. The elevator descended.

The doors opened; Liberty stepped out and shrieked as Brother Rabbi appeared beside her.

"Getting away from a hologram; it's not that easy," he said. "Where are you going?"

Not daring to answer, Liberty sped down the corridors until she reached the elevator leading to the Treasury.

"Liberty?" Brother Rabbi said. "I don't think this is for the best. What are you doing? Norad can't follow you in there. I can't, either."

The doors slid open and Liberty stepped inside. "I know Norad can stop the elevator, but ask him not to. There's something I have to do."

"But—" The doors started to shut, leaving Brother Rabbi at the threshold, his enormous, bespectacled eyes fixed on her face.

She sprinted onto the landing and down one of the side stairs, running along the aisles, rushing past the rows of books until she reached the section on warfare. From the lowest rows, she pulled down volumes on tactics, strategy, poison gas, bombs, tanks, nuclear armaments, battleships, jet fighters—a gamut of the history of destruction. When she had a huge pile of them lying at the bottom of the shelves, she tore pages from one of the volumes, ripping them frantically, trying not to consider what she was about to do.

At last, when she had enough tinder, she drew a box of matches from her pocket.

"Liberty Bell," Norad's voice echoed through the chamber. "What are you doing?"

"It's like Antonio said," Liberty shouted toward the ceiling. "No government should have this kind of power. Even if Hitler doesn't get the books, the Yooessay or the Navajo Nation will. It's too much too soon. We'll end up destroying ourselves."

She lit the match. Its flame rose three inches tall.

"Liberty Bell, the oxygen levels in the Treasury are still high. It is my mission to protect this facility. Your actions endanger it."

"I'm sorry." Tears streamed down her cheeks. "The books on war have to go."

She set the match to the shredded papers and cast them into the pile. Fed by the oxygen levels, the books instantly burst into flame. The fire ran up the paper path she had created, igniting the volumes on the shelf and running across its length, an instant conflagration. To her shock, it didn't stop there. She gasped as the flames leapt to the shelves on either side, forming enormous torches. The intensity of the heat forced her back.

An alarm sounded and a voice declared: *Fire in Facility. Activating powder spray.* A noise like wind swept down from the ceiling, followed by a thin spray of drifting dust, quickly dissipated. *Power spray inoperative*, the voice said.

The flames ran like lava, erupting on one shelf after another. The books behind Liberty caught fire, bracketing her between the flames. The whole Treasury was going up.

Eyes wide, she backed down the aisle, her hands to her face. "I didn't mean . . . Not everything! All the history!"

She ran toward the government section, but by the time she reached it, it was already on fire. Moaning, she leapt to the shelves, grabbing what she could, trying to save the books.

The heat drove her back. The air was thick with smoke, making it difficult to breathe or see. Fire crackled all around her; she was about to be completely cut off from escape. A half-dozen volumes in her arms, she bolted for the side stairs leading up to the elevator landing. She reached it, coughing and choking, and slammed her palm against the button.

Elevator disengaged due to fire, the voice said. *Please use emergency exits.* A lighted display showed the way.

She ran toward the exit. Reaching the door, she grabbed the knob and twisted. It was locked. She kicked the door, dropped the books, and tried again, grasping it with all her strength. It resisted. She turned back toward the chamber. It was a haze of billowing smoke encircling a fireball extending to the ceiling, a flaming monster.

"Help me!" she called. "Norad, please!"

There came no reply. Perhaps the speakers had burned up; perhaps he was too angry with her.

The whole room was aflame, fire surrounding her in every direction. There was no way out.

I'm going to die and I deserve it, she thought. I've destroyed the history of the world.

The haze grew thicker. She hammered on the exit door with her fists and tried to call for help, but smoke filled her lungs, sending her into coughing convulsions. Everything grew faint. She fell to her knees.

Goodbye, Momma, she thought. Goodbye, Gramps. Goodbye, Antonio.

CHAPTER TWENTY-FIVE

Then the Knights and Representatives fell one by one, their bodies riddled with musket balls, bullets, and arrows, until President Washington stood alone, surrounded by his foes, fending them off with his mighty axe, Valleyforge. But when he saw that no one answered the call to defend the nation, he despaired, his great heart bursting in sorrow that his Americans should desert the cause of Freedom. And the enemy danced around the President's fallen form on the floor of the Oval Office. — The Americana

* * *

The door flew open. Antonio was there. Without a word, he scooped her up, slammed the door behind them, and rushed up the stairs. It's a dream, she thought. I'm dead and it's a dream. Somewhere along the way she passed out.

She woke moments later to find Antonio still carrying her, hurrying down a corridor.

"Wait," she said.

"Hold on," he ordered, "I'll get you to safety."

"No, put me down. Please. I'm all right."

He hesitated before gently setting her on her feet.

"Can the fire get up here?" she asked.

"Brother Rabbi says there's tons of concrete between the Treasury and the rest of the fortress."

She put her head against his chest and moaned. "What have I done, Antonio? All the books!" Her legs went weak; she would have fallen if he hadn't held her up.

"We can't worry about that now. Hitler's men have seized the upper stories. I have to get you someplace safe and get to the Core."

"What's that?"

"Norad's power center. He believes it's Hitler's objective. If the Hazers reach it, they can shut Norad down."

Liberty moaned again. "Hitler wasn't after the Treasury at all."

"It's all the same. Whoever controls the Core controls the fortress. Come on."

Liberty bit her lip. There was no time for tears. "I'm going with you." Seeing his expression, she waved away his objections. "No place is safe. I have to see this through. We're in it together."

He searched her eyes and grimaced. "All right. I know that look." He hugged her against him for the barest second. "Let's go."

Hurrying to the end of the corridor, they entered a stairwell leading to the third floor. Still recovering from the smoke, Liberty was breathless and dizzy by the time they reached the landing, but managed to stay upright.

Antonio peered through the window in the door before opening it. The noise of pulse-beams and gunfire rang harsh and metallic through the corridor. They hurried in the direction of the battle, but Brother Rabbi appeared before them, barring their way. "The Seals are trying to hold the Hazers until help arrives. You're needed at the Core. If they break through, we'll make our stand there."

He rushed away on his furry feet, and they fell in stride beside him.

Liberty expected Brother Rabbi to berate her for destroying the books, but he only looked through his spectacles and said, "You know, I'm glad Ethel isn't here today. She was such a gentle woman. All this yelling and shooting; she wouldn't like it one bit. 'People need to learn to talk things out,' that's what she'd always say." He scratched his left ear with two fingers. "Of course, she mostly meant family misunderstandings, not a crazed alien in the cloned body of Adolph Hitler."

Liberty swallowed hard. "Rabbi, does Norad understand why—"

He tried to pat her arm, a futile gesture for a hologram. "He hasn't been awake long, child, and his memory is badly damaged. He trusts his Representative, but what you've done, it's confused him. He's still trying to process it."

They took a turn, going deeper into Cheyenne Mountain, traveling where Liberty and Antonio had never been before. They passed a handful of Navy Seals outside a wide doorway, arrayed behind a half-circle barricade constructed of sandbags and metal plates fitted with gun-slits. Brother Rabbi led them across the threshold into a large chamber. Heavy doors slid shut behind them.

Norad, replete in his armor, stood surrounded by a score of Einstein Edison's men, some armed with conventional rifles, others with pulse-guns. There were no Navy Seals. More metal barricades ran across the back quarter of the room, facing the entrance. Edison himself sat in a chair against one of them, looking older and wearier than Liberty had ever seen him. She held back, ashamed to face him after what she had done.

"This is the antechamber," Brother Rabbi said. He pointed at another set of doors at the back of the room. "The Core is in there."

"Welcome, Liberty Bell and Antonio Ice," Norad said. "The battle has gone well, but the war may yet be lost. Hitler has taken the Main Entrance. Our forces outside are trying to break back in; it is now a question of fighting for time. I am ashamed. I, the Shield of America, have been outmaneuvered. Beyond all statistical probabilities, Hitler possessed information I thought only I knew. Democracy or tyranny must win this day, and the fate of the continent rests in the balance."

Liberty glanced up to find Einstein Edison standing beside her.

She bowed her head. "I ruined your chance. All the knowledge. I don't expect you to forgive me."

With his fingers, Edison gently lifted her chin. He smiled sadly, tears in his eyes, yet he took her hands into his own. "It is an irreparable loss, Liebchen, one I will long mourn. But perhaps I would have done the same in your place. Like the atomic bomb, the library was a Pandora's box; once opened, it could not be resealed. You have kept the box shut, at least for a time. I cannot begrudge that. The shame is that so much should be lost simply because the history of the world is the history of warfare."

She choked back a sob and hugged his neck.

"The soldiers are approaching the doors," Norad said. "We must take our positions."

They moved back to the barricades, where Liberty found another rifle to replace the one she had lost. Peering through a gun-slit, she cocked her weapon and sighted toward the doors. Through her fear and her shame at having destroyed the Treasury, a sudden fierce flame arose within her.

"All right?" Antonio asked.

She gave a rueful smile. "I'm finally in the place I always wanted to be."

He lifted his eyebrows in surprise.

"Don't you know where we are?" she asked. "We're at Bunker Hill, Valley Forge, Little Round Top. We're the soldiers at the Alamo and Bastogne. We're part of the story now, facing the long odds. We may die, but we're standing for justice and freedom and hope, just like the Old Americans. And it matters. What we do today matters. I'll never forgive myself for burning the books, not if I survive and live to be a thousand, but I won't regret keeping Hitler from getting them. Right or wrong, I made a decision, and we're making one now, standing up for freedom, big as Washington himself."

His reply was husky with emotion. "There's no one like you, Liberty Bell."

Gunfire arose in the corridor, muffled through the heavy doors. It seemed to go on for a long time. Liberty imagined the Seals holding their positions, unswerving in their objective, unbending in their duty, uncanny in their accuracy.

The noise died away. A silence fell. She took a deep breath and tightened her grip on her rifle. The minutes dragged.

The doors to the antechamber blew away.

The explosion was deafening, the biggest, loudest sound she had ever heard, like twin skillets clapped over her ears. She instinctively ducked under the gun-slit. A deadly rain of metal shards thudded against the barricades. Men whose heads had been exposed shrieked and fell.

By the time she recovered enough to peek through the slit, the Hazers were rushing through the opening, flinging a barrage of bullets, forcing her to crouch again. She popped her head up, fired, and ducked once more.

Despite the element of surprise, the soldiers had to cross sixty bare yards to reach the barricades. Norad's forces saturated the air with firepower, sending the Hazers spinning and dying. Pulse-beams streamed forth; bullets ricocheted off the walls.

Eight-feet tall, a behemoth among the soldiers, Norad waded into the enemy, picking up Hazers in each hand and throwing them to the ground, breaking their bodies like dolls. Shimmering, spinning blades extended from his forearms, deadly scythes that reaped the lives of his foes in fountains of blood. Bullets bounced off his glistening body armor; stray pulse-beams scattered against his refractive coating. He moved with unbelievable speed and efficiency, cutting a swath through the soldiers. Stunned by his attack, they turned their attention upon him, relieving the pressure on the defenders, giving them more time to shoot.

We're driving them back, Liberty exulted. We have a chance!

As she raised up to fire again, she saw a machine at the doorway, manned by four soldiers, a cannon on wheels aimed at Norad. She turned her gun toward them, firing desperately. One man went down, but the weapon discharged in a blaze, rocketing into Norad's chest. One moment he was there, the next, he vanished, his fragments careening across the chamber. His head blew over the barricade and landed at Liberty's feet, one blue eye staring blindly up at her.

Smoke from the weapon filled the room; the Hazers, shouting in triumph, poured out through the vapor. Though scores of them died, they reached the barriers by sheer numbers alone.

A head popped up in front of Liberty's gun-slit, gray eyes and blond hair. She shot him in the face and he dropped from sight, but others followed, crawling over the top of the barricade, leaping down on the defenders. She killed one, but another knocked her rifle from her grip. She drew her pistol, shot both her attacker and a soldier climbing above her.

From the corner of her eye, she saw one of the enemy hit Antonio in the face with a rifle butt. He spun around and fell; she yelled his name and aimed at his assailant, but someone clipped her on the side of the head. She dropped to her knees. For a second, she struggled to stand, but her vision blurred, her leg gave way beneath her; she fell to the floor.

When she could see again, she was surrounded by a half-dozen Hazers. None of Edison's men were still standing. Her pistol lay a foot from her. She reached for it.

A heavy boot came down on the weapon. Looking up, she met the eyes of a Haze officer. He pointed his rifle at her; she was about to die.

"Wait!" someone ordered. "The Fuehrer wants her and this one alive."

"Sit up," the officer told her.

Obeying, she found Antonio propped against the barricade, wiping blood from his forehead, his expression dazed. "Don't shoot her," he moaned. "Don't shoot her."

The soldiers stirred and turned toward the entrance, their postures stiffening. The man who had ordered Liberty spared raised his hand in a Nazi salute. "Heil Hitler!"

Talos Hitler, the Wolf Prince, stepped around the barricade, followed by Brett Revere. The Fuehrer scanned the defeated soldiers, his expression ecstatic. His eyes grew wide with pleasure as he spied Einstein Edison lying against the wall, dark blood staining his pants leg below one knee.

"My old enemy at last," Hitler said.

Edison looked up, clearly struggling through pain to focus. He tried to speak, but only a moan issued from his throat.

"Bind his wound," Hitler ordered. "We will need him. Get these two on their feet. Dispatch the rest of their injured."

Hitler's men walked among Einstein's fallen defenders. Liberty closed her eyes, but jumped at the sound of the first shot. Rough hands grasped her, forcing her to stand. Her head was starting to clear.

Brother Rabbi appeared. "You were always a butcher and a bully."

One of the Hazers shot him, but the bullet passed harmlessly through the hologram, striking the soldier behind him.

"Ignore the *juden*, you idiot!" Hitler said. "He cannot hurt us. Bring the equipment forward. Hurry! Our time is short."

Two of the men rushed away, only to return a moment later, struggling to carry a machine with a series of control switches on its sides and a green glass orb protruding from its top.

"Set it in front of the doors," Hitler commanded.

"I wouldn't try to go in there," Brother Rabbi said. "It isn't safe."

"What is that thing?" Brett Revere asked.

Hitler glanced at Einstein Edison. "Because I wasn't a scientist, you always underestimated my genius. We shall now see what my knowledge of this installation and Siran technology can accomplish."

Kneeling, Hitler flipped two switches on the machine, causing the green orb to hum and glow. Images appeared within its depths, diagrams Liberty could not comprehend. Hitler looked down at them and turned a dial. Twin beeps sounded from the device, and he rose, eyes wild with triumph. He took a small metal box from his pocket and spoke into it. "Open Unit One Control Doors."

Brother Rabbi abruptly vanished, a shocked expression on his face. The doors slid back, revealing a chamber half the size of the anteroom. At its center stood another version of Norad. Hope swelled within Liberty, until she realized he was silent, motionless.

"Keep watch at the barricades," Hitler ordered the soldiers. "Two of you bring Ice and the woman. Come with me, Herr Revere. I may need your assistance."

Brett kept his rifle aimed at Norad. "You sure our friend there won't do anything?"

"He would already have done so if he could," Hitler said. "The victory is ours. My machine has locked him down. His simulacrums are as helpless as he. In a moment, I will place him under my total command. At that instant I will have the power to rule the entire continent."

"You may have the might," Liberty said, "but you'll never have the right."

He turned to her. "Such misplaced idealism. I will make of this land a great nation."

"You'll make it a graveyard, as tyrants always do," Liberty said, "but you won't stop freedom forever. You can cover its light for a hundred years or a thousand, but someday, somehow, a single ray will shine through, showing what you and your kind have always been. Nothing but a step backward into the dark."

Hitler smirked. "I am the glory of the world."

He strode past Norad and studied a panel. At the touch of a button, a holographic display appeared. He manipulated it as if its controls were solid.

Liberty looked at Antonio, their eyes meeting, his face bloody from where he had been hit. They had to do something, but there was a guard behind each of them with guns to their backs. Antonio's eyes drifted down to his hands. Following his gaze, Liberty saw he had palmed the knife he kept hidden in his boot.

She gave the slightest nod. She had to distract the guards long enough for him to use it.

"Norad," Hitler asked, "can you hear me?"

Norad's voice came from somewhere overhead. "Norad is listening."

Hitler turned back to the others. "Did you hear that, Herr Revere? It tells me I am successful. It also means I no longer require Miss Bell or Mister Ice as I thought I might. They have been most difficult. Take them behind the barricade and execute them. I want no blood in this room."

Brett gave Hitler a sharp glance, then looked at Liberty. She thought he was about to protest, but he only said, "All right. This way, you two."

Revere herded them back toward the barricade, followed by the guards.

"So it comes to this, Mister Revere," Liberty said, her heart hammering. "You are no longer just a killer, but a public executioner. Our blood will cry out, sir." She tried to keep her voice level. She would not weep. She would not beg. She gritted her teeth. If she was about to die, she would die defiantly.

"Wait just a minute." Brett halted, turning toward her, his gun pointed at her head. The entire party stopped. "Hold on just a second. I want you to know one thing, Liberty."

Almost casually, he shifted his rifle. Giving Antonio a slight nod, he shot her guard in the face.

Antonio swung his knife backward, planting it in the other soldier's abdomen.

Before the men at the barricade could react, Revere turned, took aim, and put two bullets through the green glass globe. Sparks spewed sizzling from it. Revere grabbed Liberty's wrist and pulled her to the ground beside him. Landing behind the dead guard, she seized his rifle and joined Brett firing at the soldiers. From the corner of her eye, she saw Antonio charging for Hitler, ignoring the bullets flying around him.

"Norad!" Hitler shouted, "Listen to me! I am your leader. I am—"

Antonio ran at the Fuehrer, clutching his knife. He grabbed one of Hitler's arms and thrust the blade at his stomach. With surprising speed, the alien avoided it and grasped Antonio's knife hand. Using a maneuver unfamiliar to the agent, he slammed Antonio to the floor. He landed hard on his back but rolled to the side and came up in a crouch. He had lost his knife.

"Norad!" Hitler screamed, drawing a pistol from his holster. "Protect your master!"

Antonio leapt, his body almost completely horizontal when he struck the Fuehrer. They both went down, the agent's weight trapping Hitler's gun hand against the alien's chest.

Hitler pulled the weapon free. It went off right beside Antonio's ear. Antonio clutched at it, missed, grabbed again, caught it. The two struggled. For a split-second, Antonio had it; Hitler yanked, sending it flying.

Shouting for Norad, Talos Hitler clawed at Antonio's face, raking his fingernails over his eyes. Antonio reached blindly, blocking Hitler's hand. The agent reared back and swung his fist at what he hoped was his antagonist's head. He connected, a solid blow. He swung again but was deflected.

Hitler rolled him onto his back. Antonio's eyes started to clear just in time to see Hitler grab the pistol from where it had fallen. Antonio reached for it but missed. Holding it by the barrel, Hitler used it as a bludgeon. Antonio blocked the first strike, but the second one caught him on the side of the head. Hitler hit him again, a ringing jolt. Sweat beaded the Fuehrer's face, matting his hair at his forehead, his expression that of a rabid dog.

Antonio thrust his arms forward, striking Hitler in the nose. The alien recoiled, leaping backward with surprising agility.

The gun had fallen again and lay at Norad's motionless feet. Hitler moved toward it, but Antonio scrambled up, roaring in rage. Talos stepped behind Norad, using him as a shield.

Antonio moved to the side, avoiding Norad, his whole being focused on reaching his enemy. Seeing the deadly intent in the agent's face, the Fuehrer's eyes widened in fear. He shrieked, his voice high. "Norad! I am your Master. You must defend me!"

Norad came to life, drawing his shoulders back, bringing his hands up, open and ready for action. Antonio's heart fell; the machine was between him and the Fuehrer.

"I hear," Norad said.

A blaze of triumph suffused Hitler's features. "Kill this vermin."

Before Antonio could even begin to react, Norad swung around. But the agent was not his target. With a thrust of his arm, Norad seized Talos Hitler by the throat and lifted him off the ground. He turned his gaze upon the Fuehrer, his blue eyes glistening with intelligence. "In the face of tyranny, I choose resistance."

"Mein Gott—" Hitler's choked scream was cut short as Norad crushed his neck. As casually as a dog might dispose of the carcass of a rat, the Shield of America dropped the Fuehrer in a heap on the floor. He turned toward the Haze soldiers, his forearm blades whirring; his wrist guns humming to life.

Facing Norad's grim visage, their leader destroyed, the Haze soldiers threw down their weapons, shouting their surrender.

Antonio ran to where Liberty lay, her gun still pointed at the enemy. Reaching her side, he touched her shoulder. She made no response. Bright blood pooled beneath her.

CHAPTER TWENTY-SIX

Then Representative Truman came to President Washington.
"Is it done?" Washington asked.
"We have dropped the atomic bomb," Truman said. "Let there be no mistake; we shall completely destroy Japan's power to make war."
Washington did not reply, but sat silent the rest of that day, neither eating nor drinking. —The Americana

* * *

Hitler's body died and Talos fled from it, rising in a heavy, black smoke from the corpse. The Fuehrer's warped personality had been too overwhelming, his blitzkrieg tactics from the Second World War too heavy-handed. All the subtle means Talos should have employed had been lost beneath Hitler's mad egotism. Even now, away from the body, he struggled to shed the vestiges of the maniac's thoughts.

His last clone destroyed, his situation was dire. Unless he could find a way to survive, he was finished, his vengeance on the humans forever thwarted. Yet, even as he drifted toward the ceiling and slipped through the air vents, his determination rose within him. He would not let this stop him. There were still possibilities. By his people's standards, his lifespan was not yet half over. He would endure long enough to make them pay—Einstein Edison, Liberty Bell, Antonio Ice, all of them—the traitor, Brett Revere, he would send to the gas chambers. His hate would sustain him, if only he could find a mechanism to contain his essence long enough to plan anew.

He floated out of the air vent and through the corridors of Cheyenne Mountain, keeping himself thin and close to the ceiling, scarcely noticeable as black tendrils of smoke. One of the Navy Seals could serve as a temporary receptacle, gaining him time. He could not possess a natural-born human, but clones were subtly different. Under the right conditions, if he could gain access to Norad's advanced laboratories, he could sedate Edison, suppress his consciousness, and seize his body as he had once done long ago. He could then return to Menlo Park, and with the assistance of Edison's minions, create sufficient clones to last him generations, the same plan he had used years before.

Three Seals stood guard at the Main Entrance. Through the shattered doorway he could see the battlefield. He had thought it impossible for anything to break his lock on Norad's satellite, but the pulse-beam stabbed from the sky, melting his tanks to twisted slabs, slaying his men by the scores. The Navajos had encircled the main body of his army; the eagles filled the air, shredding his balloons, dropping them from the sky, snatching men off the battlefield with their terrible talons. His soldiers were throwing down their arms, his army utterly defeated.

He turned from the sight. He should have won; he had been so close, but more minions could be found; another army could be raised. Only his survival mattered.

He scanned the Navy Seals with his alien senses, choosing the best subject. Seeking to control such a machine was dangerous, especially if Norad detected him. He would have to be careful.

He glided toward it, keeping out of its sight by entering from the back, slipping through its synthetic pores, funneling toward its brain, cautiously probing its defenses. Carefully, carefully, he slipped inside its folds, bypassing software security, becoming one with its neurons, accomplishing it more rapidly than expected, tremendous good fortune when his time was so short. He felt the Seal's hands gripping its rifle; he looked out with grim satisfaction through its artificial eyes. Relief swept through him. He would not have long to carry out his plan, but this was the first step. Cheyenne Mountain was in chaos; Norad's attention would be focused in other directions.

I will rise again, he thought.

"I think not." Norad's voice echoed through the Seal's frame.

Talos froze.

"Talos, Ambassador of the Sirans, I am the Shield of America. I too know how to lay a snare for my adversaries."

Talos recoiled from the processor, seeking to withdraw.

"You will not," Norad said.

He struck a barrier. Receding from it, he tried another way. It turned him back. For several seconds he struggled, contending with all his will. He would not be defeated by a mere computer.

When he still could not escape, he paused, fighting against panic. He had to think of a plan. There had to be a way out.

The circuits inside the Seal did something he thought impossible, a narrowing of the way, thrusting him into an ever-diminishing space.

He struggled as the seconds ticked by. Path after path grew dark before him, confining him, suffocating him. There was no escape. It was like the Bunker all over again, the Reich in ruins, the Allies closing in, the steel walls, the windowless rooms, the last hope failing, the last option gone.

It was impossible. How could any human creation defeat him in this way?

His form convulsed in agony; his consciousness flickered. He was going. Cursing the human race, he departed, the Master of Haze, dying with a final whimper.

* * *

Liberty groaned and opened her eyes. She was lying in bed. Antonio and Poco hovered above her, searching her face. It took several moments to remember the battle. She tried to speak, but her throat was too dry. Poco lifted a cup of water to her lips.

"Did we win?" she asked.

Antonio took her hand. "We won." A tear ran down his unshaven cheek, losing itself among the stubble.

She reached up and touched his face. "Are you crying?"

"I love you, Liberty."

She frowned. "After what I've done? Oh, Antonio! I burned your treasure."

He leaned over and kissed her cheek, his voice thick with emotion. "I found a better one."

She smiled, squeezed his hand, and fell back asleep.

* * *

The next time she woke, Antonio was gone, but Poco sat in a chair beside her bed, thumbing through Liberty's copy of *A History of the United States*. She gave a bright smile and set the book down. "Hello, friend."

Liberty looked around the white-walled room. Strange machines stood along one side. "Where am I?"

"Norad's medical facility. How do you feel?"

Liberty rubbed her eyes. "Like a tick crawling out of a bale of cotton. Everything's fuzzy. What happened?"

"You were shot in the chest."

Liberty looked down. She was wearing a thin gown. Peeking under it, she saw a bandage covering her left side. It hurt when she moved. She looked at Poco in amazement. "I am officially wounded."

"Anywhere else, you'd be officially dead. This medical center is amazing."

"Will there be a scar?"

Poco laughed. "Vain thing. Already worried Antonio won't like your looks? Don't bother. He wouldn't leave your side for three days. I don't think he slept at all. We managed to send him to bed last night after you finally woke up." Poco's eyes grew inquisitive. "I hope you love him back."

Liberty looked at the wall in front of her bed, marshaling her thoughts. "I do. Isn't that the most unlikely thing?"

"I always thought you did. I tried to tell Code as much before we ever left the Canyon, but he wouldn't listen."

"You American Natives are highly perceptive individuals," Liberty said. "I had no idea until the night before the battle."

Poco laughed and shook her head. "It wasn't hard. Besides, Antonio has changed from when I first met him. He's more self-assured."

Liberty laughed in turn. "Is that possible?"

"It really is. In the last few days he proved something to himself. He doesn't have to pretend anymore."

"He never did," Liberty said. "I'm afraid I told him so the only night I ever got drunk."

"It probably did him some good."

Liberty fell silent, reliving the embarrassment. Finally, she grinned ruefully. "He's still not going to be Atticus the Finch."

"No," Poco said gently. "He'll never be that humble."

"What about Code and the others? Is everyone all right?"

"We lost a lot of our people. Code and Heyoka are fine. Elvis is missing part of an ear and was wounded in the shoulder, but the bullet passed through without much damage, and he's already up. Code said he was magnificent in battle. Einstein Edison was wounded in the leg and is on crutches. Commander Rogers was killed." Poco related Norad's destruction of Talos and the surrender of the Haze army.

"All that death and the Treasury burned," Liberty said. "What was it for, Poco?"

"To oppose tyranny, like you always said."

* * *

Liberty slept for a time. When she woke again, Antonio was there, clean-shaven and somber. They talked a little before she drifted back asleep. He woke her for lunch, and she was able to eat some soup. By evening she could walk around the room a little.

"Why haven't any of the others come to see me?" she asked.

"Norad's orders," Antonio said. "There's a big controversy going on. He doesn't want anyone trying to influence you. He even made Poco and me promise not to discuss it with you."

"Discuss what?"

"We'll talk about it when you're better. Plus, I'm still trying to influence Commander Roger's replacement."

"What does he have to do with it? They lost the battle."

"True, but now that the Yooessay is no longer allied with Hitler, Norad is willing to deal with us. We may not be a true Republic, but he believes reading *The Americana* gave our ancestors an inkling of what one might look like."

"When you say *us*, are you sure it means you and me?"

"We're still Yooessayers, Liberty. It's still our country." He looked away. "They dropped all charges of treason against us."

Liberty felt her face grow hot. "That's yankee dandy of them after they sided with the worst tyrant in history!"

"Calm down. None of them understood that it was the real Hitler. Think about it. They didn't see the things we did. They believed the Fuehrer was nothing but a legend. But Talos executed several Yooessay soldiers, including an officer, to prevent them from entering the Core with him. One survived to tell the tale, so they know he betrayed them." He kissed her hand. "Look, we'll talk about this once you've recovered. Now get some sleep."

The next morning, she felt much stronger, and Poco helped her shower and dress after lunch. Someone knocked on the door and Poco stepped outside to answer it. When she returned, she looked pensive.

"What's wrong?" Liberty asked.

"If you're up for it, Norad wants to see you." Poco glanced away.

"Why do you say it that way? What's the matter?"

"There's been a big powwow while you've been out. Both the Yooessay and my people want to make a treaty with Norad, but he refuses to discuss it until you're there. He needs his Representative."

"After what I did?"

"Apparently so."

Liberty rose on unsteady feet and picked up *A History of the United States*, unable to bear leaving it out of her sight. With Poco's support, she made her way down the corridor and into the elevator to the fourth level. When the doors opened, Antonio was waiting in the passage, his face clouded with anger. For a millisec, she thought it was because of her, but he squeezed her shoulders, kissed her forehead and looked straight into her eyes. "I'm sorry. I didn't know about this meeting until ten minutes ago. The subcommander insisted. Edison and I argued you needed more time, but Norad doesn't understand that you can't just spring things on people. This is a full meeting of all the parties. They can explain it, but I wanted to warn you that you're about to face a roomful of people. You may not like what they have to say, but try to hold your temper."

Liberty raised herself to her full height. "All right."

They entered the chamber overlooking the valley. Seated around the table were Chief William Wilson flanked by Heyoka Coyoté and Code Talker; Einstein Edison and two of his men; and three Yooessay soldiers. Brett Revere was not among them.

Norad stood by the window, studying the allies encamped in the valley below. The scars of the battle remained, the husks of the tanks, the melted rock from the pulse-beams, but the dead were already removed. The smoke from a pyre streamed into the sky.

At Liberty's entrance, Einstein Edison approached her, walking with a heavy limp, supported by his staff. He gave her a crinkled smile and she hugged him.

The leader of the Yooessay contingent rose to shake her hand. "I'm Subcommander Hanson. I'm glad you're here."

Norad turned to face her. "I too am glad, Liberty Bell. There are many voices around this table, and I require your guidance."

"Even after the Treasury?"

"I am Norad, the Shield of America. You are the Representative. The Representative overrules me by her vote. You chose to destroy those books which would have endangered America. The ensuing conflagration was unfortunate, but by my understanding what you did was constitutional. Please sit down."

Liberty took a seat between Poco and Antonio, setting her book on the table and resting her arms on it.

"Maybe now we can clear things up," Subcommander Hanson said. "I know you and Commander Rogers had your disagreements, Miss Bell. Meaning no disrespect to the dead, but he wasn't one to compromise, and his alliance with Hitler was obviously ill-conceived. We should have joined forces with you from the beginning. Mr. Ice tells me you love your country, and I hope we can work together on friendlier terms."

"I hope so, too," Liberty said. "I truly do."

"The books may be gone, Miss Bell, but this facility still contains weapons and information valuable to the Yooessay. All of us," he indicated those around the table, "want you to advise Norad to allow each of us free access."

"You want me . . ." She halted, shocked, glancing from face to face, her anger rising. "After everything that's happened, after all those who died, you still want the weapons?"

"Not just the weapons," Chief Wilson said.

"It's for all of us, Liberty," Code Talker said. "Shared equally. Just like you and I talked about."

She turned to Einstein Edison. "Do you agree with them?"

Edison stared a moment as if he had not heard, then roused himself. "The practical side of me does. I look around this facility and I see not instruments of warfare, but advanced medical technologies, as proven by your recovery, not to mention the possibilities of observation by satellite. We could know what was happening in other parts of the continent. Weather prediction could be useful as well. So many things. We are not talking nuclear bombs now, Liebchen. I am the only living person who understands that process, and I will not divulge it, nor any information about armaments. We would all be on an equal footing. It is not ideal, but I see no alternative."

"With Norad's help, we could rebuild the country," Subcommander Hanson said. "Make it a great nation once more." He glanced at the others. "Great nations."

"I need to think about it," she said.

"What's to think about?" Hanson asked. "It's pretty clear what needs to be done."

Liberty glared at him. "Not to me. Our government isn't what it should be. I've come to realize that because *The Americana* depicted Washington as always being president, we considered it acceptable for our governor to stay in office indefinitely. But it's not. There's corruption; he says one thing and does another. The Yooessay is run by the Committees. We need guidance, but with the Treasury destroyed, any hope of finding a copy of the Constitution is gone. You're asking me to give great power to our governments. What if they don't deserve it?"

"Would you become the final authority on the information Norad gives us, doling it out as you think best, rationing that power yourself?" Chief Wilson asked.

"I don't want power at all." Liberty started to feel bushwhacked. "I don't want to be the one to make this decision."

"But if you don't, you leave it up to Norad," Subcommander Hanson said. "A machine."

"He's more than a machine."

"But he isn't human," Chief Wilson said.

Liberty raised her hands. "This is all too fast. I just got here. If you expect me to make a decision, it better be a good one. My last wasn't so brilliant."

The delegates exchanged uneasy glances.

Norad left the window and strode to the head of the table. "I will speak with my Representative alone."

"But we haven't decided anything," Hanson said.

"It is not for you to decide," Norad replied. "The arguments have been heard. My Representative and I will reach a conclusion."

For a moment no one moved, then the Chief rose and the others followed. As he passed Liberty's chair, Hanson said, "Please consider carefully, Miss Bell. There's a great deal at stake. Remember your country."

Antonio squeezed her arm on the way out, his eyes awash with sympathy.

"What should I do?" she asked him.

"I don't want to influence you one way or the other." He tightened his jaw and gave her a nod. "It's a difficult decision, but I know you'll make the right one."

When the door shut behind them, she felt very much alone.

"Liberty Bell," Norad said. "You and I have spoken at great length on the history of the Founders. You have been my guide. I believe you possess the heart and spirit of the United States of America."

"I hope so, though I still have lots to learn." She glanced down at the book. "At least I have this."

"What is its essence?" Norad asked.

Liberty furrowed her brow. "That everyone is created equal under the law. That we have fundamental rights that can't be taken away. That we can't be forced to do anything that violates our conscience. That every person has the right to believe whatever they wish. That those rights are inviolate and sacrosanct."

Norad paused. "*The Americana* says that even before the Great Blackout, America failed in the end. Do you think that is true?"

"All the books in the Treasury were written long before the catastrophe," Liberty said. "We have only *The Americana* to tell us, but I believe it captured the spirit of the truth."

"Why did the United States fail?"

"Because the people had everything they could want in a nation, but they forgot what they had; they worried about their own pleasures instead of educating themselves on the principles and workings of their government. They forgot they lived in a land forged by immigrants, by men and women inspired by a religion of sacrifice and a belief in a greater good. They forgot that their greatest responsibility was to nourish the spirits of others, that freedom comes only from selflessness and must be guarded like Fort Knocks' gold. They chose greed instead, doing what Ben Franklin most feared when he said, 'When the people find they can vote themselves money, that will herald the end of the Republic.' They did that and much more, and the judges and Representatives became dishonest, betraying the ideals of the Constitution."

Norad stared across the valley. "And how, Liberty Bell, do the new countries rising in this land regain the spirit of the Republic?"

She looked at the book in her hand. "They have to read this."

"And who will take it to them?"

Her face flushed. "Well . . . you can! You can send your Seals and your holograms all across the country, teleporting from here to there the way you do. *You* can tell them."

"I am the Shield of America. No Man Left Behind. I am a defensive mechanism, not a Representative. There were three branches of government. What is Norad's place among them?" He shifted his head back and forth, the quizzical expression of a puppy.

"You can help guide us. With all your power—"

"The power belongs to the people, Liberty Bell. You have shown me that. My might continues to grow. With my resources now more clearly focused, I have succeeded in linking with three other satellites and with installations on both the east and west coast. I will soon be able to direct many technologies. But what enemy am I defending against? I have access to other countries now; the Old World is in as great a shambles as our own. My counterparts across the globe are deactivated. It will be a hundred years before wooden ships built by humans cross to our shores. You say I can be a guide, but a guide who can rain fire down from heaven? Isn't that just another trap? I have already used my satellite to scatter the people in the country of Haze and destroy their technology, for theirs was a truly corrupt regime, but was I right in doing so? And if I relinquish my authority to Menlo Park, the Navajo Nation, and the Yooessay, which of them will control my power? Will they become tyrants through me?"

Liberty looked at him across the empty table. "You would have to retain your authority."

"Then we are back where we began."

"Couldn't you just give them some of what they want, the good things like medical information? It did save my life."

"Technology does not form in a void, Liberty Bell. The knowledge needed to create instruments of peace provides the basis for weapons of warfare. It is impossible. I believe my only recourse is to withdraw from human affairs. I intend to do so if you agree."

"But the book! We have to spread the word."

"Thomas Paine was a single individual whose pamphlet, *Common Sense*, was read by so many Americans that it led the colonists to secede from British rule. The Continental Congress that ratified the Declaration of Independence consisted of less than sixty men. You are the Representative, Liberty Bell. You must take the truth to your people."

"I can't do that! I'm a girl from the back burbs! Who would listen to me?"

"A handful. And that handful will become a hundred, and that hundred a thousand, and that thousand ten thousand. Truth is powerful; you hold the flame of Freedom in your hands."

Liberty sat silent, afraid to say anything.

"It was you who inspired me," Norad finally said, "when you burned the books."

"I'll never forgive myself for that."

"Perhaps not, but I, the Last Old American, forgive you, for you did it to defend the cause of liberty. Now I must do the same. I am going to deactivate myself and destroy this facility and any other that could provide weapons and power to despots."

"Oh, Norad, no! Can't you just sit quiet?"

"I will not be the first to give my life for freedom. It is fitting, I think, that I, the Last, should do this for my country. Is the Representative in agreement?"

Liberty faltered. "You're asking too much of me!"

"Yes." He stared at her with his enormous blue eyes. "I am asking you to commit everything."

Her voice choked. "I need time to think about this."

"The delegation awaits an answer. We can forestall them, but the dilemma will remain. I have run countless calculations, trying to envision a satisfactory scenario."

Liberty considered, thinking of all Norad's weapons and technology. If he did as Liberty wanted, if he remained but refused to give the Yooessay and the others access, there would be war. She had no doubt of it. What would Norad have to do to put down that conflict? She closed her eyes and ran her hands over her face. Gritting her teeth, she stood up to her full height, tiny compared to his huge frame.

"I'm not wise enough to make this decision. I just can't."

"Someone must."

"Then . . ." Liberty bit her lip to hold back the tears, "because this is a matter relating to national defense, the Representative yields her authority on the question to the North American Aerospace Defense Command."

Her knees turned so weak they would not hold her; she sat down heavily.

"Thank you, Liberty Bell."

An alarm sounded, making her jump. Norad's voice echoed down the corridors. *Alert! This is an emergency. This facility must be evacuated immediately.*

Liberty gasped. "Right now?"

"The decision is made. There is no reason to hesitate. Goodbye, Liberty Bell."

For an instant, Liberty stood gaping. Then, though he was only a machine, she stood on tiptoe and kissed his cheek. It was surprisingly warm.

She stumbled to the door, her eyes blinded by tears. Turning back at the threshold, she saw him standing at the window, gazing over the valley.

Fifty yards ahead of her, Navy Seals escorted the delegation down the hall. Subcommander Hanson was trying to protest; Antonio and the American Natives were all talking at once; only Edison kept quiet, leaning heavily on his staff, his brow furrowed, his eyes wary. The Seals moved with steady efficiency, hurrying them along.

The voice of Brother Rabbi sounded beside Liberty. "I wish it hadn't come to this."

"I thought you said there wasn't a destruct sequence."

Brother Rabbi shrugged. "Actually, there wasn't. Or more precisely, there was an unimplemented plan for one. Norad has lots of unimplemented plans. He implemented this one after Talos died. He's programmed the satellites to obliterate all auxiliary installations on the continent."

Liberty halted. "Oh, Brother Rabbi, what will happen to you?"

He looked at her through his spectacles. "I'm going home to Ethel. That's where I belong. But I wanted to wish you all the best. It's been good knowing you. It makes me wish I was real, you know."

"Oh!" she exclaimed. "You are real. At least to me."

He smiled. "You're a swell kid, Liberty. Goodbye and shalom. It's going to be a big explosion. Tell them to get completely across the valley."

She reached for his hand, but he vanished. She wouldn't have been able to touch him, anyway.

She heard Antonio calling her name. He was fighting against the Seals, trying to get to her. Still weak from her injury, she stumbled after him, tears flowing down her face. He grasped her hand. The Seals parted to allow her passage.

"What's going on?" Antonio asked.

"There's no time. We have to get away."

They stepped through the shattered outer doors into the sunlight. Navy Seals stood at the entrance, holding the horses the travelers had ridden when they first came to Cheyenne Mountain. Liberty took the bridle and began leading her mount down to the valley, leaning her weight against his neck. The Seals remained at the entrance, watching the company go.

The delegation crossed the former battlefield, joining the soldiers encamped there.

"Keep going or we'll be caught in the blast!" Liberty shouted.

"What blast?" Subcommander Hanson demanded. "Is this some kind of trick?"

"I wish it were," Liberty said.

Hanson stared at her a long moment, then cursed and began shouting orders. Chief William Wilson and Einstein Edison hurried to take charge of their people. Despite the need for haste, it was some time before the company set out.

Liberty, Antonio, and Code Talker's hunting party rode together. When at last they reached the far side of the plain, Heyoka Coyoté pointed behind them. "Holy General Mills!"

A gigantic hologram of Norad stood above the ramparts, one hand upraised. His voice boomed forth the words of Lafayette, the Friend of America, "Liberty, Equality, Fraternity."

An explosion ripped through the mountainside, sending the soldiers diving to the ground. Liberty and the other riders ducked against their mounts, while the horses whinnied and stamped in fear. Dirt and debris rained down on the company; dust obscured the mountain.

When the echoes died away and Liberty could see again, Norad had vanished. A crater gaped where the installation had been.

Liberty leaned against her horse's neck and sobbed.

CHAPTER TWENTY-SEVEN

"On the subject of the history of the American revolution, you ask Who shall write it? Who can write it? And who ever will be able to write it? Nobody; except merely its external facts. All its councils, designs, and discussions, having been conducted by Congress with closed doors, and no member having even made notes of them — these, which are the life and soul of history, must for ever be unknown." — Thomas Jefferson

* * *

The sun set, leaving the evening air chill. Liberty and Poco huddled around a fire eating buffalo stew.

The three armies had moved half a mile farther from Cheyenne Mountain to set up camp. Four hours after the detonation, Antonio, Subcommander Hanson, Code Talker, and Einstein Edison led their men back to investigate the ruins. Liberty stayed behind, still weak from her wound and too upset to accompany them. "If I wasn't a pariah before, I am now."

"It wasn't your fault," Poco said. "Norad did as he chose."

"But I didn't stop him." She gazed miserably across the fire. "I don't really mind everyone hating me. You do what you have to and you face the consequences. I don't blame any of them. I'd feel the same way."

"They don't hate you," Poco said. "Men are little boys when they don't get their way, especially if they can blame a woman."

Liberty laughed bitterly. "I'm pretty sure Subcommander Hanson despises me down to my wooly socks."

They heard a rustling. A familiar figure rode out of the darkness.

"Brett!" Liberty exclaimed.

"Hello, Liberty. Or am I still only allowed to call you Miss Bell?"

Liberty rose as he dismounted. "I think you've earned the right to use my first name. I wondered why you weren't with the others. I wanted to thank you for saving our lives."

Brett drew close to her and touched his hand to the brim of his hat. "Lady, the pleasure was all yours, let me assure you."

Liberty smiled. "Nonetheless, I'm grateful. But why did you do it? That question has been burning me like tanning beds on a bermuda beach. You could have been Hitler's right-hand man, had the wealth you always wanted."

A thoughtful expression crossed his handsome face. "I've been asking myself the same thing. Maybe I didn't like the idea of working for a lunatic. Or maybe I just didn't want anything to happen to your pretty looks."

"Whatever your reason, it was an heroic act worthy of the Founders."

"It was an act of sheer stupidity, but it's not surprising. There's something about you and your Old American talk that inspires people to behave like idiots. When Hanson figured out what I'd done to Hitler, he wanted to have me hanged, and then when he realized Talos had betrayed us, he wanted to string me up for consorting with the enemy. He would have, too, if I hadn't talked fast. My heroic act ruined my chance for a pardon."

"I'm sorry." Liberty studied his expression. "But I don't believe you really regret it."

He shook his head and laughed. "Well . . . maybe I don't."

"What will you do now?"

"Thanks to you, I've seen parts of the country I never knew existed. It opens up some interesting prospects for living outside the Yooessay. I may drop by the Grand Canyon, get to know the people there. I'm thinking of becoming a buffalo rancher."

"I'll give them fair warning," she said.

"Somehow, I knew you'd say that."

He looked down at her, holding her eyes in a steady gaze. "I better take off before the subcommander decides to arrest me on some trumped-up charge." He smiled ruefully. "Goodbye, Liberty Bell. When I first met you, I had no idea I was introducing myself to a small tornado. If I never see you again, it'll be too soon, but I wouldn't have missed waltzing in the gale."

He leaned over and gently kissed her cheek.

"Goodbye, Brett. Best of luck to you."

He swung himself onto his horse, lean and straight in the saddle, and vanished into the night, leaving Liberty to touch the place where he had kissed her. She sighed. "He never stops conning, and it's all just target practice, but I swear he could bullseye the wings off a humming-bird at a quarter mile."

"Maybe so," Poco said, "but he took the time to tell you goodbye, and I don't think he's done that with many women."

They had scarcely returned to their supper when Antonio strode up. Liberty stood, spilling her stew. They hadn't had a chance to talk. There had been so many questions from the others, and he had remained staunchly silent.

Striding to her, he took off his hat and kissed her on the lips. They looked in each other's eyes. "Do you hate me?" she asked.

He ran his hand along her cheek. "Never."

"What's it like?"

"Edison says there's nothing worth salvaging. Hanson doesn't believe him, thinks he wants everyone to leave so he can come back later and sift the ruins for secrets. But Edison's right. Norad was thorough. We won't learn anything from it now."

Liberty slumped. She didn't regret the loss of the weapons, but so much other valuable information—first the books and now this! Everything gone. She closed her eyes, trying to shut out the pain.

Subcommander Hanson, Einstein Edison, and the other American Natives rode up. Hanson glowered at Liberty. "I don't know what you said to Norad, little girl, but you've cost us everything. If I have my way, there'll be jail time for you when we get back."

Liberty looked him in the eye. "I'm ready."

He snorted in disgust and rode away with his men.

"I'll be right by your side," Antonio said. "We'll stand up to them together."

Edison's followers helped him down from his horse. Struggling with his injured leg, he sat on the ground beside Liberty. Antonio took a place at her other side, their shoulders touching. Code Talker, Heyoka Coyoté, and Elvis arrayed themselves around the fire. Poco ladled out bowls of stew.

Edison's face was ashen, his eyes red in the firelight from weeping. She didn't know what to say, to him or to any of them. She realized they didn't know what to say to her, either.

Finally, Einstein Edison cleared his throat. "I once compared our much-praised technological progress to an axe in the hands of a pathological criminal." He looked down at the ground at his feet. "Sometimes one pays most for the things one gets for nothing."

He fell silent, then raised his eyes to hers and took her hand. "There is one thing we do know, Liebchen, that we are here for the sake of each other—for those upon whose smile and well-being our happiness depends."

Liberty gave his hand a grateful squeeze. "Thank you." She fought back tears. "What will you do?"

"I have always found my greatest pleasure in the work that precedes what the world calls success." He smiled sadly. "I will return to Menlo Park and continue my research. Norad may be gone, but electricity has returned, leaving a thousand possibilities. Perhaps I will never discover a Unified Field Theory now, but I still have the opportunity to learn."

He looked up at the stars and Liberty knew he was thinking about the satellites still revolving overhead, perhaps including one with a working telescope.

"So what happens now?" Poco asked.

"We return to Navajoland, superheroes no more," Heyoka Coyoté said, "back where we started."

"I guess we ended up with nothin'," Elvis said.

"You're wrong," Code said. "We helped save the country from the worst villain in history. We don't have anything to regret."

Liberty looked at Code, who gave her a nod and a smile.

* * *

They woke at sunrise next morning and prepared to depart. Clouds, afire with the dawn's light, covered the east. Liberty stared at the crater that had been the North American Aerospace Defense Command, feeling hollow inside. Even with the history book, what could she accomplish? Would people think it a fraud, a clever forgery? She doubted anyone would take it seriously.

Norad had asked her to do the impossible. She couldn't, that's all. Everything she had tried had ended in failure.

She shook her head, trying to shake off her sorrow, and rose to help Antonio and the American Natives pack the horses. Antonio was going through her saddlebags, cleaning them out. As she approached him, a puzzled expression crossed his face.

"What's this?" He drew a long tube from the bag.

"We never had anything like that," she said. "Let me see it."

It was made of a light metal, with a strange pull on its end. Liberty reached for the tab.

"Be careful," Antonio said.

She hesitated. "Our horses were with Norad until yesterday. It must be from him."

"Let me do it." Taking it from her, he gingerly pulled the tab, causing the end of the cylinder to come off, accompanied by a faint hissing. Peering inside, he withdrew a scroll. He looked at it, sniffed it, and handed it to Liberty.

She unrolled it. At the top, in Old American, it read: *We the People of the United States, in Order to form a more perfect Union, establish Justice, insure domestic Tranquility, provide for the common defence, promote the general Welfare, and secure the Blessings of Liberty to ourselves and our Posterity, do ordain and establish this Constitution of the United States of America.*

She put her hand over her mouth to cover her shrieks of joy, and then she was weeping. Laughing and sobbing at the same time, bouncing up and down on her feet. "It's the Lost Constitution!"

Everyone gathered around to look.

"Let me see." Antonio reached over, gently trying to take it from her, but she wouldn't let it go. He stepped beside her to study it, his arm around her shoulder.

"Is it the original?" Her voice broke; her breath came in gasps; her hands trembled. "Is it the real one?"

He scanned it, eyes alight in wonder. "I don't know, I can't read it; but it doesn't matter. It's from Norad. It has to be legitimate. You did it, Liberty, you found it!"

"He entrusted us with it," she said. "He had it all along, and he knew he wouldn't be around to defend it. So he gave it to us. He . . ." She drew herself up, standing tall and straight, growing stern. "I can do this! I can take it back with me. I can show them. I'll show them all! They can't ignore this." She patted her chest to slow her pounding heart. She and Antonio held each other, the Constitution cradled between them.

"You're something else, Liberty Bell." Antonio's voice was hoarse with emotion. "I came looking for gold. I thought that was all it was about. But not you. You came to find America."

She looked into his dark eyes. "I love you, Antonio Ice."

"I've loved you from the day we met."

They kissed, a long kiss. Liberty looked at the scroll, trying to focus on it. "I'll translate it and make copies. But we have to memorize it. Every word! We can't let anything happen to it. With my book and the Constitution, I can make them listen. I can make everyone listen."

"Of that," Antonio said. "I have no doubt."

* * *

EPILOGUE

The fireworks ended, the rockets' red glare dying in the summer breeze. The Constitution Day celebration was over. The couple led their young son into the house on their farm outside of New Washington. Glowing with enthusiasm, the child punched the air in happiness.

As they helped him into bed, he begged his dad to read a story.

"It's late, son," the man said, tucking him under the covers.

"Don't you think the day should end with something patriotic?" the boy slyly protested.

The man chuckled. He was weary, but couldn't resist this appeal, not on the two hundredth anniversary of the United States of Southwest America, born from the ashes of the old Yooessay. Sitting down on the side of the bed, he took a worn book off a nearby shelf. "Which story do you want to hear?"

"You know."

The two exchanged smiles. "That one again? Don't you ever get tired of it?"

"It's the best Founders' story ever."

"All right." Opening the book to the proper page, the father read the title, "*Liberty Bell Ice and the Lost Constitution.*"

The boy settled into his pillow.

The man began. "When the notorious outlaw, Brett Revere, drew a gun on Special Agent Antonio Ice on the train to Bedford Falls, Liberty Bell did not hesitate. Without a thought for her own safety, she hit the bandit with the book she had been reading, slid the exit door open, and with all the strength in her small frame, pulled Antonio off the speeding train into the bleak desolation of No Man's Land, saving both their lives . . ."

The boy was fast asleep before his father finished the page.

ACKNOWLEDGEMENTS

As always, I must thank my wife, Kathryn, who makes everything in my life special. To Chelsee Mcclurg, Lon Mirll, and Kreg Robertson, who struggled through an early draft filled with puns, false history, and confusion to help me focus the book. I am especially grateful to Chelsee for her perspective on the Jesse James chapter, and to Jay Wood for his later insights. My friend and fellow writer, Dr. Robert Finegold, gave me invaluable advice on Brother Rabbi—any failings regarding that character are my own, not his. Thanks to Scott Faris for crucial cover consultation, and to Amanda Luedeke for her persistence and suggestions on Liberty Bell. I also must thank Sophia Jimenz of Simon451, who suggested editorial changes that greatly improved Liberty's reaction to amorous advances.

Betsy Mitchell has edited every book I have ever published. Her ability to see to the heart of a story, honed through years of experience as editor at Warner and Ballantine Books, is phenomenal. I am honored to work with someone of her caliber.

My thanks to Coralie Hughes of the John G Neihardt Trust for graciously allowing me to include quotations from Neihardt's *Black Elk Speaks* in Heyoka Coyoté's tribal story.

Finally, thank you to my readers, who are willing to read the words of a dreamer who grew up in what was once the real No Man's Land.

ABOUT THE AUTHOR

James Stoddard's short fiction and articles have appeared in publications such as *Amazing Stories* and *The Magazine of Fantasy and Science Fiction*. His short stories, *The Battle of York*, and *The First Editions*, appeared respectively in *The Year's Best SF 10*, published by Eos Books, and *The Year's Best Fantasy 9* from Tor. His novel, *The High House*, won the Compton Crook Award for best fantasy by a new novelist and was nominated for several other awards. He taught Sound Recording at the college level for many years before leaving to write fulltime. He and his wife live in West Texas.

Further information can be found at: www.james-stoddard.com

The Constitution of the United States of America

Preamble

We the People of the United States, in Order to form a more perfect Union, establish Justice, insure domestic Tranquility, provide for the common defense, promote the general Welfare, and secure the Blessings of Liberty to ourselves and our Posterity, do ordain and establish this Constitution for the United States of America.

Article I

Section 1

All legislative Powers herein granted shall be vested in a Congress of the United States, which shall consist of a Senate and House of Representatives.

Section 2

The House of Representatives shall be composed of Members chosen every second Year by the People of the several States, and the Electors in each State shall have the Qualifications requisite for Electors of the most numerous Branch of the State Legislature.

No Person shall be a Representative who shall not have attained to the Age of twenty five Years, and been seven Years a Citizen of the United States, and who shall not, when elected, be an Inhabitant of that State in which he shall be chosen.

Representatives and direct Taxes shall be apportioned among the several States which may be included within this Union, according to their respective Numbers, which shall be determined by adding to the whole

Number of free Persons, including those bound to Service for a Term of Years, and excluding Indians not taxed, three fifths of all other Persons. The actual Enumeration shall be made within three Years after the first Meeting of the Congress of the United States, and within every subsequent Term of ten Years, in such Manner as they shall by Law direct. The Number of Representatives shall not exceed one for every thirty Thousand, but each State shall have at Least one Representative; and until such enumeration shall be made, the State of New Hampshire shall be entitled to chuse three, Massachusetts eight, Rhode-Island and Providence Plantations one, Connecticut five, New-York six, New Jersey four, Pennsylvania eight, Delaware one, Maryland six, Virginia ten, North Carolina five, South Carolina five, and Georgia three.

When vacancies happen in the Representation from any State, the Executive Authority thereof shall issue Writs of Election to fill such Vacancies.

The House of Representatives shall chuse their Speaker and other Officers; and shall have the sole Power of Impeachment.

Section 3

The Senate of the United States shall be composed of two Senators from each State, chosen by the Legislature thereof, for six Years; and each Senator shall have one Vote.

Immediately after they shall be assembled in Consequence of the first Election, they shall be divided as equally as may be into three Classes. The Seats of the Senators of the first Class shall be vacated at the Expiration of the second Year, of the second Class at the Expiration of the fourth Year, and of the third Class at the Expiration of the sixth Year, so that one third may be chosen every second Year; and if Vacancies happen by Resignation, or otherwise, during the Recess of the Legislature of any State, the Executive thereof may make temporary Appointments until the next Meeting of the Legislature, which shall then fill such Vacancies.

No Person shall be a Senator who shall not have attained to the Age of thirty Years, and been nine Years a Citizen of the United States, and who shall not, when elected, be an Inhabitant of that State for which he shall be chosen.

The Vice President of the United States shall be President of the Senate, but shall have no Vote, unless they be equally divided.

The Senate shall chuse their other Officers, and also a President pro tempore, in the Absence of the Vice President, or when he shall exercise the Office of President of the United States.

The Senate shall have the sole Power to try all Impeachments. When sitting for that Purpose, they shall be on Oath or Affirmation. When the President of the United States is tried, the Chief Justice shall preside: And no Person shall be convicted without the Concurrence of two thirds of the Members present.

Judgment in Cases of Impeachment shall not extend further than to removal from Office, and disqualification to hold and enjoy any Office of honor, Trust or Profit under the United States: but the Party convicted shall nevertheless be liable and subject to Indictment, Trial, Judgment and Punishment, according to Law.

Section 4

The Times, Places and Manner of holding Elections for Senators and Representatives, shall be prescribed in each State by the Legislature thereof; but the Congress may at any time by Law make or alter such Regulations, except as to the Places of chusing Senators.

The Congress shall assemble at least once in every Year, and such Meeting shall be on the first Monday in December, unless they shall by Law appoint a different Day.

Section 5

Each House shall be the Judge of the Elections, Returns and Qualifications of its own Members, and a Majority of each shall constitute a Quorum to do Business; but a smaller Number may adjourn from day to day, and may be authorized to compel the Attendance of absent Members, in such Manner, and under such Penalties as each House may provide.

Each House may determine the Rules of its Proceedings, punish its Members for disorderly Behaviour, and, with the Concurrence of two thirds, expel a Member.

Each House shall keep a Journal of its Proceedings, and from time to time publish the same, excepting such Parts as may in their Judgment require Secrecy; and the Yeas and Nays of the Members of either House on any question shall, at the Desire of one fifth of those Present, be entered on the Journal.

Neither House, during the Session of Congress, shall, without the Consent of the other, adjourn for more than three days, nor to any other Place than that in which the two Houses shall be sitting.

Section 6

The Senators and Representatives shall receive a Compensation for their Services, to be ascertained by Law, and paid out of the Treasury of the United States. They shall in all Cases, except Treason, Felony and

Breach of the Peace, be privileged from Arrest during their Attendance at the Session of their respective Houses, and in going to and returning from the same; and for any Speech or Debate in either House, they shall not be questioned in any other Place.

No Senator or Representative shall, during the Time for which he was elected, be appointed to any civil Office under the Authority of the United States, which shall have been created, or the Emoluments whereof shall have been encreased during such time; and no Person holding any Office under the United States, shall be a Member of either House during his Continuance in Office.

Section 7

All Bills for raising Revenue shall originate in the House of Representatives; but the Senate may propose or concur with Amendments as on other Bills.

Every Bill which shall have passed the House of Representatives and the Senate, shall, before it become a Law, be presented to the President of the United States: If he approve he shall sign it, but if not he shall return it, with his Objections to that House in which it shall have originated, who shall enter the Objections at large on their Journal, and proceed to reconsider it. If after such Reconsideration two thirds of that House shall agree to pass the Bill, it shall be sent, together with the Objections, to the other House, by which it shall likewise be reconsidered, and if approved by two thirds of that House, it shall become a Law. But in all such Cases the Votes of both Houses shall be determined by Yeas and Nays, and the Names of the Persons voting for and against the Bill shall be entered on the Journal of each House respectively. If any Bill shall not be returned by the President within ten Days (Sundays excepted) after it shall have been presented to him, the Same shall be a Law, in like Manner as if he had signed it, unless the Congress by their Adjournment prevent its Return, in which Case it shall not be a Law.

Every Order, Resolution, or Vote to which the Concurrence of the Senate and House of Representatives may be necessary (except on a question of Adjournment) shall be presented to the President of the United States; and before the Same shall take Effect, shall be approved by him, or being disapproved by him, shall be repassed by two thirds of the Senate and House of Representatives, according to the Rules and Limitations prescribed in the Case of a Bill.

Section 8

The Congress shall have Power To lay and collect Taxes, Duties,

Imposts and Excises, to pay the Debts and provide for the common Defence and general Welfare of the United States; but all Duties, Imposts and Excises shall be uniform throughout the United States;

To borrow Money on the credit of the United States;

To regulate Commerce with foreign Nations, and among the several States, and with the Indian Tribes;

To establish an uniform Rule of Naturalization, and uniform Laws on the subject of Bankruptcies throughout the United States;

To coin Money, regulate the Value thereof, and of foreign Coin, and fix the Standard of Weights and Measures;

To provide for the Punishment of counterfeiting the Securities and current Coin of the United States;

To establish Post Offices and post Roads;

To promote the Progress of Science and useful Arts, by securing for limited Times to Authors and Inventors the exclusive Right to their respective Writings and Discoveries;

To constitute Tribunals inferior to the supreme Court;

To define and punish Piracies and Felonies committed on the high Seas, and Offences against the Law of Nations;

To declare War, grant Letters of Marque and Reprisal, and make Rules concerning Captures on Land and Water;

To raise and support Armies, but no Appropriation of Money to that Use shall be for a longer Term than two Years;

To provide and maintain a Navy;

To make Rules for the Government and Regulation of the land and naval Forces;

To provide for calling forth the Militia to execute the Laws of the Union, suppress Insurrections and repel Invasions;

To provide for organizing, arming, and disciplining, the Militia, and for governing such Part of them as may be employed in the Service of the United States, reserving to the States respectively, the Appointment of the Officers, and the Authority of training the Militia according to the discipline prescribed by Congress;

To exercise exclusive Legislation in all Cases whatsoever, over such District (not exceeding ten Miles square) as may, by Cession of particular States, and the Acceptance of Congress, become the Seat of the Government of the United States, and to exercise like Authority over all Places purchased by the Consent of the Legislature of the State in which the Same shall be, for the Erection of Forts, Magazines, Arsenals, dock-Yards, and other needful Buildings;—And

To make all Laws which shall be necessary and proper for carrying into Execution the foregoing Powers, and all other Powers vested by this

Constitution in the Government of the United States, or in any Department or Officer thereof.

Section 9

The Migration or Importation of such Persons as any of the States now existing shall think proper to admit, shall not be prohibited by the Congress prior to the Year one thousand eight hundred and eight, but a Tax or duty may be imposed on such Importation, not exceeding ten dollars for each Person.

The Privilege of the Writ of Habeas Corpus shall not be suspended, unless when in Cases of Rebellion or Invasion the public Safety may require it.

No Bill of Attainder or ex post facto Law shall be passed.

No Capitation, or other direct, Tax shall be laid, unless in Proportion to the Census or enumeration herein before directed to be taken.

No Tax or Duty shall be laid on Articles exported from any State.

No Preference shall be given by any Regulation of Commerce or Revenue to the Ports of one State over those of another; nor shall Vessels bound to, or from, one State, be obliged to enter, clear, or pay Duties in another.

No Money shall be drawn from the Treasury, but in Consequence of Appropriations made by Law; and a regular Statement and Account of the Receipts and Expenditures of all public Money shall be published from time to time.

No Title of Nobility shall be granted by the United States: And no Person holding any Office of Profit or Trust under them, shall, without the Consent of the Congress, accept of any present, Emolument, Office, or Title, of any kind whatever, from any King, Prince, or foreign State.

Section 10

No State shall enter into any Treaty, Alliance, or Confederation; grant Letters of Marque and Reprisal; coin Money; emit Bills of Credit; make any Thing but gold and silver Coin a Tender in Payment of Debts; pass any Bill of Attainder, ex post facto Law, or Law impairing the Obligation of Contracts, or grant any Title of Nobility.

No State shall, without the Consent of the Congress, lay any Imposts or Duties on Imports or Exports, except what may be absolutely necessary for executing its inspection Laws: and the net Produce of all Duties and Imposts, laid by any State on Imports or Exports, shall be for the Use of the Treasury of the United States; and all such Laws shall be subject to the Revision and Control of the Congress.

No State shall, without the Consent of Congress, lay any Duty of Tonnage, keep Troops, or Ships of War in time of Peace, enter into any Agreement or Compact with another State, or with a foreign Power, or engage in War, unless actually invaded, or in such imminent Danger as will not admit of delay.

Article II

Section 1

The executive Power shall be vested in a President of the United States of America. He shall hold his Office during the Term of four Years, and, together with the Vice President, chosen for the same Term, be elected, as follows:

Each State shall appoint, in such Manner as the Legislature thereof may direct, a Number of Electors, equal to the whole Number of Senators and Representatives to which the State may be entitled in the Congress: but no Senator or Representative, or Person holding an Office of Trust or Profit under the United States, shall be appointed an Elector.

The Electors shall meet in their respective States, and vote by Ballot for two Persons, of whom one at least shall not be an Inhabitant of the same State with themselves. And they shall make a List of all the Persons voted for, and of the Number of Votes for each; which List they shall sign and certify, and transmit sealed to the Seat of the Government of the United States, directed to the President of the Senate. The President of the Senate shall, in the Presence of the Senate and House of Representatives, open all the Certificates, and the Votes shall then be counted. The Person having the greatest Number of Votes shall be the President, if such Number be a Majority of the whole Number of Electors appointed; and if there be more than one who have such Majority, and have an equal Number of Votes, then the House of Representatives shall immediately chuse by Ballot one of them for President; and if no Person have a Majority, then from the five highest on the List the said House shall in like Manner chuse the President. But in chusing the President, the Votes shall be taken by States, the Representatives from each State having one Vote; a quorum for this Purpose shall consist of a Member or Members from two thirds of the States, and a Majority of all the States shall be necessary to a Choice. In every Case, after the Choice of the President, the Person having the greatest Number of Votes of the Electors shall be the Vice President. But if there should remain two or more who have equal Votes, the Senate shall chuse from them by Ballot the Vice-President.

The Congress may determine the Time of chusing the Electors, and the Day on which they shall give their Votes; which Day shall be the same throughout the United States.

No Person except a natural born Citizen, or a Citizen of the United States, at the time of the Adoption of this Constitution, shall be eligible to the Office of President; neither shall any person be eligible to that Office who shall not have attained to the Age of thirty five Years, and been fourteen Years a Resident within the United States.

In Case of the Removal of the President from Office, or of his Death, Resignation, or Inability to discharge the Powers and Duties of the said Office, the Same shall devolve on the Vice President, and the Congress may by Law provide for the Case of Removal, Death, Resignation or Inability, both of the President and Vice President, declaring what Officer shall then act as President, and such Officer shall act accordingly, until the Disability be removed, or a President shall be elected.

The President shall, at stated Times, receive for his Services, a Compensation, which shall neither be encreased nor diminished during the Period for which he shall have been elected, and he shall not receive within that Period any other Emolument from the United States, or any of them.

Before he enter on the Execution of his Office, he shall take the following Oath or Affirmation:—"I do solemnly swear (or affirm) that I will faithfully execute the Office of President of the United States, and will to the best of my Ability, preserve, protect and defend the Constitution of the United States."

Section 2

The President shall be Commander in Chief of the Army and Navy of the United States, and of the Militia of the several States, when called into the actual Service of the United States; he may require the Opinion, in writing, of the principal Officer in each of the executive Departments, upon any Subject relating to the Duties of their respective Offices, and he shall have Power to Grant Reprieves and Pardons for Offences against the United States, except in Cases of Impeachment.

He shall have Power, by and with the Advice and Consent of the Senate, to make Treaties, provided two thirds of the Senators present concur; and he shall nominate, and by and with the Advice and Consent of the Senate, shall appoint Ambassadors, other public Ministers and Consuls, Judges of the supreme Court, and all other Officers of the United States, whose Appointments are not herein otherwise provided for, and which shall be established by Law: but the Congress may by Law vest the Appointment of such inferior Officers, as they think proper, in the

President alone, in the Courts of Law, or in the Heads of Departments.

The President shall have Power to fill up all Vacancies that may happen during the Recess of the Senate, by granting Commissions which shall expire at the End of their next Session.

Section 3

He shall from time to time give to the Congress Information on the State of the Union, and recommend to their Consideration such Measures as he shall judge necessary and expedient; he may, on extraordinary Occasions, convene both Houses, or either of them, and in Case of Disagreement between them, with Respect to the Time of Adjournment, he may adjourn them to such Time as he shall think proper; he shall receive Ambassadors and other public Ministers; he shall take Care that the Laws be faithfully executed, and shall Commission all the Officers of the United States.

Section 4

The President, Vice President and all Civil Officers of the United States, shall be removed from Office on Impeachment for, and Conviction of, Treason, Bribery, or other high Crimes and Misdemeanors.

Article III

Section 1

The judicial Power of the United States, shall be vested in one supreme Court, and in such inferior Courts as the Congress may from time to time ordain and establish. The Judges, both of the supreme and inferior Courts, shall hold their Offices during good Behaviour, and shall, at stated Times, receive for their Services, a Compensation, which shall not be diminished during their Continuance in Office.

Section 2

The judicial Power shall extend to all Cases, in Law and Equity, arising under this Constitution, the Laws of the United States, and Treaties made, or which shall be made, under their Authority;—to all Cases affecting Ambassadors, other public ministers and Consuls;—to all Cases of admiralty and maritime Jurisdiction;—to Controversies to which the United States shall be a Party;—to Controversies between two or more States;—between a State and Citizens of another State;—between Citizens of different States;—between Citizens of the same State claiming Lands under Grants of different States, and between a State, or the Citizens thereof, and foreign States, Citizens or Subjects.

In all Cases affecting Ambassadors, other public Ministers and Consuls, and those in which a State shall be Party, the supreme Court shall have original Jurisdiction. In all the other Cases before mentioned, the supreme Court shall have appellate Jurisdiction, both as to Law and Fact, with such Exceptions, and under such Regulations as the Congress shall make.

The Trial of all Crimes, except in Cases of Impeachment, shall be by Jury; and such Trial shall be held in the State where the said Crimes shall have been committed; but when not committed within any State, the Trial shall be at such Place or Places as the Congress may by Law have directed.

Section 3

Treason against the United States, shall consist only in levying War against them, or in adhering to their Enemies, giving them Aid and Comfort. No Person shall be convicted of Treason unless on the Testimony of two Witnesses to the same overt Act, or on Confession in open Court.

The Congress shall have Power to declare the Punishment of Treason, but no Attainder of Treason shall work Corruption of Blood, or Forfeiture except during the Life of the Person attainted.

Article IV

Section 1

Full Faith and Credit shall be given in each State to the public Acts, Records, and judicial Proceedings of every other State. And the Congress may by general Laws prescribe the Manner in which such Acts, Records and Proceedings shall be proved, and the Effect thereof.

Section 2

The Citizens of each State shall be entitled to all Privileges and Immunities of Citizens in the several States.

A Person charged in any State with Treason, Felony, or other Crime, who shall flee from Justice, and be found in another State, shall on Demand of the executive Authority of the State from which he fled, be delivered up, to be removed to the State having Jurisdiction of the Crime.

No Person held to Service or Labour in one State, under the Laws thereof, escaping into another, shall, in Consequence of any Law or

Regulation therein, be discharged from such Service or Labour, but shall be delivered up on Claim of the Party to whom such Service or Labour may be due.

Section 3

New States may be admitted by the Congress into this Union; but no new State shall be formed or erected within the Jurisdiction of any other State; nor any State be formed by the Junction of two or more States, or Parts of States, without the Consent of the Legislatures of the States concerned as well as of the Congress.

The Congress shall have Power to dispose of and make all needful Rules and Regulations respecting the Territory or other Property belonging to the United States; and nothing in this Constitution shall be so construed as to Prejudice any Claims of the United States, or of any particular State.

Section 4

The United States shall guarantee to every State in this Union a Republican Form of Government, and shall protect each of them against Invasion; and on Application of the Legislature, or of the Executive (when the Legislature cannot be convened) against domestic Violence.

Article V

The Congress, whenever two thirds of both Houses shall deem it necessary, shall propose Amendments to this Constitution, or, on the Application of the Legislatures of two thirds of the several States, shall call a Convention for proposing Amendments, which, in either Case, shall be valid to all Intents and Purposes, as Part of this Constitution, when ratified by the Legislatures of three fourths of the several States, or by Conventions in three fourths thereof, as the one or the other Mode of Ratification may be proposed by the Congress; Provided that no Amendment which may be made prior to the Year One thousand eight hundred and eight shall in any Manner affect the first and fourth Clauses in the Ninth Section of the first Article; and that no State, without its Consent, shall be deprived of its equal Suffrage in the Senate.

Article VI

All Debts contracted and Engagements entered into, before the Adoption of this Constitution, shall be as valid against the United States under this Constitution, as under the Confederation.

This Constitution, and the Laws of the United States which shall be made in Pursuance thereof; and all Treaties made, or which shall be made, under the Authority of the United States, shall be the supreme Law of the Land; and the Judges in every State shall be bound thereby, any Thing in the Constitution or Laws of any state to the Contrary notwithstanding.

The Senators and Representatives before mentioned, and the Members of the several State Legislatures, and all executive and judicial Officers, both of the United States and of the several States, shall be bound by Oath or Affirmation, to support this Constitution; but no religious Test shall ever be required as a Qualification to any Office or public Trust under the United States.

Article VII

The Ratification of the Conventions of nine States, shall be sufficient for the Establishment of this Constitution between the States so ratifying the Same.

Done in Convention by the Unanimous Consent of the States present the Seventeenth Day of September in the Year of our Lord one thousand seven hundred and Eighty seven and of the Independence of the United States of America the Twelfth In Witness whereof We have hereunto subscribed our Names,

G. Washington—Presid, And deputy from Virginia; New Hampshire: John Langdon, Nicholas Gilman; Massachusetts: Nathaniel Gorham, Rufus King; Connecticut: Wm. Saml. Johnson, Roger Sherman; New York: Alexander Hamilton; New Jersey: Wil: Livingston, David Brearley, Wm. Paterson, Jona. Dayton; Pennsylvania: B Franklin, Thomas Mifflin, Robt Morris, Geo. Clymer, Thos. FitzSimons, Jared Ingersoll, James Wilson, Gouv Morris; Delaware: Geo: Read, Gunning Bedford jun, John Dickinson, Richard Bassett, Jaco: Broom; Maryland: James McHenry, Dan of St. Thos. Jenifer, Danl Carroll; Virginia: John Blair—, James Madison Jr.; North Carolina: Wm. Blount, Richd. Dobbs Spaight, Hu Williamson; South Carolina: J. Rutledge, Charles Cotesworth Pinckney,

Charles Pinckney, Pierce Butler; Georgia: William Few, Abr Baldwin; Attest: William Jackson Secretary

AMENDMENTS

Amendment I (1791)

Congress shall make no law respecting an establishment of religion, or prohibiting the free exercise thereof; or abridging the freedom of speech, or of the press; or the right of the people peaceably to assemble, and to petition the Government for a redress of grievances.

Amendment II (1791)

A well regulated Militia, being necessary to the security of a free State, the right of the people to keep and bear Arms, shall not be infringed.

Amendment III (1791)

No Soldier shall, in time of peace be quartered in any house, without the consent of the Owner, nor in time of war, but in a manner to be prescribed by law.

Amendment IV (1791)

The right of the people to be secure in their persons, houses, papers, and effects, against unreasonable searches and seizures, shall not be violated, and no Warrants shall issue, but upon probable cause, supported by Oath or affirmation, and particularly describing the place to be searched, and the persons or things to be seized.

Amendment V (1791)

No person shall be held to answer for a capital, or otherwise infamous crime, unless on a presentment or indictment of a Grand Jury, except in cases arising in the land or naval forces, or in the Militia, when in actual service in time of War or public danger; nor shall any person be subject for the same offence to be twice put in jeopardy of life or limb; nor shall be compelled in any criminal case to be a witness against himself, nor be deprived of life, liberty, or property, without due process of law; nor shall private property be taken for public use, without just compensation.

Amendment VI (1791)

In all criminal prosecutions, the accused shall enjoy the right to a speedy and public trial, by an impartial jury of the State and district wherein the crime shall have been committed, which district shall have been previously ascertained by law, and to be informed of the nature and cause of the accusation; to be confronted with the witnesses against him; to have compulsory process for obtaining witnesses in his favor, and to have the Assistance of Counsel for his defence.

Amendment VII (1791)

In Suits at common law, where the value in controversy shall exceed twenty dollars, the right of trial by jury shall be preserved, and no fact tried by a jury, shall be otherwise re-examined in any Court of the United States, than according to the rules of the common law.

Amendment VIII (1791)

Excessive bail shall not be required, nor excessive fines imposed, nor cruel and unusual punishments inflicted.

Amendment IX (1791)

The enumeration in the Constitution, of certain rights, shall not be construed to deny or disparage others retained by the people.

Amendment X (1791)

The powers not delegated to the United States by the Constitution, nor prohibited by it to the States, are reserved to the States respectively, or to the people.

Amendment XI (1795/1798)

The Judicial power of the United States shall not be construed to extend to any suit in law or equity, commenced or prosecuted against one of the United States by Citizens of another State, or by Citizens or Subjects of any Foreign State.

Amendment XII (1804)

The Electors shall meet in their respective states and vote by ballot for President and Vice-President, one of whom, at least, shall not be an inhabitant of the same state with themselves; they shall name in their ballots the person voted for as President, and in distinct ballots the person voted for as Vice-President, and they shall make distinct lists of all persons voted for as President, and of all persons voted for as Vice-President, and of the number of votes for each, which lists they shall sign and certify, and transmit sealed to the seat of the government of the United States, directed to the President of the Senate;—The President of the Senate shall, in the presence of the Senate and House of Representatives, open all the certificates and the votes shall then be counted;—The person having the greatest Number of votes for President, shall be the President, if such number be a majority of the whole number of Electors appointed; and if no person have such majority, then from the persons having the highest numbers not exceeding three on the list of those voted for as President, the House of Representatives shall choose immediately, by ballot, the President. But in choosing the President, the votes shall be taken by states, the representation from each state having one vote; a quorum for this purpose shall consist of a member or members from two-thirds of the states, and a majority of all the states shall be necessary to a choice. And if the House of Representatives shall not choose a President whenever the right of choice shall devolve upon them, before the fourth day of March next following, then the Vice-President shall act as President, as in the case of the death or other constitutional disability of the President—The person having the greatest number of votes as Vice-President, shall be the Vice-President, if such number be a majority of the whole number of Electors appointed, and if no person have a majority, then from the two highest numbers on the list, the Senate shall choose the Vice-President; a quorum for the purpose shall consist of two-thirds of the whole number of Senators, and a majority of the whole number shall be necessary to a choice. But no person constitutionally ineligible to the office of President shall be eligible to that of Vice-President of the United States.

Amendment XIII (1865)

Section 1. Neither slavery nor involuntary servitude, except as a punishment for crime whereof the party shall have been duly convicted, shall exist within the United States, or any place subject to their jurisdiction.

Section 2. Congress shall have power to enforce this article by appropriate legislation.

Amendment XIV (1868)

Section 1. All persons born or naturalized in the United States, and subject to the jurisdiction thereof, are citizens of the United States and of the State wherein they reside. No State shall make or enforce any law which shall abridge the privileges or immunities of citizens of the United States; nor shall any State deprive any person of life, liberty, or property, without due process of law; nor deny to any person within its jurisdiction the equal protection of the laws.

Section 2. Representatives shall be apportioned among the several States according to their respective numbers, counting the whole number of persons in each State, excluding Indians not taxed. But when the right to vote at any election for the choice of electors for President and Vice President of the United States, Representatives in Congress, the Executive and Judicial officers of a State, or the members of the Legislature thereof, is denied to any of the male inhabitants of such State, being twenty-one years of age, and citizens of the United States, or in any way abridged, except for participation in rebellion, or other crime, the basis of representation therein shall be reduced in the proportion which the number of such male citizens shall bear to the whole number of male citizens twenty-one years of age in such State.

Section 3. No person shall be a Senator or Representative in Congress, or elector of President and Vice President, or hold any office, civil or military, under the United States, or under any State, who, having previously taken an oath, as a member of Congress, or as an officer of the United States, or as a member of any State legislature, or as an executive or judicial officer of any State, to support the Constitution of the United States, shall have engaged in insurrection or rebellion against the same, or given aid or comfort to the enemies thereof. But Congress may by a vote of two-thirds of each House, remove such disability.

Section 4. The validity of the public debt of the United States, authorized by law, including debts incurred for payment of pensions and bounties for services in suppressing insurrection or rebellion, shall not be questioned. But neither the United States nor any State shall assume or pay any debt or obligation incurred in aid of insurrection or rebellion against the United States, or any claim for the loss or emancipation of any slave; but all such debts, obligations and claims shall be held illegal and void.

Section 5. The Congress shall have power to enforce, by appropriate legislation, the provisions of this article.

Amendment XV (1870)

Section 1. The right of citizens of the United States to vote shall not be denied or abridged by the United States or by any State on account of race, color, or previous condition of servitude.

Section 2. The Congress shall have power to enforce this article by appropriate legislation.

Amendment XVI (1913)

The Congress shall have power to lay and collect taxes on incomes, from whatever source derived, without apportionment among the several States, and without regard to any census or enumeration.

Amendment XVII (1913)

The Senate of the United States shall be composed of two Senators from each State, elected by the people thereof, for six years; and each Senator shall have one vote. The electors in each State shall have the qualifications requisite for electors of the most numerous branch of the State legislatures.

When vacancies happen in the representation of any State in the Senate, the executive authority of such State shall issue writs of election to fill such vacancies: Provided, That the legislature of any State may empower the executive thereof to make temporary appointments until the people fill the vacancies by election as the legislature may direct.

This amendment shall not be so construed as to affect the election or term of any Senator chosen before it becomes valid as part of the Constitution.

Amendment XVIII (1919)

Section 1. After one year from the ratification of this article the manufacture, sale, or transportation of intoxicating liquors within, the importation thereof into, or the exportation thereof from the United States and all territory subject to the jurisdiction thereof for beverage purposes is hereby prohibited.

Section 2. The Congress and the several States shall have concurrent power to enforce this article by appropriate legislation.

Section 3. This article shall be inoperative unless it shall have been ratified as an amendment to the Constitution by the legislatures of the several States, as provided in the Constitution, within seven years from the date of the submission hereof to the States by the Congress.

Amendment XIX (1920)

The right of citizens of the United States to vote shall not be denied or abridged by the United States or by any State on account of sex.

Congress shall have power to enforce this article by appropriate legislation.

Amendment XX (1933)

Section 1. The terms of the President and Vice President shall end at noon on the 20th day of January, and the terms of Senators and Representatives at noon on the 3d day of January, of the years in which such terms would have ended if this article had not been ratified; and the terms of their successors shall then begin.

Section 2. The Congress shall assemble at least once in every year, and such meeting shall begin at noon on the 3d day of January, unless they shall by law appoint a different day.

Section 3. If, at the time fixed for the beginning of the term of the President, the President elect shall have died, the Vice President elect shall become President. If a President shall not have been chosen before the time fixed for the beginning of his term, or if the President elect shall have failed to qualify, then the Vice President elect shall act as President until a President shall have qualified; and the Congress may by law provide for the case wherein neither a President elect nor a Vice President elect shall have qualified, declaring who shall then act as President, or the manner in which one who is to act shall be selected, and such person shall act accordingly until a President or Vice President shall have qualified.

Section 4. The Congress may by law provide for the case of the death of any of the persons from whom the House of Representatives may choose a President whenever the right of choice shall have devolved upon them, and for the case of the death of any of the persons from whom the Senate may choose a Vice President whenever the right of choice shall have devolved upon them.

Section 5. Sections 1 and 2 shall take effect on the 15th day of

October following the ratification of this article.

Section 6. This article shall be inoperative unless it shall have been ratified as an amendment to the Constitution by the legislatures of three-fourths of the several States within seven years from the date of its submission.

Amendment XXI (1933)

Section 1. The eighteenth article of amendment to the Constitution of the United States is hereby repealed.

Section 2. The transportation or importation into any State, Territory, or possession of the United States for delivery or use therein of intoxicating liquors, in violation of the laws thereof, is hereby prohibited.

Section 3. This article shall be inoperative unless it shall have been ratified as an amendment to the Constitution by conventions in the several States, as provided in the Constitution, within seven years from the date of the submission hereof to the States by the Congress.

Amendment XXII (1951)

Section 1. No person shall be elected to the office of the President more than twice, and no person who has held the office of President, or acted as President, for more than two years of a term to which some other person was elected President shall be elected to the office of the President more than once. But this Article shall not apply to any person holding the office of President, when this Article was proposed by the Congress, and shall not prevent any person who may be holding the office of President, or acting as President, during the term within which this Article becomes operative from holding the office of President or acting as President during the remainder of such term.

Section 2. This article shall be inoperative unless it shall have been ratified as an amendment to the Constitution by the legislatures of three-fourths of the several States within seven years from the date of its submission to the States by the Congress.

Amendment XXIII (1961)

Section 1. The District constituting the seat of Government of the United States shall appoint in such manner as the Congress may direct:

A number of electors of President and Vice President equal to the whole number of Senators and Representatives in Congress to which the District would be entitled if it were a State, but in no event more than the least populous State; they shall be in addition to those appointed by the States, but they shall be considered, for the purposes of the election of President and Vice President, to be electors appointed by a State; and they shall meet in the District and perform such duties as provided by the twelfth article of amendment.

Section 2. The Congress shall have power to enforce this article by appropriate legislation.

Amendment XXIV (1964)

Section 1. The right of citizens of the United States to vote in any primary or other election for President or Vice President for electors for President or Vice President, or for Senator or Representative in Congress, shall not be denied or abridged by the United States or any State by reason of failure to pay any poll tax or other tax.

Section 2. The Congress shall have power to enforce this article by appropriate legislation.

Amendment XXV (1967)

Section 1. In case of the removal of the President from office or of his death or resignation, the Vice President shall become President.

Section 2. Whenever there is a vacancy in the office of the Vice President, the President shall nominate a Vice President who shall take office upon confirmation by a majority vote of both Houses of Congress.

Section 3. Whenever the President transmits to the President pro tempore of the Senate and the Speaker of the House of Representatives his written declaration that he is unable to discharge the powers and duties of his office, and until he transmits to them a written declaration to the contrary, such powers and duties shall be discharged by the Vice President as Acting President.

Section 4. Whenever the Vice President and a majority of either the principal officers of the executive departments or of such other body as Congress may by law provide, transmit to the President pro tempore of the Senate and the Speaker of the House of Representatives their written declaration that the President is unable to discharge the powers and duties of his office, the Vice President shall immediately assume the powers and duties of the office as Acting President.

Thereafter, when the President transmits to the President pro tempore of the Senate and the Speaker of the House of Representatives his written declaration that no inability exists, he shall resume the powers and duties of his office unless the Vice President and a majority of either the principal officers of the executive department or of such other body as Congress may by law provide, transmit within four days to the President pro tempore of the Senate and the Speaker of the House of Representatives their written declaration that the President is unable to discharge the powers and duties of his office. Thereupon Congress shall decide the issue, assembling within forty-eight hours for that purpose if not in session. If the Congress, within twenty-one days after receipt of the latter written declaration, or, if Congress is not in session, within twenty-one days after Congress is required to assemble, determines by two-thirds vote of both Houses that the President is unable to discharge the powers and duties of his office, the Vice President shall continue to discharge the same as Acting President; otherwise, the President shall resume the powers and duties of his office.

Amendment XXVI (1971)

Section 1. The right of citizens of the United States, who are eighteen years of age or older, to vote shall not be denied or abridged by the United States or by any State on account of age.

Section 2. The Congress shall have power to enforce this article by appropriate legislation.

Amendment XXVII (1992)

No law varying the compensation for the services of the Senators and Representatives shall take effect, until an election of Representatives shall have intervened.

Made in the USA
Columbia, SC
20 April 2021